HOLLYWOOD
THE BAND

A TALE OF SEX, DRUGS, AND ROCK AND ROLL

STEVEN JORDAN BROOKS

Copyright © 2023 Steven Jordan Brooks.

All rights reserved. No part of this book may be reproduced, stored, or transmitted by any means—whether auditory, graphic, mechanical, or electronic—without written permission of both publisher and author, except in the case of brief excerpts used in critical articles and reviews. Unauthorized reproduction of any part of this work is illegal and is punishable by law.

This novel is a work of fiction. The names, characters, events, places, and incidents portrayed, depicted, or used herein are either the product of the author's imagination or are used fictitiously.

Any similarity or resemblance to any real persons, living or dead, real events or locales, past, present or historical, or any other story is purely coincidental and unintentional.

ISBN: 979-8-88640-890-4 (sc)
ISBN: 979-8-88640-891-1 (hc)
ISBN: 979-8-88640-892-8 (e)

Because of the dynamic nature of the Internet, any web addresses or links contained in this book may have changed since publication and may no longer be valid. The views expressed in this work are solely those of the author and do not necessarily reflect the views of the publisher, and the publisher hereby disclaims any responsibility for them.

THE EWINGS PUBLISHING

One Galleria Blvd., Suite 1900, Metairie, LA 70001
1-888-421-2397

CONTENTS

Characters vii
Prologue ix

PART I:
"PLEASE DON'T LET ME BE MISUNDERSTOOD"
The Animals

Chapter 1   "There's Something Happening Here" 3
                Buffalo Springfield

Chapter 2   "The Times They Are A-Changin'" 9
                Bob Dylan

Chapter 3   "Born to be Wild" 19
                Steppenwolf

Chapter 4   "Purple Haze is in my Brain" 28
                Jimi Hendrix

Chapter 5   "From the Beginning" 38
                Emerson Lake and Palmer

Chapter 6   "Changes" 45
                David Bowie

Chapter 7   "Summer in the City" 50
                Lovin' Spoonful

Chapter 8   "Captain Jack Will Get You High Tonight" 66
                Billy Joel

Chapter 9   "We're an American Band" 81
                Grand Funk Railroad

Chapter 10 "Hollywood Nights" 87
                Bob Seger

Chapter 11 "Take a Walk on the Wild Side" 100
                 Lou Reed

Chapter 12 "If You're Going to San Francisco" 113
                 Scott McKenzie

Chapter 13 "Eight Miles High" 120
                 The Byrds

Chapter 14 "After Midnight" 125
                 Eric Clapton

Chapter 15 "You're so Vain" 130
                 Carly Simon

Chapter 16 "Can't Find My Way Home" 141
                 Blind Faith

Chapter 17 "Both Sides Now" 154
                 Judy Collins

Chapter 18 "R-E-S-P-E-C-T" 161
                 Aretha Franklin

Chapter 19 "The World is a Ghetto" 168
                 War

Chapter 20 "Stop! in the Name Of Love" 175
                 The Supremes

Chapter 21 "American Woman" 183
                 Guess Who

Chapter 22 "You've Got a Friend" 193
                 James Taylor

Chapter 23 "I Am Woman, Hear Me Roar" 201
                 Helen Reddy

Chapter 24 "Don't You Want Somebody to Love" 210
                 Jefferson Airplane

Chapter 25 "School's Out" 223
                 Alice Cooper

PART II:
"TAKIN' CARE OF BUSINESS"
Bachman, Turner, Overdrive

Chapter 26 "Feelin' Stronger Every Day" 231
                Chicago

Chapter 27 "Surf City, Here We Come" 239
                Jan and Dean

Chapter 28 "It Ain't Easy" 255
                Three Dog Night

Chapter 29 "Band on the Run" 263
                Paul McCartney

Chapter 30 "You've Got to Change Your Evil Ways" 274
                Santana

Chapter 31 "La Bamba" 285
                Ritchie Valens

Chapter 32 "Kicks" 291
                Paul Revere and the Raiders

Chapter 33 "20th Century Fox" 296
                The Doors

Chapter 34 "Ain't No Sunshine When She's Gone" 305
                Bill Withers

Chapter 35 "Wild World" 314
                Cat Stevens

Chapter 36 "We Won't Get Fooled Again" 324
                The Who

Chapter 37 "Money" 341
                Pink Floyd

Chapter 38 "War, What is it Good For" 355
                Edwin Starr

Chapter 39 "What's Goin' On" 366
    Marvin Gaye

Chapter 40 "Long Time Gone" 373
    Crosby Stills and Nash

Chapter 41 "Homeward Bound" 385
    Simon & Garfunkle

Chapter 42 "This is Your Song" 392
    Elton John

Chapter 43 "Listen to the Music" 403
    The Doobie Brothers

Chapter 44 "All Right Now" 412
    Free

Chapter 45 "All the Young Dudes" 425
    Mott the Hoople

Chapter 46 "I'm Just a Singer in a Rock and Roll Band" 441
    The Moody Blues

Chapter 47 "I Went to a Garden Party" 452
    Rick Nelson

Chapter 48 "Good Times, Bad Times" 459
    Led Zeppelin

Chapter 49 "The Tracks of My Tears" 468
    The Miracles

Chapter 50 "You Can't Always Get What You Want" 477
    The Rolling Stones

Chapter 51 "I Just Want to Celebrate" 486
    Rare Earth

CHARACTERS

THE BAND
Jason Tucker	Keyboards/Gay
Mike (Michael) Stewart	Bass/Former Hippie/Political Activists
Jefferson Thomas	Drums/Black/Former Black Activist/ Viet Nam Vet
Bill Franklin (William Franklin III)	Guitarist/Ex Junkie
Gloria Fox	Female lead singer/Navy Brat/Liberated Woman/Ex Biker

MANAGEMENT AND CREW:
Frank Barcelona	Manager/Drug Dealer/Viet Nam Vet/ Ex POW
Eric Watson	Assistant Manager/Drug Dealer/Viet Nam Vet/Ex POW
Rick Martin	High Powered Industry Manager of Headline Mgmt
Mark Taylor	Roadie, Sound/Drug Runner
Pete Simons	Roadie, Lights/Drug Runner
Alex Castillo	Roadie/Drug Dealer

MUSIC BUSINESS:
Brian	Original drummer
Doug	Original Guitar player
Stan Rosen	Small Time Agent
Isaac Cohen	High Powered Hollywood Agent for Creative Artists Talent Agency

Steve Gold	Entertainment Contract Law Attorney
Mr. Grant	Owner of the Hollywood Star Nightclub/ Drug Customer
Derek Elliott	English Record Producer
Rob Allen	A&R person from The Empire Records Group
Mr. Greenwood	President of the Empire Records Group
Pat Johnson	Production and Publishing Company Owner
Jonathan Cooper	Musician/Former Rock Star
Scott	Rich Investor/Middle East Prince
Sue Stone	Publicist/Public Relations/Press Agent
Helmut	Photographer
Maggie	Fashion Consultant
Ken	Stage Director
Sally	Choreographer

FRIENDS, FAMILY:

Sunshine and Speed (Vic)	San Francisco Hippies/Political Activists
Chuck and Greg	Gay Bar Owners
Sarah Lewis	Gloria's Roommate/Mike's Love Interest
Brent Richmond	Criminal Law Attorney/ New York, LA
Debra	Bill's Girlfriend in Boston
Mr. and Mrs. Tucker	Jason's Parents
Jack Carver	Mike's Father
Margaret	Mike's Mother
Mr. & Mrs. Franklin	Bill's Parents

MISC:

Carmine	Mafia Hood
Vinnie	Mafia Boss
Luigi Barcelona	Frank's Father/Mafia
The Boss	Head Inmate
Leroy and Hank	Inmates
Russ Walker	Federal Agent/Drug Dealer
Brad	Groupie of Gloria
Detective Morgan	Police Detective
Detective Anderson	Police Detective

PROLOGUE

"The Times They Are A-Changin'," Bob Dylan once wrote. This truly could be the anthem for the seventies—a time of change due to the impact and influence of the sixties. The seventies are remembered not by its economic, social, or political importance but perhaps as the end of an era like the passing of a violent storm. For many, the sixties was a time of new ideas and new ideals—a time for questioning and re-evaluating conventional wisdom, values, attitudes, beliefs, and morals—an era of the peace and love generation, hippies, anti war demonstrations, and racial unrest. It was a political time when a generation dared to question their leaders and forefathers. It was also a time of contradictions. By the seventies, the perils and struggles of the decade before would soon be forgotten, but the effects of these changing times would be felt for a long time to come. The sixties had left its mark. From their questioning and dissatisfactions, change did occur—sometimes like a violent revolution, sometimes like a quiet whisper. Change in radical ways, change in subtle ways—but change nonetheless. Life was different.

At the center of this cultural, political, and social upheaval there was music. Music was a reflection of the time. It created anthems. It reflected a new attitude for a new age. It spoke of war. It spoke of love. It made us cry. It made us laugh. It made us feel. It made us think. It made us wonder. It made us question. It was both cause and effect. It had a profound influence on a new generation. Yes, by the seventies one could truly say "The Times They Are A-Changin'".

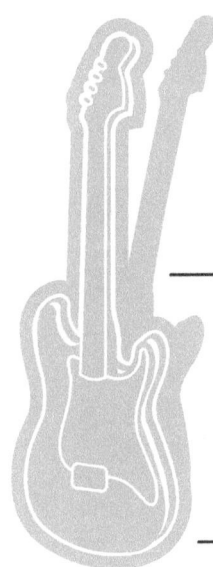

PART I

"PLEASE DON'T LET ME BE MISUNDERSTOOD"

The Animals

"THERE'S SOMETHING HAPPENING HERE"

Buffalo Springfield

"Power to the people! Power to the People!" The crowd roared with raised fists. The campus quad was a sea of students who had gathered at the amphitheater for a political demonstration.

A speaker continued his speech, his voice echoing between the surrounding buildings of higher learning. "We cannot allow this university to continue its policies of racism; its support of the military industrial complex by supporting the war in Viet Nam, the ROTC, and the draft; and to deny us of our civil right of free speech. This university is a microcosm of our society and our government. A government founded on the principles of life, liberty, and the pursuit of happiness. A government of the people, by the people, and for the people. A government that currently refuses to listen to the will of the people. Is there only one way for the voice of the people to be heard?—A revolution! I say give back the power to the people!" He raised his hand in a fist as a cheer erupted.

"The people have spoken!" He shouted over the roar of the crowd.

"Then be it so," he continued as soon as the crowd quieted down. "For when a government refuses to listen to its people it is truly time for that government to go up in a blaze of glory." With these words the speaker took an American flag then set it on fire.

The flag was soon engulfed in flames. The crowd cheered as they watched it burn. He waved the burning flag high into the air, a symbol of our nation going up in flames. The smoke from the burning flag rose between the tall university buildings and into the clear blue sky on this typical warm Southern California spring day.

The quad was in the center of campus. It served as the heart and soul of the university due not only to its central location, but also because it was the hub of activity for college life. It was surrounded by various buildings housing mostly classrooms but also offices or research facilities for different departments or schools. A large library stood at one end of the quad with a theater at the other end. The largest structure on campus was the administration building looming over the quad like some overlord of the school. Some of the older buildings were made of red brick, but the more modern ones were constructed of white concrete. It had a fairly modern look, for this was not an old campus. It was constructed mostly in the post war 1950s and '60s when California led in education, and the population was growing at rapid rates. Large areas of grass and trees lined sidewalks with benches every few feet connecting the buildings to each other. The university offered a sense of isolation from the outside world in much the same way most typical campuses did. No cars, parking lots, or streets were visible from inside the campus, and no other buildings could be seen over the tall buildings housing this place of higher learning.

"The war in Viet Nam must end," the speaker continued as the smoldering flag lay on the ground at his feet. "We have voiced our demands by our protests and demonstrations to no avail. Our voices will be heard! As a nation, we have supported the war not only by the lives of our citizens and our military might, but by our actions. Why are we at war? The mighty American Oil Co. has oil rights in the east. The Bank of the United States has been supporting the war with loans, loans to American Oil and others to help secure their interest in oil for future profits. Let them know we want the war in Viet Nam to end. Let them know we want peace. This war must stop!" The speaker raised his arms while the crowd erupted in another cheer.

"What right do we have to interfere in a civil war in another country? What right do we have to force our views, policies, politics, and way of life on another country?" He paused as the crowd cheered. "We have no right. We have no right to force our ways onto another nation. We have no right to be the bully on the block of this planet we call Earth. Why must we be the police force of the world?" He paused again. "This is a war of power. America wants to show its might and power in the world, and American politicians are using this war to show the world that we are strong. This war is none of our business. We would not be there if it were not for oil. Many other nations in the world have problems, but do we get involved with them? No! This is not a fight against Communism. This war is not about making the world safe for Democracy. This is not about 'Truth, Justice, and The American Way'. This is about money and Capitalism and American Imperialism. I say to you—Stop the War!"

The crowd roared with approval, then started shouting, "Stop the war!" as he stepped back.

After a few moments the next speaker stepped forward, paused to let the crowd chant, raised his hands to quiet the crowd, and then continued. "This war is not about Democracy. It is about power and money. But do not be fooled! Making the world safe for Democracy is just the smoke screen that our government wants us to believe. Even if it were about these ideologies, these principles of Democracy and Capitalism, who are we to impose our way on someone else? On another nation? They try to keep us believing in this cause. They do this by using fear: fear of Communism; fear of Socialism; fear of other religions, peoples, and cultures; fear of another way of life. Fear can be a powerful tool. But do not be misled, this is not about ideology. This is about power. This is about money. This is about oil. Banks that are financing the war are near. We must let the nation know that this is unacceptable. We must end this war now!"

Again the crowd shouted a chorus of "Stop the War!" repeating it many times. The speaker stepped back while another speaker stepped forward to take the podium.

"We are here today to change the policies of America as well as the policies here at our own university, for if we want America to change, we must start in our own back yard. We know that this very university is a training ground for officers. The R.O.T.C. is training officers for the military right here on our campus. This we cannot tolerate. This must come to an end."

"R.O.T.C. off campus!" The crowd shouted.

"We also have many other issues here in America that need to be dealt with: racism, poverty, education. Let them know we want justice for all. This is a struggle for power and money. For us, it must begin here at our university.

Our own campus displays racism with a lack of professors of ethnic minorities, and the failure to recognize the need for black studies programs and women studies programs. Programs we have continually asked for. We must set the example and let our dissatisfaction be known.

We must deliver our demands and not leave until they have been met. We must show the world we have spoken. We will not take no for an answer. Therefore, until our demands are met our only recourse is to go on strike. Our only alternative is to shut it down!"

With these words the whole crowd erupted in a chorus of, "On Strike! Shut it down! On Strike! Shut it down!" The voices reverberated between the buildings creating an even louder echo.

The speakers descended from the podium. They locked arms then walked through the center of the crowd which parted to allow them to pass. The crowd turned and followed them chanting, "On Strike! Shut it down!" They left the quad and walked toward the administration building.

Helicopters were flying overhead. The crowd's attention was drawn upward to see the line of policemen in riot gear lining the tops of every building—guns drawn. Inside the Administration building the faces of people, thought mostly to be administrators and professors, were watching in anticipation.

This was a real political demonstration like the ones from the sixties. But this was not the sixties, this was the seventies, and there were still some battles to be fought. Along with the crowd there were two students, Michael Stewart and Jason Tucker, caught up in the excitement. They didn't know each other, but the two of them had watched, listened, chanted, and now followed as the crowd walked toward the administration building. It was like a newsreel from the past. But it was not the past, it was not a newsreel. It was the present, and it was real.

The crowd turned the corner approaching the administration building only to be confronted by a sea of police in riot gear—gas masks on, guns drawn, ready for action. The police had formed a line at the top of the stairs leading up to the main entrance.

The crowd walked to the bottom of the stairs and stopped, still chanting, "On Strike! Shut it down!"

The sound of a bullhorn pierced through the roar of the crowd. "You must disburse. This is an unlawful assembly. By order of the University, the City of Los Angeles, and the state of California you have been ordered to disburse."

The crowd went silent. It was a standoff.

After what seemed an eternity the bullhorn spoke again. "You have been warned. You have five minutes to disburse or action will be taken. This will be your last warning."

Silence again.

Jason, who had been following the crowd, was now a little worried, unsure of what he should do next. He was frozen there as if time stood still, curious as to the outcome, afraid to leave because of the angry crowd and what they might do, and afraid to stay because of what the police might do.

The police began to advance down the stairs. The crowd held its ground; many sat down and locked arms to further demonstrate their protest by instigating a sit-in. The police began grabbing protesters. They tried to get them to stand in order to place them under arrest. Angry protesters at the front began hitting the police, screaming obscenities as they were dragged away. Others went limp, making it difficult for the police to take them away. Police threw a tear gas canister into the crowd—pandemonium began. Students scattered in all directions, police on their heels.

Jason wasn't sure where to run, but he knew that he must.

Just then a hand grabbed him. "Follow me." The stranger pulled him by the arm. Jason turned. He recognized a student in one of his music classes. Jason followed him across the campus quad, between the buildings, through the parking lot, and across the street, running and panting all the way. They began to slow as distance separated them from the demonstration. Eventually, it turned into a walk as they both felt comfortable and far enough from harm's way. Soon they were off campus, but they were still cautious, constantly looking behind them to see if anyone was following. A few of the students had taken a similar route, but mostly the street was filled with students coming and going to class—unaware of the assault. They could still hear the noise of the crowd and the voices from the bullhorns echoing from the tall buildings just a short distance away, but the noise faded as the distance became greater.

"I live in an apartment building just down the street. I suggest we hang out there till this thing blows over," Mike offered, still walking.

Jason nodded in agreement. "OK," he said panting.

They stopped in the courtyard of the apartment building which was more like a college dorm even though it was off campus. They turned to see if they were being followed; they saw only the usual students coming from or going to class.

They looked around to see what appeared to be just another spring day in Los Angeles, a day not unlike any other, where it always seemed like the weather was warm and sunny—never changing. But the weather, just like the times, had changed. It was the seventies, both in the temperature and date. A seemingly insignificant time in itself compared to the decade before when the violent storms of the sixties seemed a thing of the past. It was a time when the hardships of the decade past had brought about many changes just as spring changes bring new life after a winter of hardship. And just as a stormy winter turns into a mild spring, the sixties had turned into the seventies. Life was returning to normal after a turbulent past. A past that had spilled over from the storms of the last decade with this day a remnant and a remembrance of times past with some battles still unresolved.

"THE TIMES THEY ARE A-CHANGIN'"

Bob Dylan

It was through politics and music that Jason Tucker and Mike Stewart met on that spring day of 1971. Although they had taken a few classes together at the Los Angeles University, their paths had not crossed until this day of politics and changing times. They were about to begin a new episode in each of their lives just as spring brings about renewal and change.

"Man, what a trip. That was fucking close. Are you OK?" Mike asked.

"Uh, Yeah," Jason responded. "I didn't expect it to get so crazy."

"This is like the old days!" Mike exclaimed. "I thought we were all over this shit. Ya know. The demonstrations and all."

"Uh huh, that was pretty wild," Jason agreed still a bit out of breath.

The two stopped. They were silent as they both reflected on what had just occurred.

"I'm Mike, Mike Stewart. I think it best we lay low until all this is over. This is where I live. Wanna join me?" He unlocked the door to his apartment.

"Thanks, you're probably right." Jason turned to follow him.

The two entered the apartment exhausted and out of breath.

It was a small one bedroom apartment that looked like a typical student pad. The walls were covered with psychedelic '60s posters, a concert poster from the Rolling Stones tour, and a few other posters of various rock bands announcing tours or engagements. Jason took a seat on the sofa. In front of him was a large construction spool which sat in the middle of the living room and functioned as a coffee table. It was covered with guitar picks, magazines, old beer bottles, and ashtrays filled with cigarette butts and marijuana roaches. On one wall, bookcases made from cinder blocks and pieces of board housed his stereo, some books, and an extensive collection of albums. Various guitars, both acoustic and electric, on stands lined the other wall in what should have been the dining room; an amplifier stood in the corner. A frameless single mattress and box springs were on the floor in one corner where Mike obviously slept. Jason noticed a door to the bedroom.

"That's where my roommate Doug sleeps. He's the guitar player in the band I'm in. We share the place. Actually, it was his place first, but when we started playing together he let me crash here since I needed a place to live. It's just temporary until we can get a two bedroom or something larger. I do pay him some rent though which helps him out. He gets the bedroom unless we have chicks over. Then it's kind of a free for all. But he lets me use the bed if he's alone, and it's just me and a chick." He paused "What's your name?"

"Jason, Jason Tucker," he replied.

"I recognized you from Advanced Musical Composition and from your recital. You really play beautifully" Mike took a seat on the sofa.

"Thanks. I thought you looked familiar." Jason now recognized him from class.

Mike was tall and thin with black shoulder length hair. He wore his Levis and Rolling Stones concert T-shirt like a true rocker, and, with his rock star good looks, he certainly fit the part.

"As you can see music is my life," Mike said. "Someday I hope to make a career out of it. You know rock and roll. That's why I was taking the class, to learn more about music theory and composing. You must have musical aspirations as well."

"Yeah, I hope to make a career of it as well; playing, composing, or arranging, maybe even for the movies doin' soundtracks or something. I really love my music. I hope to be a professional some day."

"Far out. Hey, let's check out what's happening." Mike walked over and turned on the small TV "See if there's anything about the demonstration on the news. I saw the news cameras on campus when we were there." A blurry picture with a lot of snow came on the screen. Mike adjusted the wire hanger which served as an antenna to see if he could get better reception. He hit the side a couple of times. Finally, a faint picture began to take shape. The voice of a newscaster spoke out.

"Campus demonstration erupts in violence," the news anchor said. "And now for some live footage of the event."

The coverage switched to a reporter that was on the scene at the campus quad where Mike and Jason had just left. He was dressed in a blue blazer, white shirt, and dark blue tie. The campus buildings, which Jason and Mike immediately recognized, were in the background. He spoke into the microphone he held in his hand. "Students clash with police here on the campus of Los Angeles University. Violence erupted when police moved in to quiet the demonstrators. This was an anti-war rally that got out of control when demonstrators tried to take over the administration building. Here is some footage of what transpired just a short time ago." It showed coverage of what had started out as a demonstration with a few clips of the speakers. It showed the students walking to the administration building and the standoff. Then it showed how the demonstration turned to violence. It looked as if it had turned into a full fledged riot. Police were combing the area in riot gear. Bottles were being thrown at the police by the demonstrators. A police line was walking through to try to disburse the crowd. All in all it was a pretty ugly scene. Pictures of police beating, arresting, and physically hauling off demonstrators followed. The demonstrators scattered with the escalation of the violence as the police made their presence known. "Many arrests were made." The commentator continued. "A strong police presence remains here on campus, but many of the demonstrators have disbursed. The campus has been completely closed down for the day in an effort to quell the violence. Campus officials will determine whether to open the campus tomorrow or not."

"Gee, looks like we got out just in time," Jason commented seeing the news coverage.

"Fuck, you got that right. I saw you standing there looking lost, like you weren't sure where to go." Mike looked up to see his reaction.

"You were right about that. I didn't really expect to see the police show up, especially in riot gear. I couldn't believe it when they attacked the students. I mean I've been to demonstrations, but it never went this far. I've never been involved in anything like this. I've just seen it on TV."

"Um, doesn't happen too often, at least not so much any more," Mike commented.

"I remember seeing it on TV a couple of years ago. Were you here when they had the big demonstrations?" Jason asked. "I saw it on the news back in Atlanta."

"I was only here for some of it. I was in Berkeley most of that time. We had quite a bit of action there also. I was one of those out there fighting causes." Mike raised his hands, clenched his fists, and assumed a fight stance.

"Yeah, I guess I got caught up in the entire political thing as well, but mostly from the sidelines. Never anything this big or this militant. I hadn't planned to, but I was really against the war." Jason laughed and nodded in agreement.

"Yeah, me too. I really felt it would make a difference—you know protesting against the Viet Nam war, trying to get R.O.T.C off campus. I even supported the efforts to get a black studies department. I felt it was time our voices were heard. I even joined the SDS for a while, you know the Students for a Democratic Society. Sounds like you missed the big riot a couple of years ago. You know when all the arrests were made, and the police beat those people." Mike asked.

"Yeah, I missed it. I was still in Atlanta."

"I was here. I was lucky. I ran and got away. But a lot of my friends were beaten pretty badly. It was a really ugly scene. It's amazing how all that seemed so important, you know with The John Birch Society preaching their ultraconservative point of view, and then resurfacing as the American Independent Party. It's no wonder our radical factions, as they called us, eventually gave rise to the Peace and Freedom Party. If nothing else, they were forums to present different viewpoints and attitudes for a people who I think had grown lethargic. Sometimes it is necessary to make waves. Perhaps it opened the minds of some people for political and social alternatives—to let people know that it's necessary sometimes to question or disagree with the powers that be. I believe that it's only by radical action that the voice of the people be heard, people who should demand and fight for those changes."

Jason leaned forward, engaged in the conversation while the TV flickered in the background with continuing coverage of the campus demonstration.

Mike's voice rose with excitement. "You see one of my main reasons for being here at the University is only to maintain my student deferment to avoid the draft. I do believe in all those causes as well. I was just as involved as you seem to be; however, I see the times from a sociological point of view also. You see sociology is my major. Kinda means nothing I guess.

Anyway, I see this era as a time of change not just in politics, but in different ways as well—sociological and cultural ways for instance. I guess to use the old cliché' I saw this as the 'dawning of the age of Aquarius'—the promise of a new age. However, what had begun with a spectacular sunrise has now turned into just another day." Mike laughed a little at his metaphor then turned to the TV to see the continuing coverage of the campus riot. "Wow, this is certainly quite a demonstration."

"Sure is," Jason agreed.

Mike turned to Jason again to continue his conversation. "However, I do feel the new attitude of this generation did have an impact on the values and morals of the American people. I see the movement as a rejection of old ideals. Economically it was a backlash of American Capitalism which had triumphed so well in the prior generation—a generation of world wars and the Great Depression—when people survived through great hardships and eventually prospered. However, in trying to survive in a time when it was a struggle just to have a meal on the table I feel that they had grown too materialistic—placing money, wealth, and things as the top priorities in their lives. Because of this, they were anxious to give their children all the material things they fought so hard to get, and to protect their children from similar hardships which they had endured. But for their children who had never experienced hunger or the want of material goods the priorities had changed."

"I know what you mean," Jason admitted.

"I do feel the change is a positive one," Mike continued. "I see the new age as one of sharing—working for the common good; not just for oneself. I believe, at least to a certain extent, that the old goals of money and materialism have been replaced by happiness and love and peace. We now strive for the good of mankind, not just the betterment of each individual often times at the expense of others. We are less self-centered, less egotistical. I see this era as a celebration of life. I probably was caught up in the ideology of the times. I think some of these changes are great. I see their effects and attitudes slowly growing—taking root in this new generation. I also see a new tolerance and acceptance of other people and cultures, with no judgments made no matter what race, creed, color, or class they are. I firmly believe in these new principals. I can see their influences creeping in to our everyday lives." He paused, taking a deep breath. "Sorry, I didn't mean to get on my soap box. I guess it's all the sociology classes."

"Right on, I totally agree with you." Jason was a bit surprised at Mike's intelligence for to look at Mike, you would imagine him to be a rather uneducated street stoner type.

"I tell you, if it weren't for music I'd be crazy. Music is what I dig most—that, and of course the drugs. I like to experiment with different states of consciousness. I'm interested in expanding my conscience or perhaps expanding reality or exploring other realities." He stopped. "Shit, I can get all philosophical about it, but in the end drugs are something I merely enjoy, nothing more. Hey, do you get high? Wanna smoke a joint?"

"Sure," Jason replied.

Mike took out his stash which was in an old cigar box filled with marijuana and rolling papers. He rolled a joint, lit it, and then passed it to Jason. "That Chopin piano piece you did yesterday at the recital was amazing." Mike had heard Jason play at a recital he was required to attend. Jason had played a particularly difficult piano piece as part of his musical training and a requirement for his degree in music.

Compliments made Jason uncomfortable. He was quite at a loss for words, but smiled in recognition of Mike's compliments. He took a hit of the joint, coughed, and then passed it back to Mike. "Uh, Thanks. I didn't even know you were there." Jason bowed his head in modesty.

Jason was an accomplished musician—a pianist, not just a piano player and a true master of the instrument. He not only had ability, but played with emotion and a true sense of style. His main goal in life was to be a professional musician. He had been classically trained since he was young. He had transferred to Los Angeles University on scholarship because of the reputation of its music department which was well known in the music world. He gave private lessons on the side to make some extra money. Jason had the ability to make his piano feel by turning those notes on a page of music to pure art and emotion. Hearing him play Chopin could bring tears to anyone's eyes. He was a quiet, shy, introspective type; intellectual, yet philosophic by nature. He had striking good looks with long blond hair; blue eyes; and a tall, thin, muscular athletic type build. He looked like the perfect model for the California beach boy type. All he needed was a surfboard. He enjoyed the outdoors as much as he enjoyed his education for he loved to learn, see, and experience new things.

"It was awesome. You must be a music major." Mike took another hit then passed the joint to Jason.

"Thanks... um. And yes, I am majoring in music. I've been playing since I was ten, mostly piano, but also some woodwinds. I play flute, clarinet, and saxophone. It allows me to play in the school band and orchestra and helps me with my composition skills."

"I'm only going for a minor in music." Mike offered. "I dig music, but a different kind. I wanted to take some music classes to learn more about theory, composition, and stuff. Uh, I didn't become a music major because I had a tough time with the piano proficiency exams and shit. I don't have a piano to practice on. Besides, I wanna play rock music, not that classical stuff. Don't get me wrong, I love classical music, but my heart is in rock. Are you taking Advanced Composition for your degree?" Mike asked.

"Uh huh, it is required. I'd like to do some more composing. I've been writing music for a long time, but I felt that I needed the music theory to become a better composer and to better understand music and structure. I really want to write a whole orchestral piece someday. I really dig Ravel, Debussy, Stravinsky, Copeland, and probably Gershwin."

"Some of my favorites too." Mike felt enthused that they shared some similarity in musical taste. "I love most of the impressionist, modern, and contemporary composers. I even dig some of the romantics, but my favorites are mostly things after that. I just dig 'em more than Bach and all those old classical and baroque composers. Not that I don't like or can't appreciate the other composers, but the more modern stuff is just more my taste. I think it has more passion and emotion. I believe music should have passion and feeling. Ya know what I mean?"

"I agree." Jason was feeling more comfortable and relaxed as the tensions from his earlier experience left him. "I wouldn't even mind doing the music score for a film or something."

Mike grabbed a hospital clamping device that was used in surgery.

"These hemostats make great roach clips." He used it to clamp the small remaining joint so that he could pass it to Jason.

"So what d'ya plan to do with your sociology degree when you get it?" Jason inquired.

"Um, oh nothing. What can I do? Study some primitive tribe in Africa? Join the Peace Corps? No, I really wanna pursue a career in music. Ya know, the big time—rock and roll. That's why I came back to L.A. San Francisco is dead, politically and musically. It's all happening here now. Someday I will be a rock star!" Mike said emphatically.

"Yeah, I noticed the posters. I see we have similar taste in rock as well." Jason took another hit, coughed, and then passed it again to Mike. "What instrument do ya play?"

"Mostly bass. I play guitar and do some singing also." Mike put what was left of the joint in the ashtray. "In bands I mostly play the bass though. I just took to bass more for some reason and it makes it easier to sing. I started playing bass first many years ago quite by accident. I eventually picked up the guitar. I've played both in bands, but found more work as a bass player. They always seemed to be in demand. There are plenty of good guitarists out there. It seems like everyone wants to be the lead guitarist. Besides, there are many guitars players much better than me. I decided that at least I could be an excellent bass player. I'll never forget the first time I changed. I was in this band with two guitarists playing rhythm guitar, but they needed a bass player. I had mostly played rhythm, not lead. The guitarist was a lot better than I was, so I brought in my bass. I have been playing bass mostly ever since. I do write songs on regular guitar, but when it comes to a band I really connect to playing bass much more." Mike continued as he picked up his guitar and started playing chords, runs, and other things on the guitar. "Yeah, I wanna make it big. I mean I can do the same things all these musicians are doing. I hear some of the shit on the radio. I know I can do better. All I need is a break. Maybe someday I'll be discovered. Someday, someone will realize my talent and give me a chance. All I can do is to keep trying. It's a tough nut to crack, but I plan to do it!" He paused lost in thought for a moment then returned to realty.

"For now playing is how I support myself. I play in this band called Axis. We got the name from the Jimi Hendrix song and album <u>Axis, bold as love.</u> We play cover songs at clubs and parties to make money. I think we're really good. It's a power trio: bass, drums, and guitar—sort of like Cream or Jimi Hendrix. I feel all we need is the chance. But those record companies just don't wanna listen. Instead, they put out that crap ya hear on the radio. I just wish I had that chance. Someday I will. But for now at least I can make a living at it. Uh, you should come hear us play sometime."

"That' be cool, I'd like that," Jason responded.

"We're playing next week at the Campus Club, you know that night club just off campus. You ought to stop by."

"That'd be far out." Jason agreed.

"D'ya like Emerson Lake and Palmer? I just got their new album."

"They're one of my favorite groups. I like the classical influence, and of course, Keith Emerson is a great player and plays all those different keyboards." Jason smiled. "I just love 'Lucky Man.' Such an incredible song."

"Yeah, I thought you'd like 'em. One of my favorites too, man. I really dig the way Greg Lake plays bass, and he does have an amazing voice."

"I'll put it on. It's incredible." He put his guitar down and picked out the new album. "What other groups do ya like?" He asked as he pulled the record out of the sleeve and placed it on the turntable.

"I guess The Beatles, The Stones, Jimi Hendrix, The Doors, The Who, Led Zeppelin and Jethro Tull especially for their way of creating a composition almost like classical music but for rock music. Of course, I also really dig Elton John and Billy Joel for all that piano stuff they do."

"Shit, those are some of my favorites as well. <u>Who's Next</u> is such a classic album. I can't believe we have so much in common. It's like finding an old friend." He put the arm of the stereo on the record, and the music began. The first song played before he spoke again.

"Pretty cool, huh." Mike turned to see Jason's reaction.

"Yeah, really great stuff." Jason seemed very impressed indeed.

"I could do that! I know I can!" He reiterated confidently. "All I need is a break." He paused only to become pensive. "But it's really tough. The music business is full of idiots—people that don't really know what good music is. Just one big bureaucracy. It's all politics. Not what you can do or how talented you are—it's who you know." Mike stated authoritatively. His defeatist attitude allowed him an excuse for his lack of ambition and success. He could easily explain his failure due to outside sources—sources beyond his control. Mike was somewhat arrogant and just intelligent enough to be cynical, a comfortable and safe place for him to be. "I just hope someday I can break through that wall."

"Man, it's dark outside." Jason noticed as he looked out the window. "I've been here for hours. I think it's safe to go now. I guess I better split. It was great meeting you, and thanks for the joint. Uh, I'll see you in class or next week at the club."

"Far Out,' said Mike. "See you around."

"BORN TO BE WILD"

Steppenwolf

Jason arrived at the small nightclub to see Mike play. As he entered, he could hear the band playing "Sunshine of your Love" by Cream. The Campus Club was a typical college hangout. Its collegiate theme made it look more like a frat house than a nightclub complete with books; sports equipment like footballs, baseball bats, and tennis racquets; as well as pompoms and banners, all in the school colors of the campus which was only a few blocks away. Jason saw the band playing on a small stage at the back. Tables and chairs were placed all around except for a small wooden dance floor directly in front of the stage. A bar ran almost the whole length of one side of the club. Behind the bar, a small kitchen offered food, mostly burgers and pizza, but just enough to legally allow patrons under the age of 21 to enter. Jason noticed that most of the patrons were students or at least in that age bracket. Jason went to the bar, ordered a beer, and sat down to watch the rest of the set. The band was quite good, overall Jason was impressed. The next song was "Jumpin' Jack Flash" by the Rolling Stones. Jason recognized many of the songs they played since all were major hits of the day or classic rock songs from groups like The Beatles, Deep Purple, Doobie Brothers, Black

Sabbath, The Who, The Eagles, and Creedence Clearwater Revival. It was a three piece band: bass, drums, and guitar with everyone taking turns singing lead as well as singing backup harmonies. The drummer was solid providing a strong foundation. The guitar player was versatile and seemed able to play any style of music whether it was rock, and soul, rhythm and blues, or pop. He could make any song sound just like the record. He especially noticed that Mike was really good on stage. They finished their set then put their instruments away. Before leaving the stage they all huddled around each other to discuss something which appeared to be important and serious. It was almost like a football team planning their next strategy. Jason wasn't sure if they were discussing the set, the next set, or something entirely different. Mike was the first to leave, followed by the guitar player and the drummer who was wiping the sweat off of his forehead with a small white towel.

Jason stood up and waved. Mike immediately spotted him and smiled. He approached him with the other band members following.

"Band sounds great!" Jason offered.

"Uh, Thanks," Mike said. "And thanks for showing up. Not a bad gig really, playing here on weekends. Usually has a pretty good crowd, and it keeps my chops up. Let me introduce you to the rest of the guys. This is Doug." the guitar player reached out his hand to offer a handshake. "And this is Brian." the drummer did the same."

"Nice meeting you," Jason said.

Brian, the drummer, was much shorter than Jason had thought. His size had been obscured by the drum set he was sitting behind. What he lacked in height, however, he made up in width. Not fat but very stocky. The sleeveless shirt which was drenched with sweat revealed a very fit, muscular body, almost the physique of a body builder with large arms and a big chest. He was a real rugged man's man. Not real handsome but not unattractive either. His long black shoulder length hair was dripping with sweat from the workout on the stage.

Doug, the guitar player, was tall and thin with curly brown hair and round wire rim glasses. He looked rather geeky, more like a long haired accountant than a rock musician with his sport coat, collared shirt, and nice jeans.

"You guys are sounding great," commented Jason to the other musicians.

"Thanks," they all chorused in unison. The conversation continued until Doug and Brian left to get a drink at the bar and to check out the girls. Mike and Jason talked music until Mike had to return to the stage.

The set continued with songs by Led Zeppelin, Stevie Wonder, and other hits.

Mike returned to talk to Jason during the breaks while Doug and Brian usually gravitated to the bar, striking up conversations with some girls. It wasn't long before they had picked up a couple of young ladies and had their arms around them. Jason could see this was going to end up in someone's bedroom. The girls were laughing, showing the guys their interest, and the guys were ready for some action after the gig.

Doug came over to the table with the girls. He introduced them to Jason and Mike. "This is Barb and Janet, and these are their friends Patty and Meg." Doug pointed to each of them as they were introduced.

All replied with a seductive hello.

They talked for a short while until the band had to return to the stage leaving Jason with the girls. After each set the band returned to continue the conversation.

Just before the midnight set Doug announced, "Hey let's all go back to our place after the gig. It's not far from here. We can get high and party. How about it?"

"Yeah, how about it?" Mike responded turning to the girls.

The girls began to giggle. They all agreed.

He then turned to Jason. "You're welcome to join us. There's one for you."

"Er. Thanks for the offer," he replied. "But I have to get up early tomorrow and give a piano lesson. Maybe next time."

"That's cool." Mike smiled.

"In fact I should be going now. It was a pleasure meeting ya'll. Have fun." Jason stood up to get ready to leave. He said his good-byes then left as the guys continued talking with the girls. He knew that the girls were part of the benefits of playing at the club.

The girls did stay until the last set. They waited for the band to pack up, and then followed them home to Doug's place. The girls entered the apartment and sat down next to the guy they wanted. Obviously they had discussed their conquests, agreeing on who they had dibs on. Mike rolled a joint while Doug passed out the beers. They sat and talked for a short while as they passed the joint and drank the beers. The girls were obviously easy prey for the guys. All they talked about was how great the band was and what songs they liked the best, complimenting each of them on certain performances. They were ready and willing, and the boys were eager to please. Doug was the first to make his move, putting his arm around Barb as they talked. It wasn't long before Doug was kissing Barb while his hands wandered all over her willing body, feeling her breasts at first through her clothes then eventually venturing under her shirt, feeling her up while her body language expressed satisfaction and desire, succumbing to their carnal nature. Mike was soon to follow suit with Janet, his date for the evening. That left Brian the drummer with two girls on his hands, but neither seemed to mind. They were all over him as he took off his shirt displaying his well built chest like a proud peacock as the two girls ran their hands over it. It wasn't long before the guys were able to take off the girl's tops displaying their young perky breasts. They were showing no signs of inhibition. Since it was Doug's apartment, he invited his girl into the bedroom and closed the door leaving Mike and Brian with the other girls in the living room. Mike took his to the mattress on the floor where he slept. It wasn't long before clothes started flying. Brian stayed on the sofa with the other two. It wasn't long before they were all naked as well, bodies writhing in ecstasy. It was an evening of free love and wild sex, enjoyed by all.

Monday, Jason saw Mike on campus.

"Band was great. I really had a good time hanging with you guys." Jason put his arm on Mike's shoulder who was sitting on the grass waiting for his next class.

"Thanks"

"Looks like you had quite an evening after the gig." Jason smiled at him as he sat down.

"Yeah, it was a blast." Mike laughed as he turned to Jason. "Those chicks were hot."

"Do ya do that often?

"Uh, yeah, I guess. One of the perks of being a musician. It was all fun. Besides, we were all consenting. We all had a good time." Mike laughed. "Might as well make the best of it. Besides, who are we hurting? We're having fun, they're having fun, no strings attached, all consensual. Uh, I like to play the field a bit. The girls are into it. It's all just about getting off and feeling good. You know if it feels good do it. What's the harm?"

"I can dig it."

"You see that's another thing this generation has given us, this new attitude toward sex. I really dig this new free love generation. I love the new sexual freedoms and the de-mystification of sex and sexual attitudes, where sex isn't just something done after marriage. I believe that the whole idea of relationships is changing, as have sex roles, now all being less defined. People are often opting to share their life together without the legal paper. Who really needs the marriage license anyway? That has historically been the custom. It just seems so old fashioned. Now it's only their desire to continue the relationship which keeps them together. To me that seems more healthy, more realistic." Mike seemed to be rationalizing his actions as much as he was expressing his attitudes and beliefs.

"Right on, I agree with you."

Jason did go see the band on a fairly regular basis. He enjoyed listening to the band, hanging out with them, and meeting new people. Wherever they were playing it usually ended up the same. The band always seemed to pick up girls for more fun after the gig. Sometimes they all convened at Doug's apartment, sometimes they would go to the girl's place, or sometimes they would split up. For the band every night was a different gig and a different girl, a scene that was repeated many times.

Jason seemed to like the lifestyle even though he seldom participated in the after gig festivities. Only occasionally would he join them but just to get high, always leaving in a short time saying he had music lessons early the next morning. The sexual exploits were just not his thing. He did, however, love the feeling of freedom, of complete self-expression and openness, and how uninhibited the band was about each of their conquests and about their sex life. In a way it was honest and free—without limitations. Something Jason liked very much.

Mike ran up to Jason as they left class one afternoon "Hey man, they just announced the L.A. date for the Led Zeppelin tour. They just released a new album and are on tour to promote it. Wanna get some tickets and go? It should be an amazing show."

"Works for me." Jason thought it would be fun. He looked forward to going to a real rock concert with a band he really liked. "Where are they playing?'

"At the Forum."

"Is that some sort of concert hall?"

"No, not at all. It's a big indoor stadium. All the big groups play there. It holds a lot of people. It's actually a big sports arena. The Los Angeles Lakers play there, you know the basketball team. They also have other sports events there like hockey. It's sort of our version of Madison Square Garden; you know the one in New York."

"Where is it?" Jason asked again.

"In Inglewood, not far from here. It's near Los Angeles International Airport south of Hollywood and south west of downtown L.A., just off the 405 freeway."

"Sounds like fun to me. Count me in."

"I'll get the tickets if you can drive. I can even get some pot. It ought to be a bitchin' evenin'." Mike turned and left.

The night of the concert Jason picked up Mike at his apartment.

"This should be incredible." Mike entered the car excited about the evening before them. "But we need to smoke a doobie before we get there." Mike took out a small stash of already rolled joints. He lit one up then passed it to Jason.

"You've got that right." Jason took a hit and held it in. He passed the joint back to Mike as they drove on.

Once they were near to their destination they could see the huge round stadium in the distance poking up from the flat car filled parking lot. It was a grand circular building with white columns which seemed to support the roof giving it the look of a Roman Coliseum. They got to the stadium, paid for parking, and then lit up another joint in the parking lot before going into the concert.

"I can't wait to see these guys in concert. They should be really happenin'." Mike finished the joint then exited the car with Jason right behind him. They started to walk, joining the large crowd of people which continued to grow the closer they got to the building which loomed in the distance. As the approached the round building, it seemed to get larger with each step. When they finally arrived, they stood and looked up at the huge building with the columns rising up taller than they had expected. They felt dwarfed by it sheer size. They walked around until they found their section. They handed their tickets to the ticket taker then walked inside. A promenade circled all the way around the stadium where food, beverages, beer, and tour stuff—mostly t-shirts and other memorabilia were sold. Mike immediately went to the stand and bought a Led Zeppelin tour t-shirt and a tour poster. "Just gotta have it." He put the t-shirt on over the one he was wearing.

They entered the arena which Jason thought was at ground level but soon discovered was actually about half way up from the ground floor which was at the bottom of a deep pit. At one end of the floor was the huge stage brought in for the concert.

"Man, how many people does this place hold?" inquired Jason.

"Uh, I think around 18,000 for concerts," Mike answered.

"Shit, I never knew that these places were so big inside."

They found their seats. Not great seats, but at least they could see everything. They sat down and immediately started checking out the stage. It was a portable stage about five feet off the floor and filled with equipment. The drum set sat on a three foot high riser at the back of the stage. Lights and monitors lined the front while amplifiers lined the back walls. On both sides speakers were stacked for the sound system which was playing rock music. A large scaffolding system was erected on the sides and over the top of the stage to house additional sound and lighting equipment. Mike immediately began to check out the equipment, naming all the types of amplifiers and equipment they had on stage. They could barely contain their excitement. The air was electric as the crowd waited with anticipation for Led Zeppelin to take the stage. It wasn't long after they sat down that the lights began to dim. Immediately, the whole crowd stood up ready for the opening number. The lowering of the lights seemed to be the cue as the now darkened stadium was lit up by the glow of lighters and matches as everyone seemed to light up a joint at the same time. The smell of grass was everywhere as the audience cheered and the excitement built to a crescendo.

The band entered playing "Good Times, Bad Times," one of their signature songs, in an explosion of lights and sound. The music was almost deafening and the lights changed with each chord to accent the music. Mike and Jason did not talk during the show, instead focusing their attention to the stage and the performance. They sat silent during each song then cheered when each song ended. They only occasionally exchanged glances of approval as they both got into the music. Mike occasionally lit up another joint then passed it to Jason with a nod of approval. The show was high energy and well-paced with all the hits everyone wanted to hear. The Band played songs from all their albums, but the highlight seemed to be a slow song on the new album called "Stairway to Heaven." All in all it was an exciting show for all. Mike and Jason were glad to have shared this experience with the crowd and with each other. The last song was "Whole Lotta Love" which again brought the whole crowd to its feet. They left the stage while the arena stayed dark. The audience stood cheering, applauding, and pounding their feet for more. Eventually, they returned for a few more songs. Finally, after two encores they left the stage. The concert was over.

"Man, that was fuckin' awesome!" Mike exclaimed as the lights started to come back on. "What did ya think?"

"Fuckin' incredible! A real outstanding show! Robert Plant is an excellent singer, and the band is really outta sight as well." Jason was energized having seen his first real rock concert.

"Yeah, I really dig the way Jimmy Page plays guitar. And did ya check out that drummer? He sure can play. That drum solo was incredible."

"Yeah, it was a fucking fantastic show."

"I dig that new song 'Stairway to Heaven', a classic," commented Mike.

As they walked to their car, all they talked about was the show, reliving some of the songs, the moments, and the experience. Both filled with an excitement they would never forget.

"Ya see that's what I wanna do," Mike commented as they drove home. "I wanna be a rock star, play stadiums. Play my music to large crowds. I know I can do it, if I could just get a break."

"Yeah, you guys sound pretty good," agreed Jason.

"We have a long way to go, but I think we could do that. We're as good as any band I've seen. We just need a break." Mike sounded confident. "Someday I'll be on that stage. You just wait and see."

All the way home they continued talking about the show and Mike's ambition.

Mike and Jason started hanging out together more frequently on and off campus. It became more and more evident that they had a lot in common especially in their musical taste, but they also had similar political views. Jason enjoyed the evenings with the band, so he went to see them and partied with them often when they had a gig on weekends. He also liked getting high with Mike and just listening to music and talking. In addition they went to concerts to check out their favorite bands. They saw Deep Purple, The Moody Blues, Jethro Tull, The Who, Pink Floyd, Emerson Lake and Palmer, and The Rolling Stones, all playing pretty large stadiums. The shows were outstanding. It was fun for all concerned. Each time Mike saw a show he relived his dream

As time went on Jason was beginning to like the rock and roll life style: going to rock concerts, getting high, hanging out with the band, watching them pick up chicks. It seemed like life was just always a party. Between college, Mike's gigs, and concerts, Mike and Jason were becoming very close friends.

"PURPLE HAZE IS IN MY BRAIN"

Jimi Hendrix

It was a beautiful warm June day when staying inside seemed a waste. It was the end of the school year. Mike and Jason met after finishing their last final exams. Another year completed. With classes over, no gigs, and a free weekend; it seemed a good time to celebrate.

"Hey, man, just finished my last final. Glad that's over." Mike seemed relieved as he approached Jason in the quad.

"Me too," Jason agreed. "Another semester completed."

"I just got some Purple Haze from a friend." Jason looked puzzled. "You know some acid, LSD. I was saving it for a special occasion, and I think this qualifies. It'd be fun to drop a tab with you if you're into it and have nothing to do. It's still morning, and there's plenty of daylight. I dig droppin' acid outdoors in nature. D'ya like the outdoors?"

"Yeah, sure do, but I've only done acid a couple of times before."

"Oh, it'll be great. I think your trip all depends on the environment. Ya know. Where you are, and who you're with. I think we get along well, and it would be an incredible experience. Well, I know this place we can get to pretty quick. We can backpack in and camp all night. We'll just hike until we drop, and then set up camp for the evening and trip out. It ought to be warm enough tonight. Are you into that?"

"Sure, man. Sounds bitchin'," Jason agreed.

It was with excitement and anticipation that their trip began. After packing their things into Mike's van, they drove to the Angeles Forest, about an hour drive from campus.

One of the big draws of the Los Angeles area and partly responsible for its population increase was its close proximity to a variety of terrains, features, biomes, and climates. Within one or two hours one could be in the alpine pine covered mountains, the beach, rolling hills, forested oak valleys, or deserts. With its temperate Mediterranean climate, the temperatures in the basin varied little during the year, while a great variety of other climates were close by and accessible year around. On a winter's day one could even be snow skiing in the morning at one of the many ski resorts, then end up surfing at the beach—all in the same day. Even in the heat of summer one had the option of getting some relief by heading to one of the cool beaches or mountains.

"I love the beauty of nature. Isn't it great that places like this are so close?" Mike began as they drove to their destination. "L.A. just has such a variety of natural settings. I am so glad we have places like this preserved for the future. That's one thing this generation has done right. They have fostered a renewed respect for our natural environment and a concern for the world as a whole. I, too, advocate a return to nature, to the preservation of the earth and nature, and to protect our natural resources; to not pollute them like in times past. Ya know what I'm sayin'?"

"Sure do. You are really passionate about this aren't ya?"

"Just another of my causes."

When they got there it was still the afternoon. They parked the van in a large overnight lot, grabbed their back packs, and began their journey.

It was a beautiful area. The uphill path took off to the right toward the canyon. It ran along side a creek bed where a small trickle of water ran over large rocks, boulders, or sandy bottoms. The trail was lined with large trees, mostly oak but mixed with some pine, manzanita bushes, and lots of sage brush. It was a symphony of sight and sound—the green trees, the large brown boulders, the blue sky, the babbling brook, the birds singing, the leaves rustling. All enhanced the beautiful experience. The sun shining through the leaves of the trees created a dappled pattern of light and shadow while the shade kept them cool from the warm sun. It was a perfect beginning to their trip together.

"Here, take a tab. We'll walk till we drop. It's an excellent way to get high." They both took a tab of LSD then set out on their journey.

"I feel like something out of a JRR Tolkien novel. You know like Bilbo Baggins in <u>The Hobbit</u> or Frodo Baggins in <u>The Lord of the Rings</u>—setting out for our journey to the unknown." Jason's voice became bold and heroic.

"I dig those books—probably my favorites. The spirit of adventure, the journey, and all that," Mike admitted.

"Mine too," Jason agreed.

"This is gonna be a great trip. I haven't done acid in a long time, probably since I lived in San Francisco!" Mike exclaimed as they began their journey. "Those were some fun times. Hey, I know you're from Atlanta, but what was it like there? What were your folks like?"

"Well, uh. I guess you could say I came from the perfect American household. One of those strong southern families with church on Sunday, southern hospitality, and family dinner served with a good helping of family values." Jason began, feeling very comfortable and less inhibited about talking about his home life. He wasn't sure if it was just his strong connection with Mike, the drugs, or a combination of the two. Either way he felt a little more relaxed and able to open up about his past. A good feeling even if it were drug induced.

"It was like one of those 50s black and white TV sitcoms—sort of a cross between 'Father Knows Best' and 'Leave it to Beaver'." He laughed. "Dad in a suit going to work every day; Mom doing the housework in a dress. You should've seen us goin' to church on Sunday. Mom wearing a nice dress, pearls, and gloves with matching shoes and hand bag; and Dad and me in suits. Very formal. We had a small stucco house in the suburbs of Atlanta, one of those post war tracts built in the early fifties. I was part of that post war baby boom and my parents pride and joy, especially being their only son. My sister came along later. Often times they had me play the piano at parties or social events. They just loved to show me off to their friends at parties."

As they walked, the terrain changed. The canyon had narrowed with steep walls lining the creek bed and path. Sunlight shone on the top but did not penetrate into the narrow ravine. Large boulders lay in their path forcing them to cross the creek many times as they continued their journey.

Jason felt the drug come on stronger. All his inhibitions seemed to go away, and the warmth of the friendship allowed him to continue. "Dad, he was the strong authoritative type with a strong sense of responsibility. He never missed work and was always the family man, for his family gave him the greatest enjoyment in life. We were all that mattered to him. He wanted to give me all the things and opportunities he didn't have as a kid, like an education, so that I could get a good job and make a lot of money. He was from a rather poor family. He never wanted me to struggle like he had. But he sort of had life planned out for me: college, a good career, nice wife, kids to carry on the family name, home in the suburbs with a station wagon and a dog. You know—the American dream. However, he and Mom both did encourage me to always be happy. They never forced me to do anything, only the things I wanted to. But they did expect me to carry through with whatever I started. I think he would rather have wanted me to be an accountant or lawyer or something—a regular guy with whom he could watch Saturday football. But music won out for me. It was something I wanted to do.

They did, however, make me earn the things I wanted. I remember when I first started playing the piano. They encouraged me, but I had to pay for my own piano lessons. I used my allowance and money I got from mowing the neighbor's lawns, even though I still suspect they were helping by subsidizing payments on the side. But they were always there, be it a recital, a band concert, or whatever. They were always there supporting me and my dream. They were very proud. I think their proudest moment was when I received a scholarship to attend college, although I think a little shocked to find out I wanted to go away to college—and to California no less. You know, land of fruits and nuts. But it was time. I had to leave and start a life of my own. I needed to get away from the people and things in Atlanta. I just didn't fit in there. I guess those things they taught me like independence and responsibility really did pay off.

Looking back, I think the hardest thing for me was to gain Dad's respect. For a long time he was resentful that I wasn't handling my life the way he had planned. I remember my first summer home from college. It was the first time he had seen me with long hair and what he called funny clothes. They were very conservative, die-hard Republicans. We have complete differences of opinion on a number of subjects and we had some pretty heated discussions because our views and ideas were very different. For a while, we didn't talk at all. Finally, just before it was time for me to return to college, I just said to him, 'Look Dad, what the hell have you got to complain about. Maybe we do have some differences, and maybe I didn't turn out just the way you had planned, but basically I'm a good kid. I get good grades. I've never been in trouble. I got a scholarship to go to college. I just don't see why we can't just respect each other for what we are and forget the differences. Cause you are my dad, and I love you.' Well, he gave me a big hug We haven't had any trouble since." Jason, realized just how high he was, couldn't believe the things he had been saying. He had never opened up to someone like this before. But somehow it felt all right with Mike. "Boy I sure went off on a trip."

"It's cool, man. Thanks for sharing. I can really feel the acid coming on. In fact, I'm getting pretty fucked up. How 'bout you?"

"Yeah, me to. Pretty spaced," Jason agreed. "Check out the shadows, they're getting pretty long. The sun will be setting shortly. It reminds me more and more of <u>The Hobbit</u> when he was taking a long journey into the forest. This is a very beautiful area. Thanks for inviting me."

"No problem." Mike trudged on taking in all the sights and sounds as the drug took its affect.

It wasn't long before the sun would be setting behind the mountains. The scattered clouds turned a bright orange creating a beautiful sunset. As the sun set, the sky turned a beautiful shade of purple.

"Look! Purple Haze! Just like the acid!" Mike commented.

They continued their journey in the shade as the sunlight began to fade.

"Look, I am too high to keep on talking. Besides, I'm tired of listening to myself talk now that I've spilled my guts," Jason said. "Let's hear about you and your family."

Feeling touched by Jason's story Mike began, "You were lucky you *had* a father. I never really knew my dad. Um, he died before I was born. Mom said he was an Air Force Pilot—a real hero. She got pregnant during one of his shore leaves. He died overseas in a plane crash long before I was around. She never told me much else about him. In fact, she's almost secretive about him. I guess it was one of those quick military romances. I always picture it as one of those old black and white Hollywood love stories, like <u>From Here to Eternity</u>. The handsome young pilot or soldier meets the pretty young girl on leave. They fall in love. Then he must return to the war not knowing that he is soon to be a father. He has a son at home, but he never returns. He is killed in combat leaving the woman to raise his son all alone.

Anyway, for my whole life it was just me and my mom. I remember what a beautiful woman she was, a beauty queen no doubt from some small town in Pennsylvania. That's what brought her to Hollywood. She came to be a big movie star. I've seen some of the movies she was in, but she only got bit parts—strictly small time. She sure did know a lot about Hollywood though, and always kept up with the stars and everything. Then I came along. That sort of put a halt on her career. She knew she couldn't raise a child, pursue her acting career, and have enough money to support us both. So, I guess with the money she got from my dad's death she bought a house in the Valley and got a job as a waitress. I know she missed the movie business a lot. She talked about it all the time. She showed me around Hollywood quite a bit since it was her old stomping grounds.

She tried her best to be a good mother. Although we didn't have much money we managed to live in a fairly nice part of town. Just close enough for me to be able to attend the good schools with all the wealthy kids. She wanted to give me the advantage of being around the right people for the right influences in hopes of helping me in the future. She hoped I would get some breaks through those kids. But it worked in quite the opposite way. All the rich kids just made fun of me. Although I lived in that part of the valley, I didn't live 'South of the Boulevard', Ventura that is. I had no dad, and Mom was a waitress. Not the sort of kid the children of attorneys or doctors wanted to hang around. I was second class to these snobs—certainly not worthy of being one of them. What I wouldn't have given to have had a father and a normal life like the rest of the school. I longed for a family that went on picnics on weekends, and a dad to go to ballgames with. I would've given anything to have a home like yours, with a mom and dad—but I had no one—no father, no friends, and no social life.

The kids always made fun of me, whether I was mowing their lawns or pumping their gas. But I earned some extra money and bought my first guitar. The only mistake I made, being a naive kid, was I didn't know the difference between a bass guitar and a regular guitar. So I bought a bass by accident at the local pawn shop. That's how I ended up starting on the bass. I was bound and determined to show these kids. I was gonna practice and practice, and someday become a rock star. I wanted to show those kids that I was just as good as they were.

Then I met this girl and fell in love with her. But she left me because I wasn't good enough for her. She only wanted to marry the right kind of guy. Ya know, a doctor, or attorney, or something.

I became even more determined, so I left for San Francisco to make my fame and fortune. I stayed there a couple of years in a commune. It was sort of the first time I felt I had a family. I had a lot of fun and did lots of drugs. Boy, did they have good drugs there in the sixties. Eventually, I decided to come back to LA and return to school, mostly for draft reasons, but still determined to make it in rock. A dream I still have to this day."

"You take this music thing pretty seriously don't ya?" Jason asked. As he walked, the twilight overcame them. It was starting to get dark.

"You're damn right I do!" Mike exclaimed. "This ain't just some stupid dream, or something to do while I'm in college. Music is my life. Someday I'll meet some musicians who have the same ambition as I do.

Quit playing other people's songs and write my own. I know I could do it. I know I can write songs just as good as that easy pop shit that we play. I even think I could do better. It can't be that hard." His voice grew more and more confident as he continued. "I wanna see gold records on the wall of my Beverly Hills home. I want limousines and champagne and lots of drugs. I wanna tour the world, stay in first class hotels, and party with the greats of rock: people like Mick Jagger, Rod Stewart, Elton John, and Eric Clapton. All I have to do is write some songs, get a record company to hear it, get signed, put out a record, make it a hit, and go on tour. Ya know what I'm sayin'?"

"You make is sound so easy," Jason said.

"Well, it ain't, but I'm gonna do it."

He paused staring at Jason, as if he had an epiphany. "Ya know. I think we could do this thing together. You're an amazing talent. I know we could write some great songs together especially with your composition skills. I think we'd work well together. I am an excellent bass player you know, and have made a science out of rock and roll. I know we can do it, and I can't think of anyone better I'd like to be successful with."

"Uh, sounds interesting." Jason paused in thought. "But I was planning on pursuing a different type of career in music. You know classical or even scoring movies. Although, you do make it sound pretty appealing, and seeing you guys playing at the clubs and going to those concerts makes it seems like a pretty cool life style," Jason replied.

"We could be great. I just know it. With out talent how could we miss?" Mike's enthusiasm was growing.

"You're right, we could do it," Jason responded

"You're damn right we can." Mike was resolute. "And we could be just as big as any of 'em. We have the talent."

Thoughts of being a rock star made Jason's head spin. It defied most of his classical training, but the underlying factor, which Jason saw clearly, was the fact that he truly felt that they could do it. He had the realization that it wouldn't be that hard, and he felt they had the talent. It was certainly worth a try.

It was an epiphany for both. Each saw themselves as rock stars. Suddenly, their fantasy came back to reality as darkness surrounded them.

"The band I'm working with is really strong. I don't think they'd mind spending some time working on originals, so long as we still do the hits as well. We all have to eat and make money, and that is what the clubs want—songs people already know. The first thing we'll need is some original songs, but that shouldn't be too hard. After all those concerts I've seen and records I've listened to. Between your musical background and my rock background just think of the awesome music we could create. We could be at least as good as those guys I've seen on stage."

"Damn, you're right—we *could* do this." Jason was actually getting excited about the possibilities. "Besides, school is over for the summer, and it wouldn't really interfere with my education. Hell, what've I got to lose" And if it doesn't work out, I always have school and my education. I can teach or do something else in the music business. Why not give this rock and roll thing a try."

"You know we could still do Top 40 for money until we get signed," Mike added. "So at the very least you could make some extra money. We could do this. This is exciting, and damn it—we can do it!"

Jason's head was spinning with the prospects. "Man, I don't think I can walk another step. I am spaced." Jason stated as he dropped his backpack.

"Yeah, I'm pretty fucked up. Besides, we lost our light."

"This will be our quest, like Bilbo, or Frodo. Our quest is to become famous rock stars!" exclaimed Jason.

"I wonder what kind of adventure we're gonna to have. What perils will we face? What interesting characters will we meet? It is kind of an adventure isn't it? But our own adventure; our own quest." Mike jumped up on a large rock, holding his hand in the air as if he was holding a sword.

"Kind of our own fellowship, but instead of the ring it'll be the fellowship of the music." Jason joined him in a heroic pose.

"Cool. I like the metaphor. I dig the way you think." Mike laughed as they stood there like two warriors.

They had reached a beautiful open spot. It was a small meadow surrounded by trees with the creek running just off in the distance. The sun had set and they were enveloped by darkness. The only light was the moon and stars. They set up camp, pitched their tents, and sat down for the night. All they talked about was the rock band that they were about to form and the rock stars that they were to become, traveling the world playing concerts and making records. They didn't sleep all night from excitement, from the drugs, and from talking about their future together. As the sun arose the next day, they both felt that this was the dawning of a new day. They had decided their destinies. They had seen their future, and they viewed the world in a new light. They were about to embark on a journey together—it would be a quest all their own.

"FROM THE BEGINNING"

Emerson Lake and Palmer

Mike drove down Wilshire Boulevard on his way to Jason's. He lived just off this main thoroughfare of Los Angeles not far from downtown in an older section of the city. With its tall palm trees, Wilshire was the quintessential California road. In the distance amongst the other high rises he could see the City Hall obelisk with its pyramid top, a famous landmark of Los Angeles which he recognized from the TV show Dragnet. He turned up the radio when he heard "Satisfaction" by the Stones play. With the radio blasting, he was reminded of how varied this street was and how it had served as the main artery from which the urban sprawl of Los Angeles had grown west on its journey thru Beverly Hills and Santa Monica until it reached the Pacific Ocean.

Finally, he found the street Jason lived on. With the song over, he turned down the radio as he turned onto the street to look for Jason's address. It was in an older neighborhood, at least by Los Angeles' standards. The shady tree lined street had homes that were probably built in the 1940s. These were all custom homes with no two looking exactly alike, mostly California bungalow style of that era with a few Victorians as well. This street showed signs of a changing neighborhood with some homes kept up very nicely while others showed their age and neglect with many falling into disrepair or desperately in need of some work, paint, or landscaping. In its day, this had probably been a very nice upper middle class neighborhood. However, the flight to the suburbs in the 1950s and '60s had taken its toll on this part of city as people moved out to the suburbs for newer tract homes and nicer neighborhoods, leaving not only the homes but this whole area of the city blighted, tawdry, and forgotten. Many homes and neighborhoods were very unkempt or even deteriorating, seedy, and nasty. Now only pockets of nice homes were left, and even these bordered on some areas that were marginal at best. This was one of those streets which struggled to keep up the neighborhood, but it could go either way.

He checked the address of the large two story house to make sure it matched the one Jason had given him. He parked then got out of the car. He approached the typical California bungalow style house with a large front porch that looked out onto the shady tree lined street. A large oak tree stood in the center of the well manicured lawn and nicely landscaped front yard. The house was one of the well kept ones. It showed signs of renovation and pride of ownership.

He opened the side gate and walked down the driveway to the back as Jason had instructed him to do. Behind the main house adjacent to the garage there was a guest house where Jason lived. As he approached he could hear music, mostly piano with a singer. He arrived at the door of the tiny guest house and knocked.

It had been a week since their hike. Now it was time to put their words into actions—time to work on some music together and really see if this was going to work. They had decided to get together at Jason's place since he had a piano. It was easier for Mike to bring his guitar and amp than for Jason to lug his big piano anywhere.

Jason opened the door. "Come on in," he said with enthusiasm. "I was just listening to the new Billy Joel album. It's awesome. He really knows how to tell a story with his lyrics, and he is an excellent piano player as well. I really dig his songwriting."

"We'll have to check it out. I really dig him as well."

Mike entered the small guest house. It was really only one room. It had a small kitchen area with an old table and chair which served as his dining area. An upright piano sat in the corner of the room with a bust of Beethoven sitting on top of it and music scattered across the top. Next to it was a Fender Rhodes electric piano which Jason had brought from Atlanta so at least he had something on which to practice. It was not the real thing, but it was portable and at least something. Once here, he found a used upright which more suited his needs for giving lessons, practicing, and composing. A mattress and box springs sat on the floor of the other corner. One wall was lined with bookshelves, made from cinder blocks and boards, filled with books, records, and music. Jason was able to give lessons here as it did afford him some privacy. He did not have to disturb the residents of the main house when giving lessons or practicing. It was simple but a bit bohemian although it was fairly neat and tidy for a college student.

"Is this OK to practice for now?" asked Jason.

"Yeah, this works. What about the people in the front house?" Mike asked.

"They're pretty cool. They let me play anytime I want, in fact they like it. They work during the day mostly. They rent this back guest house out to students for some extra money. I even get a break on the rent in exchange for giving piano lessons to their daughter—a pretty good arrangement. I even get high with 'em sometimes. They're pretty cool people."

"It's bitchin' that you have a place where you can rehearse. The band has a difficult time finding a place to practice. We usually get to our gigs early to rehearse there, or sometimes we can rehearse acoustically at the apartment. Occasionally, we have to rent a rehearsal space." He looked around the room. "I can't believe you have a real piano. Although, I'm not sure we can use that in the band at first. It may be difficult to lug around. You may just have to use the electric one as it'll be easier to transport."

"Not a problem. That's why I have it. I brought it from Atlanta due to its portability. Someday I'd like to have a full concert grand piano, but at least for now I can practice and give lessons on the upright.

However, since most of my students have their own pianos or at least the family does, most of the time I give lessons at their place," Jason explained.

"However, I think it'd be better to write using the upright piano instead of the electric one. I can use the acoustic guitar or the electric one. It'd be really bitchin' if you could get a synthesizer and maybe a Hammond B3 as well. I love the set up that Keith Emerson of Emerson Lake and Palmer has or even the Moody Blues with all their keyboards and that great sounding mellotron, but all that'll have to be for the future." Mike was dreaming again and getting way ahead of himself.

"What kinda guitar do ya have?" asked Jason.

"For bass I play a Fender Jazz Bass. I dig the sound, and it works great with a three piece band. I have a Fender Stratocaster guitar. I also have a Martin acoustic guitar."

They decided that the best way to approach the band with their new idea was to do some writing first. That way they had something to show them by presenting their idea of becoming rock stars with a couple of songs. He knew that the band was really interested in just doing cover songs to make some extra money. Not becoming rock stars.

"I have some songs of my own I'd like ya to check out. See how this works out. I wanted to see what you thought. See if you had any ideas." Mike picked up his guitar. "Check out this riff."

"That's far out. Does it have lyrics?" Jason watched as Mike played.

"Sure does, check it out." Mike began singing the song.

"Cool lyrics. How about starting with a piano thing at the beginning? What key are ya in?"

"A minor." Mike played him the chord on his guitar.

"Check it out." Jason started playing the piano. In no time he made up an opening piano part. "Something like this. Er, then adding the band gradually? Sort of like a classical piece. Ya know. A theme and variation type of format. We can build on the theme until we get to the first verse. Also, how about putting in a bridge? I think it needs some sort of a transition between the verse and chorus."

"Let's try it. Show me what ya mean."

"Lemme try some things." Jason played around a bit until he added another section between the verse and chorus for a bridge. It all worked with the song beautifully.

"That totally works." Mike was impressed. "That's just what the song needed."

"How about after the second bridge we modulate to another key then go into a guitar lead. I'll set it up on the piano. We can gradually add the bass and drums then progress into a screaming guitar lead, and finally back to the chorus," continued Jason showing off his composition skills.

"That's brilliant. I dig your ideas. By the way, do ya sing?" Mike asked.

"Well, I don't think I have a great voice, but I have taken some lessons. I'm certainly willing to give it a try," Jason replied.

Minutes turned into hours as they continued to work that day. The creative juices just kept flowing. They knew immediately that this collaboration was going to work.

"This is fuckin' fantastic!" Mike exclaimed with a good deal of enthusiasm "I really think we work well together. This is really gonna work out great! It's an even better match than I had thought."

"Yeah, this rock and roll thing is pretty fun," Jason agreed.

"I dig what you add to the original songs, and you really pick up the pop stuff quickly. That last song we wrote I could hear on the radio or an album for sure. Man, this is gonna be fucking incredible!"

"I agree." Jason tried to hide his excitement. "I can't believe we have been working so long. I really dig working with you as well. I think this is gonna be fun."

"We certainly seem to be on the same page musically. I think we should seriously write some more songs together. We're really gonna take the music business by storm." Mike was really enjoying this new collaboration. "We could be the new Lennon and McCartney. Stewart and Tucker. Has a nice ring to it." He laughed.

Satisfied with the collaboration, Mike began the discussion. They talked at length about their future together and the future of the band.

"I think the best way to do this is to first add you to the band Axis. That way Axis can continue doing the Top 40 gigs. We can all make some money. And you can get used to playing with us and vice versa. We can see how this whole thing is gonna work out. We could always use a keyboard player. Just playing as a three piece is very limiting. However, we should have some of our set ready. I can teach ya some of those songs first and see how it goes. Then we can start working on originals as well. We'll have to convince them that adding you will make the band better, more commercial, more versatile, and more marketable—which means more gigs. They all know you, but they may have some resistance to adding another player as that means less money for us since we'd have to divide up the take four ways instead of three. I think we can get some better gigs and some better paying ones though. We ought to bring that up. What d'ya think?"

"Sounds like a good idea to me," agreed Jason.

"I'd also like to approach them with our idea of being an original band so they can be part of this dream. See how they take to the idea. However, I think we should work on some more original songs first. Really see if this collaboration is gonna work. Then we will have something to present to 'em. Man, I wanna break into the music business big time, and this could be our chance."

"Works for me." Jason was getting somewhat excited as he sat tinkling on the piano.

Both were excited about working together.

Jason and Mike continued working together almost every day for the next couple of weeks. They worked on cover songs from the Axis set, so that eventually Jason knew most of their set and would feel confident to start working with the band. They wanted it to be an easy transition. They even worked on some other new Top 40 songs that they felt they could present to the band as additional material now that they had keyboards. Jason was also at every gig the band did so that he could study even more how the band interacted and how the songs and the sets went. They worked well together as a songwriting team and had worked out quite a few original songs. Mike's influence musically was in giving the music the hard rock edge it needed. But his most important asset was lyrics. Mike had a poetic way of writing words to songs. He had a backlog of songs or poems that could be made into songs which Jason was able to write music for. Jason had a natural talent for writing melodies and arrangements and turning them into compositions. The standard verse, chorus, bridge, chorus type of structure was easy for Jason to adapt to. His study of music and composition theory made the transitions flowing and natural. He sometimes even gave it a classical edge. Once they got started the songs just seemed to flow. The more they worked together the more it became evident that this was really going to work out well.

Jason also began singing. He discovered his voice wasn't half bad. They seemed to work well together vocally. Their voices harmonized and blended well together. Both could sing lead adequately or could back each other up. This would add to the group as well. Jason even got to play some sax or flute on some of the songs which added even more diversity.

All in all it was a good match. The more they worked together the more they both enjoyed it. The ideas seemed to flow. The interaction was incredible for all the material: cover and original. Now all they had to do was convince the band.

"CHANGES"

David Bowie

Finally, with most of the Axis set learned, some new cover songs, and quite a few original songs completed; they felt that they were ready to propose the addition of Jason to Axis. Jason just hoped he would fit in with the rest of the band. It would take some rehearsing to add him, but they felt confident that it would be an easy transition requiring few rehearsals since Jason knew the material so well. They also had to convince them of their long term goals and make the whole change appealing. They had planned their speech carefully to make the players understand their goals and vision in its proper perspective, and to try to get the same enthusiasm and commitment that Jason and Mike felt. They had their strategy, now it was time to implement it.

A rehearsal and band meeting was called to discuss business in general. Mike felt it a good time to bring up the matter. He invited Jason without letting the band know. Jason arrived at the rehearsal during break time.

Mike lit a joint then passed it around. "Ya'll know Jason." They nodded a greeting. "Did you know that he's an excellent keyboard player? He can also sing and play the flute and sax as well."

"Yeah, I think we knew that," Doug replied suspiciously.

"Well, uh. I'd like for him to be a part of the band. I think it would be a great addition. We'd be able to play a greater variety of material. So, with the addition of Jason playing keys and woodwinds, we can play all the old songs which will give 'em a new dimension, and we can do some new and different kinds of songs as well. It'd make us more versatile and more marketable." Mike could tell that they were not enthused. So he continued; reiterating his proposal and his reasons, hoping it would change their mind while not giving them a chance to talk. "There are so many more songs that we could do with the addition of a keyboard player alone. And he does sing and has a really good voice. Plus he plays the flute and sax which just makes for an added bonus. I think he'd be a real asset to the band."

Doug and Brian looked at each other with a look of skepticism and disinterest.

Mike continued, not even allowing them to speak. "More importantly, Jason and I have been talking a lot. We both believe that this band has some excellent players and real talent. We see no reason why we cannot make more of it. We've been going to concerts and seen those other bands play that have record deals. We believe with the talent already present in this band there's no reason why we can't do the same. All the potential is here. All we need to do is work a little harder. We could be one of the recording and touring bands instead of just another Top 40 band playing nightclubs. We could continue to make money doing the pop stuff while concentrating on some new original material. We could even play some of the originals at the gigs."

Doug looked at Brian with a look of disapproval.

Mike picked up the less than enthusiastic reception he was getting and continued. "I've been working with Jason. He already knows the songs we do. It wouldn't take a lot of extra rehearsal time to bring him up to speed so that he could be added easily. We even worked on some new Top 40 material that we can learn. It will add a lot more music to our set list that includes keyboards. Ya know what I mean?" Mike continued not expecting an answer. "We've also been working on some original material that we'd like the band to try…"

"I'm really excited about working with the band." Jason interrupted. "Mike and I have been working hard on your set list so that I know all the songs that you play. And I think our originals are pretty damn good. We'd like to try them with the band and see what ya think. We'd like this to be a band thing with everyone contributing."

They paused hoping for some positive reaction, but instead were met with relative silence.

The first to respond was Brian seeming more to be thinking out loud. "Um, Just so long as it doesn't take too much of my time. I guess it means less money for us all, but perhaps we could get some better paying gigs. I guess I have nothing better to do. As long as I'm a part of this thing what've I got to lose? Yeah, count me in," he finished with a small amount of interest.

Doug seemed less than interested and somewhat impatient as he began. "Uh, well, as a matter of fact. I've been thinking a lot about this band lately, and, er, I guess this seems like a good time to bring up how I've been feeling lately. I just don't think this is the right thing for me. I think I want to go in a different musical direction. I've been doing more and more recording sessions. I make a lot more money doing sessions than playing these gigs. Besides, it's more my style. I do a lot of commercials. I know they're only jingles, but they pay really well. From my contacts doing commercials I've started getting some work doing movies. Ya know, soundtracks and shit; as well as some television. I've been working with a lot of really excellent musicians. I much prefer working in a studio doing session work than doing a live gig. I play all kinds of music, not just rock. As I musician, I really like the variety. I still dig rock and roll, but also like playing other stuff as well. I just think I would be happier doing sessions rather than playing night clubs and gigs. I just want you to know that this has been on my mind for some time now. I've wanted to bring it up but just haven't. Now seems the perfect time."

Mike was a bit taken aback. Surprised at the response

"I don't mind staying and playing the gigs until you find a replacement, but I think we should do them as the original three-piece. I don't wanna learn anything new, and I don't wanna split up the pot much more. We get paid so little as it is. To add another member would just mean less for us. You can work on the new stuff with Jason, Brian, and the new guitar player, but I won't be. I would like to get away from doing the Top 40 gigs as soon as possible. Uh, I hope you understand. This is nothing personal. I dig you guys, and it has been fun. I just think I'd like to go in different musical direction. I'll stay, but only for a short time. I would appreciate it if you'd find another guitar player to replace me as soon as possible."

Mike and Jason looked at each other. It was difficult for them to understand why these people did not see the same vision they had. Try as they might they could not get Doug to share their view. Doug wanted to go his own way. For Jason and Mike he was blind to one of the best opportunities he would ever have.

Brian then turned to Mike. "I also think it's time you found your own place, Mike. You've been crashing in my living room since you got here and the place is just too small. Perhaps you could crash with Jason. I don't want to be a drag, so I'll give ya some time, but please make some other living arrangements."

Mike was crestfallen. He was hoping for the same excitement and enthusiasm from the other players that he and Jason felt. Instead he was faced with nothing but negativity, the loss of one of the members, possibly the break-up of the band, and to top it off, nowhere to live. Even though he tried not to take it personally, he felt hurt. He just could not understand Doug preferring to play sessions over performing live. It was something beyond his comprehension. Mike lived for the live show and the admiration, respect, and popularity it offered him. How could he not want that?

"Shit, Man, this could be your chance. We're gonna make it big. You just wait and see. Those record companies will want to sign us to a contract soon, and I know the album will sell."

"Sorry guys. I just wanna go in another direction," Doug apologized.

This made Mike even more determined to prove it to Doug. Make him sorry for the choice he had made. The lack of understanding and the failure to see their vision made Jason and Mike even more determined to succeed.

Finally, Mike acquiesced. "Doug, we're sorry to see ya leave, but I understand. I wish you luck. Brian, how about you? Are you still in?" he asked.

"Yeah, I think we have some potential, and the money is OK. Count me in. I'd like to hear some of this original stuff though," said Brian.

"Sure bet, thanks," said Mike.

They would continue to work the Top 40 gigs for the time being, while searching for a new guitarist.

"SUMMER IN THE CITY"

Lovin' Spoonful

"I can't believe that we are losing Doug," said Mike one evening during break time at an Axis gig.

"Yeah, really a fuckin' drag." Brian agreed. "At least he is cool about playing with us until we find a replacement."

"Yeah, I think we should take time to find the right replacement since he has agreed to continue. Besides, I gotta find a place to live as well. Hey, I have an idea. How 'bout we find a place together."

"I'd be OK with that." Brian agreed. "I would love to have a place where I could practice. I can't practice at all where I live now. It's just an apartment that I share. No way could I play the drums there. I am sure the neighbors would complain."

"We will check with Jason to see if he wants to go in as well. We'll work on that. I've also been thinkin' that we need a new name. After all, it will practically be a whole new group with new instrumentation and a new sound."

"Don't really matter to me." Brian said sipping his beer.

"We could still work under the name of Axis with Doug, but for the new group let's change the name to reflect the change. Even after we replaced Doug we could still work under the old name of Axis at the clubs where we worked before just to get our foot in the door, but we would change it whenever possible."

Just then Jason walked up. "How about Purple Haze?" He offered having overheard the conversation while he was getting a drink. "You know in memory of that hike, and the acid we took when we had this idea."

"Hey man, didn't see you arrive. What's happening?"

"Nothing much, just talking about stuff. Purple Haze is a cool name," said Mike.

"Nah, I don't think the name should have any drug reference." Brian stated.

"Yeah, you're probably right."

"We'll think of somethin'. But for now, Brian and I were thinking of getting a place together. A real band house. We need somewhere to audition guitar players and to rehearse. What do ya think? Do you wanna go in with us?"

"Uh, I guess. I can probably do that so long as I have a place to give lessons."

"It'd be great!" Mike was really enthusiastic about this idea. "It would serve as the base for all band operations. We could practice any time we wanted. I think it will be fun sharing a place together. We can rehearse, write music, and party—a real band house. In fact maybe that should be our first priority especially since we don't have a place to audition a new guitar player. It'd make us look more legit."

"Yeah, you're probably right."

So it was decided to get a house together, and this seemed like the perfect time. After all, it was summer, the semester was over for Mike and Jason which made it a good time to move on and get settled before the next school year started. There was enough money to pay the rent if they pooled their resources. With the upcoming gigs for Mike and Brian with Axis, Brian's day gig working at a record store, and Jason still giving music lessons, it seemed possible to find something they could afford. Mike might have to get a day job as well, but that would be worth the sacrifice. Their budget was small, so they searched many parts of the city. They decided to look in the older section of Hollywood where prices were reasonable. It was also convenient for everyone, being close to the college and near Brian's work. They also thought there would be many opportunities since Hollywood still had a reputation for entertainment. It was filled with lots of clubs as well as music and entertainment related businesses including record companies. The thought of making it in Hollywood was, after all, their dream, and it was well known as the entertainment capital of the world.

They finally found a house that would suit them and their budget. The house itself was a throw back to the glory days of Hollywood. It had probably been a pretty nice house in the thirties, but time had taken its toll. It was a run-down frame house called a bungalow. It was probably ready for the wrecking ball, but it would serve their purpose and their needs just fine. The yard was mostly weeds and what was left of a lawn. The few remaining bushes were either dead needing to be removed or had become overgrown and were badly in need of pruning. A large palm tree stood in the middle of the front yard with another one in the back yard. The house desperately needed a paint job—but it was homey and comfortable. It had a lot of rooms that they could use for other band members. Best of all it had a garage that they could turn into a rehearsal studio with some work on sound insulation. They figured this would give them the opportunity to work more on the songs. It was perfect.

They moved in a month later. Each person had his own bedroom and the living room served as a common area and a place where Jason could give lessons. They sound proofed the garage with carpet remnants they had picked up at the local carpet stores and made it into a rehearsal studio and a place to store their equipment. They could leave it all set up there as well. They furnished the living room with thrift store furniture which was cheap. It looked more like a flop house, but it was theirs.

They were excited about living in Hollywood where fame and fortune seemed within their grasp. The name itself represented stars and glamour and magic. They felt that living in Hollywood was like living in an international cultural icon and a piece of history—a town synonymous with the entertainment industry. Living here they felt that they were truly on their way to stardom.

Hollywood, sometimes referred to as Tinsel Town, is actually only a district in the City of Los Angeles situated northwest of downtown Los Angeles. The film industry started in Hollywood when many movie studios moved there. The all year sunshine allowed filming year round especially since most of the filming was done outside. The first studios began in the early 1900s but flourished for many years. Although now, most of the movie industry has moved to surrounding areas such as the Westside where 20th Century Fox and MGM Studios is located, or the San Fernando Valley where Warner Bros Studios, Universal Studios, and Disney Studios is located. Many television studios also began in Hollywood but many also moved to the valley as well. There are still some studios in Hollywood like Paramount. There are also a lot of support services in Hollywood like film editors, special effects houses, movie and equipment rental houses, and sound stages.

They were sitting in the back yard one day smoking a joint while taking a break from rehearsal. "Baba O'Riley" by the Who played in background.

Mike began to sing along with the lyrics. "Out here in the Fields/ I fight for my meals/ I get my back into my living/....I don't need to fight/ to know I'm right/ I don't need to be forgiven." He passed the joint. This is such a bitchin' album, an anthem for our generation. I wish we could write like that. He sat silently listening. Then all of a sudden he stood up and began singing along again. "Teenage wasteland/ Its only teenage waste land/ They're all wasted!" He screamed these final words and held the joint up high over his head." He laughed and sat down.

The next song on the Who's Next album began. It was "Bargain." "Check out the lyrics to this one. It is about a chick, but I relate to it as being about all that we have to give up to make it in music."

He started to sing along "I'd gladly give up all I had/ To find you/ I'd suffer anything and be glad/... I'd pay any price just to get you/ I'd work all my life and I will/ To win you I'd stand naked, stoned, and stabbed/... I'd call that a bargain/ The best I ever had." He paused and listened. These words seem to have some deep effect on him. He continued. "To catch you/ I'm gonna run and never stop/... I'd pay any price just to win you/ Surrender my good life for bad/….. I'd call that a bargain/ the best I ever had." He stopped as the song continued.

"See what I mean. This is about what we have to do, and what we have to give up to make it. And we are gonna make it big in this town someday, just wait and see." Mike spoke with determination. He turned to Jason as he passed the joint. "It's all here, just waiting for us. All we have to do is to get our break into the business." He motioned to the Hollywood skyline visible from the back yard. "Ya know, my mom tried to make it in the business. She wanted to be big star. I guess I get my drive from her. I want to show her that I can make it here. Prove to her it can be done. I guess that is one of my driving forces."

Mike sat quietly for a while. He was feeling nostalgic. The move to Hollywood seemed to have brought about some old memories.

"My mom used to talk about Hollywood a lot when I was growing up." Mike reflected on his past. "I know she wanted to be a movie star or something. I guess she got some work here, but never really made it. She sure had some stories though." He turned, facing the guys. "She had this fascination with Hollywood and everything Hollywood. She was always reading magazines and books about it and the stars. That was her dream, but one that never happened for her. Probably 'cause I came along."

In the distance they could see the famous Hollywood sign.

"Man, you can see the Hollywood sign from our backyard. Very cool! Did ya know that it was originally an advertisement for the Hollywoodland housing development? They were selling lots just below the sign in the hills. The "land" part of the sign was torn down leaving the sign just saying Hollywood. It eventually became the international symbol of Hollywood." Mike stated as he passed the joint to Brian.

Just to the right of the Hollywood sign was the Griffith Park Observatory, looming over Hollywood like a castle.

"And there's the Griffith Park Observatory. I remember that from that movie with James Dean. Uh, <u>Rebel Without a Cause</u>" Mike stated. He pointed to the iconic landmark.

"Sort of like us." Jason laughed

Mike seemed lost in thought, contemplating something serious. "Hum…. <u>Rebel Without a Cause,</u> huh" he said almost to himself. Finally, he spoke out, voicing his epiphany. "That's a great idea for a song. That could be the title. We can also use it for the first line of the verse. Make it kind of angry with lots of angst. Sort of a 'Baba O'Riley'—a real anthem."

"That's a bitchin' idea. We need to start workin' on that immediately."

"There it is." This time Mike stood up, looked out again, and pointed at the Capitol Records Tower. It was a distinctive building due to its round shape that stuck up above the Hollywood skyline. It was built in the mid-1950s to look like a stack of records with a needle representing a phonograph needle standing on top like a beacon. The low, late afternoon sun made it glow like some ominous medieval tower. "The Capitol Records building, standing there like some fortress—virtually impenetrable—only available for those who work hard and make it in the industry. This building symbolizes our goal, our destiny."

Jason and Bryan stood up, staring at the building.

Mike now raised his guitar like a sword, and, with his hand on his hip like some heroic character, he continued. "Just like <u>The Two Towers</u> in <u>The Lord of the Rings</u>."

"What a perfect place to begin our assault of the tower to someday make it in the music business." Jason commented, picking up Mike's metaphor.

"We have a goal and a challenge. To me, this building symbolizes everything we want. It represents our assault on the business." Mike continued. "Someday we'll be able to just walk into that tower like we own the place. That tower is our goal. It is our quest—and gaining entrance will be our conquest. That tower represents everything we're striving for. It will be a difficult journey, but we will seize the tower just like in <u>The Lord of the Rings</u>." Mike put his arms around his friends' shoulders in a gesture of camaraderie. "We will make it to that tower someday." He proclaimed.

The three just stood there in stoned silent contemplation. They felt like the characters in <u>Fellowship of the Ring</u>, with a seemingly insurmountable task before them—all working toward a goal, plotting their path, and working out their strategies to one day gain entry into that tower which, for them, represented all of the music business. They knew they were going to have to fight for it, but felt that someday they would gain access. This building represented their goal.

"Hey man, I just drove by the Palladium. The Rolling Stones are playing there next month. We should get tickets," Mike said as he entered the living room of the band house one day after school.

"Yeah, we can't miss that concert." Brian agreed.

"How 'bout we go get tickets then go explore Hollywood while we're there," said Jason.

"Sounds cool, but I have to work. Just get me a ticket," said Brian

"Will do."

"C'mon Jason. I just got this book about Hollywood I've been reading a lot about its past. It's pretty interesting. Let's go check out the city." Mike grabbed the car keys then almost dragged Jason out the door. "Make it an adventure."

"Works for me." Jason showed little reluctance. "It's time we went out to explore Hollywood."

They parked near the Hollywood Palladium then walked up to the box office. "Look, Lawrence Welk is here every week taping the weekly show." Jason pointed to the huge marquee that was almost the length of the whole building. "My mom and dad watch that every Saturday night."

They bought their tickets and began their adventure.

They walked a short block to Sunset and Vine.

"This was the former location of NBC studios west coast. It was called Radio City West for many years until NBC moved to Burbank," Mike said.

They turned the corner onto Vine Street and stopped. There in the distance stood the Capitol Records Tower rising up like an ominous fortress. Its round stack of records shape made it distinguishable and unmistakable. It was even more impressive the closer they got.

"There it is again—the Tower, symbol of our ambition. We just can't seem to get away from it. Someday we will gain access to that castle even if we have to storm it." Mike stated pretending like he was a knight.

They both laughed.

"Ya know. That might be a good idea for a song. Call it 'The Tower.' It could be about everyone's goals, wishes, and aspirations—sort of a hard driving power song."

"Yeah man. It sounds like a bitchin' idea for a tune."

"I think that the Capitol Records building seems like a good place to begin our Hollywood Adventure. On to the Tower, Sir Jason."

They walked up Vine Street.

"See that theater where Merv Griffin is doing his TV show? That's the old ABC studios. All the television studios were here at one point, but most have moved."

"Interesting," Jason remarked enthusiastically.

As they approached the corner of Hollywood Boulevard and Vine Street, the familiar and iconic Capitol Records tower was growing closer, larger, and more real with each step. They approached it with anxiety and excitement. They looked up at the tall building with the big double doors that formed the entrance. Close up it was even more like a fortress. They felt like Dorothy, the Tin Man, The Cowardly Lion and The Scarecrow when they approached the palace of the Wizard in the <u>Wizard of Oz</u>, standing and looking up at the huge door, a bit frightened and overwhelmed, but wanting so much to be let in.

"Can I help you?" A guard inquired as they approached the building. He seemed to have appeared out of nowhere which startled them. "Do you have an appointment?" He said in a low intimidating voice as he grabbed his clip board.

"No, just checking it out, "they said shyly and dejectedly as they walked away.

"Oh well, someday they will know who we are," commented Jason.

"Good day Mr. Tucker and Mr. Stewart. I love your new album." Mike stood there tall and straight as if at attention pretending to be the guard. "I heard it went gold in just 10 days. Congratulations to both of you," continued Mike pretending to be the guard and pretending to open the door for Jason.

"Why, thank you, kind sir. I am so glad you like it." Jason played along with an air of importance and arrogance in his voice.

"Would you be so kind as to sign my copy of the album? It would mean so much to me. I've always been a big fan." Mike handed Jason an imaginary album.

"But of course." Jason grabbed the imaginary album, pretended to sign it, then passed it back to Mike.

"Oh, thank you kind sir. I shall cherish it always," said Mike still playing the part of the guard while bowing to Jason as he walked by.

"Think nothing of it." They both erupted in laughter.

"There's the Hollywood Palace, an old vaudeville house that now does concerts." Mike added as he looked across the street.

They walked back a half a block to the corner of Hollywood and Vine, a cross street famous as a place where many entertainment-related businesses once flourished. They had been so mesmerized with the Capitol Records Building that they hadn't even noticed that they had walked right past it already.

"My mom told me about this corner. She said she used to hang out here."

Just down the street, on Vine, they noticed a sign saying The Hollywood Brown Derby.

"That can't be *the* Brown Derby. Isn't it supposed to look like a brown derby hat?" Jason asked.

"I always thought so," replied Mike.

Their curiosity got the best of them. They walked in just to look around or maybe have a drink. It was dark inside, so it took a minute for their eyes to adjust. They entered the building only to find one couple eating at one of the booths along the wall. All the other booths and the tables in the center of the room were empty. Above the booths were many framed pictures of stars, all signed with a thank you to the Brown Derby."

An older man with gray hair approached with menus in his hand. He was the host. He was dressed in an old haggard suit that was so outdated that he looked like he was from another era. It did not seem to even fit him as it hung loosely on his thin frame. "Would you like a table?" he inquired.

"No, we were just curious. We had heard so much about this place we thought we'd take a look. I hope you don't mind?" asked Jason.

"Not at all. We get a lot of tourists and people curious about this place in here." The host seemed glad to have someone to talk to. "In its heyday, this place was full of stars. It did all happen here. I remember it well. In the past, many of Hollywood's stars would dine, make deals, hob nob, or just be seen here. It was a place of glamour. Did ya notice all those office buildings around here, especially on the corner of Hollywood and Vine?"

They both nodded yes.

"At one time they were the offices of many Hollywood agents, producers, and other industry folks." He seemed anxious to tell the story of this famous eatery. "Sadly, they've all moved to places like Beverly Hills, West Hollywood, or the San Fernando Valley. But in its day this was the center of Hollywood. It's still a street corner full of history, but nothing like it once was."

"But I thought it looked like a hat?" Mike questioned. "I've seen pictures of it on TV."

"Oh yes. There are actually two. That one was built first. They expanded to this site later. That one is more famous because it does look like a brown derby. It is actually located on Wilshire Boulevard. Many people make that mistake for it also had quite a history and was another famous stomping ground for the rich and famous. It sat across from the famous Ambassador Hotel. The Ambassador had hosted many Academy Awards Ceremonies. It was also home to the famous Cocoanut Grove, a night club in the glory days of the past where the stars would dine and dance the night away. Many famous recording artists like Frank Sinatra, Judy Garland, and Bing Crosby performed there, and many even got their start there. It was certainly the glory days of Hollywood. Its reputation was tarnished when it was the site of the shooting of Robert Kennedy in 1968."

"Oh, I know where that is; it isn't far from where I used to live. I've passed it many times but never knew it was so famous. I guess I never noticed the hat." Jason offered.

"Are you sure I can't offer you a table?" the host inquired again.

"No, but thanks for the information," said Jason. "We'll have to come back another time."

They rushed out like people who did not belong.

They left and walked to the corner onto Hollywood Boulevard There stood The Pantages Theater, one of the Landmarks of Hollywood Boulevard. It was situated on the eastern end of the main part of the town called Hollywood. This palatial art deco theater was originally built as a legitimate stage theater featuring vaudeville acts, and stage productions. However, soon after its opening in 1930 it was turned into a movie theater due to the depression which left many people without the funds to pay the high price of a live theatrical production. In addition, due to the economic downturn, movies became all the rage leaving live theater almost a thing of the past. It was an impressive building that they both recognized from pictures, newsreels, news clips on television, movies, movie premiers, or from hosting the Academy Award Ceremonies. They could almost see the stars of the past arriving in limos to walk the red carpet to see who would win the coveted award.

They decided to walk from one end of Hollywood Boulevard to the other. As they walked, they couldn't help but feel the fame and the history that this street represented. They felt like they were living in some Hollywood glamour movie. The street itself had a reputation all its own and a name recognition known throughout the world. It had once been the street of dreams with famous movie houses that hosted Hollywood premiers, theaters, shops, and famous restaurants. They walked reading the names of stars and other famous people of the entertainment business that were placed on the sidewalk on The Hollywood Walk of Fame. Some they recognized; others they had no idea who they were—stars of a bygone era. As they walked they noticed many other people, mostly tourists, walking down this street looking for their favorite celebrities.

As they continued their walk down Hollywood Boulevard, they soon discovered that it wasn't quite what they had expected. Instead of the movie stars there were a lot of tourists mixed in with what seemed to be the locals: mostly street people, runaways, drug addicts, pan handlers, and people that looked like they were homeless. Many who had probably left home to seek fame and fortune were left to the streets to fend for themselves often resorting to prostitution, drugs, or other things. The only stars left were the ones on the sidewalk where names had been placed for everyone to see and walk over. Instead of glamorous restaurants and upscale shops they passed mostly tawdry store fronts which housed cheap souvenir shops, t-shirt shops, tacky restaurants, or other shops selling cheap clothes or trinkets. Signs of the era of glamour had long past. Most of the places to eat seemed to be just pizza stands, hamburger joints, and a few coffee shops—not the elegant eateries they expected. They could see that many of these places had once been very nice, but were now showing signs of age or were simply not well kept up. Perhaps in the past this had been the playground of the stars, but no longer. All in all there were no stars, no glamour, no elegant restaurants, and no nice retail shops. All had been replaced with cheap tacky places geared to the tourist industry. The glamour they had expected was just an illusion, like a flickering movie on the silver screen—as fleeting and unreal as the movies themselves. Hollywood Boulevard had become a street of broken dreams, remnants of a bygone era.

"Hollywood sure wasn't what I expected. It's kind of seedy really."

"Yeah, you've got that right. Not what I expected either." Jason looked around as they continued their journey.

They reached Graumann's Chinese Theater which was located at the western end of the main part of Hollywood Boulevard near Highland. They had seen it on television many times mostly for Hollywood premiers or the Academy Awards, when stars would walk the red carpet to some Hollywood extravaganza. It was more grand than they had imagined; a real palace which paid proper homage to the movies. Its towering front showed the grandeur of the movie industry in its hey day. The elaborate Chinese architecture and art work made it look even more mysterious and ominous. It had all the style of a live theater but it had been built solely for movies. They thought it would be fun to look at all the hand and foot prints of many of Hollywood's stars of past and present that were Graumann's Chinese Theater's current claim to fame. They joined the tourists as they looked for the footprints of famous people, exclaiming each time they found someone they knew or trying to fit their own hand or footprints into those of the stars. Across the street stood the famous Hollywood Roosevelt Hotel In the past it was a place of glamour where stars stayed and played, but now struggled to be even a glimmer of its past glory.

The Pantages and Graumann's Chinese served as the bookends of the main section of Hollywood Boulevard and downtown Hollywood. They decided that this was far enough for their journey today.

As they stood in front of Graumann's Chinese theater Jason spoke first. "Even though Hollywood has gotten a bit run down, it still does have the name, and it still is exciting to be here, being some guy from Georgia. A bit disappointing, nonetheless, I think what Hollywood represents is important. It is still an icon in the world of entertainment. Hollywood still represents the entertainment industry and all its glory. What's important is what goes on here behind the scenes instead of the town itself." Jason stopped. He looked around taking in all the sights and sounds—lost in thought. After a few moments he continued "Perhaps Hollywood is more a state of mind—where fame and fortune can be achieved—where stars are made. And even though the town doesn't show it, I still think all this is pretty neat."

"We're gonna be big in this town someday. We've come here like many others to seek fame and fortune, but we will make it. You just wait and see," Mike announced confidently.

They returned home after their day, ready to take on a new adventure—one that could change their fates forever. They had both been to Hollywood many times, but now this town had new meaning. It was not just a town anymore, it was an attitude.

"I have some great ideas for some new songs. One is called 'Empty Sidewalks.' It's kind of sad and somber, all about loneliness. Another one is 'The Tower,' the hard driving power song we talked about. I have one more called 'Hollywood Dreams,' sort of lilting and ethereal like the Moody Blues." Mike presented the song ideas to Jason. They wrote three new songs together based on their experience.

With all its faults, Hollywood would prove to be the perfect place to have their band house. It was near many record company offices, managers, and agents' offices, and a wide variety of night clubs that would serve them well on their quest for fame and fortune.

They discovered that much of the club scene had moved to the Sunset Strip area of West Hollywood which was only about three miles from their house. The Sunset Strip had been center of the music scene since the 1960s and was filled with night clubs with names like The Whisky, The Roxy, and The Troubadour. Also, many of the music industry businesses, like managers, agents, attorneys, publishers, concert promoters, and publicists had moved to the office buildings on or near the Sunset Strip.

Just past the strip was Beverly Hills, home to the big mansions and homes of stars. And although theirs was a simple house, they could all dream someday of living in one of the mansions in Beverly Hills or the foothills beyond. For the band, it marked the start of their career together.

It was the night of the concert. As they approached the Hollywood Palladium, Mike, Jason, and Brian saw the search lights scanning the sky showing the importance of the event. It was like a real Hollywood gala—lights and people everywhere. They could see the marquee announcing tonight's act. "THE ROLLING STONES—THE GREATEST ROCK AND ROLL BAND IN THE WORLD." Limousines pulled up depositing some obviously very important people to the front of the beautiful and well lit building.

"This is pretty exciting." Jason commented. "I feel like I'm going to an old Hollywood premier or something. It reminds me of the glamour of the old Hollywood that I've seen in the movies and TV so many times."

They entered the elegant art deco building. The large lobby was carpeted and had beautiful crystal chandeliers hanging from the ceiling, remnants of a different time. Drink and t-shirt concessions lined the walls. "My mom told me that she used to go dancing here a lot. She saw some pretty big acts and famous stars here. She even saw Frank Sinatra sing with Tommy Dorsey who I guess was the first act to perform here when it originally opened in 1940 as a dance hall for big bands. She especially loved to go and watch him perform. It was the glory days of Hollywood, with stars dancing the night away to big bands in a luxurious hall. Can't ya just picture it in your mind? Search lights, tuxedos, evening dresses, and limousines." He paused as they all pictured the glamour of old Hollywood. "Many people have performed here over the years like Frank Sinatra, Barbara Streisand, The Who, and Jimi Hendrix. In later years it became the home to the weekly television show, 'The Lawrence Welk Show', a reminder of a bygone era."

They entered the large ball room. From the ceiling hung large chandeliers perfect for a diner club with ballroom dancing and fine dining. But tonight there were no chairs and tables. They had been removed so that everyone could stand and watch the group. At the other end was a huge ornate stage that would easily accommodate a big band. It was elegant and stylish. Tonight, however, it was set up for a rock concert with large scaffolding holding sound and light equipment.

The lights dimmed, and the Band began with the song "Brown Sugar". They could not stand still. They watched Mick Jagger as he pranced around the stage while the band rocked out. They performed for about two hours. They did "Satisfaction" as their encore. It was an exciting set. They couldn't help but get totally into the music, only nodding their heads and smiling at each other during the songs.

"Man, what a fan-fucking-tastic show!" Mike was the first to comment after the show. "They are a really awesome rock band. Mick Jagger is incredible. What an amazing front man. He really knows how to work the audience. And that band sure knows how to rock."

"I agree man. That was really awesome!" Jason remarked.

"You've got that right!" added Brian.

"They played a lot of their new album. I think we should learn some of those songs, especially 'Gimme Shelter' and 'Street Fighting Man' Those songs really rock. That's the kind of band I wanna be in—one that can rock an audience like that the whole time. It really got the crowd going."

Jason and Brian nodded in agreement.

"I just know we could do that," commented Mike, more determined than ever.

They returned home excited again with renewed interest in making it big in Hollywood.

"Man, I think I have the perfect name." Mike spoke up. "There is a group called Chicago, and a group called Boston, and a group called America, why not Hollywood!" Mike exclaimed. "It is where the band was formed. It's where we live. I really think we should call the band Hollywood."

"Great idea! The name not only has national recognition but also international recognition." Jason added. "It represents fame, fortune, glamour, glitter, the entertainment industry, dreams, and aspirations. Hollywood represents all that we're striving for. It is the town that we want to conquer. I think Hollywood would be a great name."

All agreed.

"Then it's settled. The new name of the band is HOLLYWOOD.

"CAPTAIN JACK WILL GET YOU HIGH TONIGHT"

Billy Joel

"Thanks for comin' by. You're a really good player, but we just don't think it fits the direction that we are going as a band. We wish you the best of luck." Mike shook the hand of the guitar player who had just auditioned.

"Thanks for the opportunity," the guitar player said as he packed up his gear.

"That guy was great if we wanted to be like some R & B band." Jason said after he had left.

"Yeah, he was," Brian agreed. "And what about that country guy who played like Buck Owens. He'd probably be great if we were Merle Haggard or even Johnny Cash. Good for what he did, just not for us."

"At least they were better than that asshole we had earlier. You remember the hard rocker dude with the long wild red hair and the strange clothes—he looked like a fuckin' clown with his striped pants and that god awful shirt. He couldn't even play. He was so fuckin' loud we couldn't hear anything else—blasting everything at full volume.

And what he played was terrible—just a lot of noise." Mike commented. They all laughed.

"Yeah, he was pretty awful and such an arrogant egotistical asshole to boot. Even if he did play well, I wouldn't want him in the band anyway." Jason added.

"I didn't think this would be so difficult." Mike commented sadly.

"And I didn't think there would be so many different kinds of guitar players out there," added Jason feeling a bit disillusioned and disheartened.

They were deep into auditioning for a new guitar player. Since they were forced to make the change they felt it best to take the time to search for the right player, not just any replacement. They wanted someone who would make the band even better. Someone who would be the right musical fit for what they wanted to accomplish and the direction they wanted to take. This was a very important decision especially for Jason and Mike, so they went about their search in a methodical fashion. In addition to their musical ability, it had to be someone who shared the same musical attitude, direction, influences, and taste. They also needed a musician who shared their dream, someone who believed in them and the band. They had to have the same kind of dedication and drive; someone who was willing and ready for the hard work that was ahead. Of course the right personality was also important. It had to be someone that they could get along with. They would be spending a lot of time together and this was going to be a long association. At times it seemed that they were looking for more than merely a band member, but for a partner in life—almost like a spouse. They knew, however, that the right guitar player was crucial to their success and the success of the band. They wouldn't stop until they found that perfect person to fit that role.

They placed ads in the local music papers and on the local music store bulletin boards. They contacted everyone they knew. They scouted the clubs. They did everything they could think of. The audition process began with long hours of interviews, auditions, rehearsals, or inviting many of them to the gigs so that they could see Doug who they were to replace. Auditions included Jam sessions just to check out their feel then some work on material in general including the original material and the cover songs from their Top 40 club set. They wanted to see their abilities and find out where their head was at musically. A long and steady stream of guitar players went through their rehearsal studio, and there were certainly some characters, each, it seemed, with a variety of problems or inadequacies. Some had egos as big as the sky itself. Some were so strange that they were not even sure they were from the same planet. Some had few skills. Some had good skills but often times their musical direction was just not what the band was looking for even though they may have been quite good in their own field. There was a wide variety of musicians with a wide range of abilities and interests that represented the whole spectrum of music: from funk to R & B, psychedelic to country, rock to old standards. They had no idea of the variety of guitar players there were in this city. The few times they thought they had found the right person, the band was a hard sell. It was difficult to get anyone decent interested in just staying with the band. Most of the good players were highly suspicious. They wanted to know where they were at in a business sense or what connections they had. They were looking for the next big act to join and many wanted to join only if they already had a record deal or at least connections. It was almost mercenary. They wanted the deal now and didn't want to waste time trying to get a deal as many had already been down that road unsuccessfully. It seemed no one could see the potential. Most believed only in themselves and their own ability. They especially did not believe in Hollywood or Jason and Mike and their ability and dream. There were a few compliments, but none encouraging enough to make the task even more difficult than they had anticipated. It was a reality check for them all. They had to fight hard to keep their dream alive with so much disinterest.

It was about a month into the auditions when Mike went to the local rock and roll music store to buy some guitar strings, guitar picks, and the usual. Mike went there often for supplies or just to hang out and see what was happening around town. Music World was the kind of place every musician eventually went to, if only to just look around, see the latest in equipment, and sometimes just to be seen. The store had everything: a wall of guitars ranging in price, drum sets, rooms full of amplifiers and other sound equipment, all the newest keyboards, and all the latest in new advances and electronics for rock musicians. Gold records of groups and artists that shopped there lined the walls above the instruments, and framed 8X10 signed photographs of many famous groups lined other walls. Their clientele ranged from the beginner to the rock star and everything in-between. It was not only a store, but a good place to be known. Their ad for a guitar player had been on the bulletin board for weeks now. They had gotten a lot of calls and auditioned a lot of musicians, but no one was willing to commit or it was just the wrong person.

Mike was glad to see his usual salesman, Bill, and immediately walked over to him. "Hey. What's happenin'?"

"Not a whole lot, what d'ya need today?" Bill responded.

"Uh, Well, I could use a good guitar player for starters." Bill could hear the frustration in Mike's voice. "Boy, this looking for a new player is just a drag. I never thought it'd be so difficult."

"Well, ya know, I play a little guitar. I didn't know you were looking, but I'd like to give it a shot. I play in a couple of bands but nothing really serious. We don't really gig a lot, just rehearse or jam once in a while," Bill replied. "I'm always looking for something else—something more serious."

Mike was surprised and at a loss for words. He was a little reluctant for although he liked Bill, he was very unsure of his ability. Bill was rather shy and introverted, especially about his playing, and Mike was so used to the braggers. He assumed this guy probably couldn't play that well, so he didn't want to waste his time. In addition Bill just wasn't the type he had been looking for. Bill was tall and very thin to the point of looking emaciated and sickly as if he had burnt-out from too many drugs. He wore old rock t-shirts and baggy jeans which seemed to be three sizes too big for him. He wasn't at all attractive, not the rock star idol type in his look or his attitude. But he thought he should at least give the guy a chance.

"Sure. Why not? What time you off work tonight?" Mike finally asked.

"About seven," Bill answered immediately. "I could be there by 7:30."

"Well, why don't ya come over then? You can meet the band. We can jam and see how it goes. Maybe even smoke a bowl."

"Works for me." Bill seemed very interested. "I'll see ya tonight."

Bill agreed. Mike was pleased at his foresight. He thought this would be a good opportunity to see what this guy could do, get rid of him quickly, and not waste a lot of time.

Bill arrived promptly after work. Mike showed him to the converted garage which served as their rehearsal studio. Brian's Rogers drum set was set up against the back wall. The Fender Rhodes keyboard was on one side and on both sides of the drum set there were amps, one for the bass and one for guitar, both Fender. Carpets and rugs lined the walls and floor for sound-proofing.

"Bitchin' rehearsal space. Where's the rest of the group?" Bill asked.

"I think they're inside," Mike answered. "They'll be out shortly. Why don't ya get set up? By the time you're ready they oughta be here."

"Ok." Bill turned and started bringing in his equipment for the audition. He had one Marshall Amplifier, two guitars, and a suitcase of other equipment including cords, and musical paraphernalia.

"What kind of ax do ya play?" Mike asked.

"Uh, I brought my Fender Stratocaster and my Gibson Les Paul. I wasn't sure what kind of sound you guys were looking for, so I brought both. I also have some others at home. A Fender Telecaster, and a Martin acoustic guitar. Er, I like the Marshall amp; it has a real rock sound. I also have a Fender at home that I use for other gigs, especially smaller quieter ones, but I really dig the rock sound of the Marshall. I actually have a Marshall stack with two speaker cabinets, but that is a bit of overkill for the audition and some clubs. It all depends on the size of the room." As he spoke he took out various devices which he placed on the floor around him—fuzz boxes, wah-wah peddles, an echoplex, and other electronics which he wired to his guitar for different sounds.

Mike was somewhat impressed with his sensible approach. "Sure got some good gear," Mike complimented him, impressed with his guitar set up.

"Uh, thanks—one of the advantages of working at the music store. I get a discount, and I really don't have anything else to spend my money on. Besides, this is what I really want to do. I thought it'd help me find the right gig with the right band—always looking for a good opportunity. I just haven't had one up until now."

Bill hooked up all the equipment, turned on the Marshall, and immediately started to do a screaming guitar lead to warm up.

Mike stopped dead in his tracks and watched.

"Wow! You sure *can* play!" Mike was unexpectedly impressed with his playing. "We're gonna have to get some more sound insulation."

"Sorry, was that too loud?" Bill asked shyly.

"No man, it was incredible, just a bit unexpected I guess."

Just then Jason and Brian entered the rehearsal studio having heard the playing.

"Man, you sure can play. Who is this?" asked Jason.

"Oh, this is Bill. He works at Music World. He plays guitar so I invited him over to audition."

"Oh, that's right. I almost forgot," Jason commented. "We've seen so many. We heard you playing from inside. You really know how to play that thing."

"You sure have some chops," Brian added.

"Uh, thanks," Bill replied.

"Yeah, can't wait to give this guy a try," Brian said.

After a quick greeting, introductions, and some small talk, they all took their places. Mike began to play a standard Blues progression. "How about we start with some blues in E?"

Bill immediately joined in. Jason went to his keyboards, turned on his equipment, and started to play along. Brian grabbed his drumstick and took his place behind the drum set. They went through the standard blues progression which Bill performed incredibly: very musical and rockin', yet tasteful.

Mike, Jason, and Brian threw all kinds of ideas and all the standard progressions at him. Bill played them like a pro. All were immediately impressed and pleasantly surprised with his ability and feel. Mike was feeling embarrassed that he had been hoping to get rid of this guy but his embarrassment soon left as he became more and more excited about his playing. They really seemed to click. Bill seemed to fit right in with the band. It was as if Bill knew what to play intuitively. However, they were mostly impressed with his leads which demonstrated his true rock mastery of the instrument. They each looked at each other with a nod of approval. They knew that this guy was hot.

They worked on some cover material. Most were standard rock songs that every guitar player knew, and songs that the band played at gigs. He was more than competent at playing them.

"We should try some of our original material. See if he has a feel for our stuff." Jason piped in." Check it out." He nodded to the other members. They started playing one of the original songs they had been working on to see what Bill would add. What he did add sounded perfect.

They moved quickly into the other material Jason and Mike had written, never speaking a word except to convey a key or a change of progression. Bill was able to pick up the songs easily and followed along extremely well, putting in what he thought would fit. He actually played them beautifully. He seemed to know just where to go and what to add. His greatest asset was his ability to listen to everyone so that what he played fit. He never over played. He just played something that would fit the song and work with what was already there, never interfering with the bass or keyboards. But when it was his turn to take the lead he could really take off, soaring with an appropriate lead—sometimes screaming, sometimes rhythmic, sometimes mellow; but always very tasteful, lyrical, and musical.

In the course of the evening they worked on a number of songs both cover and original. Bill seemed to pick up things real fast, and he just seemed to fit right in.

"Wow, sounds fuckin' fantastic!" Jason exclaimed.

"Yeah, you're really giving me a workout," said Bill still strumming his silent guitar with the amp turned off so that only the strings could be heard. "I really enjoyed that. I dig the way you guys work."

It was almost magical. The excitement grew. The band had never heard these songs sound so good. Whether they played cover songs or Mike and Jason's originals, these were the parts they had wanted to hear all along. This was how the songs were supposed to be. They also gave the band a new identity. While Doug was an expert at imitating records, Bill made the songs more original sounding, playing everything his own way with his own signature style, even the cover songs. At last Mike and Jason heard their songs done right, rock enough, hard edged enough, but also with sensitivity and taste and at the right volumes at the right times. It was about two hours before they took a break. All were rather tired but pleased with each other.

"I dig the way ya play," Mike began. "But, gotta have a break"

"Ya wanna beer or somethin'?" Brian asked.

"Uh, sure," Bill responded.

"I'm ready to smoke a bowl also," said Mike "I'll get it ready."

"Some cool tunes, man. Are they yours?" Bill asked.

"Uh huh, mostly Jason's and mine." Mike answered. "We work together a lot. Currently, I write most of the lyrics, and Jason and I work on the music together. But it's really a joint effort. We do a lot of collaborating. We would welcome you to join in on our efforts. I'm glad ya like 'em. I dug what you did with 'em," Mike continued rolling a joint.

"We've been working on 'em together a lot, but they never sounded like this before." Jason tried to hide his enthusiasm. "You really have a great feel for 'em."

Mike turned to Jason and Brian. "Can I talk with you guys inside for a minute? Bill, we'll be right back."

As soon as they left the studio Mike began. "This guy is fuckin' incredible. We need him in the band. What d'ya all think?"

"I agree. He'd be a real asset to the band," Jason agreed.

"I agree as well," said Brian

"Plus he's seems like a cool guy, and he works at Guitar World so we can get discounts." Mike was selling him.

"Let's offer him the gig," Brian made the agreement a consensus.

After a brief discussion, it was decided that he was the right guitar player for the band. Now all they had to do was convince him.

"We had a very short discussion. We really would like you to be part of the band. We all agreed. We think that you're gonna fit in incredibly." Mike offered with enthusiasm.

"Yeah, man. We all dig your playing." Jason nodded in agreement.

"You'd be an excellent addition to this group," said Brian. "How about it?"

"Sounds interesting, I really dig the band. You guys seem alright, and I like the material a lot." Bill responded enthusiastically.

Mike passed around the beers while Jason lit up a joint.

"So what's the story with this band anyway?" Bill asked. He took a hit then passed the joint to Mike.

"Well, we're currently playing some Top 40 gigs to make money, but we really want to do original material and break into the big time—get a recording contract, make some great records, go on tour. I think with a great band we can do it."

As Mike, Jason, and Brian continued their hard sell dissertation they had so well rehearsed with the other players they had auditioned, they noticed Bill getting more and more excited. He continued to play even with the amp turned off, only stopping to take a drink from his beer or a puff from the joint being passed around. He never put his guitar down, clinging onto it like a child clings onto its blanket for security.

"I hope you're interested," Mike ended.

"Well, I've only been in a few groups but nothing really serious, and I haven't really gigged a lot before. But after hearing some of the material, I think this could really be bitchin'. I really dig your direction in music. I haven't really done the Top 40 thing, but I'm sure willing to give it a try. And the extra money sure wouldn't hurt. I can also get discounts on equipment if we need something. I guess what I am trying to say is yes. I am interested. Count me in," Bill replied decidedly.

"I dunno about you, but I sure am excited. I think your playing is great—partly because of your technical prowess, but also because you play with heart and soul. You make that guitar sing. You are a very tasteful player. You have incredible chops, but you only play what works for the song."

Bill really did communicate with his guitar. Shy as he was, all the feelings were drawn out when he was playing. He had the ability to make that instrument talk.

"How d'ya two know each other?" asked Jason.

"Just from Music World," Mike replied.

Mike was suddenly reminded that he knew very little about Bill. As they got high Mike told him of his background and about San Francisco and college.

Jason followed his lead telling him of his past. They were hoping to get Bill relaxed enough to talk. They knew he was shy, but they wanted him to open up. They wanted to get to know him as a person as well. They loved his playing, but they hoped him and his personality would fit in.

"Well, enough about us. Where are ya from?"

Bill still clung to his guitar; strumming, playing, and fingering even though the amps were turned off so that the only sound was the metal strings. "Originally from Boston, but I spent a lot of time in New York," Bill replied shyly, appearing reluctant to continue with only the booze and drugs to help loosen him up.

"What brought ya out here? And how'd ya get started on the guitar?" Jason inquired.

"I, uh, just needed to get away from New York and some of the people there. It's, uh, kind of a heavy scene with the drugs and all," Bill replied still uneasy about discussing his past.

"Yeah, I bet they have good drugs in New York. I know we did in San Francisco. What was the scene like in New York?" Mike was really curious now.

"Well, I, er, kind of got into some heavy drugs in New York. It all started out great. The art scene was really happenin'. It was fun goin' to all the hip clubs and parties, especially in Greenwich Village. Of course there was The Factory. Ya know, Andy Warhol's place. I got involved with them and met a lot of people—Warhol, Jim Morrison, Velvet Underground, and Bob Dylan. It was very cool—a real happening scene for artists and musicians of all kinds. There was also a lot of drugs."

"Sounds very cool. I know what you mean. I left San Francisco for the same reasons. Look," Mike replied in an attempt to better gain Bill's confidence, "you're among friends here. Besides, if we are in a band together there will be few secrets. We are not here to judge." Mike had a way of exuding acceptance, understanding, and fairness without judgments. "We'd just like to get to know you better, so don't be shy."

"Cool, Thanks. Anyway, I even went to Woodstock that summer of '69 to the music festival. It was amazing—great music and great drugs—one of the most unforgettable experiences of my life, a community connected by drugs and music. The whole vibe was just wonderful—a real trip. I met some cool people, and for the first time I felt connected. I especially remember seeing Jimi Hendrix. I couldn't believe how incredible he was. That was when I really knew that I wanted to play the guitar like him. That weekend changed my life." He grew thoughtful as he stared off into space remembering that eventful weekend, almost reliving it in his mind—lost in his own thoughts.

Finally, Mike interrupted him after a few minutes, bringing him back to reality. "Sounds bitchin', man. I can't believe you were there."

"Yeah, it was pretty cool."

"Why'd ya leave Boston in the first place?" Jason asked thinking that by starting at the beginning this might help drag some more information out of him.

"I, er, to get away from my folks. Uh, we just didn't get along. So I, uh, left." With that question Bill seemed even more uneasy. This seemed to be a particularly bad subject as indicated by his tone of voice, his body language, and his avoidance of talking about it. He quickly skipped over the Boston era. "I hated Boston. It was time I started a life of my own. So I took off. I drifted around for a while until I ended up in New York. New York was a happening city during that time. But it was a tough life, and New York is an expensive city. I was homeless for a while. Then, I met some people who at the time I thought were friends. At least they gave me a place to sleep, and it was better than livin' on the streets. They were mostly communes and flop houses. But I learned to survive."

Bill was beginning to feel more comfortable now. He was still clung to his guitar like a security blanket, playing along as he spoke. Mike wasn't sure if this was due to the drugs or his efforts to make him relax, but he hoped the latter. They were starting to feel some camaraderie among the four of them.

"So what happened?" Brian asked.

"Well, I, er, made some good connections and got into dealing to survive since I needed to make money. Somehow this seemed the easiest way. Plus I could feed my own drug habit. I moved up in the New York drug world pretty fast. I eventually met Captain Jack. No one knew his real name; everyone just called him Captain Jack. It was sort of like one of those Film Noir art movies or an Andy Warhol drug movie. You know the type—dark alleys leading to wild psychedelic parties. Boy, was I impressed. Captain Jack had lots of money and drugs, a great place in the Village, and very cool friends: mostly artists and musicians. The scene in the Village was just so happenin'. I can see it now—big rooms everywhere, psychedelic lights, and continuous parties—very underground. I soon found out most of his money was from smack. Ya know, heroin. And man, I, ah, sure dug heroin. Uh, you ever do heroin?" Bill asked.

"No, can't say that I have. It always frightened me a little," Mike responded.

"Well, I loved it. It seemed to make me feel warm inside, like somebody cared for me and loved me and nothing else mattered. It made all the problems—past, present, and future—just melt away. It made me feel good for the first time in my life. Just like the movies. However, it started going downhill. It became a real bad scene. The drugs started getting expensive. It seemed I was dealing more and more and getting less and less. I think Captain Jack was just using me to break in some new customers, and I did. But my own habit was getting outta hand and too expensive. I couldn't even support my own habit. I was hooked. That led to some petty theft and robbery to support my habit. Of course, I eventually got caught. My life was in the gutter, sort of like the movie 'Lost Weekend,' but instead of booze it was smack. I was on a path of self destruction. I'd probably be dead if I hadn't been busted. So, in a way, I'm thankful for that. It was probably a good thing in the long run. I still think to this day that I was turned in by Captain Jack. I guess I'll never know. I wouldn't wanna fuck with him. He's one powerful pusher in New York."

"So what happened? Did ya get off?" Brian asked enthralled by this story.

"Luckily, I knew an attorney in New York" answered Bill.

"How'd you get to know a big New York attorney anyway?" Jason asked. It seemed odd that a junkie from New York would know some big New York attorney. He grew suspicious of his connections and felt that he was again holding something back.

"Er, he was just sort of a friend of the family. Someone I went to school with in Boston." He was obviously avoiding the issue. "He made a deal with the judge so that I could get off but only if I would go to rehab in a hospital and do some community service. It was my only choice and better than serving time. So, I went to the hospital to dry out. Thank God for that. Thank God for my guitar as well. It was there that I really improved my playing. I had a lot of time on my hand, so I played a lot. It helped me through the pain and made my stay and my recovery almost bearable. With so much time on my hands I did have a lot of time to practice. Once I got out I thought it best that I leave New York rather than run into the same people, especially Captain Jack. So here I am in L.A. I. uh, just want ya to know that my heroin days are over. I never wanna get involved with smack again. Oh, I do my share of other drugs, but only for recreational purposes. I'm pretty careful now. I never wanna get hooked on anything again. That was nasty shit. I hope you don't think I'm just another junkie. You know what they say, 'once a junkie always a junkie.' But I've been clean for two years, and I plan to keep it that way. You guys are the first ones out here I've told about this. Shit, I really don't usually tell people all this. I'm not too proud of my past. I keep it to myself as it turns a lot of people off. I hope I didn't blow it. I hope you still want me in the band."

"Oh course we do. This hasn't changed my mind in the slightest," Mike replied confidently with Jason and Brian shaking their heads in agreement.

"Nothing has changed. What kind of jerks d'ya think we are?" said Brian.

"This doesn't affect our decision in the slightest," continued Jason. "In fact, I, for one, am glad you opened up."

"We want this band to be very close, like brothers." Mike turned to them all. "Not just a bunch of musicians, but real friends with no secrets."

"We'll probably be spending a lot of time together, so we had best get used to each other," Jason continued.

"Thanks for understanding about my past," Bill said with a sigh of relief. "I, uh, thought I might have blown it."

"We're all in this together, man. Thanks for being honest." Mike put his hand on Bill's back to show his acceptance and understanding. "Anyway, I am no angel either," he continued. "I could tell you stories of San Francisco that aren't that different from yours. Remember, I was there with all the hippies, the Summer of Love, and all that. We certainly did our share of drugs."

"My life was a bit tamer than both of yours, but I'm cool with it. But I have done my share as well." said Jason.

"Me too," agreed Brian.

They spent more time getting high, playing, and just getting to know each other.

Finally Jason asked. "We have a rehearsal set for tomorrow night. Can ya make it?"

"Sure, after work, I get off at 6:00. I can be here at 7:00. I'd better go now. I'm really spaced. Thanks for the weed. I look forward to seeing ya tomorrow." Bill put his guitar in the case.

As he packed up and left, Mike, Jason, and Brian discussed the new addition to the band. They wondered about his family life which he had been so secretive about and how that would've driven him to New York to be a junkie. They decided not to worry about a repeat of his past problems.

No other mention was ever made of his junkie days. Bill still was his quiet shy self. Mike, Jason, and Brian knew they were one of the few people who had a glimpse into what made him tick. They could hear the pain and suffering he had undergone in his playing, and the life experience he had endured. Bill could really make that guitar sing, but now Mike, Jason, and Brian knew what he was saying.

"WE'RE AN AMERICAN BAND"

Grand Funk Railroad

Mike entered the room filled with excitement. "Have ya heard the new Led Zeppelin album? Check it out. I've just figured out this new song that we can learn. There are also some songs from the latest Rolling Stones and Beatles albums that we need to learn. But most importantly I have a new idea for a song. Check out this riff." Picking up a guitar, he played a riff and some chords that with some work would be the beginnings of a new song.

They all listened for a while. Eventually, they got their instruments and joined in, adding their parts. The start of a new song was born.

"I think it'll be a really good song when done. We should work on some lyrics." Jason said enthusiastically.

They continued working on the song for quite a while.

"Sounds great, however, we need to get back to the cover stuff." Mike brought them back to reality. "I wanna get working and playing gigs with Bill as soon as possible."

"I wish we didn't have to," Bill responded dejectedly.

"Me too, but it brings in money which we all can use."

"Besides, I think it's good practice and experience." Jason added." After all we do need to stay current, and it's a good way to learn what makes a good song and to work on a stage."

This was their routine for the next few weeks. With intensive, grueling rehearsals, Hollywood was becoming a really good tight band. Although their main goal now was to work on the original material, there were gigs to do which meant learning the Top 40 material, a task Bill both regretted and disliked as he hated doing other band's songs.

The transition had gone fairly easy. Bill had learned all the cover material that Doug had done in a very short time, allowing Doug to leave to pursue other musical endeavors. They were now ready to start doing the Top 40 gigs with Bill as the new guitar player and Jason on keys. It was time to put the new band, Hollywood, on the stage. Mike took on the task of booking them, something he also did with Axis, and something he seemed good at. Besides, he didn't have another job, and he already knew many of the club owners.

They all seemed to be getting along very well. It wasn't long before they asked Bill to move in with them at the band house since there was room. It would help them with the rent especially since Bill had a full time job. And it allowed them more time to practice. Bill jumped at the chance. It allowed him a much better place to practice with the band as well as on his own, something he could not do at his small single apartment.

Mike entered rehearsal one sunny day. "Hey, I've got some good news. I got us a gig next week at The Garage in the Valley. It's a pretty cool club. I've played there many times. We are booked under the name Axis. The club owner booked us immediately since he knows that we're good and that we'll draw a crowd." Mike explained. "Just so you know, for now I will start bookings us as Axis at the nightclubs Axis had played since it is a name that the club owners know. That way we won't have to audition. Eventually, we can tell the club owners and announce to the audience that we have a new guitar player, a new keyboard player, and a new name. For all the new clubs we will go under the name of Hollywood."

"Sounds like a plan. I can't wait." Jason seemed excited.

This would be the debut of Hollywood. They just hoped they were ready. It would be the first time they had all played together on stage.

It was late Thursday afternoon as they drove north over the hill to the flat San Fernando Valley which stretched out before them. In the distance they could see the snowcapped mountains of the Angeles Forest. The northern mountain ranges—especially Mount Wilson behind Pasadena—was the only way they could tell that this was in fact winter in L.A.

"Man, this is like old home week. You know, this is near where I grew up," Mike commented as they drove over the hill and through the valley. He looked out of the car window recognizing many sights and places he knew so well. "This is like coming home again."

This section of Los Angeles was just over the hills from Hollywood. The San Fernando Valley began as ranches, farms, and groves of fruit trees—mostly walnuts and oranges. In the 1950s, after the war, it became a bedroom community as rows of tract houses sprouted up like weeds replacing the fields of crops. The baby boom was in full bloom here as miles and miles of mass produced houses were built, all looking strangely similar but at least allowing everyone the American dream of home ownership. They drove down Ventura Boulevard through towns like Encino, Sherman Oaks, and Studio City where the wealthier people lived in the hills "South of the Boulevard." However, today their destination was Van Nuys, the heart of the San Fernando Valley and its political and social center.

"I think you guys are gonna really dig this place. It's called The Garage because that is what it once was. It's in the center of The Valley, right off Van Nuys Boulevard. It'll be packed tonight since its Thursday and Thursday night is cruise night, something Van Nuys Boulevard is famous for." Mike continued.

"Hey what do ya' think about writing a song about it—a real rhythmic, hard hitting boogie type rock song. We'll call it 'Cruisin'.' Bill, maybe you can come up with some rocking guitar line."

"Sure, I can do that."

"Sounds bitchin', man. After we check out the vibe, we'll start working on it."

They turned and drove down Van Nuys Boulevard. Mike knew that in a couple of hours this street would be a major scene of people out for the evening. Every Thursday the stores stayed open late. Some people shopped, others just walked up and down the street, while others cruised up and down the boulevard in their cars showing off their wheels. It looked much like most Main Streets in America. But the real show was the cars. Cars of all kinds, from hot rods, to anything they could get to run, with some souped up with fancy paint jobs, racing gear, or anything to make them look better. Some were so customized they were deemed unrecognizable form their original make and model. Others were just family cars that mom or dad let the kids take out for the evening. All were there checking out the scene and looking to be checked out themselves, much like the movie American Graffiti. After cruising the boulevard, it was time to rock and roll and hang out. The ones old enough usually ended up at the Garage, although since they served food the age limit was 18. This allowed for a much younger crowd than some of the other nightclubs. There they could eat, drink, dance, and listen to live music.

They entered the club ready for their sound check. It was the usual rock club, but it did have more of a younger feel to it. It was a large industrial type of building in an industrial section of town surrounded by car repair shops, warehouses, industrial businesses, and storage buildings. It had once been a car repair shop or something similar but had been converted into a nightclub. Its large size made it perfect for a rock club. A large stage about 3 feet high off the dance floor was at the back of the room. The bar ran the whole length of the right wall. The all concrete floor had an area for dancing directly in front of the stage with tables surrounding it. The walls were concrete or corrugated steel. The whole place felt very industrial which added to its ambience. The sound check went well. They left to eat and check out the cruising on Van Nuys Blvd. It was fun seeing all the great cars.

They returned to find the place packed with an eclectic assortment of people—from bikers to hot-rodders to college kids.

They took the stage. Bill and Jason were nervous. At first, they constantly watched Brian and Mike to remind them of keys, changes, and song parts. By the third set they felt more confident and relaxed. They actually began to enjoy playing. The crowd was enthusiastic—almost rowdy. It felt like a mini-rock concert. It made for a great gig.

"Not bad guys," said Mike after the gig.

"Yeah, it was actually fun," said Jason, and Bill agreed.

"There were some rough edges, and we've got a lot of work to do, but this will totally work," Mike said.

They finished out the week each day improving as they became more confident on stage and with the material.

They would play many other gigs but they grew to really appreciate The Garage as it proved to be one of the better gigs. It did at least feel like a small concert. It was a good sized club, the crowd was receptive, the vibe was good, and they could play at a decent volume—like a real rock band.

Mike kept them booked fairly regularly. They started with clubs where Axis had played. He informed the owners of the name and personnel change after the initial gig. They also added many new clubs some of which they had to audition for. Wherever they played they always made a good impression and were asked back. But most importantly, each time they did a gig they got better.

There were plenty of nightclubs throughout the city to keep the band working. The great variety of venues forced them to try new and different things. Clubs as varied as the metropolitan Los Angeles area. The East Side with its Mexican flavor, the West Side with its upscale somewhat professional crowd, Long Beach south of Los Angeles and home to a large naval base with the clubs filled with service men, South Bay with its surfers, Pasadena with its old money, and Westwood with its college students mostly from UCLA. Every club, it seemed, had a different audience with different tastes. Some were large rock clubs with a young clientele where they could really rock out on a fairly good sized stage. Others were small lounges with an older clientele and stages so small it was difficult to fit the whole band onto it. At these, the band wasn't much more than a juke box and they had to play at a very soft volume so that people could talk over the music. These they liked least, but it helped improve their playing as it forced them to listen to each other and to concentrate on their overall sound. It was difficult to hide the mistakes at a lower volume, so they were able to make everything better. The result was that the material sounded even better when the volume was turned up. They had a wide variety of material and prided themselves in their ability to adapt to any type of gig which proved to be an asset in keeping the band constantly booked. It gave them the money to support themselves, but most importantly it gave them experience of playing together on stage as a group. They were leading the life of a musician.

Some time each day was spent working on the cover songs. They were constantly fixing parts, changing parts, arranging parts, or learning new material—always trying to improve their show and keep it current. It proved to be a valuable learning tool when writing their own songs. It gave them ideas on how to write and arrange their original material. They also found that playing someone else's tunes was good practice and a good way to analyze what makes a good song and a popular hit and why.

Once the copy songs were learned the majority of the time was spent working on original material. The songs were written, re-written, revised, arranged, rearranged, and perfected countless times. And when they thought it was finished, someone came up with a better idea, and it was back for more revisions. As time passed, the songs got better: more refined and more concise. This was truly the creative process at work. For months these musicians were driven, fueled by each other's excitement, dreams, and their goals. Their love of music allowed them to persevere. Ideas became realities, and from the creative process, songs were formed. Music was their life. This project became a labor of love and dedication. Nothing could stop them now. Their creation was becoming a reality.

10

"HOLLYWOOD NIGHTS"

Bob Seger

Bill arrived home from work at about 6:00. Mike, Jason, and Brian were sitting in the living room.

"Hey guys, I got some tickets to see a band on 'The Strip'," said Bill holding up the tickets. "One of my customers just got signed. They're playing a showcase at The Whisky, and they want a full house. He gave me a couple of comps, another of the perks of working at the music store. Usually we're working, but I knew we were off that night, so I grabbed 'em. I think we should go. We should keep informed about what's happening in the business, and who is getting signed. We need to see what the competition is if we're ever gonna do anything except play Top 40. Also, I think we should make a night of it. In addition to checking out the band, check out some of the other clubs, especially the concert clubs on the Strip in West Hollywood where we can play original material. We've been playing this cover shit enough. I think it's time we found a gig that allows originals."

"I also think it's time we checked out the scene in general," Mike said.

They all agreed to go out for a night on the town.

"The Strip" or The Sunset Strip is a section of Sunset Boulevard just west of Hollywood. It is an entertainment area of Los Angeles and Hollywood with a lot of night life and where many nightclubs are located. Sunset Boulevard, or simply Sunset, as it is often called, had always been a famous street—an icon of Los Angeles with a history of its own. It had been the title of a famous movie about an aging Hollywood star, and how the star system affects people, a perfect movie to show what fame and fortune can do to someone.

The birth of Sunset Boulevard is in downtown Los Angeles where it begins its journey near Union Station, the main train station in downtown Los Angeles. In the glory days of train travel it was bustling with passengers arriving and departing from all over the United States. It served as a drop off point for many who visit the greater Los Angeles area. But for many it was also a start to a new life with the promise of a brighter future. And for some it was also a place to begin their journey to stardom. Trainloads of people arrived hoping that their path would take them to fame and fortune. For some, their dreams would be realized; for others, their journey would end in stark reality or demise.

Upon leaving Union Station, Sunset passes near Olvera Street, the original site of Los Angeles when it was simply a Mexican village and part of Mexico which had become a colony of Spain. It travels through Chinatown where Chinese immigrants ended up starting their own neighborhood. To the south the buildings of downtown Los Angeles loom skyward complete with the City Hall Tower made famous in the 50s by the Dragnet television series and still a Los Angeles icon. Sunset then winds through towns like Silver Lake and Echo Park where the ethnic diversity of Los Angeles is further displayed with older neighborhoods now populated by mostly Mexican families. It continues on to the Los Feliz area, one of the original wealthy areas of the city and home to the Griffith Park observatory, a place affording a great view of the greater Los Angeles area on a clear day with its hilltop location and where the famous ending to <u>Rebel Without a Cause</u> was filmed.

It continues through Hollywood—the symbol of the entertainment industry. Then on to the entertainment area of the city known as West Hollywood and the Sunset Strip where night clubs of past and present showcase the stars of past, present, and future. Many a career and dream were made or lost here. The tall office buildings house many music and entertainment industry businesses. They mingle with the nightclubs as a reminder that the entertainment industry is after all truly a business. This change is abrupt as the street immediately changes when it passes over to the city limits of Beverly Hills. Mansions of the famous replace the commercial buildings of The Strip. Homes to the stars line Sunset and the streets radiating out from. The mansions of Beverly Hills show off the status of the rich and famous who settle there after making it big. About midway in Beverly Hills, the huge Beverly Hills Hotel sits with its beautiful grounds and gardens and opulent building. This pink, Pepto Bismol colored hotel is famous as the hotel of the stars and other Hollywood insiders that have made it. Many deals are made there for new movies, television shows, concerts, or other entertainment related work. Many stay in the hotel or the bungalows, lounge around the pools, or drink in the famous Polo Lounge.

Leaving Beverly Hills, Sunset winds again through the foothills past large homes and mansions of those who have made it in towns like Westwood (also home to the UCLA campus), Brentwood, and Pacific Palisades signifying the final end to a long career.

Much like life, before ending, it passes by the Self Realization Fellowship, a place of spirituality—a place for self-reflection and meditation. Sunset Boulevard ends its incredible journey at Pacific Coast Highway in Malibu, beyond which is the great unknown of the seemingly infinite Pacific Ocean.

The four of them smoked a bowl before leaving the house. Once finished they ventured out leaving plenty of time to make it to the Whisky before the show.

"This should be fun." Jason was looking forward to their evening out.

"Yeah man, can't wait to see these guys. And to see what the record companies are looking for and what is getting signed," Brian commented.

It was nighttime when they left the house. They drove down Sunset. 'All the Young Dudes' by Mott the Hoople played on the radio as they began their journey.

The band house was just a couple of short blocks from Sunset in Hollywood. They had driven it many times and found it to be one of the most fascinating streets in the entire city. They drove down Sunset with a new sense of enthusiasm, as if seeing it for the first time.

"Sometimes, I still can't believe that I live here in Hollywood," commented Jason. "I heard about all this stuff when I was back in Atlanta."

"Yeah, I remember hearing about this back in Boston and New York as well," said Bill.

"Hey guys, there's CBS studios, right here at Gower." Mike pointed as they passed the intersection.

"Check it out. The Who are playing at the Palladium. We should get tickets," Mike said as they passed the famous Hollywood Palladium where they had gone to see many concerts.

"Hey guys, did ya know the Doors used to play at the Aquarius Theater across the street." Bill pointed as they continued their journey. The Aquarius Theater was where <u>Hair</u>, the landmark musical of the hip generation, had played for many years. It also launched the careers of many recording artists. It was originally built as a supper theater for dining and dancing, but it was converted to a regular theater years later.

They drove past Sunset and Vine. "You know there are a lot of record companies on this street as well," said Bill. "In fact there's the RCA records' building right across the street from the famous Cinerama Dome." This was a famous Hollywood movie theater and a Hollywood landmark because it was built using the design of a geodesic dome made famous by R. Buckminster Fuller. "And there's United Artists, Liberty, and EMI," Bill continued.

As Sunset continues through Hollywood it passes by the old Crossroads of the World, one of the world's first shopping malls and home to many entertainment businesses and offices.

"See that building down La Brea that looks like an English Village; that's A&M Records. You know Herb Alpert the Tijuana Brass. Jerry Moss was his partner. That is what A & M stands for." Bill pointed as they passed La Brea. "It was originally the Charlie Chaplin studios, but

A & M records bought it and turned it into their headquarters with studios and offices."

"You sure know a lot about the record business here in Hollywood," commented Jason.

"Well, it kind of comes with the territory I guess. Ya know, working at the music store and all. Gotta do your homework." Bill was pleased to be able to show his knowledge of the music business.

Leaving Hollywood proper the street started to become more winding as it reached West Hollywood at Crescent Heights near Laurel Canyon. This corner was the original home to Schwab's Pharmacy where supposedly Lana Turner was discovered sitting on a stool at the lunch counter. The road rose slightly above the flatlands into the foothills of the Hollywood Hills. Side roads stretched upward to large homes with panoramic views of the flat planes below where lights stretched as far as the eye could see.

"This is the beginning of the Sunset Strip," Mike commented. "It has always been home to many famous Hollywood nightclubs. These clubs have launched many a career.

Check it out, that's where Ciro's, The Mocambo, and The Trocadero were once located. They've all changed names over the years, but the clubs are still here. In the past they were the three most famous nightclubs located here." Mike pointed them out as they passed them. "They were the hub of the Hollywood entertainment crowd where stars played or could be seen. Ciro's was where the Desi Arnaz Orchestra sometimes played. See it there. It's now The Comedy Club, home to many up-and-coming comedians."

They passed the famous clubs of The Strip where many of Hollywood's past had begun. As they drove, they noticed that others had also changed names and use, but the buildings were still there, a remnant of the glory of old Hollywood. "Remember <u>77 Sunset Strip</u> from the television series. It's right there. It's still here although the number isn't the correct one; it's now called Dino's Lodge." Mike added.

"I remember that show," said Brian.

"Me too," said Jason.

"How d'ya know all this stuff?" asked Bill.

"Oh, some of it I read about in that book, but also my mom told me about it. She talked about Hollywood all the time. Some of these were places she hung out at when she was younger and was trying to break into the business. It was her dream to become one of the famous stars and be part of Hollywood, but she never really made it. She had to give all that up when I came along. It always made me feel guilty, like she had to give up her dream because of me." Mike became strangely quite for moment, lost in thought.

The higher the road rose the more they could see the incredible view the street offered them over the flatlands to the south with lights stretching far into the horizon. It felt as if they were above and in some way better than all those people that lived below.

"Tonight we're goin' to The Whisky, but I also wanna hit some of the other clubs. Most of this area is music clubs and other related businesses. It is the center of the rock and roll business. The offices of many entertainment related businesses such as managers, agents, attorneys, and record companies are located here in the office buildings." Bill informed them.

The Strip had made its mark on the music scene in the 1960s when it was the center of the hip generation—a place where hippies and others gathered on their way to nightclubs to see the latest rock bands or just hang out.

"Man, this could be our future." Mike vocalized his dream out loud.

"Yeah, this is what we should be working for," Bill agreed.

"We should write a song about this street, just call it Sunset Boulevard," said Mike.

"It could be about glamour, nightlife, and the journey from being a nobody to being famous." Jason added.

That's a great idea. We can use Sunset Boulevard as a metaphor of life!" Mike was really inspired now. "After all, this is a street with a life all its own. It could be a reflection of one's own journey in life, from beginning to end, birth to death. This street has it all. The train station can represent birth because for many it is the start of a new life. Some of the poorer neighborhoods near downtown L.A. can represent the poor and the start of a career when we all struggle. The nightclubs can represent the fun of youth with its lack or responsibility. The offices and businesses in the Hollywood, West Hollywood, and Sunset Strip area can represent the hard work that everyone must eventually do and the responsibility everyone must face. The rich mansions of Beverly Hills and beyond can represent success. Finally, the journey ends up at the ocean which can represent death. It really is a metaphor of life, career, and the journey we are on with each place representing the stepping stones everyone must take in their life." He grew more and more excited. He really felt like he was on a roll now "It is especially appropriate for people in the entertainment business. A rags to riches story in the form of a street." His head was swimming with ideas.

"Wow, sounds like a fuckin' fantastic idea!" exclaimed Jason.

"I can't wait to start writing it."

Finally, they reached The Whisky. It was a small club. A row of booths lined the back wall filled with important looking types. Reserved signs sat on the tables, some stating Elektra Records.

"Must be the record company execs and their guests," Bill confidently pointed out.

Smaller tables and chairs sat in front of the booths on a slightly lower level. They found a table and waited to see the band perform. About two steps down was the dance floor or open area for standing directly in front of the large corner stage which stood about 4 feet off the ground. The whole place was dark and dingy. It had red brick walls, red and black furniture. It was nothing special, but it was the famous Whisky. Groups like The Kinks, The Who, Cream, Led Zeppelin, The Byrds, Buffalo Springfield, and The Doors had once played there.

The band descended from a stairway at the back of the club where the dressing rooms were obviously located. They entered the stage. It was a four piece band: Bass, Drums, keyboards, and guitar. They introduced songs from their upcoming album and the new single that was to hit the stores next month.

"They were good but not great," said Jason as they left after the set was over.

"Yeah, they weren't that happenin'," commented Mike as they wandered down the street.

"Yeah, they were OK. But they are signed to Elektra Records which is more than we can say," Bill reminded them.

"I didn't think the drummer was that hot," Brian critiqued.

"And I didn't think the guitar player was that hot either," Bill criticized. "But they do have a hit single. Not my style, but I could definitely hear that on the radio. That's what we really need guys, a hit single."

"Well, we're working on it," Mike interjected.

They continued walking down the street. They stopped at The Roxy. It had some recording band with a new album performing, but the show was sold out. There was a billboard announcing the upcoming opening of a rock musical called <u>The Rocky Horror Show</u>, about a drag queen from outer space.

"Looks interesting," said Jason. The others gave him a strange look.

"Let's stop in at The Rainbow Room for a drink. This is where a lot of rock stars hang out," said Bill

They entered. The usual rock crowd lined the bar and filled the tables.

"Isn't that Rod Stewart sitting over there?" Jason nodded his head in the direction of the star while trying to be nonchalant.

"It sure is, and he's sitting with Jeff Beck. Ya know, the guitarist," commented Mike. "I think Rod used to play with Jeff Beck when he first got started; before he went out on his own."

"Yeah, I think you're right," said Bill.

"Hey look, Mick Jagger just walked in!" exclaimed Jason.

"Come on guys, let's not be so obvious." Bill motioned for them to be cool and take this all like it was just normal even though he was just as excited as the rest of them. "This is where all the rock bands and people in the business hang out. Are you guys star struck or something?"

"I just think it's cool." Jason was doing his best trying to act nonchalant, but inside he was excited like a real groupie "Where did Mick go?"

"Probably upstairs to the private club called Over the Rainbow. It's where most rock royalty hang out," Bill stated matter of factly.

there once on his first U.S. tour. Not really our thing, but I think we should check it out. Also, there's another club I wanna check out: The Starwood in West Hollywood. It's another showcase room where bands play original material. Perhaps we could get a gig there. We need to continue our search and our education about what is out there."

"Sure," they all agreed.

They drove a couple of blocks to the Troubadour on Santa Monica Boulevard—a short distance from the Strip. This club had originally been a club for small acoustic groups or even comedians. They had started to book rock bands to get more business. It had a bar in the front which was separate from the concert hall. Tonight the performer was a woman singing and playing an acoustic guitar.

The act started in a few minutes, so they decided to have a drink at the bar.

"Hey man, that's James Taylor at the end of the bar." Bill nodded to some people sipping drinks at the end of the bar.

"And I think that's Carole King." Jason whispered as he poked his friends in the ribs with his elbow.

They walked in to see the singer perform. The tables were lined up going out from the stage so that everyone could see the performer. This was a real showcase concert room. No dancing or open area. A stark stage with only a brick wall was behind the stage. The club was set up for people to sit, listen, and watch the group or artist performing.

"Man, she's putting me to sleep," Bill stated after the first set. "Time to move on."

As they walked out a group of obvious musicians was just arriving. Just after they walked past, Bill turned "Did ya see who that was?"

"No. Why?" Mike asked.

"That was Glen Frey, Don Henley, and the rest of the Eagles. I recognize them from the store."

"Fuckin'A. This place sure is the hang out." Mike said. He turned around to look as they continued down the sidewalk

Next stop was the Starwood at Santa Monica Boulevard and Crescent Heights. This was a very large L shaped night club with multiple rooms. The small show lounge which was usually reserved for small acoustic acts or comedians was in the back. The middle room was a bar with pool tables; a quiet place to just hang out and have a drink. At the other end was the large showcase room where mostly rock bands played, usually newly signed or up-and-coming groups looking to get signed. It looked like a small concert hall with its large corner stage which stood about four feet off the floor. In front of the stage was an open space where people could stand and watch the band or dance. In the back of the room a row of elevated booths and tables lined the two walls, just high enough for people to see over the crowd standing on the floor. It was one of the premier rock clubs—a place that many bands aspired to play.

They ended up in the showcase room with the large stage. They all watched an excellent band take the stage and perform a high energy, well executed set of really good original songs. They were quite impressed and showed their satisfaction with a nod of approval.

They arrived home shortly after 2 A.M.

"That last band was outstanding!" Mike exclaimed. "And that place is happenin'. That's where we should be playing."

"Right on, man! That was a great club." Jason was still enthusiastic about their evening.

"Yeah, we've certainly seen some good clubs," Mike admitted "We need to do this more often."

"Well, that's where we need to be," Bill agreed. "That's where the up-and-coming, the recently signed, or the recording acts play. I certainly didn't see any group better than we are, or at least any better than we can be with some work."

"You got that right," Mike responded enthusiastically.

"We just need to work hard and get booked into that scene. That is the scene that'll take us to the next step to getting a recording contract. Ya know what I mean?" Bill was almost lecturing them.

"Yeah, we have some good material, but we need some hit songs, and we need to become well known." Brian agreed.

"Uh huh, we really need to get out there and do it, not just talk about it and hope." Mike stressed the importance with this new realization.

This was in many ways an epiphany for Jason, Mike, Brian, and Bill. They were going to do everything in their power to make it. They could see the really hard work ahead, but they knew what they had to do.

They spent many of their nights off going to these clubs. Having the Starwood, The Whisky, The Troubadour, Gazarri's and a few other clubs nearby proved helpful. They could see what was getting signed and why, and what the record companies were looking for since many of the bands had been newly signed to recording contracts, They were also able to see what their competition was and what areas they needed to improve on and just how good they had to be. There were many unsigned acts trying to get that recording deal. They saw bands that were signed and had albums out. Some were great while others were just not ready yet. Some were really good, but they did not have a big enough draw to play large venues or stadiums, so they had to play the clubs until they got a big following. It was all about the box office draw: the fans, and the numbers. They saw bands that were unsigned, but they knew that some of these bands were the up-and-coming artists of tomorrow. Once in a while they would even see a real name band using one of the venues as a rehearsal for their tour. This really showed them the difference between a professional recording artist and an amateur band striving to be professional. They wanted to be professionals.

All in all they felt that they were living in the heart of the entertainment industry and on their way to fame and glory. They were truly living in a place of history, and they too wanted to be part of it—to become famous as well.

"TAKE A WALK ON THE WILD SIDE"

Lou Reed

It took quite a lot of work before they finally felt the original material was good enough, presentable, and ready to be performed in front of an audience. There were only a few clubs which allowed groups to play their own original material. Most clubs were only looking for cover bands playing Top 40 songs heard on the radio.

Bill did some checking and discovered a small club in Hollywood called Studio 69 that featured bands with original music. This wasn't one of the big clubs, but they wanted to start out small and see what kind of reaction they would get, see how it worked on stage, and make the necessary changes and improvements before trying to get booked at the big clubs. They wanted to be comfortable, confident, and ready before taking it to the larger clubs. They were nervous and apprehensive as this was somehow different. It wasn't just playing someone else's songs, these were their songs. They had put their heart and soul into them. They discovered that Monday was audition night. The date was set, and the four looked forward to it with anxiety and excitement. After much work, it was now time to try it out—time to present the fruits of their labors to a real audience.

They arrived early on Monday. Being the first of many acts was in fact a blessing as they were able to arrive early with plenty of time to set up their equipment and get a feel for the club. It was a dark and dingy place. Very much like a bar, not like the nicer clubs they had been playing doing cover songs. The dirty worn out carpet and old tables and chairs really made the place look tawdry. It was a fairly large club with two main rooms. One main room looked like a big open dance hall with a DJ booth on the back wall. It was probably a disco of some sort. There was a small bar behind the main dance floor which led to a show room where the original artists performed. They would be playing in the show room. It was a typical bar room with red candles in small jars on each table and a large mirror at the back of the bar stacked with various spirits—a nothing bar really. They looked at the one foot high stage with its tattered curtain in the back, and spot lights which looked suspiciously like garden spots, not stage spots. They didn't want to play too much during the warm-up because they did not want to give away their material before the show. So they chose to have a short sound check; just enough to get a feel for the room, make sure everything was working, and make sure they sounded good. But there was no doubt in their minds, nothing could ruin this evening. This was their new beginning, the birth of their child which they had labored with for so long. However, with the excitement there was also a reluctance and nervousness. The fear of rejection ran rampant throughout their bones. For Jason and Mike especially this was putting their ass on the line. This was their gig—their life—their creativity—their dream. Soon they would be playing their own music. They felt nervous, like they would be standing there naked for all the world to see, exposed to the masses for their approval or disapproval. Little was said before the show, just some nervous jokes followed by even more nervous laughter. It seemed an eternity before it was time to play. The old bar clock courtesy of some beer brand ticked away the minutes. The club was much darker now. As the time grew nearer the tensions grew. Finally, the club owner hollered from the back of the bar "Showtime." The four approached the stage which seemed to have gotten smaller since their sound check. After a quick tune the lights dimmed and the show began.

Jason and Mike were both sharing the task of being lead singer. Mike was a good rock singer, and Jason's voice was mellower as he did have some vocal training in college. Having two singers gave them some variety and allowed for a wider range of material. At times, especially during the choruses, they harmonized together, a trick they had learned playing cover songs and something that worked very well for them. The others sang backup vocals as well. Nervously, they started the first song. This song seemed to go on for an eternity. Nothing sounded the same as it did in rehearsal, but they went through it. The song ended. Silence was the response—no reaction—just the clatter of glasses and bottles from the bar at the back and the voices of people carrying on conversations. Another song brought about the same reaction or lack thereof. Just more loud talking, laughing, and clanging bottles. The band felt transparent—as if no one was listening. This was a cold disinterested audience with many of them too drunk to realize or care that this was a real band and not just some jukebox. Their fear of rejection was about to explode. The whole band was sweating from nervousness while Jason, almost in tears, continued to try and sing the songs he had labored so long on, but now felt himself a failure.

They continued playing their set, but all they seemed to hear was the chatter of the bar patrons paying little attention to the music. About five songs into the set, however, this started to change. It appeared that the audience was beginning to listen as evidenced by some applause which occurred at the end of the songs. It was probably out of courtesy but nonetheless at least a response. They could tell it was getting busier, but, with the stage lights on, all they could see when they all looked out was a sea of bodies in silhouette against the dim lights behind the bar.

They saw two people walk in holding hands. They ordered a beer. The lights from the bar illuminated them from behind. They drank their beers and held hands. They put their beers down on the bar, embraced each other, and then gave each other a big passionate kiss. They turned and moved toward the dance floor. As they danced, they gradually moved into the lights at the center of the floor. All of a sudden the whole band noticed they were both men! Looking around, they noticed that all the patrons were men. The realization almost stopped them dead in their tracks. They were in shock. This is a gay bar! They all looked at each other in amazement and bewilderment, trying their best not to seem surprised and continue on with the show as if nothing had happened. They all stood staring at each other not wanting to look into the audience anymore. They had all heard there were bars like this, but no one had really believed they existed. After what seemed an eternity, the set ended, and they left the stage.

They started tearing down their equipment to allow the next band to take the stage.

"Who the fuck got us this gig in a fag bar?" Brian began while tearing down his drums.

"Er, I didn't know it was a gay bar." Bill defended himself. "All I knew was that this was a place where bands could play originals."

"I think it was a surprise to us all," Mike added trying his best to defend Bill. "How were we to know that this was a gay bar? Just be cool. Why don't ya keep it quiet until we leave?"

They continued to tear down their equipment.

Mike grabbed his bass and was leaving with Jason when the club owner approached them. "Listen, I think you may have some potential. With some work it could be a real good act. This was your first gig wasn't it?"

"Er, yeah," Mike replied dejectedly, "at least playing original material. We do a lot of Top 40 gigs, but don't get much of a chance to play our original material."

"Well, I always thought I had an ear for talent, and I've had some pretty big names start here. I can give you a chance on some off night playing for the door. See how the reaction is." He could see their confusion. "That means whatever the door makes you get. I get the bar. Bring in a lot of people and you can make some good money. If you start bringing in a good crowd I can switch you to a weekend night occasionally."

Mike and Jason just stood staring at each other.

The owner continued. "It would give you a place to work on your act." The guys stood there silently, not sure how to take this "Look, if you are interested lemme know. I'll book ya. Probably start you out on a Tuesday night, two shows a night at nine and eleven. You must be set up by eight though since that is when I open the doors." Jason and Mike still stood there speechless. "You were here to audition after all, weren't you?" he asked puzzled at their reaction. "You two look dumbfounded. What's your problem? Ah musicians. You're all alike: temperamental and odd. Well, here's my card. Lemme know if you are interested. I'll set up some dates." With that, he walked off quite perplexed.

Jason turned to Mike "What do we do now?"

"Um, I dunno. What d'ya think?" Mike replied.

"Well, he is right." Jason shyly remarked.

"Believe me, I really didn't know it was a gay bar." Bill added still defending his decision. "But ya know. I say so what. As far as I'm concerned a gig is a gig."

"Yeah, we can work out our show. Besides, who would ever see us in this dive," Jason said surprised at Bill's attitude and acceptance about the whole thing.

"Ya know. You're right. Who cares if they're fags, just so long as they don't bother me. But I think convincing Brian won't be too easy," Mike added.

"Well, we can discuss it later and decide. I can't believe we got a gig at a gay bar. And I can't believe how bad we sounded—lots of work ahead. But what the fuck! It was really our first gig doing originals. What a bring-down." Mike said dejectedly.

They saw Brian approaching with a drum in his hand.

"Let's get the fuck outta here—" He said as he walked by rather hurriedly.

As they were loading up their equipment the bartender called them over and gave them a round of beers. "Compliments of Chuck, the owner."

Brian grabbed his beer then continued loading up his gear as did everyone else, trying to make room for the next band who was anxiously awaiting their turn to audition. By the time they had all their gear packed into the van, the next band had started.

"Let's stay and see what the next band is like. See what our competition is—" Jason walked back into the club with Mike not far behind.

"You're kidding!" Brian responded. "Let's just get the fuck outta here!"

However, by that time Mike and Jason had disappeared into the nightclub with Bill reluctantly following, unsure of which way to go. By the time Brian entered Mike had shots of tequila and beers waiting.

"We can't very well leave a free drink," said Mike.

Brian took his shot while Mike ordered another.

"This band sucks," Brian said. He gulped his beer while listening to the next band.

"I knew he wouldn't turn down free booze." whispered Mike while the bartender set them up again.

"On the house," said the club owner, waving to the bartender.

"Geez, these fags aren't so bad after all," said Brian now getting merrily drunk.

Jason decided to muster up some bravery and check out the rest of the club. He asked everyone else to join him. They were frightened and apprehensive as they walked into the other rooms. They stayed close to each other as they walked through the club like four scared kids walking into a deep dark forest, almost like Dorothy and her companions in <u>The Wizard of Oz</u>, but this was not the Emerald City—and this certainly was not Kansas. They followed the loud pulsating beat of the music to the main dance hall. They walked in to find the lights flashing and bodies everywhere dancing to the beat of the music. It took some time before their eyes adjusted to the flashing lights. Suddenly, almost simultaneously, they noticed there were only men, nothing but men, dancing, with each other. They looked at each other in amazement and bewilderment. They were completely speechless.

"Enough of this." Brian got up to leave. "Let's split."

Mike, Brian, and Bill decided it was time to leave; however, Jason decided to stay and see some more bands and check out the club. He had become quite friendly with the bartender, so Jason was left behind. Jason asked Bill and Mike to try to convince Brian that they should do the gig. The three agreed that it would be a good idea to have a venue where they could play their originals. By the time the other three had left they had seen two bands and Brian was quite drunk and had forgotten where he was.

The ride home found them all laughing at the whole situation, making sissy jokes and poking fun at some of the clientele. Once home they brought out joints and continued their high.

"That wasn't so bad after all, was it? But boy, this band needs a lot of work. We sounded like shit," Mike began while Bill nodded in agreement.

"Ah, what do those queers know anyway?" Brian was sucking down another beer as the ash to the joint fell in his lap. "Shit, I dropped the cherry!"

"We've been offered a gig there." Bill began reluctantly.

"And I think we should do it for the experience," continued Mike. "Think about it. It could be an alright place to get our act together, and no one will know. We can still play the other gigs but occasionally take a night off to play our originals there. It sounds like a perfect set up to me." He was trying his best to sound positive.

"Yeah, no one would ever know," said Bill trying to keep the argument going and trying to sound as convincing as possible. "And then when we're ready we can go to the better places. I wouldn't wanna blow our chance when we're not ready. And let's face it, we did sound like shit tonight."

"Yeah, we were pretty bad." Brian agreed.

"Bad. We were fuckin' awful. Then it's settled. We'll do it." Mike stated.

"Do what?" said Brian suddenly realizing the true ramifications of what was being discussed. "Play that queer bar? Are you outta your mind? I don't want nothin' to do with no fags! I ain't no fag, and I won't play at their bar."

"Come on, it wasn't so bad was it? We got free booze, and they were all pretty nice to us. Besides just because it is a gay bar doesn't mean you are gay for playing there. D'ya have any better ideas?" Bill commented.

"I don't want no fags grabbing my ass. Besides, I'd be afraid to take a piss; one of 'em would probably try and suck my dick or something."

"Shit, who'd want that little thing?" Mike laughed. "Ain't no one gonna try anything. You're just paranoid. You wouldn't have to tell anyone, just do the gig. Besides, we have the other gigs as well. They wouldn't interfere with each other. We need to start doing some original gigs. In the meantime, we could be working on finding somewhere else to play."

"Ain't no way I'm gonna play no fag club, and that's that! By the way, where is Jason?" He asked suddenly realizing his absence.

"He'll be home later, he decided to stay and check out the other bands." Mike explained.

"I'll bet he's a fag too, and I want nothing to do with it." Brian insisted. "Goddamn faggots. If he is; I'll quit."

Mike and Bill looked at each other and decided not to pursue the issue any further to make Brian more upset.

"Let's just drop it, all right," Mike grumbled, then passed the joint.

Brian took a large hit, garbled something about faggots and passed out cold on the sofa with Mike and Bill not far behind.

Much to Brian's dissatisfaction, they did return to Studio 69 a couple of weeks later. He had been outvoted. Brian kept mostly to himself, taking his breaks in the back alley or smoking a joint in his van. Jason walked into the crowd during the breaks. He talked with the customers, patrons and the owners, Chuck and Greg. After the last set, all went home—all except Jason. He had decided to stay.

Jason arrived at the door of the band house late the next day to find Brian packing his equipment. As Jason approached, Brian called out. "It's bad enough we have to play in a fag bar, but I won't be in a band with one."

Jason continued walking toward the house looking at Mike for some kind of help or approval.

"So, what happened to you last night? Is it true?" Mike questioned.

"Well, Uh, I uh, met a guy, and I, uh, spent the night with him. So, if you're asking me if uh I'm gay or not. Uh, yeah, I uh guess I am, and I'm tired of hiding it," said Jason, now in tears.

"See, he is a fag! I knew it when he didn't come home last night. I'm outta here." Brian walked in to pack his suitcase.

"You mean that you'd give up all this time and effort and our dream because Jason is gay." Mike was doing his best to defend his friend. "I can't believe you are so narrow-minded. I've known you for a long time, and I thought I knew you better than this, but I guess not. I think we all know each other pretty well, but let's face it, we all have secrets. That doesn't make us any different from the persons we think we know. Jason is the same person you knew yesterday. But you'd forget all that because he's gay?"

"The person I knew yesterday wasn't gay," Brian interrupted. "And I'll have nothing to do with fags. It's wrong. It's against nature. It's immoral. Furthermore, the thought of it makes me sick. I should've known something was different when he didn't pick up the chicks like the rest of us."

"But this is your friend Jason. I just can't believe that your prejudice is getting in the way of your friendship and our dedication to this music." Mike was getting a bit angry now. "You've known Jason for quite a while. He's the same person you knew yesterday. Just consider this another aspect of his personality. He hasn't changed, just grown. As far as I'm concerned, I think it took a lot of guts for him to admit it to himself and especially to us. I have a lot of respect for Jason. It's narrow minded assholes like you that make it worse for Jason and people like him. You stand there and ridicule and hurt his feelings. Jason is someone I am proud to call my friend. I'm actually more surprised at your behavior. I thought I knew you better."

"I should've known it would end up like this when we got him in the band," said Brian. "He has just taken over, wanting to do his material, and do this original thing which I went along with. But there are limits. Next thing you know he'll make us all gay, wear dresses or something—make that a requirement of the band. Well, I'm ashamed and embarrassed about this whole thing, and I've reached my limit. I went along with this original thing. I even went along with playing in a fag bar, but now playing with a fag. This is the last straw!" Brian exclaimed. It was evident there was no discussion at this time.

"Hey man, cool down. Here take a red, and then let's talk." Mike extended his hand with the pills.

Brian just slapped his hand flinging them all over the uncut and mostly brown grass. He stormed away and made his exit.

Jason ran into the house in tears. Mike followed close behind.

Bill was just coming out of his room. "What's all the commotion?" he asked.

"We lost Brian. He's quitting because he found out Jason is gay." Mike answered.

"So, if you hate faggots too, you may as well quit now!" Jason exclaimed. He ran to his room and slammed the door.

Mike decided to let Jason cool off. Eventually, he entered his room to find Jason still lying there with eyes red from crying.

"Bill's staying. He couldn't care less that you're gay. And you know I'm with you. We just need to find another drummer. Take some time to reorganize. We'll find someone better, you'll see. Someone really into it." Mike tried to console his friend.

"Uh, Thanks for sticking up for me out there. I, er, was afraid you would hate me too. I hate myself for being gay. I don't want to be gay. I just want to be like everybody else. But I can't hide behind being straight anymore. It's just too much. I just want to be normal, but I can't." Jason responded still sobbing slightly.

"Well, I don't really get it, but whatever happens I still consider you my friend. And we are still doing this band thing together no matter what. Ya can't get rid of me this easily. Besides, I kind of wondered since you never seemed that interested in picking up chicks when we were. I even thought that Bill might be gay since he defended playing in the gay bar so much and seldom picks up chicks—still not sure where he is coming from, but whatever."

Jason had stopped his sobbing. He looked up, showing signs of a slight grin.

"I just don't know why you didn't tell me before." Mike continued. "After all we've been through together? Mike questioned. "I guess I thought I knew you, but I guess not. It is kind of weird for me, but I am trying to understand."

"I guess I thought I could hide it or deny it or something. You know, live with the fact that I am gay but just not act on it. I really do not want to be gay. I'd give anything not to be gay. Look how it has fucked this up. And this is only the beginning. But I guess the time came for me to face this thing and stop running away. I had to accept this in myself. You have no idea how hard that is. I hope you understand just a little. I am gay, and there's no more hoping, or hiding, or running away. It just is." Jason seemed to be pulling himself together as he spoke, as if convincing himself of the very words he was saying.

"Well, uh, I'm not so sure I understand this gay thing, but you are my friend, gay or not. This makes no difference. But I must tell you I'm rather surprised. I mean you're not what I expect of a gay person, no limp wristed sissy who talks with a lisp. You're just like me. I just don't understand what makes you gay. I mean, I could I be gay too. This whole thing is very confusing." Mike seemed perplexed, almost questioning his own sexuality.

"Well, I think either you are gay or not. It's not something I chose. It's just something that is. You are referring to all those stereotypes which I was afraid of, because I don't wanna be one of those either. But they are real people. Gay people come in all different kinds with all different interests and personalities. What makes me gay is the fact that I like men, they turn me on, and women do not. I've been attracted to men as long as I can remember. I have fantasies about men, I think in the same way you think of women. If you are turned on by men then perhaps you are gay; that's a question only you can answer."

"I like men, and I like hanging out with men, but not sexually. I still get off on women. And I certainly don't wanna have sex with other men, nor am I attracted to men. I guess that's what makes me straight," Mike responded with a sense of relief.

"So, let me ask you this: can you explain why women get you off?" he stood there silently waiting for a reply. "I didn't think so. Well, it's the same thing for me and men. I can't explain it. It just is."

Just then the door opened. Bill entered the room. "I hear Brian quit. Well, I just wanted to say that I think that his reasons are completely ridiculous. If that's the way he feels I'm glad we're rid of him now instead of having problems later down the line."

"You don't care that I'm gay?" Jason asked timidly.

"Gay, Shmay. Makes no difference to me one way or the other. I couldn't care less. I've known a lot of gay people, especially in New York with the crowd I hung out with. Remember, I was living in the village which has a lot of gay bars. No one cared. It was just part of the scene—especially the music and art scene that I was involved with, you know, Andy Warhol and that whole crowd. Many of them were gay, bi, or experimenting with their sexuality. The lines there were not so defined. No big deal. I just think this is gonna be a great band. We have some very talented individuals, and I want it to work. It just doesn't matter to me. But don't let someone who has shit for brains upset you. That sort of thing shouldn't matter so don't torture yourself. That's his problem, not yours."

"Are you gay, too?" Jason asked.

"Uh, no. Not that I haven't experimented around, but just not my thing."

Jason was beginning to feel better now for he felt he was truly among friends. "Well, I guess we have our work cut out for us."

"I think this would be a good time to take some time off. We have been working pretty hard, and this whole thing was really traumatic. I have some friends in San Francisco we can visit. They'll put us up. How about we take a little vacation before we begin the task of finding a new drummer?" Mike replied.

"I could take some time off work, I guess. I'll just have to find someone to cover for me," Bill replied. "When we get back, there are some drummers from the store we can try."

"And we don't have any gigs this week, and I can cancel the other gigs until we find a replacement." Mike tried to soothe the pain and solve the problems. "It shouldn't take too much time to find a new drummer."

Jason agreed by shaking his head while Bill offered him a joint to calm his nerves.

Jason was thankful he had such good and understanding friends. For everyone, the scars of rejection would take time to heal but especially for Jason. However, because of this incident the bond between the three members was stronger. They were more determined than ever. They were ready to work and still believed in the band.

"IF YOU'RE GOING TO SAN FRANCISCO"

Scott McKenzie

The radio blasted "Ventura Highway" by America as Jason, Mike, and Bill drove up the stretch of Highway 101 from which the song got its name. They reached Ventura where Highway 101 and Pacific Coast highway merged into one road. This scenic two-lane highway connected Los Angeles to San Francisco. With the distance offering them some relief, they felt away from the pressures of the city, making their troubles seem far away.

Jason sat silently staring out the window lost in thought. Finally, seeing the ocean, he could breathe a sigh of relief. This was a much needed escape after all that had happened. This whole event had been life changing for him. He had a lot to think about. Looking out at the beauty of the ever changing sea gave comfort to Jason. He felt away from the pain and the trauma he had experienced by coming out. The ocean gave him strength. In its vastness he could not help but feel himself and his own problems insignificant.

They looked forward to their journey with anticipation and excitement in much the same way the original explorers and missionaries must have felt who had traveled this very same route many years ago when it was called "El Camino Real" or The Kings Highway. Now it was simply called Highway 101. These two main routes between San Diego and San Francisco sometimes merged into one road while other times paralleled each other when they were separated by hills, mountains, or other obstacles, with the Pacific Coast Highway following the coastline and Highway 101 turning inland to avoid the rugged terrain.

"El Camino Real" was an historic road that originally connected the California Missions. The missions are some of the state's oldest structures and designated state historic landmarks. The 21 Missions had been built between 1769 and 1823 by the Spanish who then laid claim to California and Mexico. They were the first European settlements in this new frontier, designed to be outposts as well as cultural centers of this new world by introducing the native peoples to new ideas, culture, and religion. This series of religious outposts was Spain's way to spread the Christian faith among the local Native Americans and to strengthen their stronghold on this new land. They were established by Spanish Catholics of the Franciscan Order. The missions represented the first major effort by Europeans to colonize the Pacific Coast region, and gave Spain a valuable hold in the new relatively unexplored frontier land. Father Junipero Serra had planned a series of missions about one day's journey apart on horseback. These settlers introduced European livestock, fruits, vegetables, and industry into the California region.

The Spanish occupation of California, however, also brought with it serious negative consequences to the Native American populations. In the end, the mission had mixed results in its objective to convert, educate, and "civilize" the indigenous population and transforming the natives into Spanish colonial citizens. The missions did, however, accomplish their goal of being the cultural centers of this new land. Many grew into large towns and cities that we recognize today as San Diego, Santa Cruz, San Francisco, Ventura, Santa Barbara, and San Luis Obispo.

Just as the explorers must have been impressed with the beauty of this area, so were Jason, Mike, and Bill. The road sometimes followed the beautiful California coastline overlooking the blue waters of the

Pacific Ocean. Mountains leading to rugged cliffs or sandy white beaches marked land's end. It was a beautiful landscape with green hills, valleys, or fields where green grasses were speckled with the occasional oak or sycamore trees. They even passed through many of the towns of these original missions. Their journey to San Francisco was proving to be a beautiful one indeed. It was like a breath of fresh air. A much needed break for them all.

The car was packed with things they thought they would need: food, drugs, and of course their instruments; two acoustic guitars and a flute. They had also packed sleeping bags so they could crash on the floor at Mike's friends' place. Jason or Mike traded driving while Bill mostly sat in the back seat rolling joints or playing his guitar. It was as if the guitar was a permanent attachment to him—something he was seldom without. The trip proved to be a wonderful experience for all three. They talked, laughed, and enjoyed each other's company while taking in the beautiful sights. They broke up the driving with an occasional stop for food or to smoke a joint in a beautiful scenic place by the seaside or in a field or grove of trees. All in all it made for a most wonderful trip.

Eventually, they reached San Francisco. For Mike, it was a return home to a place that he had lived for many years. For Jason and Bill it was a new experience with new sights and sounds. Jason immediately fell in love with the city. Its Victorian buildings all colorfully painted reminded Jason of what it must be like in Europe. The 1906 Earthquake and fire that had once devastated the city had resulted in a city with a distinct personality, look, and architectural style since virtually the whole city was rebuilt in the Victorian style that was popular at that time. This style was continued even after the rebuilding in an effort to maintain the architectural integrity that began at the beginning of the century. The city had a metropolitan feel to it unlike Los Angeles which seemed more like one huge expanding suburb. This city had charm. There was a bustle of activity everywhere as people walked, cable cars roared, and buses travelled to all points around the city. Since the city had been built on a peninsula of hills surrounded by a huge bay, it seemed there was a magnificent view around every corner. The

Golden Gate Bridge and The Oakland Bay Bridge connected the city with points across the bay. They all felt the excitement of being in a different place.

Mike's friends lived near the Haight/Ashbury district. Jason and Bill expected to see the Haight/Ashbury as a vibrant and exciting scene, one that they had heard and read about so many times. The name itself represented the movement for change in American culture: the counter culture, the love generation, the hippies, and the catalyst of a new age. Instead, what they found seemed somehow different from what they had expected. What had once been the capital of the love and peace generation and the politically active center of the revolutionary movement had turned into a cheap and tawdry section of town. The streets had a few head shops and radical bookstores—leftovers of a time past. The hippies and intellectuals of the new love generation had either turned into or had been replaced by burnt-out drug addicts and junkies. Many people were seen hanging out on street corners. Their dirty tattered clothes made them look homeless and poor. Some were panhandling for a bit of food. Crowds of people hung on to a time passed, but the dream had died many years before leaving only a few to carry on the traditions which had been so much a part of this new generation and the hope of a new America.

Jason, Mike, and Bill arrived at Sunshine and Speed's place just after dark. As they approached the Victorian house, Jason wondered just what kind of people they were. The door opened. A man with shoulder length jet black hair and beard greeted them. He was wearing sandals and a loincloth shirt and pants. Speed seemed truly happy to see Mike. He stretched out his arms to give Mike a big hug as if he were his long lost brother.

"Peace man, great to see ya," Speed started.

"Peace," Mike responded.

"It's been much too long... And this must be Jason and Bill who you've told us about. I hear you are both very talented." Bill and Jason held out their hands, but Speed grabbed them and gave them a big hug to extend his hospitality. "Any friend of Mike's is a friend of mine."

"Thanks," was Jason's only response. His eyes wandered around the room to see the remnants of the sixties in this apartment. Psychedelic posters filled the walls. Books were stacked up along the walls on the floor. Strings of beads separated the living room from what looked like the kitchen. Some sort of Indian design muslin material served as a door to another room. On the coffee table a brass hookah for smoking pot was visible and a dirty oriental rug covered the wooden floor. This was truly a hippie house, Jason thought to himself. His eyes reached the door to the kitchen just in time to see a woman with long straight brown hair wearing a full length loose fitting dress that touched the floor come running out. She looked like an earth mama with beads and bare feet.

"Is that you Mike?" she exclaimed running to give Mike a big hug and kiss while Mike just smiled from ear to ear.

Jason immediately felt welcome while Bill remained quiet. Not many words were exchanged at first, just lots of hugs. One could see that in a way these people were truly Mike's family and displayed the same kind of caring and concern as would any family member. Mike was in some sense home, back to a place which represented love and happiness and caring. Jason could understand why these people meant so much to him.

"I was just making some tea. Would ya like some?" Sunshine asked.

"Sure, that'd be bitchin'." Mike answered. Everyone nodded in agreement.

Sunshine returned a moment later with a tray on which sat a tea pot with tea cups.

"I hope chamomile will do. I also made some cookies. It has been so long. It's really great to see you. We have so much to catch up on."

"Hey man, we need to celebrate." Speed immediately brought out some pot to smoke. He rolled a joint then passed it around. All partook of the good drugs and good times. Jason immediately felt comfortable. He was relieved to be away from the trials of home. Bill just enjoyed getting high. Mike was happy to return to a home he once had left.

"So how is everything going? The band? School?" Sunshine asked.

"School is alright. I've really been concentrating on music and the band lately. I really think that this is what I want to do. Be a musician, make albums, and tour. These guys are awesome, and we work well together. We just lost our drummer, so we're taking some time off before we return to find a new one."

"Glad you came to visit. Sounds like you're working things out. We're happy for you." Sunshine smiled.

"So what happened to most of the gang?" Mike asked, anxious to catch up on old times and find out what was going on with some of his friends from the past.

"Oh, most of 'em have left," Speed replied. He filled a bong with pot, lit it, and then passed it around. "Only a few remain, mostly the ones who want to stay near the drugs. John is a serious junkie, very sad. He lives mostly on the streets. He comes by once in a while to borrow money for a fix. He left his ole lady who met someone and moved to Alaska to start a farm and live off the land. Charlie went back to college, probably finished by now. He wanted to be an attorney or a politician so that he could fight the system from within. You know he was always very political. Glen moved to a small town up north. I'm not sure what he's doing. Last I heard he met someone and got married. Janet got married to some real straight accountant type. She lives in suburbia-ville, probably with a station wagon, three point five kids, a dog, a cat, and a mortgage. Ron and Dory are still living together across the bay, still together after all these years. Uh, I dunno. They all just scattered. Times have changed. I don't see most of 'em anymore, but boy did we have some good times.

By the way, we're goin' to the Fillmore tonight; Bill Graham still runs it and comped us some tickets—one of the perks of having the paper. Jefferson Starship and Grateful Dead are playing. It should be an incredible show. We can even drop acid. I scored some window pane. It'd be like old times. It'd be fun. Are ya interested?"

"Yeah, that'd be bitchin'," said Mike

Bill was anxious to join them, always ready to get high. Jason reluctantly agreed thinking what better way to see a concert than on acid—especially these groups.

Mike started. "It really is great seeing you two. This is just like old times. It brings back some fond memories. Remember the summer of love-in '67? What a great time. But that whole time was wonderful. The love-ins in Golden Gate Park. Grateful Dead, Jefferson Airplane, or Janis Joplin played. We'd drop acid, mostly window pane, purple haze, or orange sunshine. We were high on drugs and high on life. We thought we were in heaven. It was outta sight." Mike reminisced. For Mike, the drugs brought back fond memories of times past. It was almost like he was there again. He could see the warm summers, the concerts in the park, and the massive crowds of people mostly long hair hippies, all dressed in tie-dyed clothes or shirts or long dresses from India. Many were dancing and grooving to the music. The scent of marijuana wafted through the air as joints were passed. It was a beautiful time.

Sunshine shared her thoughts. "It was just like a bond had formed among everyone in the whole crowd—like we were all connected. Those were wonderful times."

"We really thought we'd set the world on fire," Speed agreed, "the start of the cultural revolution and the counterculture, the sexual revolution, alternate lifestyles, and politics. Good times, man, good times."

All three seemed lost in thought. They just stared at each other or into space reliving their memories of the past.

Sunshine paused, her mind wandering back to times past: a scene of beautiful people, music playing, people dancing, everyone sharing, creative expression, and free love. Everyone was stoned or high on something. It was a real shared and common experience. It was bohemian, but it was truly a time of peace, love, and harmony. "Yeah, the times certainly have changed, and they just don't have drugs like that anymore."

"I think it was the people that made us high to some degree. There was real positive energy. United we were one." Sunshine continued. "Those were great times." Then she returned to reality and the magic was broken. "But people just aren't like that anymore. Times have changed."

It was time to get ready for their evening out.

"EIGHT MILES HIGH"

The Byrds

They arrived at the Fillmore. It was an old converted ballroom that Bill Graham had made famous by presenting psychedelic rock concerts with some of the most famous bands of the sixties. Groups like Led Zeppelin, Jimi Hendrix, The Who, Cream, and The Doors had played there. However, its biggest claim to fame was as the center of the San Francisco counterculture and home to the psychedelic sound of San Francisco—groups like The Grateful Dead, Jefferson Airplane, and Big Brother and the Holding Company with Janis Joplin. Although it had moved to a new location in the late sixties, it still had the same rock and roll ambience. It was truly a happening place and a blast from the past. Many people still dressed in tie-dyed shirts and had long hair. It was as if they were back in the sixties again. As they entered, the smell of marijuana permeated the room. Speed had passed out the LSD at the house so that everyone would peak at the right time. Now, everything seemed a bit surreal—like a Salvador Dali painting. The whole room seemed to be liquid with everything in it dripping.

They entered the main room just as Jefferson Airplane started to play. Grace Slick could be heard singing, "One pill makes you larger/

And one pill makes you small/ And the one that mother gives you/ Doesn't do anything at all/ Go ask Alice,/ When she's ten feet tall."

"They're playing 'White Rabbit'. I dig this song." The psychedelic lights were throbbing and the music was loud. Grace Slick and the band sounded wonderful. They could feel the full effect of the acid coming on now, enhanced by the music and the lights.

Jason, Mike, and Bill could see the impact a good rock band had on a crowd. They could see just how good the band was. It sounded just like the record they had heard so many times. Jefferson Airplane was followed by the Grateful Dead who played a lengthy set that lasted over two hours of mostly long songs. There was very little stage movement or show, but the songs really took Jason, Mike, and Bill on a journey into their own minds. They listened to "Dark Star" which went on for what seemed an eternity. All they could do was exchange glances and smile, knowing each of them was in a similar place. It was a shared experience—one shared by everyone in the room.

They had all fully come on to the acid by this time—completely high and in an altered state of consciousness. All their senses were heightened as the music, lights, and drugs had full control of their experience. It took them to a different world. It was as if they could see sounds, hear lights, and feel everything. The Grateful Dead was the perfect way to experience acid. The music would get quiet then crescendo to a wonderful climax only to return to a mellow place again. It was an emotional journey of sights and sound. They peaked during the Grateful Dead set with the music as their guide. It was a journey they would never forget.

Jason was beginning to see what being in a rock band was really all about—and he loved it. It transformed him and made him want it all the more. He could see the impact music could have on an audience. He fantasized being on stage, imagining what it would be like for Hollywood to perform their own material to the same sort of audience. It was invigorating and exciting. He left in a state of euphoria with visions of the future.

Bill was just spaced out, enjoying the music. His mind wandered as he watched the bands play, but mostly paying attention to the guitar players, especially Jerry Garcia from The Grateful Dead. But overall just enjoying the music journey he was being taken on.

Not much was said that night. The music, the scene, and the acid created a wonderful experience that no one would ever forget.

The next morning they awoke after noon. All gathered around the kitchen table to enjoy the breakfast Sunshine had made. Then they decided to smoke a joint to take the edge off from the wonderful event they had experienced the night before.

"I was really trippin' last night. I really got fucked up, really psychedelic." Mike commented.

"Me too. Totally cosmic. What an experience," Bill agreed.

"By the way, what's going on with the newspaper?" Mike asked inquiring about the paper of which Speed was the managing editor. It was a radical underground paper and the voice of the counterculture.

"Uh, not much. We still have quite a following, but it's not the same. Yeah, we have the Viet Nam War which should've ended by now. And of course that asshole Nixon. We really need to get rid of that crook, get him impeached or something. I can't believe how much we're still manipulating foreign governments and our involvement in foreign countries. Of course there is the expansion of our military industrial complex. There are other issues that need to be changed like legalizing marijuana and prostitution. Personally, I wish we could abolish that whole marriage thing, but I guess it works for some people. People are so caught up with their capitalist greed. The environment is suffering. There are so many causes, and there's so much to do. But people just aren't that interested any more. It's like there's no purpose politically like there used to be. They all seem too busy just makin' money now. I do still write about some political stuff, but people just don't seem to care about the causes anymore. These days they're more interested in sex rather than the revolution. That seems to be what keeps the paper going. You know what I say; give the people what they want. Besides, I have to sell papers. It's like all they're after is their own satisfaction. They don't care anymore about the world and the big issues. At least the sex thing is a lot more open. I am happy about that change in American culture."

"Right on." Mike wondered if in fact he was just more interested in sex than the political stuff himself. "But Speed, you were at the forefront of the political and cultural revolution. What happened?"

Speed continued "First of all most people don't call me Speed anymore. The name died with the revolution. Besides, I have to keep it clean, you know, with the drug inferences and all. The city has been trying to close me down for a long time now. I don't want to give them a reason to suspect anything. The name is Vic, my real name."

"I'll try, but that's difficult since I've always known you as Speed. So forgive me if I forget."

"Sure, understood. Old habits are hard to break. I still believe in all those causes, but I now focus more on freedom of the press and fighting censorship. My attitude hasn't changed, just my focus. I think I am like most people. I think the people have a right to read whatever they want. There are just some people that don't like it."

He handed Jason and Mike a copy of the latest edition which consisted of some politico-social commentary; some underground news; an entertainment section with the latest rock concerts, clubs, record reviews; and drug articles or ads for head shops. The remainder of the paper consisted of things related to sex: articles, ads for sex toys and sexual aids, ads for message service, escort service, and personal ads—not the usual ones for companionship, but, ads for people looking for sex, many about their sexual kinkiness including three ways, bondage, and orgies.

"I have a right to print this. I think sex has been in the closet for too long. This serves a real function of society. I think its time we demystify sex." Vic spoke authoritatively as if he were giving a speech, doing his best defending his newspaper.

"Right on. That's just like you. Always a cause to fight: be it human rights or pornography." Mike laughed, kidding about Vic's defensive behavior. He wondered if this was as much a cultural change as it was a change in Speed himself.

Jason's eye caught the multitude of gay establishments: bars, discos, bath houses etc. Mike immediately picked up on it.

"Uh, Jason is gay—just coming out sort of. We came here to get away from L.A. for a while." Mike proceeded to tell the story of what had happened.

"Far out! That is exactly what I mean—sexual freedom." He turned to Jason. "You're gonna dig this town. I think it must be one of the gayest cities in the U.S. Gay people are everywhere, and more arrive every day. It's like Mecca for the gay crowd. Listen, there's a large gay disco down the street. The owner is a client and a friend of mine. He's a big advertiser in the newspaper. How 'bout later tonight, we get a little buzzed and show Jason the 'hospitality' of San Francisco. It's the happening place right now with great sound and lights and music. It's great fun. I think even Mike will like it." Vic laughed. "We can have a drink. It'd be a great introduction to the gay life of San Francisco."

All agreed.

But Jason wanted to see some of the city also. So the rest of the day was spent sightseeing and smoking joints. Mike, Speed, and Sunshine reminisced about old times as they drove by the old places they were known to frequent in the past. They went to Golden Gate Park and the place where so many love-ins had taken place. They rode trolley cars; drove up and down hills. They even drove down the famous Lombard Street, the crookedest street in the world. They generally had a wonderful time in the City by the Bay. They finished up having dinner at Fisherman's Wharf overlooking the beautiful San Francisco Bay with views of the Golden Gate Bridge and Alcatraz Island, a former prison, in the background. All enjoyed the conversation and camaraderie.

"Looking at the Golden Gate Bridge makes me think of a song idea." Mike was lost in thought. "We can call it "Bridges." Make it about how people make bridges to connect with each other. How no one is really alone. We all just have to build those bridges."

"Cool concept. We'll work on it," said Jason.

Soon it was time to return home and get ready for the night out. After smoking a joint, it wasn't long before they were on their way to the gay bar.

"AFTER MIDNIGHT"

Eric Clapton

As they approached the club Jason noticed its size. This wasn't a small tacky bar like the one in L.A., but a large fancy nightclub all lit up with a line of people waiting to get in. Vic walked to the front of the line.

"How the hell are ya, Vic," said the man at the front door. "What brings you here? Changing your ways? Gonna try the other side for a change?" He smiled.

Vic laughed. "No, bringing some friends of mine from L.A. Jason over there just came out so what better place to bring him." Vic made the rest of the introductions. "This is Hal, the owner of The City."

"Welcome to The City, the largest gay disco in San Francisco. I hope ya have a fabulous time." The club owner motioned them in, giving a wink at Jason as he passed by.

They walked through a narrow hallway with black walls, the music growing louder with each step. It opened up into a large crowded room where a huge dance floor was filled with a sea of men, all dancing, while flashing, almost blinding lights pulsated to the blaring disco music. The whole room seemed to be throbbing—bodies undulating in time to the music. Two visible bars ran the length of each wall on opposite sides. Beyond the dance floor there appeared to be other rooms with tables. This wasn't some small underground secret place but a nice big place which somehow made it seem more legitimate.

But what caught Jason's eye most was all he could see was men—men everywhere—hundreds of them, all smiling, laughing, dancing together, and generally having a wonderful time. A rush of excitement ran through Jason's bones. The bar in L.A. had helped him come out, to come to grips with his sexuality, and to overcome the feeling or, even more, the fear that he was the only one. Seeing all these men dancing and being themselves right out in the open offered him even more affirmation of the feeling that there were plenty of others like him. That he was not the only one that was gay. For the first time ever he truly did not feel alone. It made him feel better about himself. He no longer needed to be ashamed of who he was. It was as if some great pressure had been released from Jason's mind. Here was a place where he could be himself, be gay, and no one would care. In some strange way he also felt as if he had come home too. He stood there awestruck.

They all got a drink and observed the whole scene. Jason was like the Cheshire cat, grinning from ear to ear.

Jason had been eyeing someone, and from the looks of it they both found each other mutually attractive. He was handsome and tall with dark hair and moustache. His Levis and flannel shirt gave him sort of a lumberjack look. The man came over to Jason.

"My name is Max. Wanna dance?" asked the man as he approached.

"Well…Uh… I." Jason glanced back at his friends hoping for their approval, who all just gave him a nod telling Jason that it was alright. "Of course I would."

It wasn't long before they were dancing, laughing, and enjoying themselves.

After about an hour, Mike and the others had had enough. They went to find Jason. They finally found him talking to Max. He walked up to Jason "We're ready to leave. Are you gonna stay or come with us?"

Jason looked at his dance partner for a sign. It appeared that the guy was still interested in continuing this evening.

"Don't worry," said Max. "I'll get ya home, at some point. Perhaps even talk ya into spending the night with me." He grinned. "We'd have a great time, and I could take you home in the morning."

"That'd be cool, so long as my friends don't mind," said Jason.

"Of course not," said Sunshine "Have a blast."

"In that case, I'd rather stay." Jason replied. "Oh sorry, these are my friends. Mike and Bill are in the band I told you about, and these are their friends from the bay area, Speed and Sunshine. This is Max."

"Nice to meet you all," said Max. "Now, how about another dance?"

Jason agreed. He told the others just to go on without him as Max led him to the dance floor.

Jason turned and shouted. "I may not be home until tomorrow."

"Fine with us." smiled Sunshine. "Just have fun."

They waved their goodbyes while Jason danced with his new found friend.

As they left, Mike looked back at Jason dancing. Jason and Mike's eyes caught each other's, they both smiled. They were both in a place that felt comfortable; for Mike an old life, for Jason a new one. They both knew the happiness they were feeling for each other and for themselves. They had both come home, each in their own special way.

Once outside the club Speed turned to Mike. "The Old Back Door Club is still around; remember the old days when we all used to go there? I thought it'd be fun to go there. They have an excellent band playing there tonight."

"I'm game," Mike responded without hesitation.

Bill nodded in agreement, always ready for a party.

As they entered Mike could see the club hadn't changed much. The place was still done in a psychedelic style with flashing lights and black light posters. Mike recognized many of the posters on the wall as the same ones that had been there for years. It was almost like seeing a ghost from the past. For Mike, it brought back some warm memories. But the club now looked old and outdated—time had not been kind to it. Mike wasn't sure if it had always been like that or it was just how it was now. Sometimes, you just can't go back again. Nothing seems as it was, and memories are sometimes better left as they were.

They entered and grabbed a table at the back where they could easily see the band.

Mike's attention was immediately taken to the drummer. He told Bill to check him out. Both he and Bill immediately agreed that this guy was good. The rest of the band was mediocre. The band's music still clung to the sixties, but their time had passed. But the drummer, he was incredible, a real pounder with good time and great licks. Mike and Bill were impressed. When the set ended Mike insisted on going back to meet the drummer. Speed said he would introduce them since he had been friends with the band for a long time. So Speed led them all back stage.

Speed introduced Mike and Bill to some of the band members. Just then the drummer walked up. He was a large black man with huge arms bulging from his very tight t-shirt.

"Man, you were great," was all Mike could come up with. "I dig the way you play."

"Uh, thanks man. Jeff's the name; actually Jefferson, Jefferson Thomas, but most of my friends just call me Jeff. My parents had this thing about Thomas Jefferson, says my ancestors were his slaves or something, and we were related somehow Not quite sure how, but that's a whole other story. You guys look like musicians or something," Jeff replied obviously enjoying the compliments.

"Yeah, we're in a band from L.A. Just up for some fun and to see some friends," Mike answered.

"We're gonna get high in the alley," Jeff said to Mike and Bill. "You guys wanna join me?" Jeff asked motioning Mike and Bill toward the back alley beyond the stage entrance.

"Sure." Mike was more anxious to talk to the drummer while Bill just went along for the ride, never turning down an opportunity to get high.

"We'll catch up with you later," said Speed.

"You've got some great chops," Mike complimented him. "What kinda drums d'ya have?"

"Rogers, of course, wouldn't have anything else, and Zildjian cymbals; the best as far as I'm concerned."

"How do ya like playing with the band?"

"This band sucks, but it is a gig. Man, seen any good pussy out there?" Jeff asked.

Mike didn't know quite what to say, his mind was on music, but this guy's mind was on sex. "Sure, isn't there always?" Mike replied sheepishly.

"Gotta find me some, tonight." Jeff turned and walked toward the back door. It wasn't long before Speed and Sunshine were looking for Mike and Bill.

"We're gonna split," Speed said. "Go home and get high. You guys joining us."

"Yeah," said Mike. "Let me just say bye to Jeff.

Jeff had found two likely candidates. Mike could see that he was real smooth with the women.

"We're gonna split. We'll check ya later." Mike said.

"Cool, check ya later," he said, and went on talking with the girls.

15

"YOU'RE SO VAIN"

Carly Simon

Jason showed up around noon the next day. He was the happiest Mike had ever seen him. Obviously this was a good thing for him.

"It looks like you had a good night," Mike commented.

"The best," was all Jason could say while grinning ear to ear like a Cheshire cat.

"Are ya gonna see him again?" Mike asked.

"Well, I got his number, but who knows? We'll see what happens. I was just happy to have such a fabulous time."

"Well, how about we go see some of the city?" Mike offered. "By the way, we met this great drummer. I want you to check him out. He's playing all week. He'd be perfect in the band and is very unhappy with the band he's working with now."

"Cool," said Jason. But Mike wasn't sure he heard a word that he said. Mike felt it best to let Jason have some time to himself to sort things out.

Just then Sunshine walked into the living room to find them all discussing their plans for the day. "We're having a free love party this Friday; of course you're all invited. Lots of drugs, drink, and sex; anything goes, so even you could have a good time Jason."

"Thanks," Jason replied. "But I think I'll be going out again. There are a few other places I wanna check out. There sure are a lot of gay places here in the city, and I wanna see 'em all. This is all kind of new to me. I hope you understand."

"Of course, I totally understand, just have a good time. I just don't want you to feel left out."

They all spent the next day enjoying the sights and sounds of San Francisco. At night they went their own way. Jason went to The City and other gay discos or night clubs he had discovered while Mike and Bill went to The Back Door Club to see the drummer perform.

The next day Mike turned to Jason. "What were you planning tonight?

"Maybe check out some more clubs; there are a lot of 'em here. Why?"

"Oh there's this drummer we told you about. I really think you should check him out. His band is playing again tonight. He really is unhappy with the band he's in, and I think we could get him to come and play with us. He really is incredible. We're gonna see him again tonight. I wish you would join us."

"That works for me. I can always go out afterward I guess, or I may even take a break."

They arrived at the club just in time for the first set. Jason noticed it was a small club with a brick wall as a backdrop and tables all around with a bar in the back. A little dingy, but it added to the ambiance. It had the feel of a time when rock and roll was more underground. The band wasn't particularly good except for the drummer. Mike was again impressed with him as he had been every night. The more he heard the more he liked this guy. He had ability, but more importantly, he knew when to use it. He was tasteful. He knew when to play and when not to play. Then out of the blue and at the appropriate time, he'd throw in some little thing that was amazing. He played to the point, no showing off, no bullshit, just right-on. He kept a solid beat to drive the band and worked well with the bass player. All in all he was a very solid player.

Mike could tell that Jason was also impressed. So at break time, they found their way back stage. Jeff was standing in the hallway with a drink in his hand. He looked larger than he did when he was seated behind his drums on stage. He was a formidable black man, with a muscular build. He must have been a body builder or at the very least someone who worked out. He had several women around him, vying for his attention. He seemed very confident and self-assured and was very outgoing with a slight air of conceit. He knew he had the looks, and he flaunted it in his skin tight clothes which showed every curve of his body especially his bulging crotch which was the object of all the ladies attention. He had a rough, almost mean, bad boy look as if he belonged to a gang or something which could be very intimidating under the right circumstances but was also a turn-on for the ladies.

Mike approached first, nudging his way through the crowd of girls. "You were smokin' out there."

"Thanks," Jeff responded.

"This is Jason, the other member of the band who we told you about."

"I play keyboards," Jason said as he extended his hand to offer him a handshake. "Not sure how much Mike has told you, but we're taking a break from gigging because we just lost our drummer. It seemed a good time to take off before we return to find a new one."

"Yeah, he already told me all that."

"It's a wonderful city you have here. We've been out seeing the sights. How long have you been with this band?" Jason asked.

"Too long; but it pays the rent, keeps me in drugs, and gets me laid often enough. I don't think this thing is gonna last too long though. There are fewer gigs, and the band isn't all that great. Besides, we have some internal problems on the direction. I think its time for me to move on. Ya wanna get high?" They all nodded in agreement.

They followed Jeff out the back door into the dimly lit alley. "Mike played me a tape of the band. Sounds cool. I really dig the material. I understand you did a lot of the writing. Very impressive. In fact this is just the type of thing I've been looking for. I'm definitely interested. But how can you make any money?" Jeff asked lighting up a joint.

"Well, we're mostly concentrating on originals, but we do the Top 40 thing for money. Besides, it keeps us playing and working on the stage together. If you're interested, I think you'd be a great addition to the band. Of course you'd have to audition. We'd have to see how it works out. In the end, it would of course be up to everyone to make the final decision, but I think you'd fit right in." Mike looked at him hoping he'd be amenable to the proposition.

"I'm very interested. From what Mike has said, you guys really got something going on. Look, I have to start the next set. Will you guys be here for the next break?" Jeff asked.

"Yeah, sure," Mike answered as Jeff entered the back door to take his place on stage.

"This is bitchin', isn't it? This guy would be a great drummer in the band."

"You really think this guy is that good?" Jason questioned.

"Uh huh. Don't you?" Mike asked perplexed.

"Uh, I guess so. He just seems so arrogant. What do you think Bill?"

"I think he's amazing. But Mike is the one that really has to work well with the drummer. He and the drummer must be in sync. They're the ones that really have to play together to create a strong rhythm section. But, I really do think he'd be an asset to the band," said Bill.

Mike, Bill, and Jason watched the next show. When it was break time they went backstage.

"What d'ya think about coming to L.A. to see if this thing is gonna work? We'll set up an audition and see how well we work together."

"Definitely! I guess it's time I paid a visit to L.A. We are booked next week but not much after that. I can come down then, if that's OK?"

"Sounds great! If you need a place to stay you can stay with us at the band house. There's room there."

"Deal." They exchanged phone numbers. "We'll see you next week. But it's getting late, and its time I found me some pussy. You guys want me to set you up with some chicks?"

"Uh, No, thanks," Jason replied shyly looking at Mike. "You think we should tell him?"

"Tell me what, you two lovers or something?" Jeff laughed.

"No, but Jason is gay. That's the reason the other drummer left. He couldn't handle it. I guess you should know up front rather than cause problems in the future or waste your time if you have any objections."

"The rest of the band is straight," Jason interjected fearing another rejection like the last. If anyone seemed like a redneck this guy certainly fit the bill.

"Nah, I don't give a shit. I am kind of used to it especially living in this town. I can't say I approve or condone it, but I guess that's from my background. But then, who am I to say? You do what ya wanna do. Our bass player is gay. Actually, it works out great, he gets the chick's attention because they all wanna fuck him, and so I just move in. It leaves more pussy for me. I just don't want any funny business. You try something, and I'll punch your lights out."

"The other thing you should know is that one of the clubs we play is a gay bar. We only play there because we can do our originals. Mind you, that's only temporary. We have plenty of other gigs at straight places."

"Fuck, you guys are making it harder and harder. But why not? Just so long as we get gigs where I can get laid. I need to dip my stick regularly, or I get cranky. Sure, I'm game. Gotta get back for the next set. I'll see you guys in a couple of weeks." He left for the stage.

"Charming isn't he?" Jason said facetiously. "He isn't exactly the kind of guy I had planned on."

"He's OK, just a little cocky."

"A little! Gimme a break! He's an asshole!"

"Look, he's OK with doin' the gay bars, and doesn't care that you're gay. Besides, he is an incredible drummer. What more do ya want?"

"Someone human would've been nice."

"Not sure what ya mean by that. Besides, you are certainly having a good time yourself. So who are you to talk? He may just be as trampy as you, just more open about it. Trust me, he'll be great," Mike said trying to convince him.

"Yeah, he is a good drummer." Bill admitted shyly while agreeing with Mike.

"We'll see." Jason felt uncomfortable. He longed to be back in the gay world again. The encounter was very unsettling for him. "I've had enough of him and this scene for now. I feel like I need to be around my own kind after that. I think I'll go to this club I've been hearing about. You guys staying?"

"Yeah," Mike replied.

"I'm outta here. We can discuss this guy some other time. For now I just wanna have some fun." Jason turned and left.

The next day was Friday, the evening of the party. Jason entered the room dressed to go out on the town.

"Are ya sure you don't wanna stay? Anything goes," Speed assured Jason.

"No thanks, there's this bath house I've been hearing about that I wanna check out, but thanks anyway."

"Have fun."

Mike and Bill helped Sunshine and Speed get ready for the party. Candles were placed all around the living room to give the right ambience while soft mood music played in the background. A variety of oils, lotions, potions, and lubricants were placed strategically for easy access. Sunshine had baked some brownies, both regular ones and hash ones, which she placed in the kitchen with other goodies, snacks, drinks, and drugs. This was the designated social area while the living room was the designated play area. Sunshine was wearing a very shear full-length outfit through which showed every curve of her body while Speed had on only a pair of thin muslin cotton pants which left little to the imagination.

The guests started arriving about 9:00. As the guests arrived, they were told to help themselves to the refreshments in the kitchen then directed to the changing room which was one of the bedrooms. Mike and Bill stayed mostly in the kitchen, smoking joints. About twenty people arrived, some couples, some singles, but all ready for a good time. There was little inhibition within the group. Some immediately got completely naked while others had on sexy outfits. Some of the women had on negligees or bustiers, some with fishnet stockings and high heels, some with nothing at all. Men were mostly naked, but a few had on sexy underwear or just a hat to portray some sort of character:

cowboy, police, or whatever. The evening started in the social area with all getting a drink, eating a brownie, and smoking a joint with some idle chit chat to get into the mood. All designed to get the group loosened up.

After some brief refreshments, they entered the living room which served as the play room. It wasn't long before Mike and Bill heard the sounds of sex. They were uncomfortable at first, but eventually, with enough drugs and booze, they too got naked and joined the party. It was erotic enough that even they could not resist the temptation. There were naked bodies everywhere in various sexual positions. It could have been a sex manual with positions as varied as the Kama Sutra, all right there in the living room. Moans and groans emanated from the crowd. The exchange of partners was prevalent with a lot of multiple partners playing as well. Bodies were writhing with all forms of sexual pleasure. There were no inhibitions, no restrictions, and all combinations were acceptable. Women with women, men with men, threesomes, foursomes, large groups, or sometimes just people being exhibitionists while the others watched. The groups changed frequently so that everyone had the chance to experience anyone they wanted to in the group. Every once in a while the moans grew to a crescendo resulting in a loud vocalization of climatic ecstasy usually followed by a long sigh and a quiet applause from the group, recognizing their accomplishment with approval. After a short break the next round would begin. Between encounters people would go to the kitchen to refresh, replenish, and get ready for the next round. The party lasted well into the morning hours with every one leaving satisfied and exhausted.

On the other side of town, Jason had stopped at a night club to have a few drinks. He had heard about these places called bath houses where men gathered for sexual experiences. He wanted to give it a try, but first needed to get his nerve up. He left the club. He hailed a cab and gave the cabbie the address.

The cabbie turned around "You sure you wanna go to that part of town?"

"Yes, I'm sure."

The cab drove down to a rather seedy industrial part of town with dark deserted streets. He pulled up in front of a very non-descript brick building with one light over a small door. It looked more like a warehouse than a club or place of business.

"Are you sure this is correct?" Jason asked a bit timidly.

"Yes," said the cabbie. "This is the address you gave me."

Just then Jason saw a guy walk down the street and disappear into the door. "Well, I guess this must be the place." He thought out loud.

Jason got out, paid the cab driver, and nervously walked toward the door. Part of him wanted to just run away back to the cab and just go home or to the bar, but when he turned all he could see was the back of the cab going down the street, leaving him there all alone. He decided that he had to do this. He entered the door. He immediately heard the low drone of music; nothing really distinguishable, mostly rhythmic like thumping sounds with some droning keyboard noises. He opened the door and entered a very small room. On the left was a window with a man sitting behind a cage of wire. He saw the sign that this was in fact the Downtown Baths. He approached the man.

"Room or locker?" The man asked.

"Uh, just a locker," Jason replied.

"That'll be eight bucks, and I'll need your driver's license."

Jason handed over the money and his driver's license. He was given a towel and a key. He heard the door at the end of the corridor buzz. He walked to the door and opened it.

The music was a bit louder, but it was the same background music. There was a long hallway. On the right was a room with lockers, so he entered. Inside the room men were changing, putting their clothes into the lockers, and leaving with only the key around their wrist and the towel wrapped around their waist. Jason did the same. He closed his locker and ventured out into the unknown. It was dark, lit only by colored lights, mostly red. He walked down the hallway. Another hallway took off to the right where he could see a series of doors. Most were closed, but as he walked he could see a few open. He looked inside the first room he saw open. The room was only large enough to accommodate the bed, which was more like a mattress on a platform, and the table—nothing else. There was a man sitting there naked. He smiled his approval and motioned Jason in, but it was too soon. He just continued to walk. He walked by many rooms, all were the same. Each time they would look up to check out the person walking by to see if this was someone they wanted an encounter with. Jason was both frightened and excited as he continued on his journey.

The whole place was like a labyrinth. There were several corridors leading to other parts of the establishment in this maze of hallways. Jason decided that he should first explore the whole place. He entered a large open room with a huge indoor swimming pool. He could tell it was very shallow as the men in it were all standing. Some were sitting on the edge while other guys were just hanging around the perimeter. Sex was everywhere. No one was talking. At the end of the pool was a glass door that was all fogged up. He entered what turned out to be a steam room. He could hardly see with all the steam. He walked around a maze of small cubby holes, benches, and a large section with men having sex everywhere. He exited the steam and left the pool area to see what else this club had to offer.

He entered another large room. There were carpeted stairs or bleachers made for sitting. At the end of the room a TV was showing gay pornography. Some guys were alone while others were playing with each other in various activities. He left and walked down the corridor to the next room. It had a large contraption made mostly of chains and leather that hung from the ceiling by chains. Jason left the room. He could feel the adrenaline pumping. He was both nervous and titillated. This was truly a place of sexual encounter; a place that Jason had never thought existed. He was a bit taken aback at the brazenness, openness, and the raw sexuality, but at the same time he was excited. He walked around exploring for a long time, trying to relax enough to have a good time. Eventually, he felt comfortable enough and horny enough for him to start enjoying the real rawness of this place. It wasn't long before he was enjoying all that this place had to offer. It was like nothing he had seen or experienced. It was exciting. Here there were no names, just indiscriminate sex, with as many as you cared to try; in small private rooms, the pool, the steam room, the video room, or the orgy room.

This experience was a sexual release for Jason who felt he could at last express himself sexually. He left fully satisfied

They had a wonderful time in San Francisco. Days had been spent sightseeing with Mike, Speed, and Sunshine as their guide. They had seen a lot: Chinatown, Fisherman's Wharf, the Embarcadero, Golden Gate Park, Golden Gate Bridge, and Lombard Street. They had ridden the old trolley cars and even took the ferry to Sausalito.

In the evenings they went their own ways. Jason spent his evenings hitting all the gay night spots he could find—picking up tricks whenever possible. If he couldn't find one or was just in the mood for sex, he would satisfy his needs by going to a bathhouse. He was like a kid in a candy store. However, Jason was wearing out.

Mike and Bill spent their evenings hanging out with Speed and Sunshine going to clubs to check out the bands, hanging out with the drummer, going to other parties, or having friends over. The evenings would usually end up with lots of drugs, wild orgies, wife swapping parties, or just plain uninhibited sex parties. It was fun at first but not really Mike's thing, and Bill only seldom participated in the sex, opting more to indulge in the drugs.

How have things been going with Vic and Sunshine?" Jason asked Mike one morning.

"Oh, just fine. It has been great seeing 'em again. But ya know. I can see just why I left. They certainly live in their own little world. They really have no goals in life. I guess it is true that you can't go home again. It's all talk. They just sit around and talk about all the bad things in this country, get involved in their sexual encounters, and stay high most of the time. I guess it just now seems nowhere to me, lots of attitudes but no action. I'm happy I have my music as a goal. It in some way gives meaning to my actions. Besides, I'm not the kind to just sit and do nothing—to stagnate, and I think that's what they do. They live in the past; still fighting the old causes, but the fight seems over. I guess we should be grateful for people like Speed standing up for our rights, especially freedom of the press, but putting out a newspaper about sex doesn't seem all that important somehow. Besides, they have really gotten into this sex thing more than the political things. They're into free sexual expression: wife swapping, open sexual experiences or whatever. I just call 'em orgies. That's OK for them, but it's just not for me I guess. I did have fun a couple of times. I thought I would enjoy it more, but I guess I really want something more—a real relationship. There was a time when I thought it was great, but I guess I have changed."

"I know what ya mean." Jason agreed." I've had a wonderful time this week. I fucked my brains out, but I couldn't imagine living a life where your only goal or reason to be was to get high or laid all the time. You know, work just enough to survive and screw all the rest of the time, sort of like a professional faggot. I couldn't get into that for too long. Mind you, it's been fun for a vacation, and I plan to do it more than I used to, but it's not my only goal in life."

"I really think I'd still like to meet someone someday and settle down. I guess I'm still a little old fashioned in that way. But I can't deny my hormones."

"Yeah, I know what you mean."

"Uh, I don't know about you guys, but I think it's time we headed home. I've had a great time, but I'm ready to leave." Mike looked at them both hoping for agreement.

"I agree. I can't believe this place. It's just incredible," Jason responded." But I'm ready as well. I think I've had enough gaiety for now. I couldn't get it up if I tried. Besides, it might fall off from overuse. "He laughed. "Let's head for home."

"Uh, yeah, me too. Besides, I should get back to work you know." Bill nodded in agreement.

16

"CAN'T FIND MY WAY HOME"

Blind Faith

"Light up a joint," Mike said to Jason and Bill as they drove down the coast highway on their way home. "We're far enough out, so we don't to have to worry about the cops."

Bill was sitting in the back seat playing his guitar as usual, somewhat oblivious to everything else around him.

"Light up a joint," Mike repeated.

"Sorry, I was just practicing." He put down his guitar then started rolling a joint.

Since they were not in any hurry, they had decided to take the long and scenic route down historic but winding Pacific Coast Highway or Highway 1 in a large section where it was separate from Highway 101. It was a beautiful stretch of highway famous for its dramatic ocean cliffs and redwood forests. Many towns along the way were well known for their scenic beauty—towns like Monterey, Carmel, Big Sur, and San Simeon where the newspaper magnate William Randolph Hearst built his fantasy Hearst Castle. But the road was the real attraction with its rugged coastline and incredible vistas. The road wound around high cliffs which dropped down to violent seas or beautiful beaches then meandered inward where huge California redwoods ran through pristine valleys. It was a long journey on a winding road but well worth the drive.

The radio started playing a new song. "Well I was running down the road/ trying to loosen my load."

"Hey this is the Eagles' new single. It's a really good song called 'Take it easy.' Check it out." Mike turned up the radio as the song played.

"Take it easy/ Take it easy/ Don't let the sound of your own wheels drive you crazy/ Lighten up while you still can/ Don't even try to understand/ Just find a place and make your stand/ And take it easy." The radio blasted the chorus.

"Pretty cool, huh? I think we outta learn it," Mike was singing along while Bill was working out the chords in the back seat.

"Sure fits the situation," Jason said as he passed the joint.

All were feeling wonderful after their time in San Francisco.

"Well, it looks like you had one hellova' time in San Francisco." Mike laughed.

"Yeah, it was pretty awesome," Jason agreed. He smiled picturing the beautiful city, and the beautiful men, all of which he had enjoyed immensely. "I had a great time." Jason sighed remembering his experiences.

"Yeah, for me too. I must admit, it took me back to the old days of San Francisco." Mike was a bit nostalgic.

"And the drugs were outstanding," Bill interjected.

"It really seems you got in touch with your gay side," Mike stated turning to Jason.

"Yeah, I really came out this weekend, didn't I?" Jason shyly responded. "I, uh, still hope you are OK with all that."

"Of course I am. But, I am curious about this gay thing," Mike said to Jason hoping he'd open up about being gay after spending time in San Francisco. "Like when did ya first know? And how? I mean I don't wanna pry, but we are good friends, and I'd like to know. I hope you don't mind me asking." Mike felt that talking about it would help him deal with being gay and the rejection he had felt when the drummer quit.

"Um, Oh, I was about thirteen I guess." Jason replied shyly but also seeming eager to get it off his chest. "I noticed something different about myself. At first I wasn't sure just what was going on. Ya know, with puberty and all that. I think it's a difficult and confusing time for anyone. All the changes you go through. And this mysterious thing called sex. Not knowing just what it's all about except the bad information you get from the other kids. Pop tried to explain it to me a couple of times but that only ended up in embarrassment for both of us. I do remember being called faggot back in those days. Probably because I just didn't fit in. I was a musician and not into sports or other guy things. I didn't even know what a faggot was, but they probably didn't either. I'll never forget when I first became concerned that I was different. It was when I got a hard-on in the boy's gym. All those other male bodies excited me. I didn't know what it was all about, but they did, and from then on, boy, was I ridiculed. I also remember all the other guys talking about girls. All that sexual shit boys talk about, you know, mostly about tits and ass and what they wanted to do. It just didn't interest me. Girls just didn't turn me on—but the boys did. Looking back I can now truly say I had crushes on some of the guys, but back then I didn't know what was going on. Oh, I had girlfriends. I tried to do the things other guys did, but it did absolutely nothing for me, sexually that is. So I ended up hanging around the girls more and more. I found I really didn't have much in common with the guys. I just loved looking at 'em. I even got myself a Playboy and looked at the naked pictures, but I found the men's underwear ads more exciting than the naked women. Boy was I confused and frustrated.

It wasn't until Dad gave me some books where I read about homosexuality that I realized that I might be one. Boy, did that depress me. Oh god, a homosexual, a sick person. I felt something was wrong with me. So I refused to be a homosexual. I denied it. I tried even harder to be straight because I knew that if I were gay it would be the end. I knew that I wouldn't be able to deal with school and my schoolmates or life in general. I was also very afraid that my parents, being such good Christians, would disown me. It was totally against everything the Church said, which meant all my upbringing. It was also against everything I had been told. It was a sin, and I was going to hell. It created a lot of conflict for me. I wanted so much to be straight, but the only thing that turned me on was another man. I became more angry and depressed."

"Was last week the first time you ever did it with a man?" Mike questioned. Bill sat strumming his guitar and listening.

"No, the third actually. The first time was when I was in high school. He was my best friend. We had grown up together. I kind of had a crush on him. I guess I loved him. I can admit it now. Well, one day during summer vacation we were out hiking at the river. We got stoned and drunk. We went skinny dipping. One thing led to another. It was like one of those romantic love story movies, but it was between two guys. In my mind this completed our relationship. It was a beautiful experience—one of the most wonderful feelings I ever had. Unfortunately, he felt differently. He wouldn't talk to me for the rest of summer vacation. Then one day after school had started I saw him on campus. I was nervous, but I went up to see how he had been, and why he had been avoiding me. He told me he never wanted to see me again because it only reminded him of the shame he felt for what had happened. He said that he wouldn't be seen around with a faggot, and that he hated me for what I was and what I did to him. He said if ever I was to tell anyone he would deny it and tell everyone how I was a faggot and had tried to rape him, but he fought me off. I was crushed. My affections had been rejected, and I had lost my best friend. I did all I could to keep my sanity and get over it. But, I did love him, and I think to this day I still love him."

"Sounds like a real drag. So what'd ya do?" asked Mike.

"Well, I haven't even thought about him in years." Jason thought back to that awful time. "It was after that that I decided that I'd ignore my homosexual feelings. I would just live with it. I thought that I could just deny it. Being gay wasn't gonna affect my life. I would live a normal, straight life like everyone else. Get married, have kids. This would be my secret. I refused to succumb to these inclinations. This was when I started having sex with girls. But that proved to be frustrating, because the only way I could get excited was to fantasize about other men. It worked for a while, but I just didn't have sex very often. That was until last week, when the charade ended, I just couldn't live the lie any longer."

"Sounds pretty tough," commented Mike. "No wonder you've been a bit cautious. Thanks for opening up to me. Kind of feels like a big weight has been lifted off your shoulders. "So, what happened after your first gay affair?" Mike asked.

"Well, uh, it was a long time before I ventured again into the world of sex," Jason continued, "especially gay sex. It took a couple a years before I was ready to try it again. So, when I turned twenty one I decided to try one of those gay bars I had read about in those trashy newspapers. Off to Hollywood I went, by myself, hopefully to find other people like me. It was in a seedy part of town. I'll never forget sitting in my car for an hour debating whether to go in or not. When I finally got up enough courage, with the help of a six pack and a couple of joints, I ventured into the place. I was frightened to death. The entrance was in a dark alley. I entered the bar. The small smoke filled room was dark and dreary. Even though the lights were dim, I could see a bar along the back wall where men were lined up. I remember wondering if this was the way all gay people have to live, always in the shadows or in secrecy. I felt like I was entering a scene from some seedy film noir movie with back alleys, dark sleazy bars, and strange people with desperate looks on their faces. The whole scene could've been in black and white. I remember thinking of all the gay references I had seen in the movies; all depressing images, where the gay people always ended up dead either from killing themselves out of shame or being beaten to death or killed because of what they were. I was petrified. I hated myself for being gay. I almost ran out in fear, but I felt that I had to continue on. As I entered, it seemed all eyes were on me. Perhaps it was my imagination or because I was new, but probably because I looked fairly obvious and scared. I got up enough nerve to ask for a beer. Then I started to focus, my blinding fear kept under control. This bar was my worst nightmare. It was everything I did not want a gay bar to be, but somehow everything I thought it would be. I ended up getting merrily drunk to try to ease the pain and to relax."

"So what happened?" Mike asked.

"Well, I did meet someone that night, drunk as I was. We went back to his place, a decrepit one room place in some sleazy hotel, really not much more than a flop house. It was awful, and I felt dirty. I returned home the next morning and took a lot of showers to try to cleanse myself from what had happened the night before. I vowed never to have anything to do with that scene again. I felt that if that was what being gay was all about I wanted nothing to do with it. So again, I vowed never again to be gay or at least to exercise that side of me. I would just have to hide how I felt because I wasn't gonna be part of this underworld. I didn't want to end up like them—lurking in the shadows or even dead. It was horrible."

"God, it sounds terrible. What changed this time? Why did you finally decide to come out now after all this time?" Mike asked. He lit a joint then passed it to him. He was happy to see Jason talk about all his hardships. The therapy seemed to be working. Jason was truly opening up. Mike knew these were the secrets of his soul and to tread softly.

"Remember when we played at Studio 69? Well, I went back a few times on our nights off. I told 'em I was just checking out other acts. Well, I met some nice people: people who were gay, but people that I could relate to. I think Chuck, the club owner and his lover, Greg must've known all along for they kept telling me how being gay wasn't so bad, once you accepted it. Also, how difficult it was for everyone coming out. He even relayed some of his stories about coming out to me, the depression, the suicidal tendencies, wanting to be like other people, and denying your true feelings. What he said made sense. He told me there was no point in depriving oneself or denying it because of fear of what others might think. I decided it was time to stop denying myself. I was tired of hiding. I wanted to stop living in the shadows. Time I accepted myself. Be honest with myself for who I really am. I was hoping the band would understand. I am thankful you and Bill have accepted me. I wouldn't want anything to jeopardize our friendships. I'm not hiding anymore. And I thank you for being my friends."

"Well, I'm glad you feel that way," said Mike.

"Personally, I have no problem with it. I am glad I know though. For me, I know that I'm not into dudes, only into chicks," Bill interjected.

"That's cool, because we did wonder especially since you don't seem that interested in chicks. It'd be OK with us if you were." Mike explained.

"Thanks, but not really interested in guys. I guess just more tolerant because of the people I hung out with. I would like to fall in love again sometime as well." Bill added thoughtfully. "I'm just looking for that right person to connect with."

They stopped at a particularly beautiful place called Point Lobos which offered spectacular views of the violent seas below from high cliffs of craggy rocks. As they talked they wandered the trails as waves crashed below them.

"So, I've told you about my first love. Did either of you have a first love?" Jason asked.

"I'll never forget my first love," Mike began. "Her name was Judy, Judy Clarke. She was one of the in-crowd in high school, you know, cheerleader and all that. She was bright and had good grades—one of the most popular girls in school. Her boyfriend was captain of the football team. They were very popular—prom queen and king and all that shit. I remember going to the football games just to see her, but she was always with her friends or her jock football boyfriend. Unfortunately, I just wasn't from the right neighborhood or the right kind of guy. We lived in a nice part of town in the Valley in an average valley tract house in Reseda. She lived in Encino, the nicer part of town. She even lived 'South of the Boulevard' as it was called, Ventura Boulevard that is. That's where all the homes are large and expensive, and all the parents were doctors, attorneys, or something else professional. These were all people who made a lot of money, something we really did not have. All the kids drove nice cars that their parents had given to them. They all planned on going to college and be even more wealthy than their parents. Their lives had already been planned for them. At least I got the bug about college. But overall, I just didn't fit in with 'em. I definitely was an outsider.

After high school I took a job at a gas station. She'd often drive in for a fill up in the car her parents had bought her for graduation. Her parents were fairly wealthy. I think her dad was an attorney or something. I felt so ashamed at first, working in the gas station. But she became friendlier as time went on.

I discovered that her boyfriend was in Europe, his graduation present from his parents. As I got to know her better we became friends and began to hang out together. We went out for coffee after I got off work or to the beach on my days off. I wanted to have a real date, but knew that she was going with the other guy.

In time, this grew into a real romance, at least for me, but for her it was just fun. We had never really done anything up to that point, just hung out together. She had her life planned. She'd marry a doctor or lawyer or someone with money, prestige, and good looks. This just left me feeling more and more inadequate.

Finally, one night she asked me to go to the beach with her. She had scored some booze from her parent's liquor cabinet. She seemed anxious to talk. We sat on the beach talking as the moonlight shone on the water. She told me that she was depressed because she was a virgin. She said that her boyfriend was expected to return shortly from Europe. He did make one stipulation when he left. He told her that when he returned he was expecting to have sex with her if she wanted to continue with the relationship. She really wanted him. He was the type of guy any girl would want. I comforted her and told her it would be OK. She was glad she had me to talk to. She told me what a wonderful friend I was and how much she appreciated me listening to her and her problems. We were very close that night, the kind of closeness you find only when someone is depressed and vulnerable. I gave her a big hug of support, hoping to ease her mind, but this hug turned into more. We felt each other's bodies. We grew more and more passionate. Next thing I knew we were making love. It was the most wonderful feeling I had ever experienced. I, like you, felt it consummated our love. It was almost like that movie <ins>From Here to Eternity</ins> where they were making love on the beach with the waves coming in around them.

Her boyfriend returned a short time later. That left me out. Try as I might she wouldn't see me. In fact, she completely avoided me. I decided I should tell her how I felt—how heartbroken I was that she was ignoring me."

"Did ya ever see her again?" Jason asked.

"Uh huh. I finally saw her about two months later. I poured my heart out to her. I told her how much I loved her, and how I wanted to marry her. She just laughed and basically told me I wasn't good enough for her. She said she'd only marry the right person with the right potential. She said it was wonderful, and she'd never forget me, but she had her future and her reputation at stake. It wasn't about love, it was about money. She was looking for someone who could keep her in the manner to which she had been accustomed. She thanked me for teaching her about sex. Because of me, she wasn't afraid when her boyfriend returned. She did tell me that sex wasn't the same with him, not nearly as good. But her relationship with him wasn't about sex; it was about marrying the right guy. She had used me only to learn about sex. I felt like a stud whore. I was majorly upset."

"So what happened to her?" Jason inquired.

"I heard from her again about a month later when she informed me that she was pregnant. She wanted me to pay for the abortion which cost two thousand dollars. I told her to go back to her jock boyfriend. She said that she didn't wanna tell him, afraid he'd figure out that he wasn't the first. There was no way I could get the money. She explained that if I didn't get the money she'd tell everyone and ask my mother for the money. My only alternative was to split. I didn't have the money, nor did my mother. And even if she did, I couldn't ask her for it. My mom had supported me for so long by waitressing at the coffee shop making so little money. I no longer wanted to be a burden to her. So, I left for San Francisco. I didn't think Judy would tell my mother if I was gone. And even if she did, I felt this was my only way out. I later found out she did marry the football player and had a son—probably mine. I guess I'll never know. But my love affair ended up not unlike yours, in emotional and financial disaster. I was devastated when it ended. I just don't know why love must hurt so much. But like you said the first love is always the best and is the one most remembered—no other will be the same. I'm really looking for another relationship like that again—to fall in love again."

"Do ya still keep in touch with any of 'em? Jason asked.

"No, I haven't seen those people in ages. I won't go back until I can go home with my head held high, proud of who I am. I wanna show those people that I am somebody, somebody important. They'll see. Someday, I'll come home as a rich and famous rock star. Someday I'll show 'em all. Then they'll all be sorry."

"What about your mother?" Jason continued to question.

"I, uh, haven't seen her in years either. She probably thinks I've overdosed, dead, or something. Someday I will return when I can rescue her from the life she lives, and when I can again face her for deserting her when things got rough for me. Someday I'll go back, but not until I'm ready. Then she'll be proud of me. I'll make her proud, but until then I'm just gonna stay away."

"And what about you Bill?" Jason asked hoping Bill would open up. He was a man of few words. They were never sure how he felt or what he was thinking.

Bill had up to this point had only listened but felt compelled to reply. "I, uh, had a similar situation in Boston growing up. My parents did have my whole life planned out for me, college, job—everything. They were very manipulative and controlling. Good Catholic family. You know the type. You could be bad and sin all week so long as we went to confession. I hate religions for that reason. It's just an old system to keep us in line instead of doing the right thing just because it's the right thing. I went along with it for a while, but I came to hate it. It just was not me. It was so phony. The last straw had to do with the girlfriend I had there. My, uh, parents intervened and ruined it. It kind of turned into a bad scene. It just showed how manipulative and controlling they were. Well, that was the last straw. I couldn't handle it anymore. That's why I ran away to New York. I wanted to get away from the folks and that whole scene in Boston." Bill's voice became strained. "I, uh, I really don't wanna talk about it. I, uh, really just wanna forget the whole thing. It brings back too many bad memories." Bill stopped, turned, and stood looking out at the view, lost in thoughtful silence with his back to them. They could have sworn they heard a sniffle, but it could have just been the sea air. He wandered off. It was obvious this was creating some painful memories for him, and he seemed to need some alone time.

Mike and Jason looked at each other. They had hoped that Bill would open up more but felt that it would be better not to pry.

"He certainly can be mysterious." Mike whispered to Jason.

"Yeah, quite an enigma" Jason shrugged his shoulders.

"Now that Bill is gone can I ask you something?"

"Sure, whatever," said Jason.

"I'm trying to understand this, but it's still hard for me to believe you are gay. I mean I'm cool with it and all. I guess you're not what I expect a gay person to be like. You are like me. But I must say I am a little concerned that you want to fool around with me like your other friends. Can we be just friends if you are gay?" Mike asked.

"I wouldn't lie and tell you the thought hadn't crossed my mind, at least in the beginning. However, I think it would ruin our friendship because what we share as friends really has nothing to do with sex. I guess there are different kinds of love, and the love of a friend is very different from sexual love. There need not always be love with sex. Sex is physical and love emotional—two distinct things. Sometimes they coincide and it's beautiful, sometimes they do not. Besides, just because I'm gay doesn't mean I wanna have sex with every male around. Nor do I ever want to try and force anyone to be like me. I am the one who is different. I am the homosexual. Believe me. I would do anything to not be gay, nor would I try to bring anyone to this side of the fence, unless of course that person thought that he might be." The confidence in Jason's tone of voice proved to Mike that this was working. He saw Jason really beginning to accept himself.

"Did ya ever think you might be gay?" Jason asked. "You certainly can have more women than you do. For me, I have a reason, for you it might be different."

"Well, I never thought about it, but after you came out, I did wonder. I don't feel very different from you as a person. But I must admit, the thought of having sex with a man just repulses me. I guess that's what makes me not gay." Mike spoke confidently. "Just because I don't wanna fuck every woman that comes along doesn't mean I'm gay, just selective even though it doesn't seem like it sometimes You know when the urge and the opportunity present itself it's hard to pass up. 'Love the one you're with,' as the song says. I know that I do my share, but the reality is I want something more meaningful. I really want to fall in love again. I've had the feeling once, so I know it's there."

"Well, you're not attracted to men, so I don't think you need to worry about your sexual preference. You must be straight. But I agree, it's so hard to find those feelings, to find love. And it can hurt."

Finally, Bill turned and spoke. "Check out the view—really bitchin'."

"Yes, it is," Jason agreed

"Breathtaking," Mike added as they continued walking.

"But what about your parents? What would they think now?" Mike asked Jason

"Uh, I'm not sure. They're very conservative. Good church going people, Southern Baptists. Totally against homosexuality. They go along with anything the church tells 'em. They would still probably disown me or something. It would certainly be a shock. That is one of the reasons I wanted to leave and come to California, to get away from them and start my own life. Certainly doesn't fit in with their religious views." he said looking out over the vast ocean.

"I'm with you there. I was brought up Catholic. A religion I certainly have no use for. I hated the hypocrisy." Bill interjected.

"I certainly don't believe in organized religion," Jason continued. "I rejected it long ago. I remember praying to be normal. Then I thought, how is it possible for me to be something that the Church says is wrong or doesn't exist. It just did not make sense to me that a God would create me as a gay person when it's wrong according to him. I think they have it all wrong. Besides, who are they to tell me what's right and what's wrong? Religions are up to interpretation. Perhaps there is some higher power, but I really don't know. I certainly do not believe in the Christian way of life. I do believe in doing the right thing, sort of what comes around goes around. I'm not doing anything to hurt anyone.

Why should I be condemned? I guess I might have a spiritual side but certainly not a religious one."

"Right on, man! I kinda' agree with you." Mike nodded in agreement. "From a sociological point of view, I think we, as a culture, have outgrown the need for religion. Seems like some old antiquated beliefs. It certainly doesn't fit into my lifestyle especially with all the altered consciousness I've experienced with drugs. Like you, I might be spiritual but certainly not religious, at least in the old sense. I do believe in the interconnectedness of everything. My time in San Francisco taught me a lot about the world and the universe as a whole." Mike was waxing philosophical. "We're just travelers on this planet going through life's journey. Life should be here for us to enjoy. There might be some cosmic higher power, but I don't believe in some personified deity that tells us what to do or controls our lives. Life is a journey in itself and should be appreciated for just that."

After a short time Jason began again. "Isn't it funny how we all just wanted to be accepted? How we all ran away in our own ways from those outside pressure. Society sure can create pressures and our peers sure can make it difficult for us."

"Yeah, it seems to be a very similar kind of situation for all of us," Mike agreed. "I'm glad we had this time to talk."

"I agree." Jason smiled. "Thanks for understanding. It's great to have friends we can open up to and be honest with."

"That's what friends are for," Mike agreed.

Even Bill who was still lost in thought and hadn't said much, seemed truly happy at the prospect of having friends like these and nodded in agreement. "Me too," he said shyly.

The three stood there in silence for a while, taking in the beauty of nature. Eventually, they returned to the car to continue their journey.

"BOTH SIDES NOW"

Judy Collins

Mike, Jason, and Bill arrived in Big Sur about lunch time after driving through some of the most beautiful coastline any of them had ever seen on a road that meandered along ocean cliffs and through redwood valleys. They wanted to stop and take in the beauty first hand—to experience its grandeur, and the sights, sounds, and smells of this ancient forest.

Big Sur was beautiful. It was a slightly inland valley—away from the violent surf. Huge redwoods lined the road and a small creek meandered nearby. The California Redwoods once forested the inland valleys near the California Coast from Big Sur to just north of the Oregon border. Now, with only pockets of them still remaining, this was one of the southern most places where redwoods still grew. The tree has a very limited growth area due to its ability to only grow under certain very limited conditions. They're known not only for their beauty, but also as the tallest trees in the world with some reaching heights of over 350 feet. Stepping into a redwood forest is like stepping into a primeval forest. These ancient trees are remnants from a prehistoric time. Even many of the current trees are more than 3000 years old. They have only two other relatives—the Giant Sequoia also found in California in the Sierra Nevada Mountains and another species found in China. The California Coast Redwood forests were once a very prominent feature of the coastal area of California. Now, much of the ancient forests have been wiped out. They became a much desired tree for logging and a valuable resource for the California economy for many years, especially in the 1800s and early 1900s. They even helped to rebuild San Francisco after the devastating Earthquake of the early 1900s. Only a few of the forest groves survived, mostly in state, regional, or national parks. The preservation of these mighty giants was helped due to the efforts of concerned citizens who did not want to see them destroyed forever.

They stopped at a restaurant for a bite to eat. It was a small town, not even a block long, with only a gas station, a small store, and a small restaurant. The small village was filled with what looked like hippies; people with long hair, tie-dyed clothes, and sandals. Some were carrying backpacks, which could have contained all their belongings, and guitars. Many were camping at the local camp grounds; just communing with nature, basking in the warm sun, and taking in the beautiful forest environment.

They finished their lunch and decided to walk around to check out the area. They wandered into a small campground. There was a large group of people just sitting around getting high in a large field surrounded by huge redwoods. They knew they would fit right in. As they approached, the group welcomed them. They asked the three of them to join them for a smoke. One guy was playing the guitar while others sang along. A few were dancing in the field. It reminded Mike of his days in San Francisco in the '60s. There was a true feeling of peace, serenity, and fellowship. They enjoyed the carefree lifestyle, something they seldom had the time to enjoy themselves.

"This place is gorgeous." Mike stated.

"I agree," said Jason looking up at the big trees.

"I am so glad that this generation has had a return to nature—a real change from the past. At least areas like this were preserved. I do think this new generation has a renewed appreciation for nature, ecology, and the environment."

I agree with you." Jason added. "I believe we are not here to use nature for our own selfishness. We should be caretakers of nature and work to keep it pristine and beautiful. We are part of nature."

Just then a long haired man wearing an Indian style shirt walked up. "Peace, man." he held up the two finger peace sign.

"Peace to you, man. I'm Mike."

"Hey man, want a hit?'" he reached into his pocket, pulled out a small metal container, opened it, and offered them a small tab. It was a small piece of a clear paper. "It's window pane acid, very pure. Only five bucks."

"Far out, man! Mike reached into his pocket and pulled out some money. They thought it would be fun to enjoy the scenery in a heightened sense of awareness. The tall coast redwood trees with the light filtering through made for a beautiful setting. What better a place to enjoy nature and make some music? Luckily they had sleeping bags in the car, so they decided to stay the night. They also had their instruments: two acoustic guitars and a flute for Jason. They thought it a perfect opportunity to do some playing together.

The acid was beginning to take affect when they decided to get out their instruments and play. The drugs created a heightened awareness of their surroundings and an even better connection between them. They began to play. The music just seemed to flow. They could feel where each other was going musically. They made a very profound musical connection that day, one that would serve them well in their future. It was raw, but it was real. Through their jamming they even started to write some songs or parts of songs. After playing for about two hours and feeling totally exhausted but extremely musically satisfied, they all fell back in the grass. They were peaking on the acid, and the ride up had been an incredible experience. A feeling they hoped would continue.

"Wow! That was fuckin' incredible! Mike commented as he lay in the grass staring up at the sky through the redwood trees. "We really can make some pretty great music together."

"Yeah, that was incredible," Jason agreed.

Bill nodded his head with approval.

"We were really tuned into each other. Really on the same wavelength. It was like we knew where each other was going. We ought to jam more often and come up with some more musical ideas, especially ones that we can eventually turn into songs." Mike was enthusiastic about their accomplishments.

"That'd be bitchin'. I think we had some pretty cool ideas." Bill agreed.

Finally, tired of playing, they decided to take a walk just to enjoy the beauty of the area. They took the trail that went through the forest and that eventually would lead to the ocean.

"Spaced out again. How about you?" Mike walked while taking in the natural scenery.

"Yeah me too." Jason was walking right next to him.

"Me three" said Bill about one step behind them. "That was some good shit; I'm getting pretty fucked up."

"Man this has to be one of the most beautiful places on this planet." Mike commented.

"It sure is." Jason agreed.

"Kind of makes me think of how wonderful this planet we call Earth really is. How we all are just part of nature, interconnected with it—and how we should be in harmony with it. Also makes me feel insignificant in the scheme of things. We all have our place on this planet and in the universe which is just so vast."

"I know what you mean. I feel the same way, especially when I look up at the sky. We are just travelers on this planet we call earth. At night when I see all those stars, I really feel small." Jason agreed

"We really are tiny in the context of the cosmos," said Mike

"Forget about all those organized religions." Jason was opening up with his feelings. "I think all there really is, is the laws of the universe—cause and effect and karma and all that."

"You guys getting philosophic again?" Bill asked. "I just enjoy it for the beauty. And with the acid, it's like seeing it through different eyes, like a different reality."

"Sorry, this place and the acid—it just brings out the Earth hippie in me I guess." Mike said. "Takes me on a sort of cosmic trip."

"Yeah man, cosmic. I'm right with you," Jason commented.

By this time they had reached the beach. They looked out at the violent shoreline which roared with waves crashing on the rocks. Bill walked to the waters edge, picked up some flat rocks worn smooth by the pounding surf, and began skipping them across the water.

They walked back to the campground. As the sun was setting, a large group gathered around a campfire in the clearing. The evening was warm and the campfire even warmer. A guitarist played, people sang and danced, and joints were being passed around. Mike, and Bill got their guitars and Jason got his flute and joined in. They even ended up playing some of their original songs which everyone seemed to enjoy. It was almost primeval. They enjoyed a wonderful evening. It was a reminder of the movement of the sixties that sometimes seemed to have been forgotten. They stopped playing, but the music continued with others playing.

"So this is where all the hippies went," Mike commented. "This so reminds me of San Francisco in the sixties—and when I met Sunshine and Speed."

"Tell me about Sunshine and Speed," inquired Jason.

"I met Sunshine in Golden Gate Park at a Sunday afternoon love-in. That sounds so outdated now, but they were real. We both dropped a tab of acid and spaced out together. She lived in a commune with some others, so she asked if I wanted to stay with them. Since I had nowhere else to go, I agreed. She was very different from Judy. Sunshine was the perfect earth mama—a real hippie if ever there was one. It was great for a while. We shared a close although open relationship. The commune was like a family. I stayed for quite a while."

"Did you love her?" Jason asked. Bill sat quietly listening.

"Uh, I guess in my own way I did, but it was very different. It was the kind of relationship that I needed at that time in my life. Sunshine and everyone else really showed me affection and caring. They weren't concerned with where I came from or how much money I had, or was gonna make—just who I was as a person. They cared about the real person and what was inside. For the first time I felt accepted for just being myself.

The relationship with Sunshine didn't last very long. She was a free spirit, like a wild horse. You just couldn't tie her down. She said love should be shared with everyone. I wanted to share with just one person. I couldn't handle her still playing around with everyone. I wanted more out of a relationship; something sincere, committed, and lasting. At least she made me feel wanted and accepted."

"I know how ya feel," Bill added. "I'd like that too someday."

"Then one day she met Speed. They sort of became a couple, but I didn't want to share her. Eventually, he moved into the house. Speed was a very politically active person, radical really. He was the editor of The San Francisco Free Press, one of those political papers, advocating the revolution, exposing government cover-ups, and advocating free love and all those radical causes. He was quite an illustrious character. He had political aspirations, and the newspaper gave him that outlet. He developed quite a national following. He used to give speeches in the park about the revolution. He was anti-war, anti-establishment, and pro peace and love. A true hippie. He was quite the radical. He talked about American values and how fucked up they were, praising money over all else. He talked about the military industrial complex and how bad it was. He really wanted to change the world. As the political movement died out, the paper gradually became more like one of those porno sheets where you advertise for sex and stuff. They just became sort of swinging couples. It was kind of sad. His revolution never started; his flame fizzled out. He just turned into an oversexed person. I'm surprised he didn't ask you to join him in a three way with Sunshine. He's real kinky. Sunshine just sits home and bakes, does macramé, and makes candles—the real hippie mama. If Sunshine had believed in marriage we'd probably be married, but I think it worked out for the best."

"Why'd ya ever leave San Francisco, Mike?" Jason asked. "It seems like it was a good time in your life. You have lots of fond memories."

"Oh, it was fun for a while." Mike paused, reflected, and then continued. "But after a while I grew tired of the scene. I didn't really want to share in a relationship. Besides, I was frustrated. I wanted to do more than just get high and talk about the revolution and that cosmic stuff. I wanted to play music and really get my life started. I had other goals. So I came back to L.A. to finish college and to work on my music."

"Man, this is good acid, talk about a spiritual cosmic experience. This certainly beats any kind of church." Bill spoke with a softness in his voice.

"I have another idea for a song," Jason spoke. "We can call it 'The Path.' It can be about how everyone takes their own path and about how sometimes peoples paths cross. We can even use that jam we were doing earlier."

"Sounds great." agreed Mike and Bill.

Somehow the whole experience had created a bond among the three of them, something beyond just friendship. Mike and Jason felt especially close. Bill had opened up a little but was still somewhat of an enigma, but they had opened up to him, and perhaps someday he would feel comfortable enough to open up to them.

The next morning they got into the car to get back on the road again. "The Long and Winding Road" by the Beatles played on the radio as the road curved in front of them.

The road home was a long one, but the distance seemed short when in the comfort of good friends, like a warm blanket. The rest of the journey was spent talking about the band, music, and their goals to make it in the music business.

For Mike, Jason, and Bill, they had peeled off some of the layers of their personality. They had caught a glimpse of the core of each others existence and perhaps their soul.

18

"R-E-S-P-E-C-T"

Aretha Franklin

Once home they spent all of their time in the pursuit of finding another drummer. They auditioned quite a few, mostly from Music World where Bill worked. There was a bulletin board there for bands looking for members or musicians looking for bands. There was a steady stream of drummers all as different as the rhythms of songs. Some overplayed, some could hardly play. Others just were not right. No one tried harder than Jason to find someone else to be the drummer, trying to make the best out of even the worst audition. He truly didn't want Jeff in the band.

Jeff finally did arrive about two weeks later with his drums. In a flurry of activity he entered the band house. "OK guys, I'm here. Let's get started. I need to get out and play some gigs. It's the best way to get laid."

Mike laughed while Jason gave a sigh of disgust.

"Hey man, this is just an audition. We haven't decided yet, and we are auditioning other drummers," Jason informed him.

"I know I can do this gig. I dig your material. End of story. Let's get started." Jeff stated with confidence.

Jeff set up his drums. They began to play. They went through their usual audition process. First they jammed for a while. Jeff did a great job and picked things up very quickly.

"Try this and see what you come up with." Mike played one of the original songs. Jeff seemed to catch on right away, much to their surprise and amazement.

"Cool." Mike smiled. He started to play again. "Now, how about this one?" They started another of the original songs.

Jeff sounded incredible. He knew just what to play to make the song better. They jammed. They played cover songs. They played original songs. They threw everything they could think of at him to see just how Jeff would work out. He performed wonderfully. But the real test was the original material. It took only an hour for them all to know that this was right. He was a great drummer with amazing skill, but who also just seemed to know just what to play. For the first time the songs had a strong rhythm section and a strong and driving back beat. This made for a solid foundation. Jeff actually listened to and played with Mike. Soon the two found themselves playing off each other, hitting accents together, working together, and complementing each other in such a way that never detracted from the song but only enhanced it—making it sound better. It sounded as if these two had rehearsed extensively. It was pure instinct that kept them playing together. It almost seemed magical. They were creating a rhythm section that was solid, clean, and tight. For the first time they sounded like a band. This was not four solo musicians playing together in some semblance of a song, but a band playing together. They were sounding the way they had always thought the band and the songs should have. It became evident that it was not only what was being played that was important, but also what was not being played that was equally important. Sometimes less was more. Mike and Jeff continued to amaze each other. They challenged each other, but most importantly they complimented each other, and, in the process, complimented the band and the material. They were able to approach the material with the same attitude and feel which made the material click for the first time. The fit was perfect.

"That was great man. You are one hell of a bass player. I really enjoyed working with ya," Jeff started.

"I agree. We really seem to work well together." Mike added.

Jason left the room at break time followed by Mike with a big grin on his face.

"Well?" Mike asked.

"I must admit. He is damn good." Jason conceded.

"Good! This guy is fuckin' fantastic. No one has made this material sound as good. No one has even come close. I think even you guys must admit it." Mike continued.

"Yeah, you're right." Jason begrudgingly admitted "His playing does complement the material, and it does sound better. But he's still such an asshole. He's loud, obnoxious, and a chauvinist. All he wants to do is fuck his way through rock and roll."

"And, uh, how many men did you have in San Francisco?" Mike snapped.

"That's not fair, asshole." Jason began to walk away.

"Hold on. I'm sorry, I didn't mean that. But anyone who can play as good as he can, must be serious. Besides, I don't think he's so bad. Just a regular guy."

Just then Bill walked out of the garage. "What d'ya think?" Mike asked motioning him over for a conference.

"I think this guy is amazing. Musically I couldn't ask for more. His feel is perfect. You heard the way those songs sounded—like never before—and he hasn't even rehearsed 'em. What're they gonna be like when he gets to work on 'em for good. I think we'd be fools to let this one get away."

"I agree." Mike stood there glaring at Jason.

"Well, I guess you're right." Jason acquiesced. "I'll just have to get over it. He is an excellent drummer, and the songs did sound pretty fuckin' good with him playing." Jason had to admit it. "Besides, I've been outvoted, and this is a democracy."

"Great, then it's a done deal." Mike turned and walked into the rehearsal garage with a grin on his face. "We'd like for you to be in the band. When can you quit and come down for good?"

"Already done, I knew I'd get the gig. And, after listening to the tape a number of times, I knew this was what I wanted to do. I believe in the music, and I think there is some real talent here. Besides, even if I didn't get the gig I knew I was gonna stay in L.A. I've wanted to come to L.A. for a long time. This just gave me a good start. There's more of a music scene happenin' here. The music scene in San Francisco is dead. I quit the band in San Francisco. I've wanted to quit for a long time. I've just been waiting for an excuse. This just gave me a good reason. Besides, we didn't have any more bookings. I was crashing at the band house there, so they have it all to themselves now. At least this way I can play some gigs immediately. But most of all, I dig this band. You've got some strong material and great potential. So I'm here for good. All my shit is in the van—just tell me where to crash. So long as it's a separate bed from Tinkerbell. I wouldn't wanna make him horny or frustrated or anything," Jeff joked.

"Look, let's get one thing straight. I don't appreciate your jokes, so lay off." Jason snapped back crossly then turned to walk out of the garage.

"Um, I'm sorry, man. I was just joking. I didn't mean to offend you. I apologize," Jeff shouted as Jason stormed out of the room. "A little sensitive isn't he," Jeff whispered to Mike.

"Yeah, a little—but he's only just come out. It's been difficult for him. Then to make matters worse, we just lost the last drummer because he refused to work with him because he was gay. That really didn't help. Therefore, he is a little sensitive, insecure, and unsure of himself. I hope you understand."

"Oh, I didn't know he had just come out. I guess I am used to people who are really out after living in San Francisco. I kid all the time. I mean nothing personal, it's just my way. I'd better go in and explain."

He found Jason in the living room about to put on an album and light up a joint. "Uh, look, man. I'm sorry. Really. I didn't mean to hurt your feelings. I meant nothing personal; I just kid a lot. Unfortunately, it sometimes gets me into trouble. I'm from a city where being gay is almost assumed unless otherwise proven different. Most of my friends just get used to me. I was just giving you a hard time. I didn't mean anything by it. Really.

You know, I think your material is really good. I think you're an extremely talented individual. Part of that comes from your sensitivity. I think a lot of that is probably a result of you being gay. I know I have a lot of admiration and respect for most of my gay friends because of their sensitivity and talent, but I think you are one of the most talented individuals I've met. If I had any objections to your sexuality I wouldn't have taken this gig. I just think you should lighten up on yourself, and not take this so seriously. I think being gay can be an asset. I'm just the dumb drummer, out there, beating the shit out those skins. But you—you have real talent."

Jason began to grin.

"That's better. Just don't lemme get to you. I'm only kidding—just busting your balls. And yeah, I can be a real asshole—but it's all in fun. You have my permission to call me an asshole back, or call me on it. Deal?"

"Well, I didn't like you at first. In fact, I did think you were a real asshole," Jason explained honestly. "And I'm still not sure, but you may be all right underneath it all. Deal. Welcome to the band."

The two shook hands. Jeff winked at Mike and Bill who were peeking around the corner to see what was happening, "I think this calls for a celebration," he said as he lit up a joint.

The next few weeks were spent teaching Jeff the material. First he had to learn the cover songs so they could begin gigging as soon as possible, and then the originals. Luckily Jeff was quick to learn. He learned all the cover songs they had been doing and taught them some that he knew. They now had quite a catalogue of songs from the last ten years of rock music to choose from depending on the gig. Songs by The Beatles, The Rolling Stones, Jethro Tull, Deep Purple, Jimi Hendrix, the Eagles and many more. They even did some soul and rhythm and blues songs from artists like Stevie Wonder, The Temptations, and Sly and the Family Stone that Jeff turned them on to that they could do with a more rock feel. They made nice additions to their set list. Jeff's influence really added to the band and its style.

Mike and Jeff hit it off immediately both musically and personally. They worked a lot together to form a very strong rhythm section. This formed the basis and a springboard for their friendship. This was a bit of a relief for Mike. He liked Jason as a friend, but found some of the personal issues to be sometimes tedious and things he really could not relate to or share with. Sometimes he just wanted to have fun. It was a nice escape from the general seriousness of life as Jason perceived. Bill was still a bit distant even though he considered him a good friend. Jeff was different. Mike liked him because he was just a guy—a real, regular guy. He was straight, and in a strange way Mike understood and respected him.

Jason and Jeff got along OK, but neither of them really understood each other which sometimes created some friction. Overall, they did respect each other, but they were both coming from different places. Jeff was outgoing enough and accepting enough to even make Jason feel comfortable despite their differences.

Jeff even brought out Bill a bit more. His personality made even him feel more at ease. Jeff was just one of the guys, and Bill felt very relaxed around him. Bill was still somewhat mysterious and stuck to himself, but they all knew that he too was a good friend. Bill was always likeable and very professional, but still quiet. But with Jeff's demonstrative and sometimes overbearing attitude it was hard not to feel liked and accepted.

Jeff proved to be a good addition to the band. He was honest and likeable and a real straight talker who said it like it was—no nonsense. But most of all he was fun. He liked to have a good time and while a very serious musician, he still made it fun. He was a real good time Joe. Jeff was a man's man—confident, macho, full of hell, and quite a womanizer. He was a character, and his up-beat, outgoing personality was infectious. Jeff had the ability to bring people out, to make them feel relaxed, and to give them confidence. He was convincing, personable, and charming. His bigger than life personality and openness was contagious. It relieved some of the tension which had been building up. He helped to create an even stronger bond between them all.

"Hey guys, they're hiring at Music World. They need some new sales people," Bill informed them one evening when he arrived home from work. "I already told 'em about you guys. They thought it would be a good idea. They're anxious to meet everyone. It'd give you some money to help pay the expenses here. It's mostly during the day. And since they want musicians to work there, they're willing to work around gigs and stuff. What d'ya say?"

"Works for me. Where do I sign up?" said Jeff without hesitation.

"Uh, yeah," Mike agreed. "I guess I can skip school for now. The draft is gone, so I don't really need to go to get my student deferment, and I don't really need that diploma. What am I gonna do with it anyway? Music is more important. Music is what I wanna' do. Count me in." Mike seemed confident of their future.

"How flexible are they? I still want to continue with school since I'm graduating soon, and I have the lessons that I'm giving," Jason added.

"They're pretty cool with all that. Just work part time. Also, you can usually find someone to trade hours with you." Bill answered.

So it was decided. They all would work at Music World. Jason would work the least amount of hours so that he could continue to give lessons and go to school. Mike decided to drop out of school. He felt that school was not going to take him anywhere. Music was the career path he wanted to follow.

Since none of the band wanted to get a serious day job, working at Music World was a viable alternative and fit in with their overall goal. Working at Music World would certainly have many advantages. Everyone in rock went there, from unknowns to rock stars. It was a good way to get your name known and keep in the know about the music scene. They could hear about local bands to know who the competition was, who was up-and-coming, and who was getting signed. They could also hear about clubs and gigs where they could play. For the big name recording artists, they would hear about who was touring, or putting out new albums. Generally, they could keep tabs on everything that was going on in the Hollywood music scene.

19

"THE WORLD IS A GHETTO"

War

The band had finished practicing and were sitting sat in the living room smoking a joint. They didn't have any gigs yet. Jason decided to go out to Studio 69 to hang out with his gay friends or pick up a trick. Bill went to the garage to play his guitar and work on his equipment.

"When we gonna gig, I need some woman," Jeff started." This is getting boring. I'm getting so horny that every time I hear running water I get a hard on just from jacking off in the shower. I mean rock and roll with no sex is nowhere."

"It won't be long now. Our first gig is next week. There will be lots of chicks there. But, I know what you mean. It's time we started playing again. It won't be long now." Mike responded.

"Yeah, man, let's get it together. By the way, I know what Jason's trip is, but what trip is Bill on. We've been working together for a while now, and he's hardly said two words. He sure is a strange bird?"

"Oh, he's just quiet. Actually, he has been more talkative since you've been here believe it or not. He really is pretty cool and a great player, just kind of an introvert. I don't know much about him except that he's from Boston and lived in New York for a while. He used to be a junkie in New York, but you're not supposed to know that. He told Jason and me. Said he didn't want anyone else to know so keep it to yourself until he tells you. He's pretty mellow; just plays his guitar and gets high. It's easy to keep him happy: guitar in one hand, joint in the other. He probably got burnt-out too soon. I think he can only express himself through his playing, but he sure can do that well."

"You are right about that."

"Where are you from?" Mike inquired. He opened a bottle of Jack Daniels, took a swig, and passed it.

"Detroit, garden spot of the nation." Jeff laughed. "Dad, at one time, did work in an auto factory there. We lived not far away from it. It wasn't exactly the best part of town, but it was home. Things were fine then; he was a good man, a good husband, and a good father—a very proud and respectful man who provided for his family. He was, however, one of the causalities of the demise of Detroit in the 1960s. Lost his job at the factory and couldn't find another. He lost his self-respect and his spirit. He was depressed and angry. He began to take it out on his family. He never really recovered. Eventually, he turned to drinking and carousing. He was gone for long periods of time and those were the good times."

"Any brothers or sisters?" Mike continued.

"Plenty, three of each to be exact—in a two bedroom apartment. Talk about crowded. Mom and Dad had a room, the girls had their own room, and the boys had to sleep in the living room. We had to take numbers just to jack off in the bathroom." Jeff laughed. Then suddenly, he grew thoughtfully silent. He was feeling the effect of the drugs, and with his new found closeness with Mike he felt that he could open up. He took another hit and another gulp of whisky. "Actually, I hated it. It was like a bad ghetto movie. Mom in the kitchen ironing clothes for someone else to make some money; Dad on the stoop sipping on a bottle of booze and hanging out with the other laid off non-working guys when he was home; children running all around with tattered clothes and dirty faces. You can almost hear the song 'Summertime' playing in the background as a soundtrack. I was kinda the black sheep. I just didn't live up to my brothers. I was the youngest. Dad liked them better. I could never compete. Besides, Dad was mostly working when they were growing up. My older brother was a real tough guy: football player, got drunk on weekends with the guys, always in trouble. The middle one was always in trouble, mostly drugs and gangs. My brothers were real jerks. They got all the attention. All through school I even had to contend with my brothers' reputations. The gangs my brothers were involved with were infamous. All the kids and teachers were expecting trouble from me just because they expected the same. So, I started my own gang, badder and tougher than my brothers. I did play in the school band, though. That was when I started playing drums. I really liked it even though it was kind of a geeky thing to do. But I wanted to be cool like my brothers and to make my dad proud. So I did the only thing that I thought he'd respond to. I got into a lot of trouble. Uh, I dunno why. It just seemed the only way to gain his approval. Why do we try to emulate those we hate? I guess I was just jealous. Nothing I did pleased anyone, especially Dad. I'll never know why Mom loved Dad, but she did. He was such an asshole. She did try her best to protect me."

"Sounds like a bad scene," Mike interjected sympathetically.

Jeff continued, seeming to open up his soul to Mike, his new friend. "I was the youngest, so I got all the torn and worn out hand-me-down clothes. Growing up I got all the shit from everyone. Being the youngest, everyone liked to pick on me. I got blamed for everything. I had to learn early on how to take care of myself. I never heard the end of having another mouth to feed. My brother once told me how Dad beat the shit outta Mom the day he found out she was pregnant with me. He had lost his job, didn't have a lot of money, and a kid was the last thing he needed. It sort of broke him. Abortion was out of the question, as was any kind of birth control. So Dad always blamed Mom for having me, and of course never wanted me. He couldn't afford the ones he had, much less another mouth to feed. After I was born Mom started using the pill secretly because she knew they couldn't afford another kid. If Dad ever found out she was taking the pill he'd kill her. He didn't want Mom to work. 'A women's place is in the home' Dad would say. But it probably wouldn't have mattered, he still beat her. I used to think Mom was clumsy because she was always bruised, but as I got older I realized that it was Dad. Sometimes beating her just because he got drunk, no other reason was necessary for him. I hated it when he was around. Other times she was beaten for taking the blame for us kids. In trying to protect us, she took the punishment. But we got our share of physical abuse as well. He beat us good from time to time. That fucking asshole! Mom took in laundry after Dad lost his job. Then she also went to work as a maid since Dad hadn't worked in so long. After that, Dad just sat around and got drunk a lot. Many of the men left their families, leaving single women to raise their kids, but my dad stayed. I'm not so sure if that was good or not. Yeah, we had a Dad, but he made life real tough for us when he was around. It would've been better if he had just left us for good. I just knew that I had to get away from that place. That's why I joined the Marines."

"The Marines! You were in the Marines? Why'd you ever join the Marines?" Mike asked.

"Mostly to get out of Detroit—I needed an escape, and it was a way out with pay. It seemed my only option. Detroit just became a real bad scene for me. Family problems, gangs, drugs, black militancy. And finally, some nasty business there in '67. Ya know, the riots and all."

"You were there at that time?" Mike asked.

"I was in the thick of it. I was already getting into gangs, doing drugs, getting into some petty criminal behavior; ya know, robbing liquor stores and shit. I was in a bad place. Detroit was really a bad scene in those days especially for a black man. Those were some bad economic times for the black man. We were sick and tired of being harassed by the police. They were using unnecessary force, calling us nigger or boy, and generally humiliating us. I got involved with some of the black militancy organizations. I became more and more militant as time went on. I really believed that we weren't being treated fairly. I wanted to be part of the cause. You know. Black Power and all that. The black people had been repressed long enough, and it was time for a change.

Then the riots broke out. It was just like those newsreels you see on TV. I don't really remember how it started. It just erupted. Detroit was like a pressure cooker, ready to blow—low income, no jobs, poor deteriorating neighborhoods. The anger was all there. It just needed something to set it off. And then it did happen. Detroit was on fire. We all got caught up in the frenzy, going around turning over cars, setting 'em on fire, lighting Molotov cocktails and throwing 'em into buildings, or whatever. It was a war zone.

I remember throwing a Molotov cocktail then running down an alley. I was alone. Suddenly, a cop turned the corner with his gun drawn. 'Stop Nigger' he shouted. I knew I was in trouble. It was me or him. I raised my gun and shot him. He fell to the ground. I never was sure if I killed him or not; didn't stay around to find out. I ran home and told my dad. That was it for me. He convinced me to leave town once the riot thing was over. If that cop was alive, I knew he'd recognize me, and I'd be in jail for a long time. So I joined the service. That was probably the only good advice my dad ever gave me. I knew it was time for me to get outta town. We didn't have any money. So I joined the Marines. I was a bad ass and knew I wanted the toughest group around. I wanted some respect. I felt I would get it with the uniform. The military was really my only way out of Detroit, the ghetto, and a bad situation."

"Sounds like a tough break."

"Are they still together? Your parents I mean," Mike asked sensing Jeff's desire to talk, and seeing how his inebriation was allowing him to open up without reserve.

"No, he's dead. I killed him," Jeff said nonchalantly. He took a strong gulp as Mike sat in amazement. "The son of a bitch was beating Mom real bad, so I stepped in and punched him. When he didn't get up, Mom went over to check on him, but it was too late. He was dead."

"Dead! Fuck!" was about all Mike could say.

"Not sure what exactly the fight was over, probably nothing, or just my dad being drunk again."

Although Jeff was rambling a bit Mike could sense the pain he was feeling. "Wasn't there a police investigation?" Mike asked.

"Sure, but no one knew I was there. You see this all happened when I was on leave from the Marine Corps. I had just finished boot camp. I was so proud that I had gotten through it. It was certainly no picnic. I never realized how tough the Marines really were. It was like all those movies of boot camp with the mean drill sergeant. But I made it through. I was being deployed to Nam, so I wanted to go back home to let 'em know and to see everyone before I shipped off. When I got home I found Mom and Dad arguing. Dad was drunk as usual and was beating her. When he saw me he told me what an awful son I was. Then he turned on me. He tried to beat me up as well. I just got so angry. I had had enough. He took away my one prideful moment and made me feel like shit again. I wasn't gonna take it anymore, and I wasn't gonna let Mom take it any more either. I laid back and belted him a good one. I guess in my rage, I didn't know my own strength. He flew across the room. Then he just laid there. I just thought he was passed out from the drinking. When he didn't get up, my mother told me just to leave immediately and never return and never tell anyone that I had been there. I obeyed. I never told anyone I was in Detroit. I just told my buds that I went into town to get some pussy and spent the time in a hotel with some whore. No one ever questioned me. She never forgave me for killing her husband. She did take the blame for me, however. I guess she knew nothing would happen to her because the cops had been there many times before to stop the abuse. There were numerous reports of her being beaten already on file and already a history of violence, so it was nothing new. She could just claim self defense. She did have the cuts and bruises from him beating her that night. She went to trial but was let off. They decided it was self defense and therefore justified. I think she felt she had already lost her husband, and she didn't want to lose her son. I tried numerous times to reach her or other members of my family, both before I went to Nam and even after, but after that incident they always hung up on me or refused my calls. She must've told the rest of the family. I guess they all disowned me. Ah, who needs those fuckin' assholes? Someday, I'll go back to Detroit, but not until I am somebody. I'll show 'em—all of 'em. They'll kiss my ass someday—you just watch." Jeff ended with determination.

Mike sat in amazement just beginning to realize the story he had just heard.

"Sometimes, I think of my dad when I play drums. I imagine that he's the drums and that I am beating him—beating the shit outta him and taking it out on the drums. It makes me feel good. At least I can release some of the anger I had for him and how he treated us all." He paused, lost in thought. "Man, enough of this shit, I'm horny. It's time we had some fun and got laid. Go grab Bill. Let's raise hell tonight. It's time for a pussy hunt."

He got up and went to the garage where Bill was playing his guitar. "What's up?" Bill asked.

"Come on, man, let's get crazy tonight," Jeff said. He handed Bill a joint, a bottle of Jack Daniels for a swig, and a beer to wash it all down. Jeff was quite high already and Bill was always in the mood for a good high. "We're stepping out tonight. Time to have some fun and find some action."

Bill was reluctant, but Jeff wasn't going to take no for an answer. The next thing he knew the three of them were getting into Jeff's van to head for the big city.

"STOP! IN THE NAME OF LOVE"

The Supremes

It was a warm California night, almost hot. They opened all the windows for air as they passed joints and guzzled beers. Although their house wasn't far from the center of Hollywood, it was seldom they ventured into the real town of Hollywood, but this was going to be a night to remember. They were on their way to the sleazier side of Hollywood tonight. As they passed all the famous landmarks, they couldn't help to think what an enigma Hollywood had become. In the eyes of the world, Hollywood was seen as a place of glamour as represented in the movies and TV. But there was also the seedy side of Hollywood filled with hookers, adult movie houses, and pornographic book stores. This was a place where hopeful future movie starlets resorted to street walking and prostitution until they got their big break which often never happened. But tonight this was where Jeff wanted to be, a place with excitement, and where all your sexual dreams could come true.

"This is my kind of town!" Jeff exclaimed seeing the ladies lined up along the boulevard waiting for customers. Jeff immediately found a place to park.

"Let's check this out," he said. They were all laughing; all so drunk that the whole thing seemed like a big joke. "In here." Jeff ducked into a pornographic book store. He picked up a magazine. "Look at the tits on this one." He turned the page then turned the magazine sideways. "I never tried this position." He was laughing along with the other guys who were getting as much of a kick out of watching Jeff as seeing the pictures of people fucking in the magazine.

"Come on, much more to see," Jeff said leaving the bookstore. He approached the theatre next door. He looked at the marquee. "Deep Throat, sounds like its right up my alley."

Mike and Bill were not really into seeing a skin flick, especially with each other. But Jeff seemed truly fascinated by the movie, poking and jabbing the other guys as he read the billboard.

"Man, I need a drink," Mike said, not because he was ready for more to drink. It was just an excuse to get away from the movie hall. He really did not want to sit and watch porn with these guys. "Let's split and find somewhere we can get a brew."

"Sure, I'm game," Jeff agreed. "We'll catch this flick later." The three walked down the street giggling about the movies like three sailors on leave for the first time in their lives. But this wasn't the three sailors in the movie On the Town. No, these sailors were looking for some action. "And I see the perfect place for it," Jeff said leading the pack like a gang of kids out for the first time in their lives.

The sign read The Pink Pussycat. It advertised live girls. After paying the cover charge, the three entered with Jeff leading them to a table at the front. The club was filled with smoke and the stench of stale alcohol. But the three musketeers were just there for the fun.

Once seated, a sultry voice from behind asked, "Something to drink boys?"

Jeff turned around. He was almost given two black eyes by the topless waitress's two huge tits which were hanging down just about eye level.

"Fuckin' A, man. With bozzangas like that you ought to be serving mother's milk." Jeff laughed. His eyes were as big as saucers as he reached over for a feel.

"No touching the merchandise," the tall dark brunette said as she grabbed his hand. "Any more of that and you're out."

"Ah, she can flaunt it, but ya can't touch it. That's the game huh."

"Look, there's a two drink minimum. What d'ya want? I got a show to do."

"Three beers," Mike chimed in, embarrassed by Jeff's mouth.

"And how about a private performance after the show?" Jeff asked laughing but obviously serious.

"I don't give private performances, and even if I did you couldn't afford it," she said as she walked away.

She returned with the six beers. "Here's your drinks. Two drink minimum. That'll be twenty four dollars."

"Twenty-four bucks!" Mike exclaimed in amazement reaching into his pocket for money, his naiveté showing.

"Yeah, twenty-four bucks. Four bucks a pop. Pay up. What do ya expect? Free entertainment?"

"Yeah, this place has real professional entertainers." Jeff laughed.

"You're really looking for trouble, aren't you?" the girl said. "What's your guys' trip; you're not the normal fair we get in here."

"Just a couple of guys looking for some action," Jeff said.

"If you're serious I can see what I can do." She winked.

"You bet sister. We're ready."

She left just as the lights dimmed. A woman entered the stage. She started performing a strip tease. She pranced, and danced, and undulated, wrapping herself around the pole that was in the center of the waist high stage that stuck out into the audience. All the men watched and gawked. Their eyes transfixed on her performance.

The three musketeers were now quite drunk. They watched the stage without a movement. Jeff was mesmerized by the bouncing girls on stage, enjoying every minute of it. Bill was just being mellow and seemed to get off on it himself. Mike was just having a good time but feeling a little odd being his first time in a place like this. Mike felt somewhat conflicted. He certainly was no prude and was open about sex especially with all the love-ins and free sex he had been to, but somehow this was different. He felt like this was objectifying women.

It was also very sleazy. At the same time, he was turned on. The more he drank, the more he forgot about his apprehensions. After all it was all consensual, the girls were there to make money, and the guys were there to enjoy the show.

About half way through the show a man walked up to the table and whispered to Jeff. They seemed to be negotiating something. Then the man walked away.

"What was that all about?" Mike asked.

"Well, I got a surprise for you all, now shush. It's not polite to interrupt the show." Once the show was over, Mike was burning with curiosity. "So what's up?"

"Well, we got ourselves a whore. However, I couldn't afford three, one for each of us, so we'll have to share. But, we got her for the three of us. I didn't realize the price of whores had gone up so much; or maybe it's because we're here in Hollywood. In Nam they were cheap. At least we got ourselves some pussy."

"How're we all three gonna fuck her? Take turns or something?"

"Sure, why not? We're friends. We don't have any secrets. Besides, it's no big deal. I used to do this all the time with my Marine buddies. It'll be fun. Let's get outta here. We need some booze before we meet our whore."

Mike and Bill were reluctant at first, but with another quart of Jack Daniels and some joints they too were ready. They were nervous as they approached the room to the small seedy hotel where the pimp had told Jeff to go. Jeff knocked. The door opened revealing a slender dark haired woman wearing a slinky dress.

"Can I help you?" she asked.

"Yeah," Jeff began. "Flash from the pussycat sent us. He told me to tell you it was time for a trio."

"I got the picture. Come on in. You can put your money on the table."

She grabbed the money almost before it hit the surface and stuffed it in her bra. She disappeared into the bathroom for a moment, then returned with nothing on and rubbing her breasts in a sexual way. "All right, who's first?" she asked.

"That'd be me," Jeff said. He dropped his pants and ripped off his shirt with no concern of the others there. He walked over to her, threw her on the bed, and began to fuck her immediately. This continued for a while until he decided he wanted a blow job. The girl obliged.

Mike and Bill felt as if they were watching some pornographic movie. They couldn't believe they were actually there watching Jeff fuck the prostitute. They knew they were next. They were nervous; but the booze, the drugs, and the excitement were also making them very excited. Jeff had remounted the prostitute. When Mike heard Jeff climax with loud grunts and groans he knew his turn was next.

Mike felt even more conflicted than he was back at the club. He had had plenty of sexual exploits, orgies, and other experiences, but paying for a hooker was just somehow different. He had never paid for sex. This was more like business, not about sex and passion. In one sense he did not think it wrong, but somehow he also did not think it right either. Paying for someone to have sex with you just seemed wrong. But, he did find it exciting to a certain extent. It certainly made it more difficult for him, but in the end with the booze, Jeff egging him on, and himself getting quite sexually aroused, he thought he would give it a try. Although feeling awkward, he took off his clothes and approached the prostitute. His dick was not quite hard from him being so nervous. The girl immediately tried to remedy that by giving him head until he was erect and ready. He then began to fuck her. Mike felt so awkward fucking this woman, seeing his friend Jeff sitting in the chair jacking off while he watched. He kept getting soft. So the whore would pull his dick out and stroke it until it got hard enough again. Finally, in what felt like an eternity, Mike came. Since he had finished the deed, he got up, walked over to the chair, and sat down.

"Next," the girl called out, not even tired from the activities. They both looked over to see that Bill had passed out from all the drinking and smoking.

"Well, we paid for three fucks, and we're gonna get three fucks!" Jeff exclaimed slurring his words due to the excessive drinking. He rose up and approached the prostitute stroking his already hard dick. But this time Jeff was much rougher. He pinned her down and demanded that she suck his dick. Then he told her to talk dirty to him.

"You like that big Marine dick!" He exclaimed.

"Yeah, give it to me." she said. "I want you to fuck me hard and long with that big dick of yours." The girl seemed to be really getting into it this time. "Yeah fuck me, come on. Now stick that big dick in my mouth. I wanna feel it throb." Her voice trailed off as she began to wrap her mouth again around his dick, moaning the whole time.

"You like that big Marine dick don't you?" Jeff said again. "Yeah, you fucking whore, you like sucking dick. Well, suck it hard. That's it, harder!" Jeff was really getting into this sex thing. Then he began to get rougher and rougher. He began slapping her around, calling her a whore, and telling her how much she liked getting fucked. Jeff had her pinned down and was fucking her hard. The girl started to fight back. "Come on bitch, you can take it. You know you like it. I'm gonna fuck the shit outta ya." The girl was trying to scream, but Jeff had his hand over her mouth.

Mike jumped up and tried to pull Jeff off the whore, but Jeff just knocked him aside with his brute strength causing Mike to land on the floor. Mike was stunned at first but quickly realized where he was and what was happening. It was like some bad pornographic movie gone wrong; and, with all the booze and drugs, it seemed surreal. But he knew he had to try something. He jumped up again to try to intervene. He grabbed Jeff to take him off the girl while trying to reason with him. Jeff just grabbed him again, but this time held him so he couldn't move.

"You had your turn. You can stick your dick in her mouth while I fuck her if you want, but don't ever try and stop me while I'm in mid fuck." Jeff's pace was quickening. Mike tried again to get him to stop, but Jeff just held him so that his dick was right over the girl's mouth. "Now suck his dick bitch. Come on. I wanna see this bitch get fucked in both ends." Jeff's strength was too much for Mike. He tried to get away but was unable to resist. He was barely able to stand up straight from all the booze. The sweat was pouring off Jeff now and his rhythm was faster and faster. Finally, in one long mounting groan, Jeff came while screaming obscenities the whole time.

As soon as Mike was able to get free from Jeff he did so. He helped the girl do the same. She lay immobile for a time.

"You didn't pay for any rough stuff. That costs extra," the girl said trying to regain her composure and not show her fear.

Mike was flabbergasted. All the while he thought she was in trouble, but all she wanted was extra money for getting roughed up a bit.

Jeff slowly rose, regaining his composure. Then both began getting dressed. The girl was still demanding more money, but Jeff refused to pay. Finally, he laid back and slapped her real hard, throwing her across the room. "You ain't getting another dime from me, you bitch." He grabbed Bill, threw him over his shoulder, and walked out of the room with Mike not far behind.

The trip home was oddly quiet. Mike was still in disbelief over what had just happened, while Jeff was beaming like a proud bull.

"What got into you back there?" Mike asked feeling very guilty about what had just transpired and feeling dirty himself for what he had done for his first time with a prostitute. Mike had never wanted sex like this, and it was worse than he had thought. "You were pretty rough. You could've really hurt her."

"I was just getting off," Jeff said with a strange grin on his face. "She's just a whore anyway. We paid our money."

Bill was just beginning to wake up. "What happened?"

"You missed it all," Jeff said "You were so fucked up you couldn't get it up. You passed out before you even got laid. Don't worry we didn't get cheated, I plugged her twice, you light weights."

"Leave him alone," Mike pleaded. "I 'm sure he feels bad enough from the drink. I know I sure don't feel so wonderful. Besides, I'm sure there have been times when you were too drunk to fuck."

"Never! A Marine is always prepared, sort of like the boy scouts. Always ready for a fuck—just like a real man. What's wrong with you guys? You're all a bunch of pussys? At least Jason is out getting laid. You guys are just a bunch of school girls."

"This macho Marine bullshit makes me sick!" Mike exclaimed. "Did you ever think about making love? Showing your real feelings? Fucking a whore doesn't make you a man. It's just stick it in and wham bam thank you ma'am. Sex can be more than pure animal instincts. Did you ever think about that, think about the other person's feelings?"

"Make love! Shit! Who wants to make love? That shit is for sissies. Feelings and emotions just get in your way. They get you into trouble and ruin your whole life. Just gimme some pussy, and I'll be happy. I don't need love. It's just a drag."

As Jeff spoke, his voice sounded more like he was trying to convince himself more than Mike. Mike suddenly realized that this was almost the same way he had treated his feelings regarding his family. This was a man with a lot of anger, and Mike could hear it in his voice "Yeah, you don't need love." Mike whispered to himself and slowly passed out wondering if he would even remember all this the next morning—hoping he would not, or thinking perhaps it was just some sort of nightmare.

"AMERICAN WOMAN"

Guess Who

The addition of Jeff made the band sound better than ever. Jeff proved to be a fast learner. A couple of weeks of rehearsal allowed the band to return to the stage relatively quickly.

First they returned to the clubs they had already played since these were easiest. Mike was always looking for new clubs. These usually required an audition, but they always got the job. Music World was also a great resource. It wasn't long before they were booked regularly.

Once the Top 40 sets were learned, the band was playing nightclubs, and money was coming in, they were finally able to attend to the more important task of learning the original material. This time it would be undertaken with added dedication and excitement. They returned to Studio 69 and took on more gigs which allowed them to play some if not all originals.

In addition to the club gigs they were able to pick up the occasional gig on campuses throughout the city including Los Angeles University where Mike and Jason had met. They played in the Student Unions at dances doing their cover material and even threw in some of their originals. They sometimes even played at concerts, demonstrations, or rallies. Occasionally, they got a gig as the opening or warm-up band for a recording band that was playing on campus in concert in the gym or auditorium. These they liked best as it allowed them to play their own material, and made them feel more like real recording artists rather than just some copy band. They would occasionally include a song by some other artist but only ones that they had changed so much that they had really made it their own so that it no longer sounded like a copy of another band. Overall, they liked playing the college gigs best. The college crowd was the most enthusiastic and most receptive, especially for their original material. They just wished there were more. The only drawback was it was usually only a one-nighter which prevented them from taking a full week at a club which was much better money.

With so much time spent together they still needed time to blow off some steam. Jeff was, as always, the life of the party. He immediately got to know most of the patrons of whatever bar or nightclub where they were working. It wasn't long before the customers were all buying the band drinks and getting them high during the breaks. The parties would usually continue on past the bar to the band house where many were invited to continue to party long into the morning hours. This almost always included Jeff's favorite hobby—sex. Jeff was always rounding up women to bring them back to the house for some fun and games. With the bars closing at two the party didn't begin until three. Bill was usually more interested in just getting high and Mike was fine either way. However, even they sometimes participated but were generally more selective and usually preferred a one on one encounter. But with Jeff, even they sometimes joined in the orgies, and multiple partners—sharing their catch of the night. It was hard to resist as naked bodies often ran through the house in a twisted game of musical bedrooms. It was all Jason could do to keep from getting molested from some of the women anxious to jump into bed with him, but Jeff was sure to accommodate them, making sure they all had a good time. Jeff even used Jason as bait to lure women who he or someone else wanted. Jeff would sometimes take on two, three, or more at a time, resulting in wild orgies or at the very least multiple women which Jeff took turns having fun with. Even Jason got a kick out of it. Jeff really knew how to have a party. These moments of fun were truly happy times for everyone—no inhibitions, no shyness, just complete openness. There was truly a party atmosphere.

On their nights off they were anxious to find new places to play and to check out other bands to see their competition. They were mostly unimpressed with most of these bands and understood why they remained unsigned. Seeing other bands perform did help boost their confidence. They knew that they were as good as most of them. It also allowed them to be critical observers as to what worked and what did not work. Information they could use for their own music and showmanship. It was a learning process, and they were doing their homework.

They had an upcoming gig at Studio 69 on Sunday. This prevented them from taking a full week's work somewhere else, so it was a night off for everyone. These were only one night gigs at a gay bar, but at least they could play their originals. These gigs were Jason's night to shine. It was his turn to take home the tricks. It was all in good spirits and the rest of the band became as comfortable in the gay bar as they were at the straight bars.

"Whatcha guys doin?" asked Jeff as he entered the room where Mike and Bill sat smoking a joint.

"Nothin'," they replied.

"Let's go out and check out the clubs," Jeff said grabbing the joint from Bill's hand. They had worked a long stretch. "Always good to see what our competition is," he said. "I want you to join me in a night out on the town. It'll be a fun evening." Jeff said passing the joint back to Mike and Bill as they sat around the coffee table in the living room.

"I've had enough of your nights out on the town. I get the feeling this is gonna be one of those nights No thanks. The chicks we get from gigging are just fine," Mike commented disinterestedly. "I'm not into hookers. Besides, I know what you are looking for when you go out. Not my scene man."

"No, you got me all wrong this time. Even I need a break sometimes. I've certainly had enough lately. Anymore and I think my dick will fall off. Besides, I think it's important that we check out the competition and check out other places to play. Come on, it'll be fun!" Jeff exclaimed convincingly. "What d'ya guys think?"

"Sure, why not. But no hookers!" Mike exclaimed.

"I have been hearing a lot about this club in Hollywood," Bill stated. "I think we ought to check it out. A lot of the musicians I talk to at Music World think that it's a good place to play. It's called The Underground. It is one of the places where bands that are trying to break into the business play. From what I hear, it's a real rock hangout, with some industry types and a bit of everything else. Perhaps someplace we could play."

"Sounds good to me," Jeff agreed "But where's Jason?"

"Out at one of his gay clubs," replied Mike.

"We'll just have to go without 'im," Jeff announced.

"Works for me. Count me in," said Mike. "Light it up and let's go."

They arrived at The Underground at about nine o'clock, just in time to get settled before the band started. The Underground had been in the heart of Hollywood for years. It had a history all its own. It was a famous hangout for the counterculture—a place where music and politics shaped the new generation in years past. It had been there since the 1950s when it was a beatnik hangout, but had been taken over by the hippies and radicals in the 1960s. It was a coffee shop by day, night club by night, but still mostly a place where the radicals of the day could exchange ideas, solve the problems of the world, and have intense political discussions. They found the name to be appropriate. It did have the air of the underground movement, politically and musically. It wasn't far from the topless place where they had spent that awful evening. And although no worse, it was certainly not much better.

As they entered the club, they were anxious to see what it had to offer as a potential place to gig as well a place to view the competition. They entered the club. It had a true rock and roll feel with posters of bands and concerts lining the red brick walls. A large collection of alternative radical magazines and newspapers, like the Los Angeles Free Press, were on the table in the hallway—all available for purchase.

Simple tables and chairs were on the floor and a bar sat at the far end. It was somewhat trashy but bohemian. It was a throwback from the days when rock and roll itself was struggling as an underground movement and itself a political statement. They had a small menu of food items, mostly burgers, pastries, and the like.

Jeff was having fun as he always did, but he seemed truly interested in what he was going to see that night. This became obvious by his interest in the band about to take the stage as he discussed the equipment and the club with a critical eye.

"Bass, guitar, drums, keyboards—same old line up. But they certainly have some top notch equipment. Just look at that Rogers drum set. Beautiful set of skins and the guitar player has a Marshall amp. I dig his sunburst Les Paul." Jeff continued to discuss the bands set-up.

The lights dimmed and the music started. The band was a loud cacophony of sound—more noise than music even for a rock band. Then in a few moments a shadowy figure entered from the side of the stage. It was a female. She approached the center of the stage. It became obvious that she was the lead singer and the front person for the band. She was extremely thin but sexy with long jet black hair that shined as the light hit it. She took her place right at the front of the stage and prepared to sing. She was like a ray of sunshine bathed in a spotlight on that stage. They noticed her shapely body. She wasn't a real beauty like a model but a beauty in her own right with an interesting look: exotic, sexy, but a bit tough. She used her thinness to her advantage as she slinked up to the stage with skin-tight jeans that looked like she had been poured into them. The slight flare at the bottom revealed small thin stilettos heels. Her top was skin tight revealing small but shapely breasts covered over with a leather jacket that made her look like a biker chick. She grabbed the microphone from the mike stand with confidence and strength and got ready to sing. She tilted her head back and with power and force delivered her first note. The first words out of her mouth left the guys spellbound. She belted out the song. They all looked at each other in amazement. They could not believe that big voice was coming from that small girl. They were impressed. As the set continued, the band didn't seem to be even playing together—no dynamics, no feel—just a lot of noise. They all agreed that the band wasn't good at all. But the singer, she had something. As the set continued she only got better.

The three were mesmerized by this girl's ability on stage. She had talent, poise, stage presence, great looks. Her voice was bluesy yet ballsy at the same time. She could really belt out a song with conviction or bring it down to almost a whisper. She sang with dynamics: pretty when need be, but when the music would crescendo she could really deliver a powerful performance. In addition, her presence on stage was incredible. She was more than a lead singer, she was a front person. During the set she also played a variety of instruments: the guitar, acoustic, or electric; keyboards, and various other percussion instruments. Not only was she a great singer, but she was versatile as a musician.

"This girl can sing!" Bill was the first to comment at the end of the set with agreeing nods from the rest of the table.

"You've got that right," Jeff agreed.

"Man, if only we had a singer like that," Mike stated.

"I don't want no fucking girl in the band." Jeff could see where this was going. "They're nothing but trouble. Remember the last band I was in had a chick singer."

"She'd be fantastic, and I can certainly see her singing our songs," said Bill.

"But what about Mike and Jason?" Jeff spoke with conviction. "You both do a pretty good job of singing now."

Mike responded. "We all know that Jason has a good voice, but I think that we could really use a true front person. It would only benefit the band. It's strange having all the singers stuck behind their instruments, especially Jason with all those keyboards. We really do need a real good lead singer and front person—someone to relate to the audience more and bridge the gap between stage and audience. Ya know, be the link between the band and the audience."

"Well, she is pretty damn good," Bill agreed. "Besides, all the great bands have a great front person. It'd just make the band that much better. I think Jason would be up for it if approached properly."

"I don't mind taking a back seat to a great singer," Mike continued. "That way I can just concentrate more on bass. We'd be a band with great vocals. With her, Jason, and myself we'd have three singers that could sing lead or back-up. And, depending on the song, we could all have our chance to sing lead especially since she does play a variety of instruments. I think it would only add to the group. Besides, I've seen and heard a lot of singers, and this girl has it. Whether she's with us or with another band, she's gonna make it someday. Why not have her on our side?" Mike replied spellbound by her performance.

"It certainly would be an asset," Bill continued, "and worth a try. And with a voice like that this band would be incredible. Besides, how many rock bands have a chick like that as a front person? This band would be fantastic. I agree with Mike. I've seen those bands and singers at concerts, clubs, and in the store. She has what it takes, and she *will* be a star whether it is with us or with someone else"

"Ah shit. She is good. I can see your point. I can see where this is going—seems like I'm outnumbered. Besides, at least I could get laid regularly. She is hot. Why not? Let's see what her trip is." Jeff seemed convinced and now eager.

"Hold on! I don't think that should be the issue. In fact, I'm not sure having sex with one of the band members is a good idea at all. That would be nothing but trouble." Bill voiced his concern. "Besides, we want her for her abilities, not as a whore. You can pay for that on your own. She should be just another musician just like the rest of us."

"Yeah, I agree," Mike stated. They both stared at Jeff in disapproval.

"Yeah, Yeah, Yeah, I guess you are right," Jeff said somewhat disappointed but knowing that this was best.

The band had left the stage for their break. They wandered into the club to see friends or get drinks. Jeff saw her standing at the bar. He immediately went over to talk to her.

"Really dug your performance," Jeff began.

"Thanks," she said. Then she walked away.

Jeff returned to his seat rather aggravated at her attitude. It wasn't long before she walked by the table.

"You've got a great voice and some real talent," Jeff said again.

"Thanks." She continued to walk away.

"Hey, I'm talking to you." Jeff was really getting annoyed at this point.

"Yeah, don't tell me. You're talent scouts, and you want a private performance at your place for an audience of three. I don't perform for small groups." She turned and began to walk away leaving the guys stunned at her attitude.

"Yeah, your certainly have come a long way in your musical career. I suppose the limo is parked outside," Jeff retorted, aggravated by her smart attitude.

The girl stopped and turned. Up close they could see how beautiful she really was. An interesting look: exotic and sexy in her own way. She had dark features which made her look ethnically neutral. She could have been almost any race or mix of races or ethnic groups. Not the girl next door—much too tough for that, but she knew how to make herself sexy and feminine.

"What's your guy's trip?" she asked.

"We're musicians also. We're in a band. We just wanted to let you know how much we appreciated your singing. Nothin' more. I'm Mike, and this is Jeff, and that's Bill. I don't think that's any reason to be rude. We just wanted to give you a compliment," Mike explained more diplomatically than Jeff.

"Yeah, I'm sorry, but being in this part of town you meet all kinds of weirdoes. A girl can't be too careful. The name's Gloria. Thanks for the compliment. I didn't mean to be rude. Just thought you were trying some old lame pick up line like most of the guys I see in here. Are you guys playing around or something or just rehearsing in the garage like the rest of the musicians I meet?"

"No we're working regularly doing a variety of gigs; clubs, colleges, whatever. The name of the band is Hollywood. We do a Top 40 thing for money, and we're working on our original stuff as well which we play sometimes depending on the gig. There's more money right now though in doing cover songs in that club scene. But we plan to get a recording contract eventually and make it big in the business. How tied up are you with these guys?" Jeff was the first to get to the point.

"It's just a gig. These guys are serious, but I'm not that impressed with the band," she answered shrugging her shoulders.

"The band is shit," Jeff said getting right to the point. "You are the only one with any talent up there. You ought to check out our band. We're really fuckin' happenin', and we work all the time. Would you consider doing something good and changing bands?" Jeff asked.

"If this is a job offer, how much does it pay? I'd love to give up my day gig. I hate being a waitress, but for now it is the only way I have of supporting myself."

"Let's just say it's a possibility. I think it'd be worth your while to check it out. It could be a good situation for all concerned," Mike said not wanting to make any commitments just yet. "We like your talent and think you might fit in nicely, but we'd have to see how compatible we all are, musically and personality wise as well. You may have to drop the attitude a bit. As far as money is concerned, it pays the bills and keeps us in drugs well enough. We also have day gigs working at Music World. There is, however, another member we must consult with before any final decisions are made. And I think we should get to know each other a little bit before making any drastic moves. We are all very good friends in the band. The addition of someone else would be a big change for us. It would have to be the right person. I do know that you could handle any of our cover material, but more importantly we're interested because our original material is just perfect for your voice. I think you'd dig it."

"Well it's worth checking out, I guess. One never knows. So where are you guys playing? I'd like to hear what you guys do."

"Well, I think it'd be better to come to a rehearsal."

"Yeah I've heard that one before. No thanks." She again turned and walked away.

"Wait, we are playing a Top 40 gig all next week in the Valley and after that Pasadena. We do play some originals, but mostly Top 40."

"Any gigs closer and mostly originals?"

"Well, we're playing at the Studio 69 on Sunday," Mike shyly admitted.

"Oh, yeah, isn't that that faggot bar? You guys gay or something?"

"Watch who you call gay," Jeff barked. "It's just a place where we can do originals. If you wanna see us do our Top 40 shit we work all the time at those clubs. We're a working band. However, I guess you should know. The other member is gay. He's the current singer, keyboard player, and also one of the songwriters. He's not here tonight. Is that gonna bother you, working with a gay guy?"

"Nah, why should it. Just keep him away from my men."

"Are you here tomorrow night? I'd like to bring him in to meet you." Mike asked.

"Yeah, we're here again tomorrow night, not sure where our next gig is though. Gotta get back on stage."

"We may leave before the end of the set. Hopefully, we'll see you tomorrow."

"I'll be here." She turned and left to take her place on stage.

The guys stayed for the whole next set, mesmerized by this girl's performance. They left before she came out into the audience.

The three left feeling as if they had seen something great, but the question now remained. What and how to tell Jason.

"YOU'VE GOT A FRIEND"

James Taylor

They arrived home to find Jason's car in the driveway.

"Well, I guess now is as good a time as any." Jeff said as he walked to Jason's bedroom and opened the door. "Toss the trick aside. We need to talk." Jeff quickly shut the door then walked back into the living room. "I think he'll be out real fast, and not in the best of moods."

Jason appeared at the door adjusting his underwear. He quickly shut the door. "Don't you believe in knockin', you fuckin' asshole!" He shouted. "Don't you ever barge in on me again like that! I happen to live here too, and I won't put up with any shit from you. It's about time you started respecting my privacy." Jason stormed out of the room and into the bathroom.

"What was that all about?" Bill inquired.

"Oh, I interrupted him and his trick." He started to laugh.

"That *is* pretty rude. No wonder he's pissed." Mike tried his best to hold back his laughter.

Just then a very handsome young man appeared at the bedroom door adjusting his clothing. "I think I'd better go. Tell Jason I'll see him at the club sometime." He left the house. All three burst into laughter.

Jason came out of the bathroom in time to hear the car start then speed away.

"He's gone. He said he'd see you at the club sometime." Jeff said trying to hold back the laughter. He walked over to Jason and put his arm around him to try and smooth out the situation. "Look, I'm really sorry. I just lost my head, even though you sure were getting some." He giggled at the pun. "You're right." He tried to be serious. "It was rude of me. I just got excited about something. Anyway, by now we should have no secrets. You've seen me and the rest of us running around naked, fucking chicks, or whatever. Come on, we're all brothers here. No need to be shy. Tell you what, next time I bring someone home I'll let you watch." He leaned over and in his charming way put Jason in a headlock. "What d'ya think you're hiding. We all know what goes on in there. And boy, it's no wonder you're so popular." He giggled again. Jason turned bright red. "Next time I'll knock harder." He giggled again. He couldn't help getting away from sexual puns. "I mean I'll make more noise, and maybe I can get your attention. Besides, it's hard (giggle) to find you when you're not in bed with someone different. You are almost as bad as I am." He giggled again with a sense of approval. "I know its hard (giggle). I mean difficult. You are like a kid in a candy store, just can't get enough. Believe me; I know what living up to that reputation is like. Ya know, thousands have tried, and none have failed. But it sure is fun trying. You are a horny little bastard and a little perverted, but I like that in a person. Besides, it gives me a challenge. You sure gimme a run for my money. Not sure who has the most notches on his belt, you or me. I think it's all good, so lighten up." By this time they all burst out laughing, even Jason.

"Yeah, I guess you are right. You know that I've fucked almost everyone in that bar." Jason laughed. "It's time I found somewhere else to go. I need new territory, new meat. At least you guys get more variety playing at different clubs."

"Yeah, well, that's kind of what we came to talk to you about. We went out to a nightclub called The Underground. It's a pretty cool nightclub—a good crowd and all original bands. I think we should see about getting a gig there. It's the kind of crowd that would appreciate our music. Besides, it would be nice to get away from Studio 69."

"Sounds good to me. I'll have to check it out," Jason agreed.

"Oh, we will be. In fact, how about tomorrow night?" said Jeff

"Sounds cool."

"But more importantly, we saw this great singer there. It got us to thinking about getting a lead singer. Have you ever considered getting a front person for the band?" Bill cut right to the point.

"We'll uh, no. I must say I haven't given it much thought." Jason was stunned. "I, er, thought Mike and I were doing fine, and that you all liked my singing."

"Oh, you sing just fine, and so does Mike," Bill continued. "Besides, you'd still be singing. Even lead sometimes. But with a lead singer you could concentrate more on your playing. You could be strong back up singers. You are both accomplished musicians, but with a front person it would take away that pressure to try to sing and play at the same time. Concentrate on what you do best. A great front person is a real asset to any band. They relate better to the audience, and they can put on an even better show. It'll also give the band some variety. I think that both of you ought to still have some songs of your own, but if we could get a fantastic singer who could also front the band we could be even better."

"Um, I dunno. I only started singing to help out. How do you feel about getting another singer Mike? You do a lot of the singing as well."

"I think it'd be great, and it would be a great addition to the band. We can all sing, all have our songs, and do some great harmonies. I just dig the idea of a real lead singer and a person fronting the band like Mick Jagger, Roger Daltry, or Janis Joplin." Mike enthusiastically expressed his approval.

Jason could sense that they were holding something back. "But there must be some point to all this."

"Yeah, there sure is. We saw this girl tonight. She's a fucking incredible singer," Jeff blurted out. "I think you'd agree if you saw her. Besides, she not only sings, she plays the guitar and keyboards. She's a real musician. We would have multiple singers in the band. It would be great for variety and great for harmonies. She could even play keyboards at times which would allow you to front the band. Also, she's hot and looks incredible on stage."

"Oh, I get the picture. You found some hot whore you wanna fuck who thinks she can sing. She probably gives great head, and you promised her she could be a star. Nothing doing! Just because she gives good head doesn't mean I have to work with her in the band. Don't you guys get enough when we play for God's sake?"

"No, Jason, you've got this all wrong. She really is fabulous. I mean it," said Bill.

"I just meant that she looks hot on stage. That'll be a great draw for guys," said Jeff.

"Just give her a chance." Mike pleaded. "Come with us to see her. I know you'll be impressed. Besides, we already discussed it—no sex with band members. Right, Jeff?" Mike and Bill stared straight at Jeff.

"Yeah, Right," Jeff responded reluctantly. He felt a bit disconsolate and wrongly accused.

"I see. You are all in this together, a real conspiracy. You are all teaming up against me. Going behind my back. I thought we were all supposed to be honest with each other."

"Hold on," Jeff started a little upset with Jason's attitude. "We haven't been dishonest. This all happened tonight."

"We hadn't even considered getting another singer until we saw this chick. This girl is awesome," Bill interjected

"She will be a star someday with or without us," Mike interrupted.

"She impressed us all so much that we discussed it tonight," Jeff continued. "Just wait 'til you see her. Even I was reluctant at first. I've worked with chicks before and don't really dig it. But believe me; this chick will be worth it."

They all seemed to be talking at the same time with great excitement and enthusiasm.

"This is not just any singer, this chick has it." Bill added. "We just thought she'd be a great addition to the band."

"She could do most of the cover songs. Maybe even make them sound better and different, but more importantly she would especially be great for the original material," Mike stated.

Jason took it all in. He could see how excited they were, and from the hard sell he knew that this singer must be something special. However, all he felt was disappointment and rejection which showed in his face.

Sensing this and feeling that they were ganging up on him, Mike continued. "Besides, we would never have considered anything without checking with you first. And that's all there is to the story—no bullshit."

"Yeah, we'd never go behind your back. This just came up unexpectedly," Jeff added trying to reassure Jason.

"Look," Mike started, "she's playing tomorrow night. We'd like you to at least see her—just keep an open mind."

"We already told her there was another person in the band to consult before making a decision." Bill added.

"We also told her that she would have to audition," Jeff added, "that we'd have to work together to see how it all worked out, musically and personality wise."

"She said that she must see the band before making any decisions," Bill said.

"So we invited her to the club Sunday." Mike said.

"To the gay bar?" Jason asked.

"Sure, why not? Besides, she already knows that you are gay, and she is OK with that."

"You told her already."

"Yeah, why not? You really have to get over this gay thing. It is no big deal."

"I guess you're right," Jason admitted.

"Come on. Tomorrow is a night off," Jeff said.

"If we didn't think this was the best thing for the band we wouldn't even be thinking about it." Mike said

"Just wait till you see her. I think you'll agree." Jeff finished confidently

"Well, I'll think about it!" Jason said rather dejectedly walking into his room only to return a few minutes later fully dressed. "I'm going out for a bit, I need a drink." He turned and walked out the door.

Jason was feeling hurt, rejected, and conspired against as he walked into Studio 69. Sitting on a bar stool he saw the trick that had just left his place only a short while ago. He was already putting the make on somebody else. Jason turned to avoid him and walked to the bar where Chuck, the owner, was bartending.

Chuck and Jason had become close friends due in large part to Jason's continued patronage of the bar, and Chuck's belief in Jason's talent and the band's potential. It was Chuck who could tell him that it was all right and to stop worrying.

Chuck was a man in his early forties: tall, thin, blond hair, blue eyes—a man who in his day must have been a knockout but had withered with years of alcohol and drug use. He had been with his lover for ten years. He had helped him through some of the worst times in his life. The bar, for Chuck, was everything. The success of the bar was a reflection of the way he treated his customers. But for Chuck they weren't just his customers but his friends and family, and the bar was his playground and his home. These were people he had laughed with and cried with and solved the world's problems with. This was his world—his true existence.

As he saw Jason approach looking depressed he immediately knew something was wrong.

"Why the long face, partner?" Chuck began while getting Jason his usual drink. "If it's over that kid, don't worry. He fucks everything he can, a real tramp. Don't let him upset you." Chuck had noticed that both were back in the bar but not together.

"Oh fuck him! I don't give a shit about him. I'd like your opinion about something, and I want an honest answer—no bullshit."

"Sure man. What's up?"

"What do you really think of my singing?" Jason asked.

"It's good," Chuck replied.

"Good?" Jason repeated.

"Yeah, good. And Mike is good also. But neither of you is great. You said you wanted an honest answer. Why'd ya ask?"

"Uh, yeah, I guess you're right. We're not that great. The guys want me to hear this girl singer. They think she'd be a good addition to the band—someone that sings great and can front the band. What d'ya think?"

"I think it could be a fabulous idea if she's good. A great lead singer and front person can be a real asset to any band. I think you should check her out and have an open mind."

"They tell me she's incredible, but I haven't heard her yet. It just burns me up that they went behind my back and talked to this other singer."

"They don't want to replace you. These guys are looking out for what is best for the band, and that includes you. Your importance is not in the singing department. It's in the songwriting and playing department. I think you're being too sensitive. You know these guys believe in you, and they are your friends. Let's face it. They wouldn't be playing here if they weren't." Chuck laughed. "You know they're a bunch of straight guys playing in a gay bar. How much more supportive can they be? You ought to give these guys a little credit. They're sticking by you and your music, and for that you should be grateful. I think you might need to swallow a little pride and see this for what it is—a chance to better the band. So go and listen to this girl with an open mind. And don't be so hard on yourself. These guys are only doing what will eventually be best for the band as a whole."

Just then the three other band members walked into the club. Jason turned around to face them. All three gave him a big hug. Jason tried his best to control himself, realizing his hurt feelings were unfounded. Jeff winked to Chuck in thanks for his support. Jeff had called Chuck to warn him and to ask him for his help and support. Chuck winked back trying to hide from Jason their secret earlier conversation.

"I'm sorry for being such a jerk," Jason said trying to maintain his decorum.

"Oh, you know we're your friends, and we too can have tough times. But in the end we all care about other," Jeff said convincingly.

"Yeah, I know that. I guess I just get paranoid sometimes and fly off the handle. I guess I've been living in my own world a bit lately, but this gay thing is a new world for me too. I think it's time I started hanging out with my friends and concentrating on the important things and forget about getting laid so much."

"Perish that thought." Jeff stopped and laughed." Nothing wrong with getting laid, and as often as possible. I'm all for that."

"But I do appreciate all your support." Jason's voice lowered.

"Ah, we love you too," Jeff said shyly. He put his arms around Jason trying to brighten up the situation followed by the others offering a group hug. "Now fuck off. Let's go see ourselves a girl singer."

"FRIENDS!" Jason exclaimed.

"FRIENDS!" All three responded.

"I AM WOMAN, HEAR ME ROAR"

Helen Reddy

It was with a great deal of apprehension that Jason entered The Underground. He felt he was ready only after he downed a couple of beers and smoked a couple of joints with the guys. It wasn't long before Jason was having a truly good time. They were all cutting up and making jokes. They were hoping this would be a successful evening. They wanted Jason to see that this was going to be the right decision. Jeff was his usual charming and fun-loving self with a roving eye for the women and a filthy mouth to go along with it. Jason wasn't sure if it was the drugs that made this place seem mysterious and seedy, or if it truly was strange. It seemed the kind of place that cheap detectives and hookers hung out in. Even the other guys didn't remember this place as being quite as trashy as it seemed tonight. The place was filled with a wide assortment of people: the usual rock and roll types; a couple of rowdy, boisterous motorcycle types in leather jackets making noise at the bar; and lots of girls most of which seemed like either groupies or ladies of the night with their pimps waiting to sell their merchandise. These were not high class hookers, but real rough trade whores. The place had all the atmosphere of a bad pornographic movie. But it was the trashiness that made it interesting. Jeff seemed to fit right in somehow. He was loud and boisterous, but Jason told himself he wasn't going to be embarrassed by him. Tonight was for fun.

As the band took the stage, Jason felt a bit nervous. He was trying his best to keep an open mind about the whole thing and being with his circle of friends made him feel more secure.

The girl took the stage. He could see her command of the stage. She was thin and quite a looker. Then she began to sing. Just like the others the night before, Jason was stunned. All four sat motionless for the whole set, their eyes glued on the girl. Her voice was strong, forceful, emotive, and confident. Even Jason had to admit that this girl was something special. They were equally impressed with her musicianship when she played the guitar or keyboards, allowing other members of the band to sing. She seemed to have no problem taking the back seat to allow other band members the opportunity to sing lead. But her true strength was in front of the band. When she left the stage all were again impressed. She first made her way to the bar. Jeff noticed her talking to one of the women in the bar. He immediately recognized her as the prostitute they had had the four-way with. He decided to keep a low profile for the moment and ignore the issue.

Then the singer approached the table.

"Hi boys, out for more action?" she began. "Cherry over there tells me one of you is quite insatiable, quite the macho man." She glanced over to the prostitute.

"Wouldn't you know she'd be here?" Jeff acknowledged that eventful evening.

"She told me all about that evening. I should've known it was you. Back for more fun? I'll get Cherry. I'm sure she'd oblige, but this time the rough stuff *is* extra. I hear Mr. Marine is quite well endowed."

Jason was puzzled. "What's she talkin' about?"

"Oh, some whore we picked up and fucked a while ago." Jeff confessed. Mike and Bill turned all shades of red from embarrassment.

"All of you!" Jason was flabbergasted. "You guys picked up a prostitute!" He laughed. "I guess I'm not the only horny one."

"Boy, from what I hear you are one mean mother-fucker," the singer said coyly." She glared at Jeff.

"You sure have a dirty mouth for a lady." Mike spoke out trying to forget that awful evening and attempting to defend their honor.

"She ain't no lady," Jason remarked, sticking up for his friends.

"Who's your charming friend?" The singer asked sarcastically.

"Jason, the other member we told you about," Bill answered.

"Oh, the faggot. I should've known."

"And you must be the whore," Jason barked back. He started to stand up to confront her, but Mike grabbed his shoulder to calm him down.

"So what brings you here tonight?" she asked Jeff. "Another hard on?"

"You know we're here to see you perform. We wanted Jason to hear you sing," Jeff responded trying to change the direction of this conversation and trying to keep the peace.

"Yeah, what time does the donkey show begin?" Jason asked feeling a bit intimidated, a little drunk, and just brave enough to be brazen.

"Look, what makes you think I wanna be in your band anyway?" The girl responded arrogantly.

"Yeah, you have such a fabulous career ahead of you here—that is until your tits drop." Jason cut in.

"Look, enough of this!" Jeff barked. He stood up trying to stop the quickly deteriorating conversation. "We really do think you have a great voice. We would like to see this thing work out. At least come to the club to see what we do. It'd be doing us and you a big favor. Remember—Studio 69—Sunday night. I think we had better leave now guys." He got up to make his exit, motioning for them to leave.

"Didn't we tell you she could sing?" Mike questioned Jason as they journeyed home.

"That woman is a bitch!" was Jason's only comment.

"Yeah, and one bitch in the band is enough," Jeff responded. There was complete silence as they all sat there stunned in disbelief waiting to see what would happen. From the look on Jason's face he was angry. Mike tried his best not to laugh, concealing it under his breath. Finally, he could hold it no longer. He burst into laughter. It wasn't long before they all followed, unable to hide the laughter. Eventually, they were all laughing, even Jason.

"I guess you're right," Jason said. "But she does it our way. I ain't gonna cater to her no matter how great she is."

"First let's see if she even shows up," Jeff said a bit exasperated.

Sunday night arrived quicker than they had expected. When she hadn't arrived in time for their first set they were worried she wasn't coming at all. Unbeknownst to them she did sneak in the back. She hung around the shadows trying her best not to be obvious which was difficult if only for the fact that she was the only female in the club. As the band left the stage, she emerged from the shadows. The face of Mike, Jeff, and Bill immediately lit up as they almost ran over to greet her.

"Glad to see you could make it," Jeff began.

"Yeah, curiosity got the best of me. You are sure confident about this band. Rather cocky really, no pun intended." She laughed.

Jason approached. "Oh, hi," he said rather condescendingly and a bit arrogantly.

"Yeah, I guess I deserve that. But ya know, I get all kinds in that bar." She tried to explain her actions and bury the hatchet. "I never know who's legit, and who's just making a come on. For all I knew you guys could've been a bunch of sex perverts wanting to do strange things. And you may still be that, but I think your music is great. And if the offer still stands, I am interested. I do see real potential." She turned to Jason. "Jason, I know we didn't start out on the right foot, but I think your song writing is wonderful. I'd dig the opportunity to sing some of your songs. That is if you would allow me to." She humbled herself trying to get on Jason's good side.

Compliments and humility were just what Jason needed. "I think that'd be bitchin'."

"Why not come to a rehearsal? We can all check each other out and see if it's a good fit for everyone. We could try the original songs and some of the cover songs we do," said Mike. "See how well we work together. You may also want to come and see us at a Top 40 gig. If it works out we can work on the pop stuff, our original material, and maybe some of your material. But one step at a time. First we need to see if we're compatible musically, socially, and all."

"Sounds good to me. I'm willing to give it a try." She aggressively held out her hand to shake on the deal, offering her acceptance.

"When are you available?' Jeff asked. "We rehearse during the day and gig most nights. We are rehearsing tomorrow."

"That works for me."

"Far out, tomorrow at noon. But I don't even know who you are. What is your name?" Jason asked.

"Gloria, Gloria Fox," she responded. "But let's set some ground rules." She spoke to the whole band "I don't fuck band members, so get any of those bright ideas outta your heads right now. And as for you darling," she looked straight at Jason. "You leave my men alone, and I'll leave yours alone." She grabbed Jason's arm and started leading him to the bar. "But it might just be fun cruising together." She paused and looked around the room. "There sure are some hot numbers in this place. Look at the blond over there. I sure would like to jump between the sheets with him."

"Yeah, he's pretty good in bed," Jason accidently blurted out remembering past experiences. "Oops, didn't mean that."

"Of course you did, darling, and I'm glad to know that you can be honest. I think we're gonna get along just fine." Gloria giggled.

All of a sudden Jason was feeling more at ease. He was enjoying the common interest they both had—the appreciation of men.

Gloria continued. "But I prefer the dark ones. You know the real macho ones like the one over there with the bushy moustache wearing jeans and a flannel shirt. Now he's probably hot in bed."

"You got that right. Unbelievable," was all Jason could say with a big grin on his face. Then realizing what he had said, he turned a bright red from embarrassment.

Gloria laughed. "Honey, I like your honesty. But, it's gonna be hard keeping my promise to leave your men alone. You sure have good taste. And you seem to have had all the good ones in here." She winked her approval.

"Yeah you've got that right, at least any one worthwhile," he said proudly feeling more relaxed, confident, and comfortable. He was pleased that he was able to talk like this with someone—something he could not do with the rest of the guys. As they walked, men were constantly greeting him or walking up to say hello. Jason acknowledged them while he continued to talk to Gloria.

"You seem to have a fan club here."

"Ah, just some old tricks and fans of the band. One of the perks I guess. This place is pretty small. I can't keep my hands off 'em. But once I've had 'em, I'm no longer interested."

"Yeah, I know what you mean, I'm the same way. Gimme a one-nighter any time. I think this one is back for seconds." Gloria laughed as a young man approached Jason to say hello. They nodded to each other, and the man passed. "You seemed to have been with most of the bar."

"Yeah, I guess its time to move on to greener pastures." He was now bragging about his conquests. Gloria seemed to love it.

"Yeah, the old cow in heat," Jeff said. He had overheard the conversation. "You know, thousands have tried, and none have failed."

"Well, you're either irresistible or a great fuck," Gloria said, "but I sure wouldn't mind taking some of these guys for a test drive."

"Jason has been like a kid in a candy store. Once he got started he couldn't stop. I guess he's making up for lost time." Mike laughed. "And boy, have you ever made up for lost time." He winked at Jason.

"Your reputation precedes you," Jeff said. He slapped him on the back giving him an at-a-boy to show his approval.

Jason's face was turning red again.

"Oh, shit, we're just giving you a hard time." He giggled. "Just like what most of these guys have given you."

"Don't worry, we'll all get our own," Gloria said. "I can see that this is gonna be fun. You guys are as big a tramps as I am. I gotta go. See you all tomorrow." She turned and left.

"She's gonna work out just fine," Jason finally admitted feeling more comfortable and at ease. There seemed to be a feeling of true camaraderie in the band and a connection with her. "I can't wait until tomorrow."

Gloria did show up the next day. It did not take long to find out that she did fit right in with the band, musically and personality-wise. After only one rehearsal it only took a few minutes of discussion before they all agreed that this was a perfect fit. She showed up a few days later at the next Top 40 gig. They offered to make her part of the band. She immediately accepted. All were excited about the future. Gloria quit the other band to work full time with them. She wanted to get this done fast. She was anxious to start performing with them.

It only took a couple of weeks for Gloria to learn all the cover songs at least enough to join them on stage. Once she was ready to start performing they immediately integrated her into the gigs they already had booked. They added her gradually giving her more and more of the vocals as she learned the material. She interacted well with the band both on stage and off, allowing each band member to have their moments as well. She took over some of the lead vocals when she could which made the songs sound different but usually better. Having a female lead singer added a whole new dimension to the band. Eventually, they were able to add other songs to their repertoire. It opened up a whole new genre of music with songs by Janis Joplin, Heart, Jefferson Airplane, and Fleetwood Mac. The guys still had songs they sang which allowed Gloria to play one of the many instruments she could play. Sometimes having a female sing a song that had been performed by a male singer made it just different enough that it sounded like their own version of a popular song. So while doing other artists material they were putting their own brand on it that made it sound distinctive and their own. Once she learned the cover songs she was ready to learn the original material which they could perform at Studio 69 or The Underground where Gloria had connections.

It wasn't long before Gloria was fully integrated into the band, and they were playing all the usual places. The energy was high in the band. They all worked hard in arranging the old material and collaborating on new material. All felt the desire to succeed. They thought that they could because they had the musicianship, the songs, and the drive.

The addition of Gloria made all the difference in the world. Even Chuck was extremely impressed when they finally returned to Studio

69. He thought it was a great addition to the band. The belief and dedication in the project made the bond of brotherhood even stronger than it had ever been. They all knew they were on the way to greatness.

Jason arrived home after school excited. "Elton John is playing the Hollywood Bowl. I really wanna see him. I think we should all go. Make it a field trip."

It was agreed, and they got tickets.

It was a month later that they all climbed into the van for their trip to the bowl. They were all excited but especially Jason for he loved the way Elton played the piano and sang, but most of all he loved his music. The Hollywood bowl was just a few blocks north of downtown Hollywood. It was nestled in a canyon on the side of a hill surrounded by the hillside and trees. Though it was only blocks from the city; its remote location isolated it from any other buildings making it almost seem far away, like it was in the country. They walked up the path from the parking lot to the isolated outdoor venue. They entered the open air theater. It was a gentle slopping hill that looked down on the huge stage which was covered with a large band shell in the shape of a series of concentric arches. They took their seats and waited for the show to start.

"This place is huge!" said Gloria. She had never been to a concert there.

"Yeah I think it holds about 17,000 people. The Los Angeles Philharmonic plays here in the summer, but they have some rock and other shows as well. Check out the box seats down in the front section. Pretty cool, huh."

The lights dimmed, and the show began. The opening song was "Saturday night's Alright for Fightin'", an up-tempo rock song. About halfway through one sole spotlight shined on Elton at the piano as he performed his hit "Our Song." He performed songs from the albums <u>Elton John</u>, <u>Tumbleweed Connection</u>, <u>Madman Across the Water</u>, <u>Don't Shoot Me I'm only the piano Player</u> and <u>Goodbye Yellow Brick Road</u> including "Levon," "Rocket Man," and "Candle in the Wind." Elton was magnificent. It was a well-paced show with both mellow songs and up-tempo rock songs. Not only did he play the piano, but he was truly a showman. They watched him prance around the stage in his outrageous outfits working the audience and interacting with the band. It was very exciting.

"That was a fabulous show!" Jason exclaimed.

"Yeah, he really did put on an incredible show!" Gloria agreed.

"He really knows how to work the crowd," Jeff added. "I think you could do the same thing, Gloria, just in your own way. You are really good at it, you just need to work on it some more."

"I agree," Mike interjected. "You have a wonderful voice and good stage presence. I think you could be great like him—a real show person."

"I'll keep that in mind," she said. "I think this was a good lesson for us all. We can all add more showmanship to our show."

"Yeah, you are right," they all agreed.

"DON'T YOU WANT SOMEBODY TO LOVE"

Jefferson Airplane

Mike got them a gig at a club near the beach. The Surf-rider was on the borderline of Venice and Santa Monica about 15 miles west of Hollywood. Santa Monica and Venice are beach communities known for their beautiful wide beaches and blue sparkling ocean. Mountains lined the coastline to the north which stretched to Malibu and places beyond. Many famous streets that begin in Los Angeles end at the Pacific Ocean in Santa Monica, streets like Wilshire Boulevard, Sunset Boulevard, and Santa Monica Boulevard. Venice, just to the south, was designed to be like its Italian counterpart complete with canals. Santa Monica and Venice had been the beach where Los Angeles played. It was especially popular at the beginning of the 20th century but had since lost some of its luster, especially Venice which now had a large population of drug addicts and counterculture people.

In Santa Monica, a pier stretched out into the ocean for the sports fishermen or the romantic wanting to see the sunset over the beautiful Pacific Ocean. People would flock there to avoid the heat and take in the cool ocean breezes offering some relief from the hot California summer.

The beaches had been popular ever since early times. There was once a street car that ran all the way through the city from downtown Los Angeles through Hollywood and Beverly Hills then ending in Santa Monica. It was the original beach city. One could almost visualize Frankie Avalon and Annette Funicello running around the beach throwing a beach ball like in some beach movie, with Gidget frolicking in the surf. Venice had a long strand, a sidewalk, right on the beach with shops and restaurants. It also had Muscle Beach, a hangout for body builders which offered many types of weights and gym equipment where they could do their work out in the California sun, showing off their muscles for anyone who wanted to watch.

The area proved to be so popular that an amusement park was built there which extended right out over the water. Pacific Ocean Park had been a thriving amusement park in the 1960s designed to compete with Disneyland, but it closed in the late sixties due to poor attendance. Now, years of neglect made it more of an eyesore. Although most of the pier and surrounding area had been burned out by suspicious fires, a few buildings and landmarks remained including a small section of the pier, a couple of rides like the merry-go-round, and a few souvenir shops. The burnt out pier had become home to many homeless people, mostly burnt-out drug addicts and street people

They approached the club in the afternoon to do their sound check for the week-long engagement. The Surf-rider was in one of the few remaining buildings at the pier. It was creepy to see the old carnival style building which had fallen into disrepair with the burnt out pier surrounding it. Store fronts lined the row of buildings, all empty now with many of them simply burned out from fire. Faded or half burned faces of clowns, rides, and other circus type pictures were on the fronts or sides of these macabre buildings. To the west beyond the buildings was the Pacific Ocean where beautiful beaches stretched as far as the eye could see. The Surf-rider was a rock club which catered to the beach crowd—a rowdy bunch, heavily into drugs and partying. It was an interesting mix of drug addicts, beach bums, surfers, and real beach people many of whom would come out of the woodwork to listen to music and drink from money they had made panhandling or selling drugs. It was by far one of the strangest clubs they had ever played, but it was a good and enthusiastic crowd. Jeff liked the tanned beach bunnies, but even Mike and Bill thought they were hot. Gloria and Jason liked looking at the boys—all tanned and muscular. Some were surfers and many hung out at Muscle Beach. But unlike Jason, Gloria could touch and play and did so whenever possible. Bill simply liked the drugs. The band was widely accepted. It proved to be a great place to learn to work the crowd as this crowd was responsive and ready to have fun. It was like a party every night. They were hired for a week but were brought back many times due to the fact that the owner truly liked the band, and they were popular with the patrons. After playing there a couple of times they developed their own crowd, and their own groupies, both male and female. This was one of many clubs throughout the city where they were beginning to develop a following. It became one of the many clubs that was part of their circuit.

It was a typical night at The Surf-rider when Gloria met a young man. It wasn't unusual for Gloria to meet someone and take him home. She fit right in with the band and their attitudes especially regarding sexual freedom. She often picked up guys when the band members picked up girls. She was as promiscuous as they were—like one of the guys. On this evening, she saw this boy staring at her while she was performing, but she too was interested in him. He looked very young, barely twenty one; blond, thin, but well-built with a surfer's body. He was probably one of the body builders that worked out on muscle beach. He was wearing a skin tight t-shirt and tight jeans showing every curve and muscle of his body. It was pure physical attraction. They were immediately drawn to each other. She went up to him at break time and introduced herself. His name was Brad. He seemed very shy unlike the usual rowdy boisterous crowd at the club, and not really Gloria's usual rough trade type. Although he wasn't the smartest guy she had met, he was handsome enough, but the more she looked the more she could not take her eyes off of his tight well-defined body. He was hot, and Gloria had to have him. They got along so well that she took him home that night.

Brad was at the club every time they played, waiting like a stage door Johnnie. Many times she went home with him or invited him to her house. It seemed fun and harmless. Over time he became completely enamored with her. Unbeknownst to her he eventually fell madly in love with her. Gloria liked the guy but certainly wasn't going to get involved. It wasn't long before his persistence was getting boring.

Then one night she left with someone else, leaving him alone.

The next night he was there waiting when she arrived.

"Uh, Can we talk?" Brad asked.

"Yeah, what's on your mind?" she asked.

"I, uh, saw you leave last night with some other guy. I can't believe you went home with some other guy when we mean so much to each other. I want you, and I, uh, love you. Without you my life is meaningless—"

"Hold on." She stopped him from continuing. "Where is this coming from? Look. We had fun. We went home together a couple of times. And while you are a great fuck, you are still just a trick. Nothing more."

"But we made love, and it was beautiful," he protested.

"We fucked, but that is all it was," Gloria said realizing this was almost like a teenage crush. "We didn't make love. I am sorry you have them confused."

"I don't believe you. We did make love," he insisted.

"How can you be in love with me? We only fucked a couple of times. Love takes time and getting to know someone. I think there is a big difference between love and sex. I don't think that the two necessarily have to be one and the same thing. In fact, as far as I'm concerned, they have nothing to do with each other. I love lots of people I don't have sex with, my friends for instance. For me, sex is something I do when I feel the urge. Although it can at times be emotional, for the most part it's purely physical—a way of enjoying oneself. Love is a profound emotion that develops over a long period of time—not after a great fuck. Perhaps if we got to know each other it would develop into love, but come on. Let's call a spade a spade. You are in love with the idea of love. We fucked, and that was that. Nothing more, nothing less."

The boy started crying in the club. Gloria grabbed him, led him out the back door, and onto the deserted beach. The sand was warm from the afternoon sun and the moon was shimmering on the water.

"But I do love you!" he exclaimed between the sobbing.

"Look I'm sorry it turned out this way. I didn't mean to hurt your feelings, but there's no sense in lying about this. Sex, I think more than anything, can stand in the way of a relationship. It's much easier to have sex with people we don't know than people we do. Having sex with people we already know can screw up whatever relationship there is. I love to have sex with a stranger—the thrill of the hunt, the mystery of what that person is like in bed. It's all very exciting and erotic, but it is not love. What you love is the illusion—not me. You don't really know me. All you know is some fantasy of me that made you feel good a couple of times. But that's all in your mind. It's not real. How can one feel love after a one night trick? Even after a couple of times. How can you love someone you don't even know? I don't love you and never will. But it was a lot of fun. So thanks for the fun. Why don't you be a man and forget the whole thing? Just chalk it up to a great time. Can't you understand what I'm saying?"

"Yeah, but I do feel that special love you talked about—with you—and I do love you. And I know we can work something out. Can't you understand my feelings?" he said trying to contain himself.

"I could see how you might have strong feelings towards me. We did have a great time and great sex. But I think this is only an infatuation. It takes me a long time to love someone."

"Couldn't we try to be lovers? Give it some time at least."

"This affair is going nowhere. Even if I did love you, I haven't got time for this sort of thing. My lover is my music. I'm married to my career, and the band members are my brothers. This is what I'm dedicated to. I have no time to nurture a relationship. It wouldn't be fair to you or anyone else. It just isn't in the cards at this time in my life."

"Will you come home with me again tonight after the gig?" he pleaded.

"Under the circumstances, I think that would be unwise. I don't wanna give you any false hope."

"But I still think it was emotional. You're just denying it. I could tell the way you were in bed. It was more than just sex. It was a beautiful, emotional experience."

"Yes I will say it had some emotion in it—pseudo-emotion. I love to pretend I'm making love. But it wasn't real. It was some mating dance like something out of a thirties movie: love, passion, the music swelling, and Fred Astaire dancing away with Ginger Rodgers. It's all part of the game, part of the fantasy, part of the fun, and part of the enjoyment. It is just not real. I'm sorry you misunderstood."

"The only thing I understand is that you're a whore and a bitch." He was now beginning to get angry. "You play games with my emotions; then toss me aside like an old shoe which has lost its use. I had thought you really felt something for me. That you had emotions, but I find you are a cold, callous, unfeeling, thoughtless bitch with no concern for the other person. I don't think you have any love in your heart because you're too busy fucking to know what real love is. You are just too self-centered to have a real relationship. I think it's your fantasy, your selfish gratification, and your illusion, making me into something I am not. Creating an illusion for yourself, with no concern for me. In the end, I get treated like just some old piece of meat. There only for your pleasure and fantasy. I think I *am* being realistic about the situation. You're just too afraid to admit it. I think I do mean something to you even though your pride or whatever won't allow you to feel these things. At least I'm honest with myself about my feelings and not living in some fantasy land where people are merely objects for one's pleasure."

"Yeah, and I assume you were a virgin too. Come on. Picking up someone in a bar is not grounds for a relationship. Grow up. This is the seventies. I think we had better not see each other anymore." She turned and walked away, a little upset at what had just been said.

Jason, who had overheard part of the conversation, approached Gloria. "Are you OK? I heard what happened. You seem upset."

"I'm Ok"

"Let's talk. I'll meet you at your place for a nightcap after the gig," he said.

"Sure, why not," she agreed.

Bill and Mike had gone home to go to bed and Jeff had met some chicks at the bar and was going home with them.

Jason arrived at Gloria's apartment. She had kept her own apartment even though she was seldom there except to sleep, opting not to move into the band house. She was on the second floor of a three story brick building in Hollywood, not far from the band house. It was probably built in the 1940s. In its day it was probably quite nice but had since become a bit run down, although it did have some charm. It had a definite Spanish look to it with curved arched windows, terra cotta roof, and some ornate tile and wrought iron work on the front. It was either mission revival or Spanish revival architecture or perhaps some sort of combination of the two. It had a small front yard with grass and large mature trees. The lobby had high ceilings with wood beams, wood paneling, and an old dusty chandelier hanging in the center. A terra cotta stairway with a wrought iron banister led to the upstairs with Spanish style lamps on the walls lighting the way. The apartment itself was rather large with large rooms. The high ceilings made it seem even more spacious. The doorways and walls were curved at the top which made it seem even more interesting. They whole room had furniture that could almost have been antiques had it been of a decent quality but was probably just from the thrift store. An old sofa and coffee table sat in the middle of the room. A bookcase housed a stereo, TV, records, and books. A worn out oriental rug covered the wood floors. A few antique style lamps and a few plants to make the place a bit greener finished the look. Overall, it was well kept and tidy.

Jason passed the bottle of tequila then lit up a joint as they sat in Gloria's living room. "Sorry about what happened between you and Brad. That must have been tough."

"Oh, he'll get over it. I'm just not into having a relationship right now. I just wanna' have fun."

"I overheard what you said. I really think we have a lot in common. I feel the same way as you about sex and love. But, it's odd hearing it come from a woman. Most people, but especially women, are more like him, wanting security and a permanent relationship. It always seems

OK for a man to be promiscuous. You know, sow his wild oats and all that. But, it's different for a woman, at least for most of society. I guess that's why gay guys are so promiscuous, because they are guys, and they can, and it's OK. I also believe there is the distinction, a big difference, between sex and love. I like 'em both. Sometimes they work together, sometimes not. For some people, sex should accompany love. I like sex without love. I guess that's why I'm able to have fun. Why do people always confuse sex with love? Love is very emotional, sex is just physical. Besides, you know how this band is—anything goes—and you've certainly seen me in action. I can be a real slut. And then there's Jeff. He's getting laid all the time. Talk about sex with no love."

"Yeah, it's always OK for guys. You're all such assholes."

"Wait a minute, what d'ya mean by that? I think there's nothing wrong with you playing around."

"I guess I shouldn't blame you. But men especially straight men can be such assholes!" She was drinking heavy now and feeling no pain. "I get so tired of being called a whore because I like to screw. For a man it's OK, for a woman she's a whore. I think this double standard stuff sucks. Why can't we enjoy it as well? You know what I mean?"

"Yeah"

"But that wasn't what upset me. He made me think about me getting involved with people, and something did hit home. It has to do with how I connect with people. It comes from my past." She seemed anxious to open up.

"What do you mean?" asked Jason.

"You see, I grew up in a military family. Dad was a navy man. We traveled all over the world. I had to learn to adapt to all kinds of situations. It was sort of like being a chameleon. You learn to fend for yourself. It's often a fight for survival. I became very good at adapting, you know, always being the new kid in the neighborhood. He was always being transferred, so I moved around a lot. That meant new friends about every two years. No matter how many times we moved, I never got used to leaving my friends. So my best defense was not to get too close—to keep my distance. I just wanted to be liked. I think it sort of hit me tonight with what he said."

"But why do you think all men are assholes?"

"Oh God! I shouldn't tell you this, but that has to do with my first sexual encounter. As I said, Dad was a navy man. He was a good father and a good husband to my mother. As a father he was very strict, but he treated me like I was special. I was Daddy's little angel. It was like one of those military movies. The military is very disciplined, very strict, and very regimented; so the men are as well. So much so that sometimes they just need to blow off some steam. I don't mean that my dad was an angel. He did his share of carousing with his buddies, drinking, and brawling. But he never did anything bad to Mom or me.

Anyway, one night I was home alone. First, I heard loud voices. Then, when I looked out the window I could see three of my dad's buddies staggering down the road. I knew immediately that they were drunk—three drunken sailors just home from shore leave and getting a bit crazy to blow off some steam. The next thing I knew they were at my door. They forced their way into the house to wait for my dad. I didn't think too much of it because they were my dad's friends and had been there often. Well, they found a bottle of whisky and proceeded to get even more drunk. They started getting playful which led to getting touchy. It all seemed so innocent at first. They were being kind of fatherly and nice to me. I was sitting on their laps and stuff. I was just too young to realize what was happening. Then they started touching me in my private places. I tried to get away, but they were too strong. Pretty soon they were holding me down and taking off my clothes. Then one of them pulled his pants down. This was the first time I had seen an erection, and it scared me. Then he put it inside of me. I was petrified. They all had their turn raping me. I was so young. I didn't even know what sex was. I was only twelve. I'll never forget how frightened I was, and how violated I felt afterward. It felt as if someone had seen right through me. I was stripped of any dignity. I felt dirty and disgusted. After they had finished, they all suddenly realized what they had done. They started to panic. I could see it in their eyes as they discussed what to do with me. I told 'em I wouldn't tell anyone what had happened and acted as if it were nothing. I was so brave. They told me that if anyone found out, I was dead. I told 'em no one would ever find out. As soon as they left, I burst into tears. I must've cried for about two hours. I bathed to try and cleanse myself, but no matter what I did I still felt dirty."

Jason was shocked. He passed the bottle of tequila then lit up another joint. "Fuck, what a story."

"I guess since then I never wanted men to have that much power over me. I assumed that that's what men wanted, so I gave it to 'em. You can't steal what's being given away. It was all about power. I learned that it was a way to get what I liked and be popular with the guys. I had already been violated, so why not. It was another way of surviving. Get in with the tough guys by fucking one of 'em and you're safe."

"Well, what happened? Did ya ever tell your parents?"

"No, I left home at a rather early age. Things changed. My parents, especially my dad, were very conservative. As time went on we just grew farther and farther apart. He became more right wing and conservative, while I became more wild, radical, and liberal. It got worse as the radical '60s happened. I think he was reacting to the whole thing which was against the way he believed. We just didn't see eye to eye on politics, race, religion, and a number of other issues. You know, he became one of those "America, love it or leave it" kind of guys. He even joined the John Birch Society. You know that ultra conservative right wing group. He was always talking about the communists, and how they were taking over America. I think he became rather paranoid. Probably stemmed from his military training and the people he associated with. He hated the hippies and everything they stood for and called 'em all commies. He hated the new morality and free love and all those radical ideas. He hated the blacks, Mexicans, and anyone who was not white. I remember during the race riots he'd sit in front of the TV screaming out 'kill the nigger' and stuff. I think he became very afraid that the America he knew, the conservative America, was changing, and he wanted it back. He was always religious, but he became more extreme. He was always trying to push his views onto everyone else. He became one of those self-righteous Christian conservatives who think that the whole world should be the way they think it should be according to their interpretation of the Bible. He longed for the simpler times—a time when people got dressed up and were more respectful. A time when communities were segregated. And life was like the cover of Life magazine or some Norman Rockwell painting. I think he had good reason to be scared. America was changing. It was not the same place. I just thought it was changing for the better, but he thought for the worse.

Besides, I had grown up. I was no longer Daddy's little angel. I guess I rebelled against him and his strict up-bringing. I became a wild, radical, tough hippie chick. He thought women should be subservient to their men, and Mom was certainly that. But I thought women should he equal and be their own person. I believed in women's liberation. The restraints and restrictions became too much for me. I could never live up to what he expected me to be and definitely couldn't agree on his beliefs, attitudes, and politics. One thing he did teach me was to be independent and to speak my mind and stand up for myself. Well, it sort of backfired on him. We started to argue all the time. The fights and disagreements got worse. He even slapped me a couple of times, saying I was being disrespectful. Then one day he threw me out of the house. He told me that while under his roof I was to abide by his rules, and if I didn't then it was time for me to leave. It was his house, and he would be respected. I just had to go. I just couldn't take it anymore. I left and I never went back."

"Wow, sounds fucked-up. Where did you go?"

"Well, I had nowhere to go. I met some bikers, and since I would put out they let me join their motorcycle group. I became one of their biker chicks. At least they took care of me. Eventually, I worked my way up to a Hell's Angels gang. Boy, did those guys know how to fuck. I decided I wanted to be satisfied, and they knew how to do it. Besides, they didn't care if I wasn't pure. It was also a kind of family. It was all about power, and I learned a lot about power from them. Eventually, though, I grew real tired of being subservient, so I left. I have a rather strong will, thanks to my dad, and it was time I did things for myself. It took some time, but I finally convinced myself that sex was OK for women also. It had been a way of acceptance and of power for me up to that point. I guess I kind of went the other way. I had experienced that power, and I wanted to be in charge. So I began treating men as they had treated me in the past, you know like a piece of ass. I guess I do that, but shit, men don't care. I became a strong supporter of women's liberation and kind of a radical feminist I guess. I wanted women to have equal rights and to have power as well."

"What happened to your Dad?" Jason asked.

"He retired from the military. He had become a bitter and angry man. Last I heard, he and Mom settled in Texas, near Dallas. I talk to Mom occasionally. She's not as severe as he is. She always tried to be the peace maker. But it'll take time to heal our wounds. I miss the old dad that I knew when I was growing up, not the one he has become. In some way, I'll always be Daddy's little girl. I guess I would someday like to make him proud of me. Maybe someday I'll return. But who knows? I sure wish I could find a man like the one I knew growing up—a good man with good, honorable qualities. He may not have been perfect, but he was kind and considerate—a real man. He always treated me and Mom well, always provided for us, and took good care of us. I'm not sure if that's just my perception or if that really is the way he was. I'm not sure what changed in him, but in the beginning he *was* a good man." For a moment she grew quiet and thoughtful, almost in a haze. Finally, she spoke softly. "I guess I really do wish I could find someone like that." She bowed her head for a moment and sat in silence. She then looked up and became lucid again. "But perhaps that is just a dream. Good men are hard to find, so for now I'll settle for a hard man, they are good to find also." She giggled trying to lighten up the conversation that she realized had become very heavy and intense.

"I surely can agree with that. But I don't think you should preclude a relationship from sex, I agree sex and love are two different things. They can coincide. And when they do, it can be beautiful—a mixing of the pleasures of the body with those of the soul." Jason found himself opening up to feelings he had long had but had never admitted. "I do also agree that sex can fuck up relationships. I guess that's why I'm so trashy and prefer one night stands. My friends are separate. Even those people I have sex with often become just friends after the sexual desire fades. But when you can find love and sex and friendship; that to me is a fulfilling relationship—something we should all look for. I thought I had it once, but he ended up being straight. That seems to be the story of my life.

But you shouldn't feel strange about screwing a lot of guys. I think it's bitchin' and liberated. I don't think women should be afraid of their sexuality either. They should be able to express it instead of worrying about some old taboo or customs. Shit, I spent too much time in the closet worrying about that."

"Right on, I agree. But there is something in me that wants to be accepted by men—and wants to be appreciated by men. In one sense it's acceptance and in another sense it's power. I call it pussy power. I use it quite well. We'll have to go out and pick us up a couple of guys sometime."

"That would be cool."

"And don't worry; with me around we'll get our share. We certainly won't starve. Don't you just love the power of sex? I can see we're gonna be great friends. I'm glad we had this time together. I think we're two of a kind."

"I agree."

25

"SCHOOL'S OUT"

Alice Cooper

The band continued to work fairly regularly all over the Los Angeles area. They had been aggressive about finding new venues to play, and it was paying off. Most importantly though was the addition of Gloria. Everyone, especially the club owners, remarked on the improvement they saw with her now in the band. Even the band had to admit she was a real asset. The band sounded and looked better than ever. They all knew that she was at least partly responsible for them working so much. They had to give her credit for helping them get more and better gigs. They now felt complete.

"Man, after rehearsal we gotta check out this new Pink Floyd album." Mike entered the main room of the band house holding up an album. "It's called <u>Dark Side of the Moon</u>. But first, we'll have to smoke a joint. Get us into the mood. Let's get rehearsal over with so that we can check it out. You won't be disappointed. From what I've heard it's really bitchin'."

Mike noticed Jason who was sitting there with his nose in a book studying while the rest of the band was just hanging around waiting for rehearsal to start. "Hey, aren't you graduating this semester?"

"Yeah," Jason responded.

"Well, congratulations." Mike patted him on the back. "Quite an accomplishment."

"Yeah, I'll be glad when it's all behind me. It's a shame you quit before getting your degree. You'd be graduating as well."

"Yeah, but what was I gonna do? There was nothin' there that I wanted to pursue as a career. You know I really only want to be a musician. Also, one of the main reasons I went to college was so I wouldn't get drafted. I had to maintain my student deferment so that I could get out of the military. Since there's no longer a draft, there seemed to be no need to keep going to school. Also, I dug the politics, but that scene has really died. The war is over and most people lost interest in the other causes. I guess like most others I lost interest in politics too. I think the smarter leaders finally saw that the best way to bring about change was to do so by entering the system and changing it from within. Even many of my friends and other political activists that I knew in Berkeley are working at or became attorneys, businessmen, or politicians themselves. I saw many of 'em ending up no better than the ones they had revolted against, and therefore, no better replacements than their predecessors. I guess I just became disillusioned and disinterested and gave up any interest I had in politics. I felt that I had to pursue my musical dream full time. So, when is the graduation ceremony?"

"In June."

"I'll be there." They all agreed to attend Jason's graduation. "Who else is coming?"

"My folks are coming out from Atlanta." Jason continued shyly." Hard to believe isn't it?" He passed the joint. "I hope you all can make it too. I told my parents about the band as well. While they're here I also want them to see us play."

"It's hard to believe that we met so long ago at that rally," said Mike.

"Yeah, The Campus is a lot quieter now, said Jason.

"Things sure are different." Mike rolled another joint.

"Let's get rehearsal done so we can check out this album."

They finished rehearsal and went into the band house. They passed the bong filled with weed around a couple of times and put on the new Pink Floyd album. They sat silently—listening intently as the album played, each in his own world, thinking of the time that had transpired.

It was a beautiful spring day. The campus quad was now filled with graduates in their caps and gowns and proud parents, families, and friends all there for support. It seemed only yesterday that it had been filled with police in riot gear and students in protest—but time had passed. It was graduation day. Jason had finally completed college He was graduating with a bachelor's degree in music. The entire band was there to show support for Jason's accomplishments. Mike was there even though he felt a bit awkward since he had decided to leave college before completing his degree. A decision he hoped he would not regret. Jason's family had even come out for the graduation. Mr. and Mrs. Tucker and his sister Debra were all there to show their support and to offer their congratulations.

"We're so proud of you son," said the two beaming parents as they approached Jason in his cap and gown after the ceremony had finished. Mr. Tucker was dressed in a conservative suit and Mrs. Tucker in a nice print dress complete with pearls, high heels, and gloves, with her handbag dangling from her elbow. It could have been a scene from Leave it to Beaver or Father Knows Best.

"Thanks, I'm glad I finally finished. It was a long road, but at least I now have my degree in music."

"Yes, we are happy that you pursued your dream, and that you did end up with a college degree. We hope you use it well." Mr. Tucker shook his son's hand. "Perhaps you can get a job in the music business playing in an orchestra or in doin' movie soundtracks or something."

"Actually, I have a surprise. The band I've been telling you about is playing this weekend. I can't wait for you to hear us. I think you'll be impressed. I think this is what I want to do, play in a rock band."

"That would be lovely, dear. We'd love to hear the band. I guess you are serious about it, although we were kind of hoping you'd get a job in music playing something different and using your training. We thought you'd be playing classical music at some symphony or some other orchestra somewhere, or at least a Broadway show. Perhaps even movie scores. But I guess this rock and roll thing is what the kids are buying these days. Whatever makes you happy." His mother gave him a big hug.

They were very proud that their son had gotten his degree in music and glad to see that Jason was pursuing his goal of being a musician, however, this was not what they had really expected.

"There's the band now," he said as they approached. "Let me introduce you." Jason made introductions between the band and his family.

Jason's parents invited everyone to lunch, so they all went to celebrate this eventful day. Jason's parents picked up the bill even for the band members. The band returned to the band house, while Jason went to spend some time with his parents at their hotel.

"There's something else I must tell you," Jason started shyly with his head down. He knew that this would be the hardest thing he had ever done, but he thought that this would be a good time to put everything out on the table since he knew that they were proud of his completing college.

"Oh, what is that dear?" responded Mrs. Tucker.

"Well, Um. I'm gay."

There was a complete pause. The silence seemed to last forever.

Finally, the mother spoke up. "Well, this is certainly a week of surprises. When did ya discover this?"

"I, uh, guess I've known all along. I just wasn't sure. But now, with all that's happening, I can be myself. I know that I must be a disappointment to you, but this is really who I am."

Mr. Tucker walked over to his son and looked him directly in the eye. "Well son, your mother and I have actually wondered about this quite a bit. We've talked about it a lot. It certainly does go against our beliefs and teachings, especially with the church. We weren't sure what to do and how to take it."

Jason was ready for the big speech and the big rejection. He felt the gnawing in the pit of his stomach as he readied himself for the worst.

Then an extraordinary thing happened.

Mother took over. "We certainly do not understand it. However, we decided that no matter what, you are still our son, and we love you."

Jason was stunned.

"Son," the father continued, "we just want you to be happy. I think that you must've had a very difficult time growing up knowing that you were different from other guys. Do you think it was something we did? Where did we go wrong?"

"No, not at all. It is just the way it is. Certainly do not blame yourselves. You were wonderful parents."

"Well, we will accept you. Any way you are. It'll be a bit difficult for us to understand, but we'll try our best."

"But please remember that we love you no matter what," Jason's mother reiterated.

Jason was taken aback. He had expected disappointment and rejection, but acceptance was just not what he anticipated.

"Wow, I thought you'd be disappointed in me."

"We are very proud of you son. Of course we'd prefer that you not be gay, but it is your life. We will accept you any way you are. You are our son, and we love you."

They both gave Jason a big hug to show their acceptance.

"Thanks," Jason said with tears in his eyes. "Thanks for understanding."

Jason was very pleased. He had graduated, he had told his parents his deep dark secret about being gay, and told them about the rock band.

The parents did get a chance to see the group play that weekend. They sat quietly listening to the band play. They were pleased that he was able to pursue his goal even though it was not what they had planned on.

After the first set, Jason approached his parents. "So what d'ya think?"

"Well, it's not really our type of music. Not Lawrence Welk." Mrs. Tucker could see the disappointment in Jason's face. "But it's not as bad as I thought it would be. You are actually quite good, not just a bunch of noise that I usually hear with this rock and roll stuff. We think you're wonderful. We're just happy that you can pursue your dream and do what you want."

Jason perked up as Mr. Tucker continued. "Besides, we know that you can always get a job teaching or something else later if you want. But if you prefer to pursue this musical career we wish you the best. Now is the time to pursue your dreams. Do it while you are young."

Jason was glad his parents had been so supportive about his career choice and his gayness. It was with sadness that he said good-bye to them the next day.

For them all this seemed like the end of a chapter and the beginning of a new one. It was time to move on to the next step in their lives and careers. They finally had formed a great line-up of musicians and talent. Hollywood was a great band. They were all working more than they ever had in music and felt like real professional musicians. They all shared a wonderful openness, camaraderie and closeness with few secrets. Mike and Jason felt like they had come full circle with Jason's graduation as this was in fact how they met and where the spark of starting a band began. With graduation over, Jason was relieved he had finished college which was a major accomplishment in his life. Also, he had come out to himself, to the band, and to his family. Mike felt he was part of one big family, something he always wanted. Bill felt at home with the closeness of his friends and was able to get high. Jeff was comfortable with everyone, felt a particular closeness to them all, and was able to get laid as much as possible. Even Gloria felt accepted, like this was her family. They all had their careers in mind and felt they were on the right path. They felt their lives were ahead of them, and they looked forward to it with great anticipation. Their spirits were high as they looked to the future.

PART II

"TAKIN' CARE OF BUSINESS"

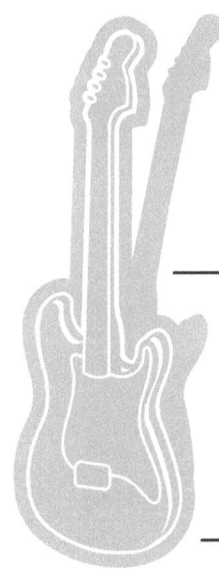

Bachman
Turner
Overdrive

"FEELIN' STRONGER EVERY DAY"

Chicago

It was a typical night as they played their set with songs like "Brown Sugar" by The Rolling Stones, "Come Together" by the Beatles, "Listen to the Music" by The Doobie Brothers, "Rocket Man" by Elton John, and "Whole Lotta Love" by Led Zeppelin. They were at The Office near downtown Los Angeles, but it could have been any number of clubs they had been playing lately. The crowd was somewhere between receptive and disinterested, but there were many people dancing as they played. A collection of girls sat eyeing the male band members, and a couple of guys were eyeing Gloria. They were all anxious to meet the musicians in hopes of a sexual encounter. Each was vying for their pick of whom they wanted. The band, of course, was usually willing to oblige. The whole scene was like a mating dance played out for all members. This seemed to be their nightly routine.

It had been quite a while now since they had added Gloria to the band. They kept themselves booked as much as possible because now there were five people to support on their income. It took some work and some hustling, but they were working fairly regularly, and they made almost enough to support themselves. They hoped for the day when their lives would become completely involved with the band. Being in the band was not just a job or a career, this was a life style. Between gigging, rehearsing, and working, it was a grueling schedule, but one they felt would pay off.

They had all hoped by now that they would have a record deal, but that hadn't happened. They wished they could at least have been able to give up the day jobs; but it gave them some security, a regular paycheck, and something to fall back on when times were tough between gigs. Jason was able to pick up more hours at Music World now that school was over in addition to giving lessons. Gloria continued to work as a waitress at a local coffee shop during the day but hoped to quit someday soon. She lived on her own and had to support herself. Besides, the perks and benefits made it worthwhile, and at least the hours were flexible.

They also thought it best to keep the connection with Music World just to keep current on what was happening in the industry and to get the discounts on equipment that they were constantly buying. The discounts they received allowed them all to buy new equipment or add to what they already had. Jason was able to buy a synthesizer and a Hammond B3 organ which added greatly to the sound of the band. Bill and Mike added new electronic devices, and Jeff added some drum pieces to his set. They also invested in a decent PA system and microphones which they could use for rehearsals as well as the clubs or gigs that didn't furnish one. They were able to buy additional equipment to fit any size gig. Because they had extra equipment and a whole other set up, they did not have to tear down everything every night. They could leave the equipment set up in the club and use the other equipment to rehearse with during the day.

They were usually working in Top 40 nightclubs five or six nights a week doing five or six sets a night. In addition they were also picking up a few gigs on the college circuit, casuals, and an occasional one-night gig playing originals. They had a large repertoire, and felt they could play anywhere. They could even integrate some of the originals into other sets including some Top 40 gigs. This allowed them a greater variety of gigs and venues. They were playing all over the city. They had become a working band and professional musicians.

The band Hollywood was getting its name known as a good club band. They were beginning to develop a following especially at the clubs they frequently played. By returning to the same clubs, they would always draw a crowd which the club owners loved. The more they worked and the more popular they became, the more money they would make. They enjoyed their popularity. At least they were a working band, and they were supporting themselves. There were plenty of nightclubs to keep the band busy—clubs like The Shore Leave in Long Beach, the Surf-rider in Venice, The Office in Los Angeles, The Garage in the San Fernando Valley, The Student Union in Westwood, and Rock Creek in Pasadena. Many of the clubs seemed so similar that they could hardly tell the difference between them from one week to the next. They only varied in small ways. However, the band had to approach each club differently to suit the clientele and the club owner. Some were small, seedy, and tacky while others were larger and a bit nicer. Some were rock clubs where the band was able to really rock out. Others were cocktail lounges where they were just a replacement for the jukebox and had to play quietly. But all were just nightclubs for playing other people's music. At least they were good at it. They repeated the same songs and the same sets night after night with little variance, but at least they were playing.

Playing in clubs had its own perks. Musicians had a reputation. They were considered to be mysterious and exciting, and known for their sexual prowess. Everyone knew that musicians were easy, unattached, and not looking for relationships which made them perfect prey for one night stands as they may never see them again after their engagement. It was like anonymous sex; no attachment, no commitment, just fun. During their breaks they would grab a beer, smoke a joint, and meet their future encounters. Jeff, who seemed to enjoy it the most, took advantage of it whenever possible. There seemed like an endless supply of girls available at every club, a plethora of females to choose from—all available and ready and willing for their enjoyment. Girls as varied as the clubs themselves: some sleazy, some classy, and of every description and type imaginable: tall, short, thin, buxom, blonde, black hair, white, black, or any ethnic group you could imagine. Gloria also had her pick of willing and available guys. And with the new sexual revolution, even Jason occasionally met some guy who was available—willing to try something new, or claiming to be bisexual. But these were seldom. Many times he had to thwart off the advances of the women or would play the decoy for the other guys rounding up chicks for them to take. It was a bit sneaky, but all in fun. All in all they were all willing participants. Most evenings ended up with a sexual encounter of some sort for some.

Of course the evening usually included drinking and drugs. Smoking a joint between sets was fairly routine and a good way to meet people and to keep the party going. They had given into the routine with the same music, same party, same sexual encounters, and same drugs; just different cities, clubs, and people. It was a repetitious schedule, but one that they all enjoyed. It was in fact fun—sleazy clubs, sleazier women. Even with the routine of it all, they did find that they were having a good time and doing what they loved to do.

Many musicians considered playing Top 40 a cop out and not truly artistic. However, the band found that there were some advantages to playing cover songs. It allowed them to try new things: musically and on stage for showmanship. They could throw in an occasional original song mixed in with the cover tunes to see what kind of reaction they would get. They learned what it took to put on a great show. They could really work on getting their act together without fear of getting the wrong reputation. It proved to be a valuable learning tool. Also, it allowed them to be working fairly steadily, playing music on stage almost every night as opposed to only once every two months which is about how often they got gigs at Hollywood original showcase clubs. They became more and more comfortable on stage. It was not just a one-time shot. Besides, they did need to make money, and since the showcase clubs paid so little, at least they were making money playing. Their reputation in the music scene in Hollywood as an original band was very important and playing out of town seemed the perfect solution.

Playing cover songs itself also had it advantages and allowed them valuable learning experiences. Musically it was teaching them how to play well together, how to write a good song, and what made a good performance. Playing great songs from great bands like The Beatles, The Who, The Rolling Stones, Jethro Tull, The Eagles, Steppenwolf, Fleetwood Mac or whoever had a hit song on the radio had its own reward. They learned a lot about how to be a successful show. Playing a variety of styles and music types allowed them to improve on their vocals and their own playing as they copied other musicians' music, riffs, and parts. They also concentrated on the song itself to figure out what made a hit single. There was a reason why some of these songs were big hits, and they wanted to learn the formula without sacrificing their artistic integrity. They learned that sometimes it was not so much what they played, but what they did not play. They needed to become a band, not four soloists showing off their abilities. They worked hard on writing, rewriting, refining, and trying new things to make each song better. It was a real education in music, for while they were all good musicians, they needed to become and sound like a band. They needed to write songs that made sense, songs that could be hits, not just a big collection of musical ideas. In playing a lot of styles they were able to discover what worked best for them. This allowed them to develop a sound of their own—distinct from anyone else.

But most importantly, they maintained their ultimate goal of becoming recording artists. They wanted so much to be an originals band performing their own material, to get a record deal, and be a recording and touring band. They did their best to book gigs where originals only bands performed. But these were few and far between with only a few nightclubs and an occasional college or other gig. And they seldom paid very well. However, these gigs were their favorites. It gave the band a chance to perform their own material. It also allowed them to observe audience reaction to ascertain what worked and what didn't work. These were perfect places to experiment.

In Hollywood, they only played at clubs where they would play their original music. It was only out of town away from the music business that they would play top forty or at top 40 clubs—never in Hollywood. They did not want to be known or get a reputation as a cover band in the music capitol of the world. They wanted to be known only as an up-and-coming rock group. A strategy they were hoping would pay off. Because there were only a few of these clubs, it was difficult to get bookings. They continued to play mostly small alternative concert clubs like Studio 69, The Underground, and a few others. Except for a few college gigs, these were the only places where they could really be the original band they longed to be. The gigs were usually only one-nighters for little money as opposed to a full week engagement at the Top 40 nightclubs. But at least it was a start. The larger, nicer ones were even more difficult to get bookings. The wanted to get booked at the more prestigious clubs like The Whisky, The Troubadour, Gazarri's, or Starwood. These were the real industry clubs. But, these clubs were not interested. They had to first develop and build a following. These clubs wanted bands with an immediate audience or a record company backing. At these clubs, record companies would often showcase or introduce a new band or promote a new record. The companies would often pick up the tab to fill the house with industry people, fans, and press, or at least furnish a good advertising budget to foster a buzz for the curious.

It was not uncommon during this time for the band to be rehearsing as many hours as possible. This all depended on work and school schedules. They also spent extra time practicing individually or in groups working out individual parts, vocals, or new songs. This was a time of hard work, serious musical challenges, and intensive rehearsals. There were many differences of opinions which were often discussed at length and at times erupted into major disagreements, but in the end they would come to an agreement or majority rule. It was the creative process at work. There was a wide variety of musical tastes, influences, and expertise. With all of their input, the songs became better and better. Although Jason and Mike were the main songwriters, they all were involved in writing songs. They all had their say in the final product. Since they were all involved, whoever wrote most of the song would take credit for it as the songwriter even though the final product was a collaborative effort. Other times it came down to a matter of degrees with two or more being the songwriters. Sometimes they worked in groups with someone doing the lyrics and someone else doing the music or any number of combinations and variations.

When it was completely a joint effort, they all took credit for writing. They would start out with an idea or a jam that eventually turned into a song or even part of a song: perhaps a bridge, hook, verse, transition, or chorus. It was all about making the song better. All in all it was the creative process at work.

Jason had the classical and compositional training. He loved classical music from Bach to Mozart to Beethoven, but was influenced mostly by more contemporary composers like Stravinsky with his wild and powerful music, Copeland with his dynamics and attention to song, and Gershwin with his use of jazz themes. He saw how these could be applied to rock in the same way that Jethro Tull, King Crimson, Yes, Moody Blues, Procol Harum, and Emerson, Lake and Palmer had done. While he brought many songs to the band, his strong point for the band was in arranging the songs. He and Mike worked together a lot and were the strongest contributors to original material.

Mike was well grounded in the more basic solid ground work set forth on the bass. He was a rock and roll aficionado. His favorites groups were The Rolling Stones and The Who, but he liked many other rock groups as well. But, he was also influenced by some good rhythm and blues with a very solid back beat like Sly and the Family Stone or Earth, Wind, and Fire. Of course he liked the simplicity of The Beatles. He wanted to make sure the bottom was there and solid, and that he and the drummer played as one—like groups such as Cream, and Jimi Hendrix. His strongpoint was in keeping a simple song format with verse, chorus, and bridge, and perhaps a lead. For Mike it was all about the song. He understood the rock format for writing a good song. Mike came up with many finished songs or collaborated with anyone.

This only helped complement Jeff who was influenced by major soul or rhythm and blues groups like The Temptations and James Brown. He always gave a strong back beat and just knew what would make each song work. He was a hard driving drummer who really gave each song a strong and solid foundation.

Bill had been influenced by all the great guitar players. His rock heroes were Jimi Hendrix, Eric Clapton, and Jimmy Page. But he was well founded in the blues which were his roots with perhaps a bit of jazz thrown in for good measure—people like B.B. King, Muddy Waters, and Chet Akins. He was always coming up with a great guitar riff or guitar rhythm that would fit the songs and the band, and even came up with some of his own that became songs.

Gloria's influences had been the songwriters, where song and lyrics were most important. Artists like Cat Stevens, Carole King, Joni Mitchell, Simon and Garfunkle, James Taylor, Elton John, Billy Joel, and The Beatles were her greatest influences. She wanted songs to tell a story and would often write lyrics that did just that. She was a true poet, and her songs lent themselves to be truly poetic and lyrical. She would often rely on the others for the music, but since she did play instruments, she had a repertoire all her own as well.

Together they needed to make this combination fit, and somehow it did. All in all, they learned that the song was the most important of all. No matter how good the musician, if the song wasn't there it just did not work. They knew that it was only through their ability to write good songs and perform them well that their dream of becoming an original signed recording and touring band would eventually be realized—making good music was their ticket. They all had the dedication. They felt that it was only a matter of time before they hit the big time. Hollywood was working hard to fulfill their goal.

"SURF CITY, HERE WE COME"

Jan and Dean

"**M**an, it's fuckin' hot." Mike walked into the room fanning himself from the summer heat. "What d'ya say we all pack up and head to the beach for the day to cool off?"

"Sounds cool, I'm off today, and we don't have a gig tonight." Bill looked up from rolling a joint.

"What about Gloria?" Mike took the joint, took a hit, and then coughed.

"Er, let's just make it a guy day," said Jeff. "I wanna check out the chicks, and she cramps my style." Jeff took a hit then passed it.

All nodded in agreement.

The guys packed up the van with stuff needed for a day at the beach and were soon on their way. They decided to drive down to Hermosa Beach, one of a number of small beach towns that Los Angeles was so famous for. Hermosa was about thirty miles south of Hollywood, but it seemed like a different world. It was located in the South Bay area of Los Angeles. Although only a 30 minute drive from the band house in Hollywood, it was very different in its look and attitude.

It was a beautiful day as they arrived at Hermosa Beach. The sun was shining as they drove into town on this warm summer day. The cool ocean breeze coming off the blue waters of the Pacific Ocean offered much needed relief from the inland heat. They got out their beach towels, a cooler with drinks, sun block, and other essentials. They found a place in the sand very close to the Pier. Hermosa Beach was all about sun, surf, and sand. There was a wide stretch of beach that separated the town from the water. In the distance along the horizon sailboats filled the ocean waters. There was a long pier on which people walked or fished. It divided the beach into two sections. On one side, surfers caught waves. On the other side, people were frolicking in the surf, swimming, or body surfing in the cool ocean water. It truly represented the California dream.

As they settled into their place on the sand they noticed the many sights, sounds, and smells of this beach community. The beautiful California coastline stretched for miles in both directions. The warm California sun shined brightly on the Pacific Ocean—the sunlight dancing on the blue waters. Waves crashed along the shoreline pounding the beautiful white sand. The roar of the surf, the laughter of the people playing, and the call of seagulls created a symphony of sounds. In the background "California Girls" by The Beach Boys was playing on someone's transistor radio. They laughed. It seemed so perfect to hear surf music, and it only added to their experience. A group of children was laughing and playing in the sand while others were splashing at the water's edge or looking for seashells. Some were making sand castles while others threw beach balls to each other. A bunch of sand volleyball courts lined the area at the top of the beach where young guys and girls mostly in their teens and young twenties played a friendly game, their tanned muscular bodies glowing in the afternoon sun. Nearby a group of guys was throwing a football while not far away another group was throwing a Frisbee. The salty smell of the ocean and the scent of suntan lotion permeated the air. Everyone seemed to be enjoying themselves. It seemed like vacation.

"This reminds me one of those beach movies or one of those Beach Boys songs. I could see why they wrote about it. I bet they used to come here." Jason laughed just as "California Dreamin'" by the Mamas and Papas played on the radio. "This certainly is the California dream."

"Anyone for a walk? I'd like to check out this town," Bill said as he got up.

They left the sand of the beach to explore this idyllic California beach community.

They approached the picturesque town rising on the hills beyond. A short wall separated the warm sand from a long sidewalk called The Strand which extended out on both sides. Lining The Strand were small beach cottages, hotels, and apartments with nothing over two or three stories. All had large patios, lots of windows, and sea view balconies looking out over the sand and ocean. Most were filled with crowds of young people laughing and partying—hot young girls in skimpy bikinis and shirtless muscular guys. The strand was obviously where people hung out, or generally enjoyed the beautiful weather—but mostly checked out each other.

"We oughta write a song about this." Mike's head was swimming with ideas as he looked out over the ocean, the waves, the beach, and the happy people. "Maybe call it 'Life is a Beach.' Make it sort of a fun party beach song. Very up-tempo."

"Sounds cool," they all agreed.

They returned to the center of town. As they walked along The Strand, Mike noticed some posters advertising up-and-coming bands for a rock club located right in town.

"Hey guys, check it out. They have a rock club here called Pier 11. It might be a cool place to play."

They all agreed to investigate. They returned to Pier Avenue. This was the focal point and the main street in the center of this small town. Pier Avenue was so named because of the location of the Pier at its end. It was lined with surf shops, beach shops, restaurants, and fast food places—all related to the beach culture. As they looked back toward the ocean, Pier Avenue seemed to extend on to infinity as the street turned into the Pier which extended out over the ocean with no end in sight on the horizon. It was quite an illusion.

They found Pier 11 about a half a block from the beach on Pier Avenue. It was a small club, but it looked fun.

"Here it is. Let's go for a beer and check it out," said Jeff as he walked in the front door.

Pier 11 was a typical beach bar with a nautical theme. Surf boards stacked in the corners hid the aged wood planks. Fishing nets, oars, life savers, shells, and stuffed fish lined the walls with other fishing gear to make it look like some old fisherman's cabin. It was a long thin room with a small stage at the far end.

They entered the club, ordered a beer, and introduced themselves.

"Nice club. Who's the owner?" asked Jeff as he paid the bartender.

"That would be me," answered the man who had served them the beers. He was tall, blonde, tanned, and wore a Hawaiian shirt and shorts. He looked like an aging surfer.

"I see that you have bands play," commented Bill.

"Yep, almost every night." The owner put the money in the cash register and got out some change.

"Well, we're in a band. We've been playing mostly in town and in the valley, but this looks like a cool place to play. How do we get a gig?"

"Monday night is audition night. You come play a couple of sets, and if I like you I bring you back for a week. I just happen to have an opening this Monday. No money in it, but if I bring you back I can give you the door on weekends and a base rate for the other nights. It all depends on how many people you bring in. Ya interested?"

"Yeah, that'd be bitchin'. We have Monday night off," said Jeff to the owner, and they had set up an audition.

They returned that Monday to audition. They played the whole evening. The audition went well, and the owner liked them. It was just the kind of party band he had been looking for. He agreed to book them for a week-long engagement. They worked out a week when he had an opening, and the band was available.

They returned about a month later and played the week. If daytime was all about the sun and the beach, the nighttime was all about the party. At night, the beach was still busy, but the small town really came alive with the numerous night clubs and restaurants. Girls and guys wore little more at night than they did during the day. All were dressed in sexy attire trying to attract the opposite sex for an evening of pleasure. Although the stage and club were small, the enthusiastic and receptive crowd made up for it. It suited them perfectly. Every night seemed like a party. It was a fun place to play and a great addition to their club circuit.

It only took them a few gigs to develop quite a reputation and a following at Pier 11. People returned to hear this great party band. The band loved the crowd, the crowd loved the band, and the owner loved the band for bringing in customers. With the band bringing in good crowds, the club owner did hire them on a fairly regular basis since this meant money for everyone. It quickly became their favorite place to play. Even though it was only a top forty gig, it was a fun crowd, a great gig, and they loved to hang out on the beach during the afternoon before the gig. It was like they were on vacation. It was the California dream. It was a wonderful way to relax, meet the locals, and even promote the band. It was also an excellent time to discuss the matters of the day, changes in songs, set order, and their goals for the future.

The sexual revolution was in full bloom here. Night or day there was a constant parade of people. Hot chicks wearing very little, showing everything they had to lure the hottest young guys. They would prance around as if on the runway of a swimsuit competition in hopes of luring the hottest catch of the day. The guys were like sharks looking for some action from the more than willing girls of the beach with the chicks being easy prey. Sometimes it was hard to tell who the shark was, the girl or the guy. They were like proud peacocks doing a mating dance with everyone displaying all their best assets in an effort to attract someone. All were good looking and hot and horny for each other. Everyone was checking out the prospects for a fun time. It was certainly consensual and mutually gratifying. It was youth personified

Best of all though was the attitude of the town. It didn't take them long to discover that this was really a party town especially with its mostly very young crowd. Beach all day, party all night, and the best drugs in the city. It seemed all people did was drink, get high, or look for someone to hook up with. They fit right in and were often invited to parties before or after the show. It seemed like life at the beach was always a party.

It was a particularly hot summer evening at Pier 11. It was the weekend, and the club was packed as the band played their set. The still evening air was thick with lingering smoke which created an atmosphere so dense it was almost like being underwater. The loud pounding music and loud voices only added to the ambiance. They were in the middle of playing a high energy set which was being enthusiastically received by the audience who reacted positively to their music with dancing, applause, and shouts of approval. Sweat was pouring off Jeff's body as he played even harder, stimulated by the energy and feedback of the crowd. Suddenly, in the back of the smoky room he saw a figure enter through the door which he thought he recognized. As the man went to the bar, Jeff was sure it was his old Marine buddy from Viet Nam. He got his drink, faced the stage to check out the band, and stood there watching them perform. Between songs Jeff waved with excitement. He finally caught his attention. This was someone he hadn't seen in many years. His friend excitedly waved back and sat at the bar to wait for the break time of the band.

"How the hell are ya!" Jeff yelled while approaching his friend after the set.

"Couldn't be better. You're sounding good up there." The man ordered him a beer. "How long ya been in L.A?"

"Quite a while. We've been gigging around. You live around here?"

"Yeah, not far."

They talked for the whole break, catching up on old times.

"So, what d'ya do here now that you're outta the service?" Jeff asked during one of the breaks.

"Uh, mostly drug dealing. I sell to the locals and run some drugs for other dealers around town. You know, it pays the bills and keeps me with pocket change. Look, how about you and your buddies come by the house after the gig for some good smoke."

"Sure, why not. I'll check with everyone else to see if that's OK." Jeff agreed. "Come on, I'll introduce you to the band…. Hey everyone, this is Frank, Frank Barcelona." The other members were gathered round the bar waiting for their drinks. "He has invited us to his place after the gig." The bartender set up the drinks on the bar.

"Drinks are on Frank here!" the bartender exclaimed.

The group acknowledged the offer and thanked him for the drinks. As the evening continued, he never let the band pay, but always picked up the tab and had drinks ready and waiting when the set was over. Each time he pulled out a huge wad of cash to pay for the drinks. They wondered where he got his money since he obviously had bucks. They found him to be generous, charming, and a fun guy to hang around.

Frank was a good looking man of Italian decent. He was average height with dark hair and dark brown eyes. He was wearing shorts and a shirt open to reveal his hairy chest. His dark tan gave him the look of a real beach guy and a man of leisure who spent his days on the beach and his nights at clubs.

The band went to Frank's after they finished their last set. It seemed like a good way to cool down after the gig. They arrived at his place just after two. Since they were playing at Pier 11 tomorrow there wasn't much tearing down of the equipment. It was a typical beach house, just a short block from the beach itself. The ground floor was the garage which put the rest of the house upstairs. Two stories of large glass picture windows offered a great view of the now black ocean with only the lights from The Strand and the pier visible. It had high wood beam ceilings that soared overhead. A fireplace sat in the corner next to the windows. The large deck ran the whole front of the house and offered wonderful views of the beach area.

Frank rolled a couple of joints and started passing them around, two at a time. The evening proved to be a marathon of drugs, for Frank had everything imaginable and in large quantities.

"I'm getting pretty fuckin' high," said Jeff. "This is some good shit."

"Yeah, only the best. It's from my private stash, not the usual shit I sell on the street," said Frank.

"You still deal this shit?" asked Jeff.

"How the hell else do ya think I can afford all this? I don't work or anything. I just deal. It has proven to be very lucrative, especially here at the beach. It seems everyone wants to get high down here. This is a party city."

"Yeah, I know what you mean. We have certainly found that to be true as well," agreed Mike.

A good time was had by all. Frank initially spoke to Jeff about their Viet Nam days, while the band carried on about their sets that night, and if they should perhaps change the order of some of the songs. They tried to pace the sets to take the audience on a journey. Pacing was everything. They also discussed the crowd. The guys couldn't believe all the hot chicks while Gloria and Jason were checking out all the hot guys. Most importantly, they discussed their career. It was obvious to Frank that these people were serious. They had dedication, drive, and enthusiasm. Frank immediately was drawn to the commitment and energy he felt from these musicians.

Frank became quite a regular of the club, always showing his support for the band whenever they played there. He even went to see them at some of their other gigs. He usually arrived at most of their gigs with a good supply of grass to entertain them on their breaks. When they did play at Pier 11, he oftentimes invited the band, his and their friends, and anyone else they met to his place afterward for an after party with plenty of drugs and booze to entertain the guests and to get a good buzz. He even had them over to his place before the gigs to enjoy the beach. Then they could shower and get ready at his house before the gig.

The band learned that Frank was the main supplier of drugs to the whole of South Bay, and many of his drugs made it into the Greater Los Angeles area and all over Southern California. He dealt in large quantities of marijuana, cocaine, LSD, hash or whatever was available. He sometimes would buy pounds of coke, thousands of tabs of acid, or pounds of pot at any one time for distribution throughout the city.

The band was introduced to Mark and Pete, two of Frank's friends who seemed to be around a lot. They helped Frank in his drug dealing operation and were a permanent part of his entourage. They were two druggies that loved to get high. Their long hair, jeans, t-shirts, and tennis shoes made them look more like stoner drop-outs into drugs and parties than anything else. But they were nice guys, and always very complimentary.

Frank enjoyed hanging around the band. They always seemed to draw a good crowd of partiers which also made for good connections for Frank who was able to get new clients through them.

Frank and Jeff spent a lot of time together reminiscing about the old Viet Nam days. They talked about all the whores and drugs that helped make their life bearable; but also about their black marketing activities—prostitution, dealing drugs, but mostly selling military supplies which were in such demand. Apparently they had quite a good business going which made them some extra bucks. Military goods were at a premium in Nam, and they knew how to make the system work for them. Fortunes could be made with the right attitude and connections, and it seemed Frank had made the most of a fairly bad situation. Buying and selling black market goods in Viet Nam had proven to be very lucrative.

Frank had been impressed by the unfaltering conviction of the band to make it big. It was the major topic of conversation. The band began to trust Frank's unbiased opinion and criticism. They were all becoming good friends.

It was a typical after-gig party at Frank's. He had invited the band and whomever they wanted to invite, Mark and Pete, and some other friends back to his place for some fun and to unwind. It wasn't a large crowd, but enough to make it fun. Jeff and Frank had met some girls. They were waiting by the side of the stage at each break and eventually for the end of the show. Gloria met some guys and asked them to go party. The guests arrived first with the band not far behind.

"We think your band is great," one of the girls said coyly as the band entered the apartment.

"Thanks," Jeff said. He lit up a joint then grabbed a beer, trying to unwind from the gig.

"This band is gonna be famous rock stars someday," Frank said as he made his move toward one of the girls. "Don't you agree?" he questioned not really expecting an answer. He put his arm around her and grabbed the girl for a big kiss and a quick feel.

Bill was busy smoking a joint, while Jeff was busy trying to get the girl to take her top off as he grabbed her breast.

Mike had struck up a conversation with one of the girls and was having a real deep conversation. Eventually, he held her hand to show his affection.

Everyone was having a wonderful time smoking, drinking, and doing drugs. Many found partners to hook up with and left while others just left due to the late hour. After a while, only Frank, the band, and their guests and potential conquests were still there.

It wasn't long before Frank had escaped to one of the bedrooms with the girl he had been putting the make on. Soon groans of pleasure emanated from the bedroom, while Jeff's girl just giggled as he put the make on her.

"Not here in front of everyone," she said. But Jeff didn't seem to care; in fact he seemed to quite enjoy being the center of attention. He showed no shyness when, after he excused himself for the bathroom, he re-entered the room with no clothes on and a raging hard-on which he paraded about like a proud peacock—a symbol of his masculinity.

At this point, Mike grabbed the girl's hand with whom he had been having this deep conversation and left to go outside to the patio, not wanting to be any more embarrassed.

"Um, let's check out the beach," he said. He led the girl out the door and down the stairs to The Strand.

Jeff seemed to want everyone to join in—in one big orgy, but Mike wasn't interested. Mike seemed to be trying to have a more affectionate one-on-one type relationship. On his return, he made it to the second bedroom and made his most earnest attempt to make love to her as if this were really a relationship, even though he knew it was only a one-night stand.

Bill had escaped to the kitchen to get higher, followed by the one girl left who had been trying to make passes at him all night even though he was not interested.

It wasn't long before Frank emerged from the bedroom unclothed and sweaty, looking for a beer. The room was empty except for Jeff who was sitting naked with one of the girls servicing him orally. Frank sat down and lit up a joint.

The girl stopped for a minute, but Jeff pushed her head back into his lap. "It's OK. We're like brothers. We share everything." This allowed Frank to make his move. Frank motioned to Jeff to go to the bedroom where the other girl was waiting for his return. Jeff left to find the girl in the bedroom waiting. It was his turn to take her for a test drive.

The girl in the bedroom was quite surprised to find Jeff instead of Frank, but it soon didn't matter.

In the meantime, Jason and Gloria were busy entertaining the two guys on the deck that Gloria had invited to the party. As a result of their busy schedule, Jason had gone for weeks without the ability to get to the gay bars to get laid, but with Gloria there this might be his lucky day. Once stoned, and after viewing the ongoing activities, these men were getting obviously hornier and hornier. It just took Gloria to get it all started. She left with one of the guys leaving Jason alone with the other. Now that they were separated and the guy very stoned, Jason made his move. Once alone and under these stoned and drunk conditions with all the sexual exploits surrounding him, it would've been difficult for even the straightest of men to not get turned on. Without realizing it, the boy soon found himself involved in a sexual exploit with Jason. After all, no one was there to see, and he probably didn't even realize what was happening.

Once Gloria had finished, she returned to see that Jason had also just finished. She gave him a wink. Jason took the cue. He proceeded to the bedroom to find the other man lying naked on the bed.

"That was hot," he said thinking it was Gloria again. Without a word, Jason proceeded to orally service the guy while he moaned in ecstasy. This continued until he reached down. Much to his surprise he did not feel what he expected to find.

"What the fuck is going on? I ain't no faggot!" the man jumped up only to fall over from his drunkenness. "You're not Gloria!"

"You didn't seem to mind a minute ago. Besides, no one will know. I won't tell, and I'm sure you won't. So just lay back and enjoy." Jason replied and went right back to the job he had been previously performing. The man was just too drunk to care or to fight him off, or perhaps even fully realize what was in fact going on. Besides, it did feel good. For Jason it was exhilarating for it made the thrill of the hunt more exciting and the conquest even more of a prize.

Long into the night the energy from the gig wore down helped by their sexual gratification. The evening lasted into the early dawn hours, but eventually everyone left except the band. The band and Frank reconvened in the living room to talk about their evening. Everyone had a big laugh.

"Gee, I think this is gonna be alright," Jason said.

Everyone agreed with a passing grin on their face before completely passing out.

Frank fit right in with the group. He was just as uninhibited as they were. He loved to party and always had the best drugs.

Frank's house became quite the party house whenever they played the South Bay. It was fun, and for Frank it was good for business. There were always plenty of people, new and old. This was after all the beach area where everyone was looking for a good time, and it was certainly living up to its reputation. All were hoping to get high at the very least, and possibly get laid.

It was a hot evening at the beach club when Frank asked the band to his beach house the next day for a band beach day. It was a night off for the band. Some relaxation and a good old fashioned buzz seemed the order of the day, and Frank surely had what seemed an endless supply of drugs. They arrived early. The band arrived just as three guys in suits were leaving. They got into a large black car and sped away.

"Who was that?" Mike asked when he got in the door.

"Just some of my business associates, nothin' that concerns you." Frank replied.

This day though seemed somehow special. The band had played particularly well the night before. Everyone was excited and still talking about their performance, trying to analyze what made it work. They sat on the deck of Frank's house with a beautiful view of the ocean, watching the sunset after a day of fun and frolic on the beach. Frank entered with cocktails. He thought it a good chance to celebrate, so he brought out his private stash: the best pot, some excellent hash, and his own coke just to keep the buzz going. He wanted to speak to the band privately, so he had asked that only the band come to his house on this day.

Frank lit up a couple of joints then started passing them around. "I've asked you here for a reason. I wanna discuss something with you all. I've been watching this band for quite a while now, and, as a representative of the average public, I think this band has a lot of potential. I really like this band and think it is going to go far. What I see that this band needs most is good management—an outside businessman that knows the ropes, can give good sound advice, take care of business, and work on getting you a record deal. Someone to handle all the boring business details so that all the band needs to do is play, create, and concentrate on your music. Let me get to the point. As you all know, my income comes from dealing drugs. I'd eventually like to become more legit and have a regular income made from legal sources. But in the meantime, I have to make a living. I would like to manage this band. I have the time since drug dealing does not take up that much of my time, and I would like to give it a shot. What do you get out of it you may ask? I think I have a lot to offer After all my black marketing and drug dealing experience, one thing I have learned is how to be a good negotiator. I know I can sell anything. I am in a position where I have a fairly good supply of money which is all made by illicit means, so I also have money to invest. I can bankroll the band. I think the investment will eventually pay off. What do I get out of it? I've always wanted to be involved in music, mostly because I really dig music. Also, this seems like a good way for me to get new clients, and will also help in laundering the money I do make.

Also, I've been talking to Jeff. He tells me what a great bunch of people you are. I think we all get along great, especially after some of those parties. I really like the way you guys interact with no inhibitions, no problems, and no secrets. I could really get into this and this whole life style. I would really like to be part of all that, and I do think that I fit in.

Finally, and perhaps most importantly, I see the drive and dedication you all have. You take this very seriously. I believe in this band probably as much as you believe in yourselves. I know that what you really want to do is break into the big time and get a record deal. I realize I have no experience in that field, but how different can it be from what I already do or have done—just different people. I know I can be a good manager. I can operate with the same enthusiasm in business as you do with your music. I think that it's about time this band started doing something besides these clubs. Started getting seen by the right people, do some studio work, make a demo, and get some better equipment. After all, you're as good as all the rest of the albums I hear. The only difference is that you don't have a record deal. I think it's about time someone started pursuing that aspect, and I'm your man. I'm willing to invest some money, take care of business, work on bookings, shop for a record deal, and give this band the chance it really deserves. If nothing else, I can keep you supplied with drugs." Frank laughed. "That ought to be worth something. I think it could be a winning situation for all."

The members looked at each other, a little taken aback by his unexpected offer, but a little enthusiastic about having someone book the gigs, take care of business, and really get their career on the move. They could see how persuasive he could be, and how he could take charge of a situation—all which worked in his favor. There was a little uneasiness with Jason which Frank immediately sensed.

"Look, I know this has become a family for you all. I'd like to be a part of that family. There will be no secrets. You all know what a black market drug dealer I am. I like a good screw occasionally. Jeff is a complete letch. I can sense the sensitivity in Mike. I think Bill is a cool guy but probably has a long history of drugs and perhaps drug abuse and must watch himself. Gloria I think can be a tart. I know Jason is gay and I'm cool with that. I'd be here for you, to help you with your problems and issues, and to avoid or at least mediate internal problems.

"IT AIN'T EASY"

Three Dog Night

Frank took the job of manager very seriously and was good at it. He was a real hustler and kept them booked as much as possible. He started by contacting the clubs where they had already played, but was also getting some new bookings as well. They were working more and more now that Frank was taking care of that side of the business. It was a relief having someone handle all the details. In addition to getting them bookings, he found out all the particulars, took care of the money with the club owners, made sure the band was there on time, and in general made all the arrangements. He even had some pictures taken and some business cards made. He made up a press packet for new clubs with pictures, a bio of the band and its members, and a list of the clubs they had played. All in all, the band was coming off more professionally. He had a good ear when they worked on material, either copy or original, and his input was appreciated. He quickly became like a member of the band even though he was not on stage.

It was a warm summer afternoon when Frank decided to invite a real agent to rehearsal. It was time that the band got some good bookings that only a real agent could get. This could mean better and higher paying gigs. Frank had been doing an excellent job of keeping their bookings going, but they were in the same old clubs for very little money. Frank felt that they were ready to move on and become more professional. He contacted Aggregate Artists International or what most called AAI. He talked with an agent by the name of Stan Rosen who agreed to see the band. This was a real break. This agency booked some fairly big acts in some big venues and also was the agency for many recording artists as well as other entertainment types like actors and directors. Not the top names but truly the up-and-coming and working people. He was a real professional agent.

Frank had invited him to a rehearsal to listen to and meet the band. This worked best for his schedule since he preferred not to travel far, and he would be booking Top 40 gigs which the band only played out of town. They were to play the set without an audience. This was difficult since there would be no friendly faces or audience reaction to work off of. Performing for the agent could be a bit intimidating. It was as if they were some circus animals doing a private show.

Only Mark and Pete were there as usual. They had become good friends of the band. They were at many of the gigs and sometimes even helped as roadies. They would supply the only moral support for this audition.

Stan entered the room. He looked like what the band thought to be a typical Hollywood agent—not at all good looking, a bit overweight, black horn rimmed glasses, expensive jeans, a designer shirt, and expensive shoes. He was a real geek with hip clothes He was greeted by Frank who introduced him to the band. Then he sat down with folded arms ready for the show. The band performed a set of cover tunes almost flawlessly although without any feeling. Performing for a single person was quite different than performing in front of a live receptive audience.

"Yeah, I can book 'em," he said rather coldly. He grabbed Frank by the arm while ignoring the band members as if they weren't even in the room. "It's sellable. But I'll tell you, it needs work. They need to turn down. Most of the clubs I book are lounges. I even book some of the lounges in Vegas which pay pretty well, but you will have to work up to that. But for these types of gigs they'll be background music.

People need to be able to have conversations over the music. Also, they need some sprucing up in the showmanship department. What kind of costumes do you have?" He glanced at them like they were just some commodity—like a car that he was buying. "You know matching shirts or something, with flowers perhaps." Frank didn't even have a chance to answer. "Well, I'll see. Call me next week for lunch, and I'll set up a trial gig. I'd like to see how they do in the type of clubs I book. Gotta run," he said waving to the rest of the band as if more out of obligation than anything else.

"Matching flower shirts, what the fuck have you gotten us into? Who the hell does he think we are, The Partridge Family? Who was that asshole?" Mike replied rather offended.

"And turn down? What the fuck is that all about?" Bill joined in. "We were playing as quietly as possible. It's bad enough that we have to play this Top 40 shit as it is, but this is goin' too far."

"He's a very big top agent, and these gigs pay well," Frank stated convincingly. "What do we have to lose? All these gigs are outta town, so no one will see us. We could even change our name for these gigs if it is that big of an issue. He books Vegas and a lot of big paying Vegas type clubs and show rooms. Look, we play this top 40 stuff anyway. Let's at least make some good money at it, and the gigs he books pays three times what we're making now."

"Have you forgotten what this is all about? This is a rock band—someday we'll be rock stars. We are not some Vegas lounge act. I refuse to sacrifice my artistry." Mike began to walk out in a huff.

"Wait a second, guys. We should listen to what he has to say. Besides, we do play too fuckin' loud sometimes. There are times I can't even hear myself sing, and no way can I hear the other harmonies with that Marshall amp blasting in my ear and you pounding the shit outta those drums. I think we could learn something playin' softer. It could help our playin' and especially our vocals." Gloria added.

"And I can't even hear my piano or my vocals either," Jason said agreeing with Gloria. "We've played quieter gigs. Remember how helpful it was. We'd have a chance to hear each other."

"But fuckin' A! We're a rock band, not lounge lizards," Mike protested.

"I can only play the drums so soft. I am a rock drummer." Jeff got up to defend himself.

"That's all fine for you to say, you make enough money with the band and working at the music store. I still have to be a waitress. I want outta that." Gloria argued.

"Well, whose fuckin' problem is that?" Jeff shouted.

Tempers flared as they fought over the direction of the band.

Finally, Frank had had enough. He Shouted. "ENOUGH! Look guys. Let's face it, we all need the money. My drug dealing can't continue to support the band either. Let's do the gig and see how it goes. It can't be all that bad. Let's just give the guy a chance. We can do a few gigs, make some money outta town, and then come back and do some real gigs." The band begrudgingly nodded in agreement. Some realized that they had been outvoted.

After the rehearsal, Frank went into the house to get some cold beers. He placed them on the floor. Jeff turned to Gloria. "Hey, pass me one of those beers, will ya?"

"Get it yourself," Gloria snapped back crossly.

"Well, you said yourself that you were a waitress." Jeff joked.

"Well, I ain't your waitress, buster." Gloria interrupted him. She was not in the mood. "And I ain't a slave to any man. So don't order me around, asshole. Just because I have to make some money because this fuckin' band can't support me doesn't make me your slave."

"Well, I just thought," Jeff responded not realizing Gloria was truly angry, "that you wouldn't mind waiting on me. Isn't that what women are supposed to do?" He laughed thinking she would get the joke. "Besides, you do it for everyone else."

"You male chauvinist pig asshole," Gloria screamed as she decked him one. Jeff was more stunned than hurt.

Jason, seeing this display, ran over to split them up. "Knock it off, you two. We just can't have this infighting. Now kiss and make up."

"Fuck, I didn't know you were so sensitive. I was just bustin' your balls and for a woman you sure have some." He laughed trying to lighten the mood. "You should know me by now, and know that I was only kidding. I'll get my own beer. Sorry if I offended you," said Jeff not wanting to carry this any further. "You have quite a right hook there by the way." He joked as he rubbed his cheek.

"Yeah, well, watch yourself buster," Gloria replied grabbing her things and leaving the rehearsal studio still very angry.

The atmosphere in the room after she left was very tense. Everyone was quiet, not saying a word.

Finally, Bill broke the silence. "Boy, she sure is a pistol." Bill laughed. "I guess that's what makes her such a great entertainer. For a chick she sure does have balls, figuratively speaking of course." They all laughed.

They did not continue to rehearse. They felt that everyone needed some cooling off.

The tension was still in the air later that week when they arrived at the next booking. Frank had landed them a gig at the Alley for the weekend. It was in Anaheim about 30 miles east of Hollywood, not far from Disneyland. Orange County was directly south and east of Los Angeles County but a world away. It had grown as a bedroom community of Los Angeles, but it had a reputation of being ultra-right wing conservative, and with its reputation it attracted more of the same. As Los Angeles experienced another wave of white flight, many people left and moved to Orange County for bigger houses, newer neighborhoods, and a safer place to raise their children. This was a place where they could live with people of their own kind and with their same values. It was an "America, love it or leave it" kind of place without the diversity, poverty, and crime of Los Angeles.

The Alley was actually a fairly nice club. It had once been a bowling alley but had since been turned into a very large night club. It was like a small concert hall with a large high stage and a room which could accommodate about a thousand people. It had a good professional sound and light system which the band immediately liked. At least they could perform like a real rock band and not some lounge act. The huge dance floor went the length of the building where the lanes once had been. The bar was at the back directly opposite of where the band was playing. It had started out as a legitimate club with up-and-coming bands and some name acts and recording artists. However, it now was mostly just a rock and roll dance club with a lot of bands playing other people's music. The club had certainly changed.

The band played well for its first two sets. They took their breaks as usual, grabbing a drink or a quick joint out back. Their break was over, and the set was to begin, but no one was able to find Jeff anywhere. The rest of the band waited near the stage. Finally, Gloria left out the back door to find Jeff, leaving the rest of the band searching the club. She noticed a car in the lot with a person in it. As she approached, it became clear it was Jeff. As she got even closer, she could see this wad of hair bobbing up and down in his lap. She knew Jeff was somewhat of a sexual athlete with a different girl every night, but doing it on band time enraged her. She sneaked up to the car and poked her head in the window as the girl continued.

"Suck it up fast honey; because if he doesn't cum now he's coming with me, you little whore." Both were taken by surprise.

"If you wanna pick up whores, please do so on your own time, asshole!" Gloria exclaimed.

With that the girl jumped out of the car. "Who you calling a whore, you bitch?" she yelled as she approached Gloria, ready for a fight. "I ain't no whore."

"Yeah, you're right. Whores get paid for it, and you're not even good enough for that," Gloria yelled back.

The girl who had been servicing Jeff immediately went for Gloria, pulling her hair and throwing punches. A fight ensued. The girls were really going at each other. Jeff jumped out of the car to try and stop the fight, trying at the same time to stuff his erection back into his pants. With everything happening so fast, his first priority was to split them up. A crowd of people had heard the commotion and rushed out. With a look of concern and aggravation he struggled to reach the girls, yelling for them to stop but impeded by his handicap. No matter how hard he tried he was still unable to stuff his large boner back into his too tight trousers. By then, the club patrons who were watching began to laugh and point. The girls heard them, saw them pointing at Jeff, and looked over at him. There he stood, looking quite foolish with his manhood hanging out. They noticed his dilemma. So in the midst of their fighting, they too began to laugh. Jeff just stood there red-faced and embarrassed, still struggling with his dangling dignity as the girls and some of the club patrons watched and laughed. Of course the fight was over. The band returned to the stage. Jeff was angered and mortified for what had transpired.

The evening continued with more problems. All of the vocal mics seemed to be constantly feeding back creating a loud screeching noise anytime anyone approached them, especially Gloria. The feedback got so bad that at times it was deafening. Broken guitar strings seemed to be happening more often than usual for Bill. Mike's guitar or guitar cord was constantly shorting out creating a loud buzzing sound or no sound at all.

With the tensions of the day and evening and all the guitar problems, Bill had been doing more than his share of drinking and drugs. As the evening continued, he became less and less able to perform and play until he was barely able to function. He was missing his cues, playing out of time, out of tune, making mistakes, and generally playing poorly. Gloria was angered, and the rest of the band frustrated.

Eventually, Gloria became enraged. Finally, she went over to Bill and whispered, "You'd better get your fuckin' act together."

He continued to play poorly. Gloria repeatedly told him that he'd better get his act together—getting louder and louder each time. She began harassing him about his poor playing.

Jeff could see the frustration and anger in Bill's face and was himself not in the greatest mood. He was still angry at Gloria for what had happened earlier. Finally, he told her to lay off.

"Mind your own business, asshole," Gloria snapped back aggravated by the events of the whole day. "I've had just about enough of you as well."

The band continued to play as Gloria and Jeff proceeded to have an argument right there on stage. They could see the anger in their faces even though they tried to hide it from the audience. Gloria belted out the songs with anger and verve as never before. Jeff beat the drums so hard that Mike and Jason thought he was going to break the drum heads. He did keep breaking drum sticks with his harder than usual playing. Every so often the ends would fly off hitting one of the band members. It was obvious to the band members he was taking out his frustration on his drum set.

All the smoking and drinking Bill had been doing was catching up with him. He could hardly stand up.

Mike and Jason had had a few as well. They were doing their best to keep it together, but even they made more than their share of mistakes and had their own problems and issues. Being the party band was taking its toll.

Gloria finally had enough. She stormed off stage in a huff and in so doing tripped on an electrical cord which made one of Jeff's cymbal stands fall. Jason and Mike watched in what seemed like slow motion. As the cymbal fell, its sharp edge severed the main power cable for the stage. This caused the whole electrical system to shut down. It had tripped the circuit breakers. The stage went pitch black except for the flurry of sparks which flew in every direction as the metal to current created a short. Frank ran up to help the band off the stage.

The crowd was silent for just a moment. Then, much to everyone's surprise, the crowd broke out into loud cheers and applause. For the first time in their career they received a standing ovation.

It took about 30 minutes to get the lights on the stage back on. When the band returned to the stage, the whole audience again started cheering and applauding. For the rest of the evening the audience was theirs. Everyone watched, listened, and waited for the next big show stopper.

Needless to say, the band was amazed, not quite sure what had really transpired.

Frank, on the other hand, had some ideas of his own. He had seen what was happening, and how it happened. He had his own agenda that he hoped he could discuss with the band. This just did not seem to be the right time. Frank felt that some ground rules needed to be set. He just wasn't sure how to approach the band. There were things that needed to be fixed, and he, as manager, needed to take control. He thought it out to himself and decided to discuss some issues with the band at the first chance possible. He was just glad the agent had not been there to see this.

"BAND ON THE RUN"

Paul McCartney

It wasn't long thereafter that they had their first gig with the new agent. It was a trial gig, but hopefully they would do well and get some more bookings.

"We need to do a great job for this agent. That gig in Anaheim was a fuckin' disaster!" Frank scolded them. "So don't fuck it up!"

They all bowed their heads in shame like a bunch of children being punished by their parents. They all agreed to try their best and really work on getting their act together.

Stan, the new agent, booked the band in a club in San Bernardino. It was about an hour drive east of Hollywood. They arrived at the club feeling a lot of reservations about the whole gig. They were wearing their new color-coordinated outfits—brightly colored flowered shirts and tight bell bottom hip huggers with huge flared legs. Patent leather platform shoes completed the outfit. The club was called The Precinct, an odd name they thought. It was adjacent to a bowling alley with only a door separating them and the noise next door. The sound of rolling balls and pins being hit could be heard in the background like distant thunder. It was a small intimate lounge, not the usual rock clubs they were used to. There was a small foot high stage in the corner. They were not certain how they were going to fit the whole band on this tiny stage. There was barely enough room to accommodate the drum set. They would have to use less equipment or stack it as best as they could. They knew it would be cramped, but somehow they would make it work. A railing separated the band from the small wooden dance floor, and beyond that some tables and chairs. The back wall and one side wall was lined with red naugahyde booths. A red glass candle sat flickering on each table. The bar lined one of the walls to the right of the stage with bar stools for the hard-core drinkers.

"This really sucks!" Mike commented feeling rather embarrassed. He was wearing his new outfit of bright red pants and matching flowered shirt. "I feel like one of The Partridge Family or The Cowsills or something. We really look ridiculous!"

"Just think of the money," Jason said in his bright orange ensemble, trying to convince everyone, including himself, that it was not so bad. "We make a lot more here than we do at those other clubs. At least its way outta town so no one will see us except those stopping in at the bowling alley—certainly not our usual rock crowd."

"It ain't so bad," said Gloria trying to sound convincing all dressed in hot pink. "I just hope no one sees us. Just think of all the money we're making here. We make more in one night here than what it usually takes a whole week to make in those rock clubs. We do a couple of these a month, and we're set for doing what ever else we want the rest of the time. We might even be able to quit our day jobs. Besides, it might be good for us to play a bit quieter. We might even be able to hear each other and make some improvements."

"We look like the God Damn Jackson 5," said Jeff. He was stuffed into his too tight yellow attire and looked like an overstuffed canary. "And I look like fuckin' Big Bird."

They laughed.

"Or the fucking Osmonds," said Bill. He was all decked out in bright purple. "I mean, we make The Brady Bunch look radical and sloppy."

The setup and sound check went well. They began to play. They felt the gig was going fairly well despite the fact they were completely unable to move onstage. That was until the bartender walked over to them in the middle of the first set.

"Turn down!" he said sternly. "You're too damn loud. I can't even hear what the customers are ordering." This only added insult to injury.

They tried to play quieter, but again he complained this time shouting from the bar. "Still too loud!" They felt they were already to the point of being too soft. They were a rock band, used to playing loud in rock clubs. Even the Top 40 nightclubs they had been playing were rock clubs which allowed them to play at a decent volume. But in this case, they were there to replace the jukebox. This was a real lounge gig with the band as background music. The hardest part was getting Jeff to play soft.

By the third set they just about had enough. They were making the best of a bad situation. They had made a few friends who they felt understood what they were doing, but for the most part they were a background band. Many of the patrons just looked at them with disgusted looks on their faces, sometimes covering their ears.

"Man, I need to get high if I'm gonna make it through this night." Mike put his bass away then headed for the back door.

Jeff wasn't far behind. "Brotha', I'm with ya."

Jeff had met some women, so he decided to invite them out into the back parking lot to smoke some joints. As he passed by them on his way to the parking lot he stopped. "You ladies wanna join us for a little smoke?" He put two fingers together and put them to his lips to mimic like he was smoking a joint just to make sure they understood.

The girls nodded in agreement and followed him out.

Mike, Jason, Gloria, and Jeff and the girls left the club out the back door. They went to the back of the parking lot. Bill was having trouble with his guitar. He said he'd join them shortly. Frank, being totally bored, was out searching for some food. As they stood passing the joint, they were discussing the gig, trying not to offend the other patrons.

As they were passing the joint, they noticed two other guys leaving the bar. Upon noticing the crowd in the back of the parking lot, they walked over to join them. The band watched them approach thinking that they just wanted to get high with them. They approached the group just as Bill was exiting the club to join them.

As they approached the group, they split up so that each of them would be on opposite sides of the circle.

Jeff acknowledged them with a nod. "Want a hit, man?" he asked holding the joint out for one of them to take.

The man grabbed the joint, while grabbing Jeff's arm. At the same time the other man grabbed Mike and Gloria. Bill stopped dead in his tracks, still about thirty feet away. Upon seeing what was happening, he panicked. He turned and ran back into the club. While he was running back into the club, he noticed two other men running from the sides of the club, anxious to see what all the ruckus was about. Moments later, two police cars pulled up through the alley with tires squealing, lights flashing, and sirens blaring.

"You're under arrest for possession of drugs," announced the man who had grabbed Jeff and the joint.

"What the fuck!" Jeff exclaimed.

"You have the right to remain silent," The other man barked authoritatively as he read them their rights. The two police cars stopped one on each side of the circle. Two uniformed police officers got out of each car with guns drawn. They approached the circle.

"Everything under control?" one said to the two men who had grabbed them.

"Yes, no problem," said the one who still had a hold of Jeff.

In a moment, two other cars sped around the corner. They screeched to a halt. The cars moved in formation and stopped so that they formed a circle around the band and the girls. These were obviously unmarked police cars. Two men in suits got out, obviously plain clothes policemen. A helicopter swooped down and hovered right above them, shining its spotlight on the ruckus in the parking lot. Now with eight police officers, two cop cars, two unmarked cars, and a helicopter, they were completely surrounded with no way of escape. They were busted.

"Fuck!" Mike stated. "Cops all over. Where'd you come from?"

"Our off duty buddies inside tipped us off, you fools. It's all over the police radio. Everyone wanted to find out what was happening and be here for backup just in case. Besides, it's a pretty slow night. Pretty stupid doing drugs at a cop hangout, wouldn't you say?" The policeman laughed nodding to his buddies who all broke out laughing, proud of their accomplishment.

"A cop bar. Son-of-a bitch! I can't believe it! This is a fuckin' drag," said Gloria.

The policemen started handcuffing them.

"You should've known with a name like The Precinct," One of the cops said and laughed. The rest of his buddies joined in the laughter.

"And we don't take kindly to your type here!" The man in the suit exclaimed.

Gloria and Jan, one of the girls Jeff was picking up on and who Gloria had just met, were the first to be put into the police car. The girl turned to Gloria and whispered, "I've got a roll of whites in my pocket. We need to get rid of 'em, or we're all gonna be in even more trouble."

So, while the police officers were busy handcuffing Jeff, Jason, Mike, and the other girls and escorting them to the other police cars, Gloria and Jan edged their way close to each other so that they were back to back in the police car. Gloria grabbed the baggie of uppers, opened it up, and took a few, but there must have been twenty in the bag. The girl took about half, swallowed them, then gave some more to Gloria who took them and swallowed them quickly, leaving only a few left in the bag which they stuffed into the seat.

The officers finished putting them into the police cars. Finally, with everyone inside the cars, the men shut the doors, got into their cars, and left. They were under arrest for narcotics. The plain clothes officers motioned to the helicopter. It turned off its light and flew off. Then they got back into the unmarked cars and left. Soon the parking lot was again quiet.

Bill had escaped to the club. He sat there shaking for a while, unsure of what had transpired outside. When he finally calmed down, he looked for Frank. After all, Frank was the manager; he'd know what to do.

The club owner who was also the bartender came to Bill asking him where the band was. "Man, its past time for you to begin your set." He stood angrily pointing to his watch.

"I think they all got busted out back. I'm not sure where they are. Last I saw them they were surrounded by police cars and officers." He told him everything he knew, and what he thought had happened.

"Shit! You bands and your God Damn drugs. This is a police hangout. Didn't anyone tell you? How stupid can you guys be? Especially with a name like The Precinct. Can't even play one night without getting high!" he exclaimed in disgust. "Well, I guess that does it for you. Pack it up. That's the last straw. Find another gig."

After about an hour, Frank returned wondering where the band was, and why Bill was tearing down the stage with a rather frightened look in his eye. "What happened?" Frank asked.

"They've all been arrested!" Bill exclaimed in a panic, sweat pouring off his face.

"Arrested!"

"We need to get 'em out." Bill was still shaking. He continued to relate the events that had just transpired.

Once they had all the equipment packed up, Frank grabbed Bill and ran to his car. They raced to the police station.

He entered to find a man sitting at a large desk that even he had to look up to. He felt like a little kid dwarfed by the desk.

After inquiring with the officer at the desk, he was informed that, "They're being booked right now. It'll take a while."

After some time and red tape, he finally discovered that bail had been set at $100,000 each. Even with a bail bondsman, they couldn't come up with that much tonight. Especially for all the bail money they needed. That much money is a lump of change Frank just didn't keep with him at all times.

"I have an old friend from the east coast who's an attorney. He got me off on a drug charge in New York. He practices in L.A. now. We can call him and get his advice." Bill timidly advised Frank.

"I didn't know that you knew any attorneys." Frank was stunned.

"Long story—just a friend of the family, really." Bill seemed reluctant to give out much information or to go into details. Frank just left it alone as he had other concerns. "Got me out of a sticky drug situation in New York once. I'll call him on Monday and see what he says," said Bill.

Frank and Bill left feeling helpless. At first, Frank was going to try and come up with some money for bail, but as he thought about it he decided to wait until Monday when hopefully they would be arraigned. That would give him some time to think. In the meantime, that would give Bill time to contact his attorney friend and see what he advised. The band would just have to sit in jail for a couple of days.

Bill arranged a meeting on Monday for him and Frank to meet the attorney in his office in downtown Los Angeles.

They entered the lavish expensive law offices, told the receptionist who they were and who they were there to see, sat down, and waited.

A tall, thin man in a very expensive suit entered. His dark hair and black horn rimmed glasses made him look like Clark Kent. "Bill, is that really you?"

"Yeah, man, it is. It has been a long time. I wish it were under better circumstances." The attorney put his hand on Bill's shoulder and gave him a hearty handshake.

"This is Frank, our manager. Frank, this is Brent Richmond." They shook hands.

"So come on into my office and tell me the whole story."

They entered the posh office and sat in two chairs that were placed in front of the large wooden desk. Behind the desk was a view of City Hall and all of the high rises of downtown Los Angeles.

Frank told him the story.

"First, let me see what I can find out. I'll make a few phone calls and let you know what's going on. You can bail them out now, that is if you have the money, or you can wait for the arraignment which should be in a couple of days. If you wait, I can be there as well to try to get it reduced. That's up to you. Just lemme know."

Frank thanked him. Then they left.

Brent found out that the arraignment was to be on Wednesday. Brent advised them to just sit tight and wait. Frank thought long and hard about it. He decided to just let them stay there in jail until the arraignment. In the long run, it would probably cost less and hopefully Brent would be able to get the sentences reduced and therefore the bail reduced. Besides, it was only a couple of days. Frank also wanted to teach the band a lesson.

Frank did want to tell them in person, so he and Bill drove to San Bernardino. Since no one had posted bail immediately, Frank discovered that they had already been transferred from the police station to the local prison since the jail was so overcrowded. They would have to wait it out there until their arraignment.

Frank arrived at the prison late Monday to break the news to them. He was able to speak to them as a visitor.

"Whatcha waiting for? Get us outta here!" Desperation was in Jason's voice.

"We're working on it. Even I don't have that kind of cash sitting around. I'll do what I can, but your arraignment is later this week. You may just have to stay here until then. These guys are tough. They're throwing the book at you. I think they want to make an example of you guys. We've already contacted an attorney, a friend of Bill's, Brent."

"Shit, man. That means we're stuck here. This fuckin' place is horrible," Mike protested.

"Only for a couple of days. I'll do the best I can and keep you posted."

They looked disappointed and disconsolate. They returned to their cells with heads bowed low.

Gloria and her new found friend were jailed together, and, with each of them on a handful of double-cross white uppers, they were buzzed. Needless to say, with all those amphetamines, they spent the whole weekend wide awake, talking, and pacing—completely unable to sleep. They got to know each other real well in a short time, for in that weekend they covered everything there was to know about each other very quickly.

The men, on the other hand, were placed in large cells with a couple of other inmates. It was just like some prison movie, and this was a typical jail cell. There were three concrete walls and a fourth wall of steel bars which included a door. Bunk beds lined the walls with mattresses so thin they were hardly worth sleeping on. At one end there was a toilet and sink which afforded no privacy. Outside the cell, a long hallway with other identical cells completed the cell block. They could hear voices coming from the other cells and the occasional loud clank of a door shutting. At the end of the hall was another steel door leading to the rest of the prison. Luckily, they were in the same cell together.

"What ya in for?" a rather large black man who seemed to be in charge questioned while smoking a cigarette. His mere size meant that he was not someone you wanted to mess with.

"Drugs." Jeff quickly responded. "We got busted smoking a joint. We're musicians. We were gigging at some bar. We went out to get high at break time, and they caught us."

"Musicians huh," the black man responded. "Well, then you must be all right. They call me The Boss. You guys must get a lot of action, I mean with the chicks. It's been a long time since my dick felt a good pussy. Sure must be nice. This is Leroy." He pointed to a small black man, who seemed to be more important just by his association with The Boss who obviously ruled this place. "He's my bitch; you know my slave and my fuck. He's the best we got here. If you're good, I may just let you have a piece of that action. Or maybe you'd like to be the receiver?"

Jason was petrified. He tried his best to act straight and macho, afraid of what they would do to him if they discovered he was gay. Jeff and Mike just gave him that look of "your secret is safe with us."

"We appreciate the offer, man" Jeff piped in although even he appeared a little intimidated but tried his best to hide it. "But no thanks, we get enough action, you know being musicians and all. Besides, we left our women at home, and I think we can wait. Whatcha in here for?" Jeff asked trying to change the subject fast.

"Murder, I got life. She was my best whore. She decided she didn't need a pimp anymore; she was going to work as an independent, so she broke off the arrangement. She threatened me by telling me she'd expose my drug activities if I continued to harass her. No one breaks a business deal with me. So I went to change her mind and make her pay for her lack of loyalty. Didn't know I hit her so hard. It ended up I killed her. Didn't really mean to. At least I taught that bitch a lesson.

Leroy here was part of a gang—armed robbery, liquor stores, and shit. Killed a couple of guys in the process, you know, they got in his way. Nothing real major though, all small time. Hank over there." He pointed to a scruffy but quiet and apparently harmless white man with blond hair and a beard. He smiled exposing the fact that he was missing a couple of teeth. He looked like a real redneck. "He killed his old lady and some other guy."

"Yeah, I caught the bitch cheating on me, right in my own fuckin' bed. Came home one night and saw someone's car parked in the driveway. I thought it might be a prowler or something. I parked my car in the garage and grabbed the nearest thing I could find, an ax. I went around to the back and peeked in the window. There they were in bed together—fucking. I went ballistic. I walked around to the front door, stormed in with the ax in my hand and started beating the shit out of 'em. It sure felt good. I gave 'em what they deserved. But, it sure made a mess, blood squirting all over the place." As he spoke, he became more and more excited. All the band could envision was some bad slasher movie. "I would've gotten away with it too if it hadn't been for the bleeding all over the highway. I had to do something with the bodies—couldn't just leave 'em there in the bedroom. I packed 'em into the back of the truck to take 'em out to the woods to bury 'em. It was dark though, and I guess I just didn't see all the blood. Bodies sure do have a lot of blood in 'em. I thought they'd never stop bleeding. Anyway, the cops pulled me over. They wanted to see what I had in the back of the truck. So, here I am."

"The police picked him up on the freeway." The boss continued the story. "The bodies were so badly chopped up they were losing a lot of blood. The bundle in the back of his pickup truck was splattering blood all over the highway and other cars, especially the windshields. Someone reported it to the police. They were so badly chopped up they wouldn't contain the blood. Pretty nasty scene really. The cops pulled him over and found the hacked up bodies in the back of his pickup." The black man said finishing the story.

The three looked at each other horrified. Mike and Jason were trying their best not to expose the sheer terror they felt. Jeff was trying to reassure them and show them that the worst thing they could do was to show the terror. Luckily, it wasn't long before lights off. Mike and Jason did not sleep at all that night, instead lay there with eyes wide open. Fear did get the best of them. The Boss was poking Leroy from the sounds of it, and Mike and Jason did not want to be next. Jeff on the other hand was taking all this in stride.

The days went by with no problems, although they were all on their best behavior, doing more than their share to clean the cell. They got over the initial indignity of going to the bathroom in front of everyone, but all were still very conscious of not bending over in the shower for fear of The Boss' wrath. He had been in here so long, who knows what he would've done. Thanks to Jeff and his wit, they were actually liked. Jeff had made the best of a bad situation. When Wednesday rolled around for their arraignments, they were almost sad to leave; oddly enough they had become friends. But at the same time, they couldn't be happier to get out.

Frank and Brent were in court on Wednesday for the arraignment. With only a small roach as evidence, Brent was able to get the charges reduced, and therefore the bail reduced. They were to return to court at a later date for the trial, but for the time being they were free. They returned home with stories and broken egos.

30

"YOU'VE GOT TO CHANGE YOUR EVIL WAYS"

Santana

The next day Frank called a band meeting at his home. The band all found places on the sofa while Frank stood there pacing with his arms folded and a stern look on his face. "There's been a lot going on lately. I think it's time we clear the air and establish some rules." He stood there like a parent scolding his naughty children.

They all sunk into the sofa like bad kids, heads bowed in shame.

"You're sounding like a fuckin' parent." Mike frowned and folded his arms in defiance.

"Well, if you wanna act like children, and this is what it takes—so be it. You are all really fucking up. And if things don't change, I'm outta here. Needless to say, we lost the agent. He wants nothing to do with us."

"No loss there," Jeff chimed in.

"We pissed off the club owner because he couldn't find a replacement band to play the rest of the week, but he hated the band anyway. There's nothing but petty bickering within the band. The band has sounded like shit these last few gigs. And to top it all off, you got arrested. The last two gigs have been nothing but disasters. Perhaps you just want to be some second rate bar band playing these dives. You can decide. Do you just want to party and have fun, or are you really serious about becoming recording artists and rock stars? This is not the band I got involved with. The band I signed up for knew they were gonna make it big. I believe in this band, and I believe that you can do it. But, you need to make some changes and decisions if you want to get better, and if you wanna make it in this business. This is a business, and this is your job. It's about time you started treating it as such. You are acting, looking, and sounding like a bunch of amateurs. You really need to get your act together."

They all listened. They knew that there was certainly a lot of truth in what he was saying and also knew that some issues needed to be addressed.

"First of all, drugs." Frank was pacing the floor like a drill sergeant, hands raised and gesturing for emphasis. "Beside the fact that you guys got busted last week, which was very stupid, I've noticed and have had many complaints about the drug use in the band. Now, I don't want to point any fingers." He paused. He surveyed each person in the room, looking each of them straight in the eyes, and focusing his attention on each individual accusatorially. "But if drugs affects anyone's playing or interferes with our performance, then it must be stopped. As you all know, I personally do not care how many drugs you do, so long as you can handle 'em. But no one is handling 'em well. I know you all think that when you're stoned you play better, but actually the opposite is true. Even I can hear the difference. You make more mistakes, you're not as tight, not as clean, the vocals are off, and the performances are just not as good. It's just the drugs you are hearing, not the reality. To be fair to everyone and to not get into who can handle the drugs and drinking and who can't, I think the drugs and drinking should stop now for everyone when we're gigging. At the very minimum, there should be limits to it. When we are working, I would prefer it be only drinking and little of that. I don't wanna see any drug use, nor can I afford another drug bust. I think we should ban the hard drugs: coke, LSD, and mushrooms, and as far a pot is concerned I think that should be kept at a minimum—only before you leave for the gig and after the gig. But not at the gig! None when we are working. I don't wanna see anyone drunk, stoned, or too spaced out from drugs or alcohol to perform again. We need to leave those days behind us. You need to start treating this like a career—not a party. Let's not lose sight of what we're trying to do here. It's not just a reason to get high. We're trying to make it in the music world. We should think of this like any other job. No, not just a job, this is about your careers, which makes it even more difficult because there are so many bands out there trying to make it. We must be that much better than the others if we're ever gonna make it in this business. We can still be a party band and get the crowd going, just without drugs. Everyone else can do the drinking and drugs. We can create a party without us doing the drugs and drinking. This is especially important at the big gigs where I say we have a no drinking or drugs rule at all—period. Save getting stoned until after the gigs or at other times. I'm even OK with a little at rehearsals to get the creative juices flowing. But not at the gigs! I say we stop the drug use now until after the gig is over and keep the drinking to a minimum if not at all."

"Uh, yeah, I guess you're right. We *have* been partying too much," Mike agreed.

"Yeah, I don't want people to see any of us too drunk or too stoned to perform," Jason expressed his concern. "It makes it difficult for everyone. I say we keep it real until after the gig. I know if affects my playing."

All agreed to have no drugs and very little drinking at the gigs.

"Next, this petty bickering between everyone must stop. This goes for everyone. Jeff you must start showing some respect for Gloria. She is a woman, but more importantly she is a valuable member of this band and a real person that deserves everyone's respect. We should respect her opinions as well. Try and act a little grown up for a change. You can treat those bimbos you pick up any way you want, but show some respect for the members of the band.

"But you know how I am. Sometimes I am just kidding or busting people's balls, sorry Gloria" Jeff defended himself.

"Well, you had better learn to be a bit more diplomatic and understanding. Just watch your mouth.

Same goes for everyone. We have five different and strong personalities. We just need to get along. We all need to treat each other with respect. We all care about each other, so let's just get beyond this pettiness.

Same goes for getting laid. Do it all you want on your own time or after the gig. Pick em' up, bring em' home, fuck all you want. But after we're done working, I see no reason to stop the after gig parties, just keep 'em after the gig. This goes for everyone. It shouldn't interfere with the band or its performance." Jeff knew he was talking about him and lowered his head in shame. "So keep it in your pants until the gig is over." He stared straight at Jeff.

"Next, I think it'd be a good idea to have a band meeting every so often to clear the air. Remember, it's us against the world. If we can't be honest with each other and discuss problems or situations, we're gonna have more severe problems in the future.

We must all remember what our purpose and our goal is. Let's keep the dream alive. I'd hate to see this thing break up at this point because of a bunch of petty bullshit. Is everyone in agreement?"

They all shook their heads in agreement, all pouting like children being punished.

Now are there any other problems in the band before I continue?"

"What about those outfits and these lounge gigs?" Mike asked. "Is that what we really wanna do?"

"Fuck no," they all chorused in agreement.

"I agree," Frank began. "That really is not the direction of this band. While I do think that we could dress up a bit more. I certainly do not see us doing anything like that again."

"Yeah, I'd rather play for less money than do that again." Jeff remarked with all in agreement.

"All agreed?" Frank asked. The band shook their heads in agreement. "Anything else?"

They shook their heads no.

"Next I wanna discuss performance. Despite all the problems we had, there were some good things that I've seen recently, quite by accident. That performance we gave last week was one of the best ones

I've ever seen from the band for a couple of reasons. You remember when the cymbal fell, and there was an argument and all hell broke loose." They nodded feeling ashamed at their own behavior "Well, because of that tension on-stage, everyone played with energy, tension, and passion. It was awesome, and the audience thought it was part of the show. It's time we started thinking about a show. Channel that energy into a more creative place—utilize it to our advantage. You've gotten to be a pretty good party band, now use that even more. Really make it a show. And that cymbal crash and the lights going off was an incredible finale. In fact, we got our first standing ovation. I don't want to see real arguments or accidents on stage, but I do want to see that same passion, energy, and show on stage every time we play. It's something to work on and discuss in the next few weeks.

Last, I think we need more help. There were so many technical problems that need to be addressed. I want to propose that we add Mark Taylor and Pete Simons to the organization. They have approached me about working with the band. They are extremely interested in being roadies and tech people." He left the room only to return with Mark and Pete who had been waiting in the other room. They all knew Mark and Pete. They had been hanging around a lot as Frank's helper in the drug business, and they had helped on a number of gigs. The band knew them as two stoner types who wanted to get high, listen to music, and party. They were in their usual white t-shirt, blue Levis, and white tennis shoes. They were both very thin, actually quite skinny, and their shoulder length brown hair just added to their stoner look. "You all know them. They've been very helpful in the past. Now, they want to be more involved. I've been working with both of them for a while, mostly in my drug dealing operations. Mark is a local boy. He's smart and hard working. I started working with him because he had some real good local connections having grown up here. He had a lot of friends from school and the beach that liked to get high. Pete is from back east somewhere. They are both hard working, and I trust them implicitly. I think they would be a real asset to the band. They can help with set up, tear down, and deal with the technical problems. Perhaps you should hear what they have to say."

"First of all, we really dig this band. We would consider it an honor to work with you guys. I'd really like to be a roadie. I'm interested in learning sound. I think I have a good ear. I can learn real fast and am willing to do anything the band needs done," Mark started.

"We know very little about you two. We have seen you around, and you have been very helpful. How about you tell us a little bit about yourself?" Gloria asked.

"Well man, I grew up in this area. I dropped out of high school because I just hated all that structure. I did, however, keep in touch with a lot of my friends: some from high school, some from the beach, but most were just my stoner friends. We got together to get high and party a lot. It was always difficult to find the drugs. I met Frank on the beach. He always had plenty and a wide variety as well. Anything we wanted. I knew I could always count on him for drugs. So he became my dealer of choice. Eventually, because of Frank, I could supply my stoner friends with all kinds of drugs, and Frank got more business. I made a bit on the side as well, which Frank was well aware of. Seemed like a good situation for everyone concerned. As Frank knows, I can be trusted. I'm very honest. I met Pete on the beach. He became one of my stoner friends. We just hit it off, so we both help Frank in his drug business."

"Yeah, we met because we had common interests: rock music, getting stoned, and partying," Pete began. "I came out here for a summer after I graduated high school, but I never went back. I called my parents in Baltimore and told 'em I wasn't coming home. I really dug the California lifestyle: parties, chicks, and drugs. Found some odd jobs to support myself. Mark and I just hit it off. I'd really like to pursue a career in the music industry working with bands. I'm more interested in lights. I've been to a lot of rock concerts. I dig the music, but I really love the visuals and the moods that can be created with the right lighting and effects. Good lights can really make the music seem even better."

"Both of us are really into music." Mark picked up the conversation "We listen to it all the time. We even talked about getting into the music business between ourselves but never knew how to get started. Then when Frank started managing this band we thought this could be our chance. After hanging around with you guys, we both decided we really wanted to get involved. We'd appreciate it if you would give us the opportunity. Also, we want you to know that although we like getting stoned, we know that you guys are serious, and so are we. Our getting stoned won't affect how hard we work or how good we do our job. Getting high wouldn't happen on the job. We always keep that as recreational. Business comes first."

"You know, they brought in a lot of people to Pier 11," Frank interrupted. "A lot of that crowd was their friends and other people they knew. They created a bit of a buzz. Word spread, which is one of the reasons the clubs was always packed when you played, and also the reason that you keep getting asked back."

"Yeah, I wanted to turn all my friends on to the band." Mark continued "I think it's a great band, and one I thought my friends would appreciate. I also think that this band could make it big. I like to think of myself as a connoisseur of rock music. I really think you guys have what it takes."

They stood there as Frank continued. "They'll need some additional training with the off stage technical side, but if they were here all the time I think they'd learn fast. They certainly have the drive, enthusiasm, and commitment. They're happy just being with the band to learn what it takes to be roadies so long as they can share in with the party afterward. I think we should try to throw a few bucks their way once in a while. They'll continue working for me doing some dealing for the time being so that should keep 'em in enough money until you guys can pay 'em."

"Eventually, we'd like to get good enough to pursue this as a career, but for now we're happy just being apprentices. We'd really dig the opportunity to learn the ropes." Mark said as they both nodded in enthusiastic agreement.

"They'd both help in the set up and maintenance of the equipment, but they need to be trained. We'll assign particular jobs for each of them and divide the jobs up fairly evenly. You can fight over who you prefer to work with. However, they should be cross trained so that either of 'em can do any job just in case only one is there. They'll come to rehearsal to learn to set up and tear down. They should learn all the songs so that they could do the sound and light cues. At some gigs it might only require one or only one might be available. I especially want someone mixing sound at every gig. That feedback was horrible, not to mention the bad balance. We need someone to control that every time we play. It is crucial. It would certainly take the pressure off of you having to worry about equipment and your own sound. I think it's a wining proposition for all. They both play guitar a bit, so they know something about music and instruments. You'll just need to teach them. What d'ya think?"

Mark spoke up. "Yeah man, we really dig this band. We would love the opportunity to work with you guys. We really wanna learn what it takes to do the behind the scenes work with a rock band. It would be a dream come true for us."

Pete stood next to him a bit timidly but with an undercurrent of excitement. "Er, we dig you all, and think your music is great. I know we can help you guys out. We just hope you give us a chance to learn. I'm sure we won't let you down."

"Give us a minute. Wait for us outside," Mike instructed.

Mark and Pete went outside to await the verdict.

"This would be great, actual roadies." Jeff began. "I would love to have some help setting up all this shit."

It took little discussion for the band to agree to add Mark and Pete as their crew. They were happy that they actually now had a road crew.

"I would like to work with Mark" said Jeff. "He can be in charge of drums, bass, and vocals since he wants to do sound."

"Cool," said Gloria.

"Sounds like a good plan," said Mike

"Then I think Pete should do the keys and guitar to break up the responsibilities."

"Works for me," said Jason. "I like Pete."

"Me too," said Bill. "And I know he plays guitar; so he can set up, change strings, tune, and do other shit."

"Then it's settled," Frank said." I'll discuss with them our new rules as well, but I don't think that'll be a problem with 'em. I know how much they wanna do this."

They called them in to give them the good news.

"Well guys. You're in." Mike was first to shake their hands. "Welcome to the organization."

"Thanks," was all Mark and Pete could say. They went around shaking everyone's hand.

"Then it's settled," said Frank. "We're creating a strong organization which will take team work and a lot of dedication. "Now let's go and show the world what a great band we have. And from now on, all problems out in the open," Frank ended sounding more like a football coach or a general leading the troops, but it worked. Everyone's faith was again restored.

They all apologized to Frank for everything and acknowledged that they had really made a mess of things. They agreed to the new ground rules and the new ideas. Frank was earning his keep as manager. They felt that this would only make them better.

"Since we don't have any gigs for the rest of week because we got fired I think we need to celebrate a bit. This will be to our new direction, our new rules, and the new members of our crew." Frank took out a couple of joints and lit them up. He passed them around as sort of a welcoming of the new roadies and a renewed commitment they all felt to each other.

The next few weeks showed a renewed interest in the band. Spirits were high. They were also concentrating on the show for the first time. They had all come to realize that sometimes what made a performance great was not just the music but was also the show. They had to make it exciting every time they performed on stage. It was not just about playing the songs. They could still play the part of the party band, as this did work for them, but now it became part of the show. They just did it without drugs. There was a renewed commitment to the music and the show. It was the epiphany they all needed to make it to the next step.

Mark and Pete were at most of the rehearsals and gigs, learning their new jobs as crew. Luckily, they had a week of rehearsals to get some training and practice before they were sent out to work on actual gigs. They were soon working at the gigs doing the best job they could and learning all the time. They picked up the information quickly and easily and with a real sense of commitment. Both were learning all about the equipment so that they could completely set up and tear down for a gig. They also had to be able to fix a variety of problems if needed including fixing cables, changing drum heads, tuning the guitars offstage, and changing broken guitar strings which happened often when the band was playing, and required them to do it backstage while the show was in progress. Luckily, Bill had a couple of guitars which he used depending on the sound he wanted, but it also meant that they didn't have to stop the set if he broke a string. The guitar would be ready for the next song.

They both needed to know the songs to get the sound and light cues. Mark concentrated on sound to make sure the overall sound mix and blend of the band especially the vocals was great. He had to learn all about PA systems and how to work the sound board for a good vocal sound and mix. Sometimes they used their own sound system; sometimes they used the clubs, so he had to be versatile. He tried to keep an overall good balance of the band and grew to be respected for his ear. This also meant turning on and off mics depending on who was singing. He even told them who should turn up or down depending on the passage of the song. Pete concentrated on lights. He needed to know every song and what mood or lighting cue would be appropriate. He would be required to adapt to whatever lighting equipment they had to work with which varied with each club.

Both enjoyed their new role with the band. They took their parts very seriously. They felt like part of the band, and they played an integral part to their success which the band appreciated. The band began to rely on them as their eyes and ears to better their performances.

Their next few engagements were Top 40 gigs. It was good that these first gigs were easy ones. It made for a good training ground. This allowed the band to work on getting their act together and to break in the road crew. It only took a couple of gigs to really see their value. It was helpful having a road crew set up their gear, make sure the sound and lights was good, and to fix any problems. It proved to be a big benefit to the band.

Finally, the court date for their drug arrest was set. They readied themselves for their day in court.

They were all dressed up as they entered the court room, men in sport coats and Gloria in a nice dress. They looked quite presentable. They sat down at a long table facing the bench where the judge would sit. The bailiff had everyone stand as the Judge entered. The bailiff announced the case. The band just sat there like a bunch of naughty school kids who had been sent to the principal's office.

"Your honor. May I approach the bench?" Brent stood up after everyone sat down and the case had been announced.

The judged motioned him to the bench. Words were exchanged.

It was quick.

The judge began, "Will the defendants please stand."

"That means you," said Brent motioning to the band.

They all stood with heads bowed.

"I understand that there is very little evidence in this case." The judge continued. "Your attorney has advised me that you are willing to plead to a lesser misdemeanor charge, pay a fine, and attend six months of drug prevention classes. He asks that we consider the time you already spent in jail when you were arrested as your jail time served. He says that you have learned your lesson and are sorry for what you have caused. Let me tell you. We do not take kindly to your type in this town. I have considered his offer, and I will agree to it. However, if I ever see you in this courtroom again I will throw the book at you. Do you understand?"

"Yes sir," they all agreed like some children being scolded by their father.

"Then I will accept this as your verdict." The judge pounded his gavel.

Brent was able to get the charges reduced. Their drug trial was done. They paid the fine and attended the classes, although usually stoned. It became more of a joke than anything else.

"LA BAMBA"

Ritchie Valens

Frank had landed the band a gig at a rock club in East L.A. They were not sure this would be their audience, but a gig was a gig. This could also be a good place to work out their sound and their show.

They were to play there a week. The first night was Tuesday. As they drove into that section of L.A. it seemed like a foreign country. It was only minutes away from downtown, but it was as if they had crossed the border into Mexico. This was an older section of L.A. that had once been a Jewish neighborhood, but as the Jewish community left for better places it had become mostly Spanish speaking people which meant mostly people of Mexican descent. Some families had been here since California was part of Mexico, but most were recent immigrants looking for a better life in the United States. The streets were lined with colorful shops and restaurants all with Spanish names and selling everything from tacos and burritos to piñatas and colorful clothes. While it seemed more like Mexico, it was truly a part of Los Angeles and part of its heritage. It was not a wealthy part of town, but a place with people struggling to make a living. It was a bit dirty, but a thriving neighborhood nonetheless. The club was on Whittier Boulevard, one of the main streets in the neighborhood. As they got out of the van, they could see the high rise buildings of downtown L.A. in the distance, a reminder how a few miles can make such a difference in this city of diversity.

The club was small and brightly painted—mostly red, green, and white; the colors of the flag of Mexico. Serapes, straw hats, maracas, and other things lined the walls to really give the feel of old Mexico. The furniture was cheap mission style, but it somehow worked with the rest of the look of the club.

Mark and Pete loaded their equipment into the club and set up the stage with the help of the band members. They did a sound check with Mark at the board. Since there were very few lights, there wasn't much for Pete to do except help.

After the sound check they all went to a local eatery for dinner that served the best Mexican food any of them had ever had. They returned to the club ready to start their first set.

There was a small group of people there. They began their set, but no one seemed to be paying any attention. They were more interested in talking to their amigos over a cerveza.

One rather intoxicated man stumbled up to the stage area. "Hey man, you know any Santana?" he asked once they finished their song.

Luckily, they had a few Santana songs in their repertoire. They nodded and started to play" Black Magic Woman" much to the satisfaction of the few patrons who were listening while sipping their beers and conversing. A big toothy grin appeared on the man's face as he stumbled back to the bar. It was a song that the band liked because they had rearranged an extended version of the song to make it their own. It had some dramatic dynamics and a nice build. This included a breakdown where very few instruments played, starting with just some percussion and other rhythm instruments. That led to a long flute solo for Jason which eventually built into a tasteful guitar solo that soared. It finally returned back to the verse creating a musical journey. The song was an immediate hit. It eventually became a crowd favorite. It made them more accepted among the local patrons who kept asking them to play it all week.

On the second night at the end of the third set a man approached the group. They were expecting more requests. Just as Jeff turned to exit the stage, he saw the man wave, but, with the lights in his eyes, he could not make out his face. Finally, off stage he could see it was someone from his past.

"Alex Castillo, is that you?"

"Yeah man. Long time, no see," said Alex.

"Great to see you." Jeff gave Alex a hearty but manly hug. "How the hell are ya?"

"Pretty cool. And you?"

"Just fine. You know that Frank is also here. He's the manager."

"Far out man."

"There he is. Hey Frank, look who's here." He shouted across the room. "It's Alex Castillo. You remember, from our military days."

"What a trip. I can't believe it's you." He walked over holding out his hand. They executed a hearty handshake. "What brings you here?"

"I live here. This is where I came from before I joined the army. After my tour I just returned home to my family. I have a lot of family here."

"Cool, so, whatcha up to?" asked Frank.

"Just doing a bit of dealing, I have some good connections in Mexico. I have a pretty steady supply of marijuana coming in from south of the border and a pretty good clientele in the neighborhood. Otherwise, I just hang around, kinda looking for something to fill up my time."

"Yeah, well, I've been doing some dealing as well. That's how I support the band."

"We should talk. Perhaps we could do some business. Some of my clients are looking for some variety. I think we would benefit each other."

"Sounds interesting."

"In fact one of my suppliers you may know. His name is Eric. He was in Nam about the same time we were. He's not one of my Mexican connections, but he always seems to have good material."

"Yeah, I knew Eric. I haven't seen him in ages. It'd be great to see him again," admitted Frank. "How's he doing?"

"Just fine. I'll invite him to a gig. It could be good for both of us."

"Great."

"Your band is great. I'm gonna spread the word. I'll get you a crowd in here in no time."

"Let me introduce you." Frank proceeded to introduce his old war buddy to all the band members.

As the week progressed, Alex brought in more and more people. The club was filled with his friends and family. By the weekend the club was packed.

Frank and Alex began to discuss some business transactions that could be beneficial for them both. For Frank, this could be a whole new area for him to explore. This arrangement could work out well for them both.

On the last day of the gig, Alex invited the band to a Sunday afternoon get-together. It was a small wood frame house probably built in the 1940s. It had a large back yard with grass and large trees. Today it was filled with friends, family, and neighbors—all bringing food to enjoy the afternoon feast. The air was filled with the spicy aroma of Mexican food as the sounds of Latin rhythms played in the background. A large group of children played in one corner. The adults sat around talking and eating burritos, tacos, tamales, chile rellenos, and enchiladas, all served with great quantities of rice and beans. After lunch, it was time for more talk and music. A few of them picked up guitars and other instruments they had brought and started to play. It wasn't long before everyone seemed to join in picking up whatever instruments they could find: mostly percussion instruments like maracas, tambourines, or bongo drums. Of course they all sang along to the familiar songs. A full jam session ensued. The sound of Latin rhythms filled the air. The band was impressed with the sense of family and extended family and friends that prevailed. Many generations were represented there.

"This is mi abuela, my grandmother," said Alex as he introduced an older woman with a serape draped around her shoulders.

"Hola," She replied.

"She speaks very little English. She was the first to immigrate to the United States from Mexico to make a better life for her and her family many years ago. Luckily, we had some family here. Leftovers from when California was part of Mexico, but they were distant relatives at best."

Alex brought over a very big strong looking man.

"This is my Papa," continued Alex.

Introductions were made, and they all shook hands.

"He's the head of the family. He had worked hard in the fields picking fruits and vegetables in the central valley for many years. I was the first real U.S. citizen as I was the first to be born in the United States. I was just the first of 8 children. Being born in the US gave me even more opportunity. I'm very proud of my Mexican heritage, but even more proud that I am an American. I joined the service because it was a great way of showing my appreciation for all this country had to offer me. Besides, I came from a big family. We didn't have a lot of money. It was my ticket out. I could not afford much else. I thought joining the service would be a good way of getting ahead, getting some training, and ending up with some benefits especially things like the GI bill, VA loans, and other veterans' programs. I went to school for a while under the GI bill, but I made more money dealing—so I dropped out."

Alex continued showing off his friends and family to the band as the day continued. The band had met many of them briefly at the gig but never really had a chance to talk with them. There was a real sense of community. It was a nice way to spend the Sunday.

The party continued into the evening. Later, it moved to the nightclub where the band was playing. They all showed up at the club to support the band for their final night there.

In the weeks to come, Alex was always around. He and Frank were doing business selling and buying drugs. He also enjoyed going to see the band as much as possible. He was at every gig and even started showing up at rehearsals just to hang around. As time went on, he began helping the band as a part of the road crew when someone was needed.

He loved the band and felt that they were really going to make it. He saw the enthusiasm and commitment in the band members, and he wanted to be part of it.

One day he approached Frank. "I would like to be involved with the band. I got nothing better to do when I'm not dealing, and it is kind of fun. Besides, I dig everyone. I like to party. I dig the drugs, and I like the chicks." he told him.

Frank told the band, and they all agreed. Alex became a welcomed addition. He was made in charge of the stage area for the big gigs. He made sure the band had what they needed on stage, and he watched for any problems. He also helped with any special effects like the fog machine or flash pods. Mark and Pete also trained him to do any job which was especially helpful for the smaller gigs when one or more of the crew was not there. He learned the songs, the set up, and everything. He fit right in. Alex was going to be a good addition to the organization, and good for Frank's drug business as well.

"KICKS"

Paul Revere and the Raiders

F lash! The stage seemed to ignite in an explosion of sight and sound. The blaringly loud music filled the room. The members of the band could barely be seen through the dense fog that covered the five foot stage. As the smoke cleared, five musicians were rocking out to the music they were playing as the lights pulsated to the rhythms of the songs. The audience stood listening to the band play. The club had a sound and light system that made them look and sound even better, especially with Mark and Pete there to follow the music cues. They were confident this was going to be a great show and one that they would certainly enjoy playing. Of course, Alex was there to make sure everything went as planned on stage, since Mark and Pete were in the sound and light booth. This was their goal—to be playing their own music for a crowd.

They were on stage at the Music Factory, one of the many rock clubs in Hollywood that would showcase new talent and original music. Although it was not one of the prestigious clubs like The Whisky or Starwood, it was still a step up from The Underground and Club 69. It was a place where many bands played in hopes of hitting it big and getting a record deal. Many recording bands had played there on their way up. Some had even been discovered there. Many record company executives frequented there to find new talent. This was their first gig in a big Hollywood premiere showcase club. Every night the club featured two bands. Tonight they were the opening act. It wasn't quite the big time, but at least it was a start. The gig didn't pay much either. They actually lost money giving up a whole weeks work at a Top 40 club, but it was worth it. This gig was for prestige and to be seen by the right people. The Music Factory was a stepping stone in their career and definitely a step in the right direction.

The first song ended. Gloria screamed, "How is everyone tonight? Are you ready to rock?" with that the band began their next song. They had made their grand entrance, now they had to finish the set with great songs, lights, sound, and showmanship—all of which they had been working on. Gloria stood in front—proud and stately—while Mike and Bill rocked out behind her. Jason was moving to the music behind his keyboard and Jeff was truly animated, pounding the drums with great ferocity.

The band had decided that they needed to make it more of a show at least when they played the original clubs. They had worked so hard on the music that they felt they had some potential hits on their hands. Now it just needed the show to go along with it.

They had added simple things to make the show flashier, more interesting, and more spectacular. This gig was the one where they pulled out all the stops. They were doing things they were never able to do as a bar band—things that would make it seem like a true rock show. They added flash pots and fog from a fog machine. They added showmanship. They really tried working the stage: moving around like rock stars, getting into the music, and working with the audience as well as with each other to make it look as if they really were into the songs. They played with more commitment. Their work as a cover band had helped them to know how to get the audience rocking, and now they used everything they had learned. They made it a big party.

They performed an exciting and energetic one hour set. They were rewarded with rousing applause from the audience with some screaming for more. They exited the stage exhausted but elated.

Mark approached the band backstage after the set was over. "Great fuckin' set guys. You've never sounded or looked better."

"Yeah, you guys rocked," Pete commented as he walked up.

"Great show guys," Alex added.

"Thanks, it's also great having you guys there to help. It sure felt good up there." Jason smiled.

All nodded in agreement. Jeff was wiping off the sweat while Bill was wiping down his guitar.

"I dug the mix. Nice job, Mark. I could hear everyone and everything. Was my guitar loud enough?" Bill asked.

"Yeah, perfect. You're dynamics were right on. And that lead you did in the second song. Wow. It really took off. I dug the way you backed off when the vocals came back in."

"Thanks."

"How were the vocals?" asked Gloria.

"Perfect. Right on top of the band—soaring just a bit louder then the music. They have a great sound system here. How was the monitor mix? Could you hear yourself?" asked Mark.

"Yes, it was perfect."

"And the harmonies were right on. Could everyone hear themselves?"

They all nodded enthusiastically in agreement and thanked him for the excellent mix.

"I also dug the way you worked the lights Pete," Jason added. "You really had some far out color combinations. It really reflected the mood of the music. You've done an amazing job of listening and picking up the cues, especially with the spotlight."

"Thanks, man, I appreciate it."

"And Alex, those cues were right on with the fog and flash pots," Jeff complimented him.

"Yeah, and thanks for helping me with the guitar when I broke that string," Bill added.

"And my guitar cord," Mike turned to him. "You were right there with a new one."

"All this really helps make the show go so much better and smoother," said Gloria.

Frank entered. "That was great. You guys sounded and looked the best I've ever heard or seen you. All that work has really paid off. I also really hope you can see the value of our road crew."

"We sure do. We really appreciate everything they are doing for us," Gloria stated. They all nodded their heads in agreement.

After the show they knew that they had to have a party. They had worked hard and deserved it. They were buzzed about the set and how well it went. They invited their friends and some people from the club they had just met to the band house. The congratulations continued for everyone, and the band felt good about the evening's accomplishments. As usual, it turned into a typical wild after-gig party.

They returned for other engagements at this and other Hollywood concert clubs interspersed with the Top 40 gigs which were still the better money makers. With the addition of the new gimmicks and showmanship, they began to gain some notoriety and quite a following of fans in the Los Angeles club scene. They were enjoying playing much more with all the work they had done. They especially loved playing at these types of clubs. They felt more like a real rock band—not just another club band. It was fun to finally put on a show and be like rock stars.

The more they played the Hollywood clubs the more the Hollywood band house was becoming known as the party house. Everyone wanted to be invited to the after show party. The band restricted their drug use until after the show, and because of that the shows were becoming more and more consistent. They actually enjoyed playing without drugs or alcohol, but once the show was over—anything was game.

The addition of Mark, Pete, and Alex helped elevate the shows to new heights, especially for the big gigs. Having a stage crew made them look and sound even more professional.

The crew was also helpful for the smaller out-of-town gigs. They had all been cross-trained so that any one of them could handle it alone. Many times they would all show up for opening night to help load in and set up. Then take turns the rest of the week so that each of them had experience in all areas of the road crew. Even so, with nothing better to do, many times they all showed up just for the practice.

The band had become closer and closer. They functioned more like a family. Although they shared a common dream, the vision and goal was a long way off. For now, they were in this together to get through the hard times. They did this without selfishness. They had each other for emotional support. After every gig they would discuss it to see how they did and what could be improved.

This feeling even extended to the crew and management. Frank, Mark, Pete, and Alex shared in the work, the dream, and the family like atmosphere. Their comments, criticisms, and enthusiasm were always welcome. With the band acting as the central focus point for everyone—they all shared in the camaraderie.

Frank was especially valuable for those difficult times. He could always be the voice of reason when disagreements arose. It helped having someone on the outside as an objective ear and an objective observer. He proved to be invaluable to the band and the band's mental health as a whole—part critic, part psychologist, part baby sitter, part businessman. He was as much a part of the band as anyone on stage.

All in all, they felt they were making progress towards their dream and having a great time doing it. The whole organization was working well.

33

"20TH CENTURY FOX"

The Doors

It was a warm summer evening. They were playing at Pier 11. During the second set Mike noticed a particularly beautiful girl enter the club. From the stage he could see her silhouette in the skin tight mini skirt which accented the curves of her beautiful body. She walked up to the bar, ordered a drink, and then sat down at a table right in front of Mike. He could see her long blond hair shining in the lights. She looked up, her big blue eyes opened wide as she watched the band perform the set. She offered a big smile with her ruby red lips. He was hooked. Mike couldn't take his eyes off this woman for the rest of the set. It was all he could do to concentrate on his music. All he could think about was this woman.

Once the set was over he decided to walk over to her to introduce himself. He put his bass away and got up the nerve to approach her. He turned to leave the stage, his heart racing in anticipation. Just as he left the stage, she got up and walked toward him. Their eyes met. They both smiled. Mike was speechless. He felt like a schoolboy with his first crush. He was usually very comfortable around the ladies, but this one was different. As he got nearer he could see her smile and wave.

But then she walked right past him. There was obviously someone else that she knew there. Mike was a bit taken aback. He stood there feeling like a fool. He knew that somehow he just had to meet this woman. He turned around to see where she was going. She looked back as she passed him. Their eyes met again. She walked right up to Gloria and began a conversation with her, but she was constantly looking over her shoulder at Mike who just stood there.

She must know Gloria, Mike thought. So that was who she had been smiling at. He turned around to go to where Gloria was standing in hope of getting an introduction.

"Mike, this is Sarah," said Gloria as Mike approached. "She's staying with me for a while in my apartment. Sarah, this is Mike, our bass player."

Sarah was a beautiful girl, very soft spoken and seemed just plain nice.

"Oh, so that answers my questions. I was wondering how you knew each other. Very happy to meet you," Mike shyly put out his hand to her.

"I assure you, the pleasure is all mine," she said coyly.

"How long have you been staying with Gloria?" asked Mike. "I never heard her mention you."

"Oh, just a short time. It's only temporary. I asked Gloria, and she agreed. We've been friends for a long time."

Sarah needed a place to stay, so she asked Gloria if she could stay with her in exchange for rent. Gloria liked the idea of having a roommate to help pay the rent especially since she was seldom there with all the gigs they were playing.

"Where're you from?" Mike was mesmerized staring right into her blue eyes.

"Iowa originally. I came out here to become an actress and do some modeling." She paused and lowered her head. "I won some beauty pageants back home and did some acting in school. I thought it would be pretty easy to get jobs out here, and it was at first. I got a few small parts and did some modeling for magazines and stuff, but this is a pretty tough town. I do OK, but it can be a struggle. But you know that. I know how much you guys are trying to make it. Gloria tells me all about your hardships."

As Mike stood there talking he became more and more interested in her. She was everyman's fantasy, and the girl of his dreams. She was sweet and innocent with just enough of naughty to make her interesting. They spent the rest of the evening together at every break. Mike could tell the feeling was mutual. They both immediately fell for each other. It wasn't long before they were in each other's arms.

"Boy, you sure hit it off with Sarah," Gloria said the next day.

"Yeah, I think she's awesome. I think we really made a connection. I hope she feels the same," Mike responded with excitement in his voice.

"Oh, she does." Gloria nodded. "She's a nice girl and could use some attention."

Mike and Sarah began to spend a lot of time together. He quickly became quite enamored with her. He hoped it would continue. She was not like the usual girls and groupies he met or had after the gigs. She was a real nice wholesome girl. Sarah ended up going to most of the gigs, spending most of her time with Mike during the breaks. The two of them were generally inseparable. They often separated themselves from the rest of the band preferring to sit quietly in a corner talking with a close embrace.

Gloria and Sarah had met when Gloria was playing in a nightclub in another band before she joined Hollywood. Over time they had become good friends. For Sarah, things hadn't gone the way she had planned in Hollywood. She was like a fawn lost in the wood. She was quiet, mysterious, and rather secretive about herself, but the kind of woman Mike had searched for his whole life.

In the following weeks they spent every possible opportunity together. They were always glad to see each other and anxious to get together whether it was at a gig or when they had free time. They talked, laughed, and enjoyed each other's company. They seemed the perfect couple. Mike was the happiest he had ever been in his whole life. He now felt that his life was complete since he had finally found his true soul mate.

It was a beautiful night as they walked hand in hand down the beach on their way to Frank's. The band had just finished playing in Hermosa at Pier 11. A whole crowd was going to Frank's to party—another evening of sex, drugs, and rock and roll. Mike and Sarah had left after the gig so that they could be alone. The big full moon hung brightly in the black sky as if watching over the dark of the night. Its reflection danced on the sea like diamonds for what seemed like infinity. It was the perfect light to show off her beauty. The cool ocean breeze was gently blowing her long blond hair. The sound of the surf created a symphony all its own. It was a magical night.

"I love you," he told her as they walked along the beach holding hands. These were words he never thought he would say, but they came from his heart. It was the perfect evening to tell her. The mood and the setting just made it seem right.

"And I you," she said. She turned to kiss him.

This was one night Mike would never forget. They walked hand in hand down the beach; no words needed to be said anymore.

It was like a fairy tale romance. The kind of relationship he had always longed for. This was his chance for true happiness. This was Mike's dream girl. And this was Mike's dream relationship. It met all of Mike's fantasized notions of love, romance, and family. It was like some romantic Hollywood movie where it always has a happy ending and the guy ends up with the girl of his dreams and the perfect family he always wanted. She embodied the American dream. He could envision the kind of life they would have together. The romance they would have for many years—walks on the beach, romantic vacations, intimate dinners, the big romantic wedding. Eventually, they could start a family, the kind of family he never had. He could see it now in his own mind: mom, dad, 2 children—preferably one boy and one girl—a dog, a white frame house with a white picket fence, green grass, and a large tree in the front yard. He could see the family dinners, the children playing in the yard, family outings in the station wagon, and picnics in the park, dad mowing the lawn or working in the garage while the wife was in the kitchen cooking. He could envision going to the baseball games, teaching his son how to play ball while mom taught the daughter how to cook. He loved the thought of watching their children grow up: going to school, attending dance recitals, football games, or band concerts. This would be the perfect family and lead the perfect life—like a Norman Rockwell painting. This was a dream he had longed for. The kind of life he had always wanted. This was his chance to finally have it.

It was out of true caring that Jason went to Mike to discuss Sarah. "You're becoming quite involved with Sarah," Jason began as they waited for the rest of the band to arrive for the gig one evening.

"Yeah, I think I love her. She's everything I've ever hoped for." Mike grinned.

"Well, I'm happy for you," Jason responded. "But do me a favor. Take it real slow. We're all concerned that you might get hurt." He could see Mike getting defensive and agitated. "Look, I'm not here to tell you what to do. I just want you to be careful. It's only because I care. We all care. I'm glad you found someone. I can see that you are really falling for this girl. I guess I just don't want you to get hurt."

"Yeah, I can see how much love means to you with all the men you and Gloria have. It's just downright trashy. Then spending your nights off at that old bar with your friends and picking up someone else."

"Look who's fuckin' talkin'! I admit I am a bit of slut, but you know, I like it. It's fun. What's wrong with it? I ain't hurting anybody." Jason defended himself.

"What about those straight guys you and Gloria pick up?" Mike asked.

"What about 'em. If they resist or aren't interested I back off. Believe me; they enjoy it as much as I do." Jason was a bit taken aback at Mike's attitude. "Also, they're just one-nighters. Not for anything really serious, emotional, or long lasting. I don't love 'em. They're just for play. But we aren't talking about me. Do all my sexual exploits matter that much to you? I thought we were better friends than that. You certainly have done more than your share with all the chicks you've picked up at the gigs. So, who are you to talk? Just because you found someone and don't pick up chicks like you used to, don't make you any better."

"Yeah, I'm sorry. I just got carried away. I'm just so confused because I love her so much. You have no idea. She's the most important thing in my life—except the band of course. You know this band is my family. But I just can't give her up, nor do I want to. She's wonderful. She makes me feel whole. She fills that void in my life."

"There's just something about her that we're not so sure about. I've discussed it with the band a little. We've never seen her in a movie or any modeling. We're just afraid that one day she'll take off and forget about you. Maybe get that big movie part or modeling job, or even make it big as an actress. Ours is only true concern. Please believe that. I'm truly happy for you if you think this is real, and you are truly in love. Believe me. I envy you for that. Just be real careful, and remember who your friends are."

Bill entered the room. "What's happening?"

"I was just telling Mike our concern over his relationship with Sarah." Jason turned to Bill.

"Be careful," Bill replied. "You never know what'll happen, or what they're after."

"That's funny coming from you. You never even seem interested in girls. I even thought you might be gay once. With Jason around there's certainly nothing stopping you from coming out. Don't you enjoy sex?"

"Sure I do, as much as anyone, except maybe Jeff," he chuckled. "I just do it myself. You know, I have more control, no expectations, no involvement, and no emotions. I know exactly what to do. I guess you might say I make love to myself or maybe my hand." Again he smiled. "I can give a lot of pleasure to myself without all that other entanglement. It's just easier that way."

"Why is that?" Jason inquired noting that Bill was in one of his seldom talkative moods.

"I think I just find it difficult dealing with another person. I have enough trouble dealing with myself. What's the big deal, this foreplay and stuff? I'd rather get myself off. And can usually do it better because I know what to do. Also, there's no expectation of me by anyone else. I only disappoint myself, no one else. Besides, I feel very vulnerable having sex with someone else. It's like I'm standing there naked, not only in the physical sense but in an emotional sense. Like someone can see right through you. It frightens me. I don't like being vulnerable. If that means not having sex with someone, well, that's the way it is. Maybe someday I will fall in love with someone, but it'll take some time for someone to get to know me. When they do, the final thing will be the sexual aspect to finalize the relationship. I want to make love, not just fuck. I think sex is very special. I'd rather keep it that way. I may not have sex as often, but I think it means so much more than just a quick fuck. It'll be perfect and beautiful—the most wonderful feeling in the world. Now, I sometimes feel that way when I play music. Maybe music is my woman. In the meantime, I'll continue to relieve my urges by beating off, getting high, and playing music. I hope you understand. Besides, I get my share. Can't really help it with this band."

"Yeah, I guess so," Jason responded. "I mean who am I to say anything or to judge you? After all I am the different one. I like boys. I just hope your expectations are not too high. I wonder if you'll ever be fulfilled."

"But I know what you mean," Mike continued in agreement. "That's how I feel about Sarah. Our relationship is the most wonderful and fulfilling thing I have ever felt."

"Just don't get hurt." Bill looked Mike right in the eye. "You might just end up gun shy like me. You see, I was in love once too, but I got hurt—real bad." Jason and Mike looked at each other stunned. Bill was opening up.

"Was it the girl in Boston?" Mike asked hoping to get some more information out of him since Bill seldom talked about his personal life.

"Yeah, I guess I never told you guys much about it. It just ended up in a bad scene. That's why I went to New York and got into drugs. I'd just like to forget the whole damn thing. I don't ever want to be hurt like that again. It was a very painful experience. I never wanna go through that again."

Just then Jeff and Frank's voices could be heard just outside the room. "I got a call from Eric. He's interested in discussing some business with you."

"Yeah, Alex told me. I thought he was long gone. Where'd you run into him?" Frank asked. "I didn't know you were still in touch with Eric." Frank looked at him questioningly.

"Yeah, haven't really seen him in years, probably since Nam."

"I thought after that Viet Nam affair you wouldn't see each other any more."

"But what do you know about Viet Nam?" Jeff asked.

"Only that you and Eric used to whore around a lot. Got caught—reprimanded or something," said Frank.

"Yeah, actually we had a nice little black market business going, running drugs, contraband, and stuff. Nothing big or anything; just small time stuff. We got caught and got our hands slapped." Jeff admitted.

"So that's why you hung out so much together in Nam."

"Yeah, once they found out, we thought we were in pretty big trouble. They ended up just giving us a warning. We lost track of each other after Viet Nam. He got in touch with me recently through Alex. He heard that I was in the band. Quite a coincidence really."

"Sounds like old home week."

"We thought it'd be fun to reconnect. Old times and all that. However, I think he was mostly checking up on you. Wanted to find out what I thought. He asked a lot of questions about you and your operation. He says he has some government connection. He says it could be mutually beneficial to both of you. I thought it might be better than dealing with those Mafia hoodlums you are dealing with now," Jeff said not knowing anyone else was listening.

"Yeah, that could be interesting."

"I thought you knew each other. What really happened in Nam between you and Eric?" Jeff inquired. "Rumor around the platoon had it that the Viet Cong captured both of you. Since we never saw the two of you again, we figured you were either dead or lost—another POW statistic. Then one day we saw them bring you back to base together. We figured you were POWs together."

"I can't believe you know," Frank said astonished. "We were held prisoners for a while—almost a year. But we were rescued. It was the most hellish year in my life. If it wasn't for Eric I would probably be dead. But we held on. How d'ya know about all that?"

"I thought it was common knowledge."

"Let's keep all this quiet—at least from the band. That's a time in my life I'd like to forget. OK? Do it for me." They entered the room.

They were surprised to find the other three sitting in silence. The three continued their conversation, pretending they had not heard anything.

"Oh, Jeff, we were just telling Mike our concern over Sarah," Jason said.

"Yeah, don't make the price too high just to get your dick wet."

"You're so sensitive." Jason laughed.

However, Two weeks later Jeff had changed his tune. He took Mike aside. "This girl is not good for you, Mike," Jeff said with real concern in his voice, something he seldom displayed.

"You're not gonna start on me too are you? I love her. And that's all there is to it. Case closed!" Mike curtly exclaimed.

"But just what d'ya know about this girl? Where she's from? What she's done? You know very little."

"I know that I love her, and that's enough for me."

"No matter what she's done?" Jeff asked.

"What do you mean?" Mike asked. "Do you know something I don't?"

"Just suppose."

"Just suppose what? I love her and that's that."

"All right, all right. But look, tomorrow I'm going out. I want you to join me. Just us. We'll have a great time. You'll see," Jeff said with a snicker. "I won't take no for an answer, or I will keep hounding you."

"OK," Mike reluctantly agreed.

"AIN'T NO SUNSHINE WHEN SHE'S GONE"

Bill Withers

It was a warm night in downtown Hollywood when Mike and Jeff left for their boy's night out. Mike, feeling as if he had been taken hostage, passed the joint back to Jeff who had a sneaky grin on his face.

"I need a drink," Jeff said. They stopped at one of Hollywood's seedy bars. Once inside Mike could see just how seedy this bar really was. But the drinks were really cheap, and Jeff kept them coming. Two hours later they were both feeling no pain.

"Movie time," Jeff said. He stood up and staggered to the door as Mike followed. Before he knew it Jeff was buying tickets to the pussycat theatre next door.

"Where are we going?" Mike asked.

"This is that new porno flick everyone is talking about, 'Head of the Class'. It's supposed to be even better than Deep Throat. They say that this new star is incredible.

Mike looked up at the poster. "Holly Wood, is that the name of this new porn star?"

"You got that right. Come on. This should be fun."

"Not one of *those* evenings again! I don't wanna see this. Let's just split," Mike insisted, but Jeff grabbed his arm, leading him into the dark theatre with a smirk on his face. He had a strange laugh like he was up to something.

The picture had just started and the credits were rolling with all the usual names of porno stars, obviously made up. Holly Wood even got her credit before the name of the picture then Dick Long and a cast of many. Finally, the movie began trying to set up some vague semblance of story line before the real sex scenes. This was like most pornographic movies—thin on plot, bad acting, bad directing, and generally cheap looking. Mike, now bored, watched without the least bit of enthusiasm. He was really hardly paying any attention to it at all. That was until suddenly a woman on the screen caught his eye. She looked just like Sarah. The more he looked, the more he thought it was Sarah, and the more he couldn't believe his eyes. Then it hit him.

"That's Sarah!" he shouted looking at Jeff who had a sad but satisfied look on his face. "What the fuck is she doing there? You knew about this all along you bastard!"

His shouting had alerted the ushers (more like bouncers) of the theater who came running in just in time to see Mike stand up with fists drawn, ready to deliver a good right hook to Jeff. They grabbed Mike who was by now a raving lunatic, muscled him out of the theatre, and threw him out into the street where he landed in the gutter.

Mike was in such shock that all he could think to do was run, his face now streaming with tears. Jeff ran outside to find Mike, but it was too late. Mike was gone. He had ducked down one of the side streets. Mike ran as far as he could, trying to stop the tears. He found himself on a small alley off one of the back streets of Hollywood. He noticed a sign with a martini glass.

"I need a drink," he thought to himself entering the bar still in a daze. He found a barstool, sat down, and ordered a beer. He was trying to hide how truly upset he was. It seemed his whole world was tumbling down.

"You all right honey?" said a voice from behind.

Mike's eyes looked up to find a tall rather unattractive looking woman staring at him. Then for the first time he got a look at the rest of the bar. It was seedy beyond belief. All he could think of was some bad black and white movie about drunks, crooks, and low life living in the back alleys of any American city.

"Yeah, I'm OK." He noticed how most of the women in this bar looked like prostitutes—fish net stockings, stiletto heels, mini-skirts. One walked up and grabbed his leg. She gave him a big wink with her long false eyelashes, and then walked on. She returned to a table with a group of other women and one large mean looking guy, the kind you would not want to meet in a dark alley.

"These are fucking prostitutes," Mike thought to himself. "Fucking prostitutes—the same as Sarah, except they do it in private, not in front of the cameras for all to see." He strained a laugh which sounded more like dementia than anything comedic. "That's all Sarah is, a fucking prostitute. The band was right." He was now talking to himself. He started out with his voice in a whisper, but the more he thought about it the louder and louder his voice got. The liquor made him unaware of how really loud he was becoming. People in the bar started to look his way as they became aware of him talking to himself but thinking that he was just some drunken derelict.

Suddenly, he shouted, "You're all whores, fucking whores!"

With that, the woman sitting next to him slapped him.

"Who you calling a whore, honey." But this time her voice had suddenly dropped. It was very masculine. Then he noticed her arms and her legs. This was not the body of a woman.

"You're a man!" He suddenly realized. "A fucking transvestite!" He looked around. He noticed she was not the only one. These were some big broads with way too much make-up to hide the five o'clock shadow and all the semblance of being a man. Mike felt it was like some seedy film noir movie, where the drunk stumbles into a real strange scene, right out of a Fellini movie. "Yeah, honey, you ought to try it some time, you just might surprise yourself. You might like it," making her last ploy to pick him up or at least calm him down.

"You're disgusting!" he shouted. "You're all sick!"

"Honey, I am more woman than you'll ever have and more man than you'll ever be." The painted drag queen retorted back, now fed up with the whole thing.

This was enough for the big burly guy who looked like he could have been their pimp. He stood up, walked over, and hit Mike so hard he flew across the room. The man continued pushing him out the door, into the alley, and into the gutter. All patrons of the bar ran out to the door of the bar where they watched him kick Mike a few more times then left him there in the middle of the dark dimly lit street. Once finished, all the girls gave a rousing round of applause.

By the time Mike was able to get up, they had left the door. He stumbled again down the street. He thought it was time he found a cab home. He discovered his wallet was missing, and he wasn't about to go back and get it. He finally reached the bright lights of Hollywood Boulevard again. He tried asking for help, but people just avoided him thinking he was some derelict.

Jeff had been searching for Mike for hours. Eventually, he felt he should call someone. He really had not expected this kind of reaction. He was truly concerned. He called Gloria at home from a pay phone.

"Have you heard from Mike?" he asked Gloria when she answered the phone.

"No, Why? Should I have?" Gloria responded rather surprised at the question.

"He knows about Sarah."

"What they fuck do you mean? What happened?" Gloria's angry voice demanded.

"I took him to the Pussycat theatre. They were playing one of her films."

"What kind of a heartless asshole are you? Mike is a sensitive human being. Something like this could devastate him. Who the fuck d'ya think you are? Don't you have any brains?"

"A least I was honest. All his so called friends were telling him lies. You knew what kind of person Sarah was, and you did nothing to protect Mike. What kind of friend is it that lets another live a lie, get his hopes up, believes in someone, only to find out it was a lie. At least I showed him the truth."

"And he'll probably kill himself over it. Where is he now?"

"Uh… I don't know. I lost him when he ran out of the theatre. I've been searching the streets for over an hour. I was hoping he might've called. You stay there and wait for him in case he gets to you. I'll keep searching and call back later."

Gloria turned to find Sarah standing there. She had been listening. "Well, I guess you heard."

"Yeah," she said tears streaming down her face. "It's time I got back anyway." She turned and began to pack.

Gloria grabbed her and slapped her. "You aren't running out on this situation! You just waltz in here. Then when things get tough you waltz right out and think you can ruin someone else's life. And now you want to forget everything and run back to your sugar daddy and return to your old habits. You'll wind up a cocaine addict again, just like you were when you got here. Don't you realize this boy loves you? And damn it! You're gonna stay and face him! You owe him that. I helped you kick the habit, now I'm cashing in on my favor. Whatever happened to that little girl I knew when she got off the bus from Iowa? So full of dreams. So full of hopes. Looking for a career as an actress and a husband that would make you happy. Now look at you. You're nothing but a two bit whore. The only difference is that you've done a bit better because you can perform on film. What has this town done to you? You think you are special to those people. Well, grow up. They just want to use you, to exploit you. They make a fortune off you. I can't believe that the fame it has brought you means that much to you."

"I don't have to listen to this. I just can't deal with seeing Mike, not after this. I gotta split." She rushed out the door.

"Yeah, go back to your fuckin' drugs, your acting. Ha! And your glamorous Hollywood crowd!"

Sarah ran down the street, tears streaming down her cheek.

An hour later there was a knock at the door. Gloria rushed to open it. She could hear Mike calling Sarah's name. She opened the door to find Mike—completely drunk and being supported by another man. "I found him wandering Hollywood Boulevard. He's kind of messed up. I was finally able to get an address out of him." Gloria grabbed the other shoulder and helped the man carry Mike in. They laid him on the sofa.

"I don't know how to repay you," she said. "I was so worried. Thank God for people like you. He could've been dead." The man left as Gloria comforted Mike. His head was buried in Gloria's arms as he sobbed for hours finally crying himself to sleep.

The band was having their band meeting a week later. Mike just hadn't been himself. It was time for an intervention. The trauma of Sarah had made him lethargic and disinterested. He seemed to have lost his drive and purpose.

Jason entered the room He had newspaper under his arm and an upset look on his face. He gave the paper to Mike who read it for a short time, threw it down, and then ran into his bedroom. Jason picked up the newspaper and found the article. The headlines read. "Porn Queen Found Dead of Overdose." He continued to read the rest of the article as all listened. It was like an old Hollywood starlet movie with a bad ending. Beauty queen moves to Hollywood to make it big in pictures only to be led to a life of corruption. A sad tale, to say the least.

Jason started reading.

Porn Queen Found Dead of Overdose

> To most people she was known as Holly Wood, star of numerous pornographic films and recipient of many awards for her performances. But for her family she was known as Sarah Lewis, the homecoming queen from a small town in Iowa where she worked her way up the beauty queen circuit to be Corn Queen for the Iowa State Fair. She came to Hollywood to make her fame and fortune as a movie star. Instead she ended up another casualty of lust and greed and drugs so prevalent in the business.
>
> She was found at the home of her producer and sometimes lover John Donaldson. "She had left for a couple weeks,"

Mr. Donaldson told the press, "just vanished. I didn't know where she was. Then late one night she reappeared. She was very upset. She said she wanted to do more movies. I could see she'd been drinking and doing a lot of drugs. For the rest of the week I couldn't stop her from doing drugs. She was hiding them, and she was out of control. It was like she was on a suicide mission. She was totally destructive. I don't know what happened during that time she was away, but something major affected her life."

Sarah left a short, simple note: "Thank you for making my life worthwhile, if only for a short time. I will never hurt you again." In many ways, it was the town whose namesake she inherited that finally broke her, and today she is dead.

The paper went on to describe her wholesome Middle America upbringing as if she were Pollyanna or someone.

The whole band went into Mike's room. He lay across the bed sobbing, Jason on one side and Gloria on the other. They gave him a big hug.

"Look, we know this must be tough on you." Frank started talking as he stood in the doorway. "But we're all here for you. We're in this together."

Mike turned and sat up; his eyes red from crying. He stretched out his arms. The whole group gave him one big hug.

"Gloria, you knew all this. Why the fuck didn't you tell me?" Mike asked.

"I met her when she first came here from Iowa, a wild eyed girl with stars in her eyes, sweet and innocent. She went downhill from there, but I always believed in her. She made it pretty big in the industry, but got really involved in drugs. She was making really good money. She was being well kept by her producer, living in his mansion. It seemed like the good life. It seemed she had everything she wanted. She did get into a lot of drugs, but I wasn't that aware of it until she told me later. Then she came to me wanting me to help her get away from all that and to get off the drugs. That was when you met her. I truly thought she was gonna change here life again. She had had enough. She really wanted to turn her life around. Please think kindly of her. She was that sweet, innocent girl that you met. She just got caught up in the seedy yet strangely glamorous side of Hollywood. She did care about you Mike, so please keep her in your heart."

Mike entered the rehearsal room late the next day. The whole band was there as was Frank.

"I wrote a song last night. It was the only way I could deal with all this. I just had to get it out. The song is called Hollywood. It's about Hollywood the city and what it does to people. It lures people in with the dreams of fame and fortune. How no one knows what is real or what is an illusion or just fantasy. And behind all that glitter, is a tarnished reality. It's also about how we all have to hide behind our masks and our feelings. It's also about Sarah since Holly Wood was her stage name. She was one of the causalities of this city. But she did the same thing to me, lured me in. She created an illusion that was just not real. Mostly it's about all the secrets we keep inside us. It's really rough, but I'd like to know what you think. It's a slow power ballad. I'd like to start with an acoustic guitar and Jason on flute. Then to the first verse. Bass and drums don't come in until the second verse and then the whole band for the chorus. I want it to be really strong." Mike picked up the acoustic guitar and started playing his song "The Song is called 'HOLLYWOOD'."

He played it. The band was speechless.

"So what d'ya think?"

"It's incredible. We should work on it right now." Jason grabbed his flute.

This was their song. They were not out to copy anyone else. This song came from a real place which made it all the better. Everyone knew it was going to be a great song.

"I thought a lot about this last night as well. I have an idea," Frank started. "I think we should dedicate the name of the band to her. And now we also have this great song which will represent her as well as the town from which we were conceived. For Mike and for all of us it'll represent the girl whose inspiration will continue to take us further, even after her death. So every time we play this song let's think about her, so that her life will not have been in vain."

They all agreed enthusiastically. As the band worked on the song, Frank disappeared only to return a short time later with a bottle of champagne to celebrate. He proclaimed. "The band name and this song are now officially dedicated to her."

"HOLLYWOOD"

"WILD WORLD"

Cat Stevens

"We got a gig at The Hollywood Star next month!" Frank exclaimed as he entered the room during rehearsal. "I'm also working on getting gigs at The Whisky, Gazarri's, Starwood, and The Troubadour. They're all starting to listen now."

The band cheered expressing their satisfaction and happiness.

"Man, that is fuckin' fantastic! I really think it's starting to happen." Mike put down his bass to hear more.

"I also have continuous bookings well in the future. You guys better get ready to work a lot."

All their hard work on the songs, the show, and the gimmicks was finally beginning to pay off. The band was starting to develop a reputation and a good following all over town, and the crowds were beginning to follow them. This worked to their advantage since club owners and bookers wanted to see a good crowd and a guaranteed box office. They too wanted a piece of the action. They wanted to see that audience in their club. This was especially important in Hollywood and the big clubs. It was easier to get gigs, and they were booked well in advance. The club owners and other bookers were anxious to see them return, but now had to work with the band's schedule since they seemed to always be booked and were in such high demand. Frank was booking them all over town. Working at the lesser known concert rock clubs in Hollywood had helped them work their way up to the bigger better known clubs, and the Hollywood Star was the first. This following also began to generate some interest in the music business. There was a real buzz about the band Hollywood.

It was with a great deal of anticipation that the date of the Hollywood Star gig approached. This could be their first real big break. This was the club for musicians, recording artists, and music industry people. The Hollywood Star was one of the main clubs for displaying original talent. Every night different bands played—some signed and some unsigned. It also served the industry, especially record labels as a venue to showcase a new artist to other people in the industry, especially the press. The club was mostly filled with Hollywood's best up-and-coming musicians, all struggling for the record deal and their chance to become rock stars. This club had the reputation of launching many careers. Many bands that had played at the Star had gone on to get record deals. Some had hit records on the charts, and a few had even gone on to become major rock stars selling millions of records and touring all over the world in large arenas. Many of the days top recording artists got their start, were discovered, or at the very least had at one time played there. It was a perfect room for really putting on a rock show with a large stage, good sound system, and professional lighting. It was a place to be seen by the major players in the industry. This could be the start of their professional career as recording artists.

They were given a Monday night to start. The bookings depended on the sheer numbers of your audience drawing power as well as the club's schedule. The bigger the draw, the more you were moved into better and better nights that would eventually lead to either opening or headlining status.

They arrived for their sound check excited. They felt that this was their first real gig in the big time. As they arrived, the parking lot was filled with limousines. They entered the club to check out the room only to find a band playing on the stage. They were putting on a real show and sounding incredible. The club manager saw Frank and rushed over.

"You'll have to wait. There's a band showcasing for Motown. All the Motown executives are here. They'll be done shortly, but you can start unloading to the back stage area so long as you are quiet, or you can sit in the back quietly and listen." Frank nodded in agreement. He advised the band who decided to stay and watch the show.

The band was really good. They put on quite a show even without an audience. It was not really their type of music, but it seemed perfect for Motown—soulful and funky. The show ended and the room was quiet—no applause, no reaction—just dead silence. Six people in the middle of the room stood up. They whispered to themselves as a man approached from the backstage area. "Hoped you liked the show," he timidly inquired. He obviously was their manager.

"We'll be in touch," one man spoke out as the others dispersed out the door to their awaiting limousines. He turned to join them, but upon seeing a man standing at the back of the hall in the doorway he waved and hollered, "Thanks Mr. Grant, we appreciate the use of your club."

Mr. Grant was an impeccably dressed older man. He had gray hair and was a bit overweight which made the fit of his sport coat seem too tight for his body. He was surrounded by young men, also well dressed. He snapped his fingers and put two fingers in the air which signaled one of the young men to light up a cigarette. He turned to another and motioned with a flip of his other hand, at which point the young man ran to the bar to get a drink. He stood up and left with his entourage following in tow. He disappeared into the back rooms of the club.

"Must be the owner." Frank looked to the house manager for confirmation.

"Yep, he's The Boss." The club manager stated.

"Where does he get all his money? He can't be that rich from running this club. I mean it's nice and all, but come on."

"Well, some say he gets it from drug money or some underground organized crime connection, but I don't ask questions. I just collect my paycheck, do my job, and keep my mouth shut. But don't let it concern you, you'll never see him. He only comes out for big industry events or showcases. Now let's get your sound check happening."

"He'll be here to see us, eventually. You'll see. This is a great band, and someday—"

"Yeah, yeah." He interrupted Frank. "I've heard it all before from you managers. Let's just do the sound check. Mitch, come down here. This is the band that'll be playing tonight. Mitch is our stage manager. He'll be helping you with everything: sound, lights, whatever. See you all later."

Frank turned, a little aggravated by this club manager's cavalier attitude, but thought it best to leave well enough alone. He went to a telephone in the club and dialed. "Listen. Find out everything you can about a Mr. Grant. He owns the Hollywood Star Club. I'll call back later." He hung up then walked outside only to find an old friend.

"Eric Watson, how the hell are you?" he shouted. He ran to greet his old Viet Nam buddy.

"Just great, thanks. Really good to see you again." They shook hands. "Jeff and Alex had told me about your band and your operation," said Eric. "I thought it was time I paid you a visit, and what better a place. Pretty impressive."

"Well, you came at a good time. How'd you find me here?"

"I invited him," Alex interrupted them as he walked up to greet them. "Glad you could make it." He shook Eric's hand, and then turned to Frank. "As I told you, he's one of my connections—actually, one of my suppliers. I thought it was time you met. He said he had a proposition for you. Thought, perhaps, you could do some business together."

"Great," Frank replied in amazement. "But whatcha doing these days? Still flying?"

"A little. I still have my pilot's license. I own a small four-seater Cessna airplane that I keep at one of the local airports. I rent it and myself out as pilot to individuals who need a plane. I take businessmen on short trips or people out sightseeing. But mostly I use it for running drugs. I also do a bit of dealing of my own on the side," Eric continued. "Alex tells me you have quite an operation. I wanna talk to you about some good deals. I think we can do some business. I have the connections, and you have the capital. I think I have an interesting proposition for ya."

"Sounds interesting. We'll talk later. I have a band to get ready. Why don't you stick around and have a listen. I have some business to take care of, but we should talk afterwards. I'll make sure you can get in tonight on our guest list as well." They shook hands while Eric nodded in agreement. Frank left to supervise the loading in of the equipment and to make sure everything was ready for tonight's performance. This one was important.

Sound check went as planned. They only had to wait for tonight when they were to play.

The band left. Frank stayed at the club to make a phone call and take care of some business. He saw Eric again.

"Band sounds real good. I'm very impressed." Eric approached Frank.

"Thanks, so what you got?" Frank asked.

"Well, here's the deal. An old buddy of mine is now a federal agent. He has quite an operation with some other feds and drug agents that he has introduced me to. You may even know the guy. I've known him since Viet Nam. We ran drugs there. His name is Russ, Russ Walker. He was the base commander in Nam."

"Base Commander Walker. Oh, I knew of him all right. If you were on that base how could anyone not know who he was? I didn't know him well, but I knew his reputation. He was a hard nosed power hungry asshole. He ruled that base with an iron fist. I can't believe he became a federal agent and a dirty one at that. I should've known. He was one conniving son of a bitch."

"That's him. So here's the deal. When there's a big bust, Walker and his team only turn in half. They don't want to get involved in petty dealing, so they sell us the other half at well below market price. The government gets a big bust; Walker gets some extra cash especially since he gets it free, while we get some good drugs to sell. He has fronted me some small quantities, but it's just getting way to big time for me. He has even larger quantities, but he wants the money in advance. All we have to do is come up with the cash and pick it up. That's where I come in. We have to fly to the desert in Arizona to pick it up. So, we can just fly out and make the deal, then fly back before anyone knows the difference. Also, I don't have the cash or connections which you do. I thought it would be a good proposition for you, and it would help me out. I get a cut of course. It's a win-win for everyone."

"Sounds interesting! What kinda drugs, and what kinda quantities are we talking? And what do we need to do?" Frank inquired.

"Mostly pot and coke, but also some acid, hash, and other stuff. It all depends on the bust. I never know what they'll get. We just need to be ready to act quickly. The quantities are vast so don't worry about the volume. So long as you got the cash, they're ready to do business. They're just waiting for my call. If you're interested I'll set it up. I understand you can use the band to launder the money and make it look legit. It'd be a great front. Consequently, we can be partners, help the band, and help ourselves."

"Count me in," said Frank.

"Cool, I'll set it up and make the introductions." Eric held out his hand for a handshake. Frank took it as a gentlemen's agreement. He held out his hand to seal the deal.

"Sounds like a deal. Now I need to make a phone call." Frank went to the phone and dialed.

"What's the word?" asked Eric.

"Big time stuff. I suggest you not get involved with this guy. Way beyond your league. All dirty money, drugs, and shit. Involved with the syndicate. Just wait outside for me."

"Thanks, that's all I need to know." Eric turned and left.

Frank went to the private section of the club. He found the door marked private and burst in. "Oh, excuse me; I thought this was the dressing rooms."

Mr. Grant had his nose to the table. He was snorting what looked like cocaine on a small mirror with a rolled up dollar bill. He was at first startled. He immediately stood up and snapped his fingers signaling the two large thugs. They approached Frank.

"I'm sorry, Mr. Grant. You have quite a club here. Interesting way to hide your real business." The thugs had him by the arms, ready to throw him out. "Wait, its cool. I think we can talk some business here." He threw out a vile of cocaine which landed on his desk. "Try it. There's more where that came from."

"You small-time dealers think you can impress me with your little connections." He snapped his fingers again.

"I wouldn't call the U.S. Government a small source. What do ya think they do with all the drugs in those big busts?"

"Hold on," he instructed his men. "What do you know about these busts?" He snapped his fingers again and turned, his interest peaked. "I've lost a lot of goods to the feds."

"Well, here is a way of getting it back. Or perhaps, I can arrange to have them look the other way for your shipments. Also, we can arrange to make life a bit more difficult for your competitors, set 'em up for a bust or somethin'. Interested?"

"Slightly, but what do you get outta this?"

"I get my take, either a percentage or some of the material. Also, there are times when I'll need a source for some drugs when my connections are dry. I think we can help each other out and do some mutually beneficial business. However, mostly I want my band seen by some industry people."

"I won't go out on a limb for any band. I have a reputation as well. You bring me the first shipment on first refusal. We'll go from there. I'll keep this little sample for a try and let you know." Mr. Grant snapped his fingers. The two thugs escorted him out of the office.

Outside the office Frank smiled, having bluffed his way into the scene. Now all he had to do was make it happen.

Eric was waiting in the parking lot as Frank approached. "I think we have a deal. Let's get the ball rolling." They shook hands and left.

The gig that evening went flawlessly. The band sounded great. They had a good crowd and good audience reaction. Curiosity had even got the best of Mr. Grant who was seen in the audience taking a look at the band. They were all happy with the way it went and looked forward to returning for another engagement.

Eric set up a meeting for Frank to meet his connections. It was late in the evening when the two sped out to a small airport in Hawthorne where Eric's plane was kept. It was a small black twin engine Cessna.

"You sure you can fly this?" Frank asked.

"Are you kidding? There is one thing that the army taught me and that was how to fly a plane."

It was a clear night. As they gained altitude, the lights of Los Angeles stretched out as far as the eye could see. It was a sight to behold. Glimmering jewels of light in a sea of darkness. The lights seemed to go on forever. It seemed like a long time before they started getting more sparse. Finally, the lights lessened once they passed Riverside. The full moon hung brightly in the eastern sky like a beacon guiding them to their destination and lighting their way. As they passed between the San Jacinto and San Bernardino Mountain ranges, they could see the snow-capped peaks of Mount San Jacinto and San Gorgonio Mountain illuminated by moonlight. They rose on either side like fortresses with elevations exceeding 10,000 feet making them two of the highest peaks not only in California but in North America. Once passed the mountains, the blackness of the desert overcame them with expansive darkness as far as the eye could see. Most of southeastern California was a vast desert created as a result of the rain shadow effect with precipitation seldom making it past the mountain ranges. In the distance they could see the lights of Palm Springs at the base of Mount San Jacinto. A long-time playground of the rich and famous where 350 days of sunshine allowed for warm days even in the coldest of winters. Because of its climate, it offered a variety of recreational activities all year long including golf, swimming, tennis, and hiking. Since it was only about a two hour drive from Los Angeles, many Hollywood stars spent a lot of time there or had second homes there. It was a place to get away from the pressures of the entertainment business, and a place to play without the eyes of the press constantly on them. A few other desert cities were visible in the distance, but they soon vanished leaving them in complete darkness. They turned left and traveled north leaving the lower flat Sonoran Desert to the higher elevations but more isolated and mountainous Mojave Desert They passed over Joshua Tree National Monument on their way to their destination.

"There it is," said Eric as he started to bring the plane down.

Frank could see the lights of small landing strip in the middle of nowhere. They landed the small plane then got out. Two lights flashed in the distance. They turned out to be car headlights. Eric took out his flashlight and flashed them back. A black car drove up to the airplane. Two guys in suits got out of the front seat with machine guns.

"Looking for Mr. Walker, Eric's the name."

A tall, dark ominous looking man in a black suit exited the back of the car.

"Eric, great to see you," said Russ.

"You too. This is Frank Barcelona, the guy I told you about. I'm not sure if you remember him. He was stationed on your base in Nam. He was infantry."

"Can't really say that I remember you, Frank. I was in charge of a lot of troops. I can't believe that our paths have crossed again. Small world."

"I never thought I'd see you again, especially under these circumstances. You were pretty straight forward. You ran a tight ship."

"Still do," he said in his military voice.

"Never thought you'd be one of the bad guys, uh, I mean good guys. Well, you know what I mean. You were such a bad ass in the army—a real hard nose. I guess it fits," Frank responded with his hand outstretched. They shook hands like two long lost buddies, with conviction and power—each trying to show their dominance over the other. This was a handshake and a power play all in one.

"I understand that we're gonna do some business together."

"I think so." Frank opened up a briefcase full of money for Russ to look over. "I think this should get us started."

Russ snapped his fingers. One of the other guys went to the trunk and took out a suitcase. He opened it in front of Frank. He gave the other guy the suitcase Frank had given him to check to see if everything was there. He looked over it carefully then gave it back to Russ.

"10 pounds of cocaine, the finest quality and pure—not cut with anything."

Frank wet his finger and took a small sampling. He tasted it then snorted the rest.

"Seems like some good material," said Frank.

"I'll keep Eric informed as to what I get in. It's a difficult business and one never knows, but I'll give my old army buddies first crack at whatever I get."

"Thanks, I appreciate that."

"I think it's gonna be good doing business with ya."

"Yeah. If you can't trust your old war buddies, who can you trust?"

The two men closed their cases. Frank and Eric turned and walked toward the waiting plane as the three men got in to the car and sped away into the night.

The plane lifted off into the darkness.

"I think this arrangement is gonna work out great," said Frank.

"Works for me," agreed Eric.

As they flew back to LA they could see the lights of the city on the horizon like sparkling diamonds stretching for miles in all directions with no end in sight. It was a beautiful sight—one they would never forget.

36

"WE WON'T GET FOOLED AGAIN"

The Who

It was the band's third gig at the Hollywood Star. They had done such a good job and had brought in a good crowd that they were asked back. They were playing there about every other month now. In addition to Frank's usual network, connections, and dealers, he and Eric were running drugs in the desert. Frank was also doing business with Mr. Grant, the owner of the club. All was running very smoothly.

They had finished their set and were backstage putting away their instruments when someone appeared at the door to their dressing room. "Hey man, I thought your show really rocked tonight," he said as he confidently entered the dressing room like he owned the place.

He was a tall, thin man wearing small round sun glasses that obscured his eyes. He had long, straight, shiny black hair that reached all the way down his back. His rock t-shirt, blue jeans, and sport coat made him look like he was someone important.

"Thanks," they all said paying little attention. They continued to get ready to leave.

He approached Mike who was the closest and the first to acknowledge him with a glance and a nod. Mike thought he recognized him as one of the members of an old '60s band but could not quite place him.

"My name is Jonathan, Jonathan Cooper." He held out his hand to shake.

"Oh, I thought you looked familiar." Mike was able to make the connection now with the name. "Weren't you in The Blue Wave?" Mike asked.

"Yeah, I played guitar," the man responded.

"Far out! I have a couple of your albums. You guys were great."

"Thanks."

"Hey everyone, this guy was in The Blue Wave. His name is Jonathan."

They all acknowledged him this time. Introductions were made all around.

"You guys were huge, and then you vanished," said Mike.

"Yeah, we broke up a couple of years ago."

"What happened?" Mike asked.

"Oh, many things—drugs, the different tastes of the record buying public, band infighting. You know—the usual. The band had run its course. It was time we moved on. Anyway, I think you guys have real potential. I've seen you perform a couple of times now. I think there is really something there. I'd like to hear more of what you guys have. Perhaps we can get together sometime and discuss some business."

"We're having a party at our house after the gig. Why don't you come by? There'll be lots of drink, drugs, and chicks."

"Can't tonight." He shrugged his shoulders.

"Then how about some other time? We're rehearsing tomorrow in our studio if you wanna come by then."

"Tomorrow would be great."

"Here is our address and phone number—say around two."

"I'll be there." He turned and left.

The next day he arrived closer to three. Mike stopped, re-introduced him to the rest of the band, and introduced him to Frank.

"I'd like to hear you play a couple of your tunes. See whatcha got. Just go ahead. Is it OK if I smoke?" They nodded that is was fine. He lit up a joint offering it to all the members each of whom refused.

After they played a couple of songs he held up his hand. "That was great. Some really good material. Do you have anything on tape?"

They all responded by shaking their heads no. "Only rehearsal tapes," Frank responded.

"So, you haven't sent anything to record companies yet?"

"No, I invite them to gigs, but I don't think they show up," Frank admitted.

"Perhaps I could help. I'd like to take you into the studio to record some tunes. I have a studio in my house. I still know a lot of people in the business. Maybe I could do something for ya. I know how hard it can be."

"Sounds interesting. When do we start?" Frank asked.

"Call me tomorrow. We can work out a time. You can just bring what you think you need. I do have amps, but you may prefer your own. The drummer needs to bring his own set though, unless he wants to play on the one I have. It's up to him. Are you gigging much?"

"Nothin' for the rest of the week since we had the Star gig. After that we are pretty booked. We do a lot of Top 40 clubs to make money. We can spend time this week on the tape. After that we are free during the day."

"Cool, talk to you tomorrow." He left as quickly as he had arrived.

"I'm not so sure about this guy." Gloria was the first to talk. "I mean he's some washed up old rock star. What can he offer?"

"Look, what've we got to lose?" said Frank. "Besides, we could get a good tape out of it if nothing else. And he says he has some connections. Let's give it a try. He hasn't asked us to sign anything."

"He must know how to make a record since he made quite a few with his band," Mike commented.

"Yeah come on. Let's give the guy a chance."

All agreed.

They called and arranged a time to meet him at his home in Laurel Canyon. In a couple of days they were on their way. They drove down Sunset and turned right onto Laurel Canyon. This was a winding stretch of road on a canyon that connected Hollywood with the San Fernando

Valley. The road followed the canyon floor with steep canyon walls and cliffs on either side. Plenty of trees and a few scattered homes were built into the side of the hills or wherever a flat area could be found. It immediately seemed like they had gone from an urban setting to a rural one. This had always been an area where people in the entertainment business lived due to its beauty and close proximity to the city while seeming remote. It was almost like living in the country. In later years it was invaded with hippies, rock stars, porn stars, and drug dealers offering them a bit of country along with a lot of privacy and secrecy with older homes tucked away on the main road or on other roads that emanated out from the main road on small streets

"You know there were a lot of rock stars that call this place home." Bill commented. "It's kinda famous for that country folk rock sound like Crosby, Stills, Nash and Young and shit. I heard that Joni Mitchell lives here somewhere. She sang about it on her album and song "<u>Ladies of the Canyon</u>."

"Cool," commented Jason.

"Check it out," said Mike pointing to what looked like some ancient ruins. "See that old foundation of a house." Concrete and some sections of brick walls could be seen, but all were overgrown with ivy, plants, and brush "That was where Houdini, the magician from the twenties, once had his house. More of a castle really, but it's long gone. It was torn done many years ago. You know that people still gather here every Halloween for a séance to see if Houdini could fulfill his final promise. He died on Halloween, but when he was alive he told people that if it were at all possible he would communicate with the living after his death."

"Really!" exclaimed Gloria.

"Yeah, but so far nothing. So much for talking to the dead." Mike laughed.

They arrived at the address on one of the small winding streets off Laurel Canyon. There was a long steep driveway leading up to the house. It was a modest house but very private. It was a bit run down and definitely ill kept with overgrown bushes and trees in the yard obscuring a house badly in need of paint. They knocked on the door. Jonathan answered smoking a cigarette. As they entered, they noticed that the house had electronic equipment everywhere. The living room was where he had the recording studio set up. It was filled with recording equipment—not exactly professional, but it would work. In one of the bedrooms there was a bed which offered the only sign that somebody actually lived there. On the wall hung a couple of gold records and singles and framed posters of concerts the band had done. It all looked quite impressive.

"Wanna get high first?" He asked lighting up a joint.

"Uh, no thanks. Not until the work is done. Too hard to concentrate," Jeff responded, and the rest of the band followed suit.

They spent the next few hours working on tunes before they even began to roll tape. They played them over and over again until they sounded better. All the while Jonathan was smoking, listening, and making comments. The Blue Wave was a heavy psychedelic band, and Jonathan was into that heavy rock sound which influenced the direction he took the band.

They set up and played it a couple of times, but every time something was wrong: the tuning, the vocals, the timing.

"This is not really working," said Jonathan. "Let's try it without vocals. Just get a good rhythm track first: bass, drums, guitar and piano. We can put vocals on later. Ya know what I'm sayin'?" Once the tracks were done they made a final mix. Fifteen hours later they had one song done. They decided to call it a night. The band was tired but Jonathan was ready to party.

He lit up a joint. "Here, now take a hit. Let's listen to what we've accomplished." They passed around joints and listened to it for hours while discussing the next step and the improvements they needed to make. They smoked and talked about how great it sounded and how they couldn't wait to finish the other songs.

The rest of the week was spent working on the tape. They spent one day on each song: laying tracks, overdubbing, and mixing. Three days later they were able to put together three songs which felt and sounded real good. It was a bit on the heavy metal side. It wasn't really what the band expected—not the way they heard themselves. But they figured that this guy knew his stuff. And if this would help them to get signed, they were fine with it. Overall, they were very happy.

Their next gig at the Hollywood Star wasn't for a couple of weeks which gave them time to prepare. Jonathan said he'd play the tape for some people to see what they thought and bring them to the gig if they were interested.

The next Star gig seemed to come quickly. There was a great deal of anticipation as they were backstage waiting to go on. All were hoping that Jonathan would come through. After the set, they waited for Jonathan to show. They thought he'd at least come backstage to say hello and hopefully he would bring some people from the music industry. Unfortunately, no one important showed up—not even Jonathan. There was a great deal of disappointment. The band was crestfallen.

They were outside and just about ready to leave when they were approached by an extremely well dressed man. He wore fashionable clothes and jewelry, like something out of a GQ magazine; not conservative, but hip, trendy, and noticeably expensive. He was strikingly good looking with dark features that made him seem even more mysterious. He had jet black hair styled just right, a big black moustache which complemented his dark swarthy complexion and dark brown almost black piercing eyes. It looked as if he was from somewhere in the Middle East.

"I saw your show. I thought it was great," he said.

"Uh, thanks," Jason responded. "Glad you liked it."

"My name is Scott. Never mind the last name you probably wouldn't be able to pronounce it. I'm really interested in your band."

By now Jason was a little put off after having Jonathan not show up. He thought here was another one.

"Do you have a tape or something I can listen to?"

Frank stepped in. "What is your interest in the band?"

"Investment, purely investment. I have lots of investments in a variety of areas. I own an airline, a chain of restaurants, and lots of real estate holdings. I'm just looking to diversify. I see that a lot of money can be made in the music business, and I'd like to be a part of it," the man responded.

"Here's a copy of a tape they just made. See how you like it. Here's my card," Frank said. He left never expecting to hear from the man again like so many people they had met.

The next day Frank received a phone call from Scott. "I'd like to meet with you as soon as possible."

"Anytime tomorrow is fine."

"Great, I'll send a car to pick you up. What's your address?" Frank was a little taken aback—a car to fetch him. Frank gave him the address and put down the phone a little dumbfounded.

The car, a black stretch limousine, arrived the next day. Frank was whisked off to the Beverly Hills Hotel. He approached the huge pink building with awe. The driver explained that Scott was staying in bungalow three. He told him how to get there and left.

Frank walked through the opulent lobby with high end shops, restaurants, and bars; then out to the lush grounds to bungalow three. He knocked on the door. When it opened, he was surprised and awestruck. He hadn't expected anything like this. It was huge. The place was filled with expensive furniture, a fireplace, and even a grand piano. With its large living room, dining room, full kitchen, and multiple bedrooms, it was more like a home than a hotel room.

Scott began. "I've listened to the tape. It's OK, but I am not sure it's really the band I heard. The band I heard live was great. That is the band I am interested in. Let me get right to the point. I have a lot of money—mostly inherited, and some I made myself with investing in various companies. I've always loved rock and roll. I am interested in investing in a band. It would be for a return, a percentage of the sales and gross receipts, but I think we could work out the details. If there is no profit, I can always write it off. So you see, as strange as it may sound, I can't lose. Nor can you. I think this band could be a real money maker. I want nothing to do with the business. I just want to be an outside private investor, a silent investor, for equipment, recording, touring—whatever the band may need. And if it's difficult to get a record deal, we can start our own record company and put out our own record. I am known to be successful at whatever I do. Are you interested?"

"Sounds good to me. But how do I know this is all real?" Frank asked.

"Don't worry. You'll know when the time is right. I'd like to set up a meeting next week with my staff, my board of directors, and my financial and legal people to discuss all this. I need to return to New York tomorrow, but I'll return with them so that you can go over all the details. Can you have a proposal ready? I want you to present both options to them: one for just signing the band and one for starting a record company. I need all the details so that we can really see how feasible this would be and what it would take to make this band a big hit. I need budgets and everything. Afterward, we can have a little party for the band. Can you have all that ready by next week?"

"I don't see why not."

"Good, I'll see you next week then." Scott shook Frank's hand and escorted him out the door.

Frank now had his work cut out for him. He had to come up with a proposal complete with budgets, graphs, cost analysis, and explanations. This included finding out what the costs were to record an album, but also what it would cost to start a record company and all its components—promotion, advertising, marketing, touring, equipment, and whatever else.

He called a meeting the very next day to delegate responsibilities. Frank and Eric would be in charge of the record company and recording side of things. This began with the costs to record an album including studio time, session players, rental equipment, producers, and engineers. Once the album was finished they needed to find out the cost to advertise, promote, and market it all over the U.S. In addition he needed to do the same for starting a record company which was almost identical with the cost of offices and staff added in. Luckily, most of these services could be hired or contracted independently so that only a small staff would be necessary, at least at first, until the company became big enough to hire its own staff for all the departments. They needed to get budget estimates to hire companies for promotion, marketing, advertising, publicity and everything else. They drafted several types of scenarios depending on what kind of company they wanted to start.

Alex was in charge of dealing with the tour expenses. He was to work with Mark and Pete and the band members for all the equipment costs including sound and lights if needed, travel, hotels, trucking the equipment, and anything else that they might need when they went on tour.

In addition they needed to explain each expense and the reason it was important to promote the band and the album. In all, they compiled a step-by-step explanation of how to promote a band. It was an education for everyone, but they felt that it was worth the effort. They really learned what it took to make and promote an album. They all worked diligently for the entire week getting proposals and estimates of costs. Frank and Eric drafted the proposals to present to Scott and his staff. The final product was a folder made up with the proposals for various options complete with budgets and graphs, along with explanations for each. They had copies made so that everyone had a copy of their proposal.

Scott had changed hotels to one on The Strip. Frank decided to take Eric along as part of the management team and for some moral support. Frank and Eric arrived for their meeting which was held in one of the conference rooms at the hotel. They were both very nervous at having to present a proposal like this, but they were both confident that they had done a good job, and that they knew their stuff. They were ready.

They looked each other in the eye and took a deep breath. "Let's do this!" Frank exclaimed. He opened the door and entered the room.

It was a typical board room with wood paneled walls and a large wooden table with high back office chairs surrounding it. At one end, there was a wall of glass with the curtains open offering a view of the city. Around the table sat a group of ten people, all dressed for success—men in suits and ties and women in business suits or other business attire. They all looked very corporate. Scott made the introductions which included CEOs, CFOs and other officers as well as accountants, lawyers, and professional people. They sat down ready for the presentation. All eyes were on Frank as they sat waiting to hear the proposition with hands folded, glasses in place, pens, pencils, calculators, and yellow legal pads ready to take notes. It was a very intimidating crowd. Frank readied himself for his presentation. He was nervous, but he mustered up enough of his confidence and started as Eric passed out the proposals.

"First of all, I wish to thank you all for you time and your interest in the band. We're quite excited. We have compiled proposals that I think cover many of the issues that need to be addressed including budgets and explanations. I'll go over them all. If you have any questions, please feel free to interrupt me.

There are three ways to draft this deal. You'll find explanations for these options starting on page 3. It's all about power, control, and money. The main difference between them involves who owns the rights and who spends the money and incurs the expenses for recording, marketing, promoting, advertising, and financing the tour. The more control, the more money it costs, but the more profits to be made. The less control the less money it costs, but the less profits that can be made. Many of these expenses overlap. I will address that later. One way is to sign directly to a record company which means getting a record deal and signing an exclusive contact with them. Another is to have a production deal. The third is to start a record company. Whichever way you decide, I suggest that you leave the manufacturing and distribution up to a company or distributor.

I will start with the last, starting your own record company. Many companies will be glad to distribute product for a fee and small percentage without any other services. You, as the record company, will have to incur the whole cost of recording, promoting, marketing, and advertising the album along with other expenses such as touring. It is more costly, but you also make a bigger percentage of the sales. You'll find that budget on page 8 with explanations following.

Next is a production company. This means that the band signs with the production company and the production company signs with the record label. This allows more control. It is, of course, more costly than signing directly with the label, but less costly that starting your own record company. You will be responsible for many of the expenses that the record company would normally incur. Everything is negotiable, but you have the contract directly with the band, not the record label; and the band is signed directly to you, not the record company.

Finally, the other option is to sign directly with the record company. This gives the record company complete control. They'll incur and be responsible for most of the expenses. I do think, however, that even if you sign directly with a record company that the organization should hire some of their own independent services just in case the record company doesn't do its job. Since they are doing most of the work and using their personnel, there is less money to be made. For you there is less risk, less outlay of money, but also less profit to be made. So there's one set of budgets for these services.

All of these services can be hired independently—and should be for any of the options, even if the record company has their own departments. However, for distribution and production deals, these services will be crucial as they will not furnish them. For a record company or production company there will be some additional expenses such as offices, staff, and stuff like that. I've addressed those on page 9 with a variety of options." Frank looked at Eric who gave him a nod of approval. As time went on, he became more confident.

"Recording costs begin on page 15. These are the expenses and costs that'll be incurred for recording an album followed by explanations, timing, and other details. This includes studio time, rental equipment, and session time for the musicians and any other musicians they might need. Also, it includes the cost of a producer and engineer if separate from the studio and other miscellaneous expenses. If the band is signed directly to the label, the label will pay for these expenses as an advance against their royalties or earnings, which means no one gets paid until these expenses are recouped by the record company.

Next is the cost of promoting, marketing, and advertising the album beginning on page 20. While there is some crossover in what each firm would do, here are the main areas. There are also different budgets depending on if the band is signed directly to a label or if you start a company that acts as a production company. Also, no matter what route you take, as I stated earlier, I recommend that you hire independent companies to perform these services so that you can get the best. If you start your own record company, eventually, if the record company is successful, you can hire your own people for these departments, but at least in the beginning I think it wise to just contract out for these services. The promotion company would be in charge of getting radio play. The advertising agency would be in charge of all forms of advertising. This would include print ads in newspapers, magazines, and other printed material as well as other media like radio and television. The press agency would be in charge of radio and magazine interviews. The marketing agency would be in charge of posters; t-shirts; give-away items such as t-shirts, concert tickets, albums; and other promotional items. The publishing company would be for the songwriters only. They're in charge of collecting money for the songwriters which comes from record sales, radio or television play, and sheet music. This is different from the album royalties that the band and musicians make. They can also be helpful in getting their songs covered by other artists. It would be a separate company and a separate deal."

He was now pacing the floor and circling the table, confident at the good job he was doing. "The last step in the process deals with a tour. There needs to be the national tour to help promote the band and the album. On page 30 you'll find all the tour expenses and equipment needed as well as what it takes to do a great show and put a band on the road. The tour is necessary mostly as a promotional tool. Even though the tour would lose money, it would in the long run really help promote the album and the band. The tour must work in conjunction with all the marketing, promotion, and advertising so that their live appearances became a media event with advertising, radio play, and interviews. Also, most importantly, is how crucial it is to have all of this coordinated so that it all works together to promote the band, the album, and the tour.

Finally, the last section has to do with potential profits or losses. Starting on page 40 you'll find the cost analysis and a complete budget for each of these endeavors. They vary slightly. At least you can get an idea of the various options you have. This'll include what the initial outlay of money will be and the potential return on your investment, taking into consideration all costs and all percentages including what the band receives. Record royalties are paid on actual album sales and vary greatly depending on which route you take. Also, the band makes their record royalties as well. It takes into consideration when you recoup your investment and how much money is to be made at various points of sales. Keep in mind that even the band won't receive any money until the initial investment is recouped. So we're all in this together."

He went over many of the budgets, cost analysis, charts and graphs which outlined the various options. He explained every page of the proposal with Eric joining in when needed. When he finally realized that two hours had passed he felt he had said enough. They finished their presentation and answered questions. It had been a difficult audience. These people certainly seemed to know their stuff judging by the way they investigated the proposals, were seen crunching the numbers, and the questions that they asking. They were thorough and businesslike. This was not about music or the band; this was about a business proposition.

"As you can see there are various options open to you depending on how involved you wanna be and what kind of company you want to start. I hope this has been informative."

They thanked him and told him that if they had any further questions they would be in touch.

Once finished, they all left. Frank and Eric were elated at the excellent job they had done, but were doing their best to contain themselves.

Scott escorted Frank and Eric up to his hotel room. It was a huge penthouse suite on the upper floor of the hotel. The living room area had a sofa and two chairs with tables and table lamps completing the look of elegance. A sliding glass door to a large roof top patio offered a view of the whole Los Angeles area. The whole city seemed to be stretched out below them. They immediately spotted the band. They had arrived separately and were waiting on the patio—checking out the view of the city. Frank and Eric gave a big sigh of relief when they saw them. They immediately went out and gave them a nod of satisfaction to let them know that things had gone well.

Scott motioned for the band to follow him. He had something to show them. They were taken into one of the bedrooms. The room was filled with all new equipment: amplifiers, guitars, keyboards, and various other electronic equipment and devices—all gifts for the band.

"This is for you," he told them. "I believe that we're gonna do business together, so I bought this in good faith to show my intentions are real." Scott grinned.

The band was flabbergasted; "Shit!" was all Mike could say.

"I hope you like it." Scott stated "I wasn't sure what type of stuff you wanted."

"No! No! It's fantastic! We're just speechless," Gloria said using all her charm.

"This calls for a celebration." Scott opened a bottle of champagne. "Let the party begin."

"Dom Perignon." Bill noticed. "This is expensive shit."

"Uh, how the fuck would he know that?" Mike whispered to the other members of the band. They shrugged their shoulders and laughed.

"So this is how the rock stars live," Bill continued as he grabbed a glass of champagne.

"I also have some blow if anyone is interested. It's in the other bedroom. Please help yourself. And the pot should be out on the table by now." They went back to the living room area of the suite just as one of Scott's helpers opened a cigar box filled with what looked like fifty joints. He placed it on the table. Just then there was a knock on the door. A group of hotel staff personnel brought in platters of all kinds of foods: caviar, shrimp, hors d'oeuvres, and everything expensive. The band was speechless.

"I do have some other guests joining us shortly. I hope you don't mind. Some are musicians also."

As the evening continued more people arrived. Scott introduced the band to his other guests and made sure the band felt comfortable. The band partied the rest of the evening with Scott and his friends. Many people in the music business were there discussing various aspects of the industry. They met many other musicians many of whom happened to play in back up bands for some very famous people and major recording artists. Scott was in heaven telling them all about his new discovery and how great they were. He even played the tape several times. Scott wanted to be a rock and roller, but instead had become a businessman with the help of family money. The band felt like rock stars. They felt that they had arrived.

As they left, Scott held out his hand. "I hope this is the start of a long and prosperous relationship."

Frank took his hand. "I certainly hope so."

"I'm flying out tomorrow, back to New York which is my home base. You can reach me there. I may need to send for you later, but don't worry. I can have my private jet bring you there. See you soon." Scott waved and smiled as the band walked out the door.

The band was ecstatic. They thought that at last they were on their way. They stayed up all night talking about it.

The next day they returned to the hotel to pick up their gear. They reached the floor only to find the door to the suite wide open. They peeked in to see the room had been ransacked. A group of men in suits were checking things out. They quickly turned around and rushed to the front desk to inquire what had happened. The desk clerk took them aside.

"He has left. He's under investigation. I suggest you stay clear." He motioned for them to leave.

"But…" Mike, said, quite surprised.

"Please stay out if you know what's best for you," he interrupted. "Or you may be investigated as well. You could be suspects." The desk clerk turned and left.

Just then a small man in a suit with the hotel insignia on it pulled them aside. "Look, I shouldn't be telling you this, but here's what I know. He had run up such a huge bill here and had exceeded his limit of credit. That's when the hotel contacted his home operation. They informed us that they were looking for him as well. Apparently he owes money all over town and all over the US. He has been running around spending money he doesn't have. They were glad to know where he was. The next thing we knew federal agents that were flown out from New York were all over the room. It appears he has been under investigation for a long time. All that money he has, over 10 million dollars, came from embezzling from large corporations—a brilliant mind gone wrong. He must've gotten word something was up because he left real early with his friends. They said he was returning to his home country because there he had diplomatic immunity. He was a prince or something from some Middle East country. They'll never get him. I suggest you stay clear, or you will also get investigated."

"But what about the gear he bought for us?"

"It was all returned. He paid for it using a bad check."

"A con man, a fucking con man. I can't fuckin' believe it. What next?" Mike displayed the sentiments of the rest of the band. "First that flake Jonathan, and now this. Fuckin' unbelievable!"

They read in the newspaper the next day how a Middle Eastern prince had fled the country after he had embezzled a lot of money but was untouchable due to diplomatic immunity.

They arrived home where Frank was waiting to hear how everything went. They told Frank the story who was also quite amazed. "I can't believe it," was all Frank could say as he shook his head. "I have some more news. Jonathan called. He now wants the band to sign a production deal. He wants fifty percent of everything the band earns. Says it's what he expects because he did the tape and wants to be involved with us. He said if we don't sign he'd spread rumors all over town and get us black listed in the business if we tried to not give him his share of the money. Says he has some record company interested, but of course that is only if we sign with him." Frank told them.

"Well, that sucks," said Mike.

"Besides, I really didn't think that tape really represented what we sound like and the direction we want to take. Ya know what I mean?" said Bill.

"I agree, it really was not us," agreed Jason.

"Well, I think we should tell him to fuck off," said Jeff. "A couple of days of taping in his home, and he thinks he owns us. Tell him we'll pay him for his time when we get a deal, but for now he ain't getting shit from us."

"Fuck him," said Gloria.

"Yeah for fifty percent I'd rather work at McDonalds. He'll never get anything. Deal's off," Jason said in disgust.

It was not without bad feelings that Jonathan was dismissed from their life. He threatened to sue, but it never happened. They never did hear from him again. It was more talk than reality—just idle threats to see how far it would go. This whole series of events they could just chalk up to experience.

"MONEY"

Pink Floyd

"Back to work," said Frank as he entered the rehearsal studio. He sensed that everyone's spirits were a bit low after what had transpired. "I know we've just had some setbacks and some major disappointment, but the show must go on." He was sounding like a coach giving a pre-game pep talk. "We have plenty of bookings for the next couple of months. The good news is that I have a few dates on hold for The Whisky and Starwood. Let's forget about all this bad stuff. The only good thing is how much we've learned, and how much these people are taking notice. We must've made an impact for them to be even remotely interested. In the meantime, we still have a job to do. I still believe that this is a great band. It's just a matter of time."

"You're right," said Jason. "We cannot let this get us down."

The band was working constantly trying not to lose their faith and enthusiasm. They continued to play the out of town cover gigs mostly and about once a month worked in one of the Hollywood showcase clubs for a one night show. These engagements had to be a month apart because of the club owner's requirement for advertising purposes. They didn't want the band to be appearing in another local venue within the same month since they had ads running announcing the bands performance. They wanted their name to only appear once for their club appearance for the monthly and weekly newspapers without any overlap or conflict. In Hollywood they played mostly off nights, during the week, but at least it was a start. The good thing was that they were playing some of the big clubs—The Roxy, The Whisky, The Troubadour, Gazarri's, and Starwood. They were becoming well-known and developing a good following in the Hollywood scene which allowed them to play more often and at the better clubs. They could even demand more money at the Top 40 gigs since they were getting more of a following. They were getting a name for themselves all over the city.

They also preferred these in-town gigs or the beach gigs as it was easier to have a band after-gig party. They had learned their lesson to not drink or smoke during the gig, but afterward—anything goes. Their reputation as a party band extended beyond the stage.

Since they had worked so well together for the presentation for Scott, Frank and Eric decided to become business partners in every way—drugs and the band. The arrangement worked out so well that it wasn't long before Eric had moved in with Frank at the beach house. It was from there that they ran their drug business and band business. They made an excellent management team. Frank was taking him along on appointments so that he too could meet all of his contacts in both the drug world and the music world. Frank was the aggressive one, while Eric was more logical and businesslike. Things were going better than either of them had planned. They all had their own connections and clients. Frank had his Mafia connections, Eric had the feds connection. Even Alex had become a valuable member of the team since he had his Mexican connections and his own clients. They had created a major business of dealing drugs throughout the greater Los Angeles area which even filtered out throughout the whole Southern California area. They had developed a large clientele of single users, but they were mostly suppliers to a vast network of other dealers in all of Southern California. They sold to small time dealers and large dealers who required larger quantities. They were moving a lot of drugs. The midnight drug runs were becoming more frequent. It seemed they were constantly flying out to the middle of the desert to score some drugs from the feds who always seemed to have a great supply. It also made it look like the band was their source of income, and therefore, created a pretty good front for laundering money. With money coming in, the band was able to get some new equipment. Eric also liked being a co-manager for the band. It allowed him to be involved with the band and party with everyone. Alex, Mark, and Pete helped sell the drugs and worked with the band. Everyone profited from this endeavor. It was a major operation that Frank had orchestrated.

It was before a Hollywood Star gig that Frank went into Mr. Grant. "Look, I've kept up my end of the bargain, now I wanna see some industry people out here."

"They have been at the gigs; you just don't know who they are. No one has been impressed—including me. The band needs some work. That stint with Jonathan didn't help either. He has been telling people all over town that you ripped him off. He made you some tapes and now you refuse to pay him for 'em. Unfortunately, he does have his connections as well."

"That's not how it was at all. He wanted fifty percent, and that was just too much." Frank's exasperation was showing.

"No need to explain it to me, I know what he's like. He has done it to a couple of my acts. He makes tapes for 'em, makes them promises, and then asks outrageous percentages. If they refuse, he bad mouths 'em. I don't think anyone takes him too seriously, but it didn't help. I wish you had checked with me first. I could've warned you about him. However, the prevailing attitude from the companies is that the band needs work. That is directly from the people from the record labels that I've seen out there who have seen you." Mr. Grant was gloating over the fact that they had gotten into trouble. This made Frank even madder.

"What d'ya mean they need some work? This band is ready." Frank was getting angry now as he defended his band.

"Yeah, they do pretty well in clubs. They are a good bar and party band which is why I and the audience like them. They have a lot of energy. But they have no album material and especially no singles. A real recording band needs singles."

"I can't keep 'em going, and we don't make any money here. If it weren't for those weeks at Top 40 clubs they wouldn't be making any money at all. And you only allow us to play here occasionally."

"Not my problem. Let's just wait and see what happens. Get 'em rehearsing. They need to write some hit singles."

"Just because you can sell drugs doesn't make you a music expert. You know I can cut your supply off any time."

"Don't threaten me little man. You small time pushers think you're so great. Now outta my sight."

Frank didn't have the nerve to tell the band that the industry wasn't responding. The band was getting pretty tired of playing Top 40 nightclubs and only a big showcase club once a month.

After one of the Star shows Frank entered the dressing room.

"You're sounding better all the time."

"Yeah, so what's happening with the business thing? I'm sick and tired of playing this shit. I hear these bands. We're just as good as they are. In fact we're better." Jason was the first to vent his frustration.

"Yeah, let's get this show on the road," Gloria added with all others voicing their agreement.

Just as Frank was about to give the band the news that the industry had in fact been out to see them, there was a knock at the door. A small head with glasses peeked in. "Just saw your show. Thought you showed some potential."

"Yeah, who're you," Jason sarcastically inquired.

"Pat Johnson, P.J. Productions." he entered the room handing out his cards. He was short, rather dumpy, almost fat, and not at all attractive. He wore a sport coat and blue jeans which seemed out of place for his personality, as if he should have been an accountant or something. He was pushy, energetic, not afraid to take control, but seemed like he was in a hurry and had other more important things to do. "Who's in charge here?"

"I am the manager." Frank stepped forward. He held out his hand to shake.

"Meet me in my office Monday, 10:00. We'll talk. Do you have a card and a tape?"

Frank handed him one of the tapes and his business card.

"Thanks, see you Monday." He left as quickly as he had arrived.

"What the fuck is P.J. Productions? And who the Fuck is Pat Johnson?" Jason asked.

"Who knows? I'll find out Monday. This could be our break."

Frank drove down Sunset ready for his appointment. The office building was at the far end of the Sunset Strip in the 9000 building. He found the large towering black ominous building almost right across the street from The Roxy, about three blocks away from the start of Beverly Hills. Frank arrived at the high-rise promptly. He didn't want to appear too eager by arriving early, but didn't want to seem unreliable either by arriving late. As he entered the building, he looked at the directory to find out what suite he was to go to. He noticed many of the important names of individuals and companies in the music business and services related to the music industry—names of managers, agents, attorneys, concert promoters, publicists, music publishers, and even a few small independent record companies. He entered the office on the 10th floor. He first noticed the walls lined with Gold and Platinum records from various groups. A large picture window looked out onto the city.

"Frank Barcelona from the band Hollywood to see Pat Johnson. I have an appointment," he told the receptionist. He sat down trying to read the trophies on the wall while still appearing nonchalant about the whole thing.

"Pat will see you now." The secretary motioned him into the inner offices. "Coffee, tea?" the secretary asked showing him into Pat's office.

"Coffee is fine." He entered.

Pat was on the phone with his back to the door staring out the large window which overlooked most of L.A. On hearing the commotion he motioned Frank in. He pointed to a chair directly across from his large desk. As Pat was finishing his phone call, Frank noticed more gold and platinum albums on the wall. In the corner was a baby grand piano stacked with cassette tapes. More tapes were stacked in shelves on the opposite side of the piano.

"I know Rod wants the song, but Cat Stevens wants to use it as his next single for himself, and Elton is saving all his songs for his next album. I'm sure we can find another song. I have plenty of other songwriters. Listen, I'll see what I can do. How's lunch tomorrow?" a pause, "Wednesday." He looked over his appointment book. "Fine, I'll have an answer or a solution by then. Chasen's OK...... I'll make the arrangements. 12:00...... see you Wednesday, bye." he hung up pressed then another button. "Hold all my calls unless my call from New York comes in." He turned to Frank. "Sorry for the delay."

Frank, for the first time, noticed that because his chair was so much shorter he was forced to look up to this otherwise short person. He had to wonder if this was intentional, some kind of short person power trip.

"I was impressed with your band. At least they show some potential. I was not that impressed with the tape however. It sounds like a different band. Nonetheless, based on what I saw live, I'm willing to offer a standard production deal. I assume you still have the entire band's publishing, and that those songs I heard were original."

Frank nodded in agreement. He began to speak but was interrupted. "I still haven't heard a single yet. Perhaps I can get one of my other songwriters to write one for you, or maybe even a song written by Rod or Elton or Cat Stevens that would suit you. Here's the deal. First we find a single. Then, I'll take you into the studio to produce a good demo with that single and some of your own songs. I'll use that demo to go to the labels. Have they been approached yet?"

"I don't think..." Frank wasn't even able to finish his sentence.

"Good. Then I'll shop the deal. The band will be signed to my production company. The production company will then sign to the label. I take all publishing, meaning I'll be their publishing company. The band can keep the songwriter's portion. I take 25% from the record company deal which is usually three points on a twelve point deal. That is fairly standard. I also get a percentage of all performances—live, taped, TV, or whatever. The contract will be for two years with four one year options, my option. In addition if you have any songs perhaps

I can place them with other artists. The first thing we can get going on is the publishing."

"Publishing?"

"Yes, publishing. That's money that is made for the songwriters. It's always separate from the artist deal." Frank was trying to interrupt since he knew what publishing was. He just could not get a word in edgewise. "All songwriters get paid publishing money. Generally a publishing company handles that. The publisher and the songwriter get paid every time the song is used by anyone, including themselves. This includes albums, radio, TV, sheet music, whatever. Even if it's on your own album you get separate money for publishing and songwriting. I represent a lot of songwriters. In fact many of my clients are just songwriters; they don't even wanna be recording artists. I'm pretty good at placing songs with other artists that are looking for songs. There is some good money in it, and I've been doing it a long time. Most publishers go through ASCAP or BMI. ASCAP is the American Society of Composers, Authors and Publishers and BMI stands for Broadcast Music Inc. I work with both of 'em. We'll just have to see who offers the best deal. They license the songs, collect the royalties, and distribute the royalties or money to the songwriters and publishing companies. It is a great way to make some extra money especially if you have some songs that you don't want or perhaps ones that do not suit the band, or songs that you could see other artists doing. So tell the band to get writing. Send me everything you don't wanna keep yourselves. Publishing is the thing I do best. It's how I really got started in the business. I have a lot of clients for whom I just handle their publishing."

"Your call from New York, line three," the receptionist interrupted on the intercom.

"Thanks, I gotta take this. I'll have the contract drafted and sent to you in a week. Also, you can pick up some invitations for you and the band to a small party I'm having. I hope to see you there. I look forward to working with you."

He picked up the phone and turned his swivel chair so that his back was now to Frank. "What're you doing with my song? I heard the studio tracks and it sounds terrible."

Frank got up and left the office. He stopped to pick up the invitations from the receptionist. He left rather dumbfounded. Never had he felt at such a disadvantage, but he was duly impressed.

The band had not been in the best of spirits. The weeks of playing had seemed to go on endlessly and they seemed to be getting nowhere. The band was on the verge of a breakup.

Frank received the contract and reviewed it. He called a meeting to discuss the proposal with the band. He explained the deal to the band as best he could and with real excitement.

"But this is no label deal," Jason said. "Who is this Pat Johnson?"

"Well, he has gold albums all over his walls. He must be doing something right." Frank tried to convince him.

"Um, I just don't think this is the right deal," Mike expressed with concern. "I want an album deal—with a real company—like Columbia or Capitol—not this bullshit. Uh, I don't know. What the fuck do these other bands have that we don't? We are great. Aren't we? Frank—what the fuck have you been doing except running drugs? Have any labels seen this act?—No!" Mike answered his own rhetorical question.

"Well, as a matter of fact, they have." The whole band stopped—shocked to hear this for the first time. "None have been interested so far. They wanna hear singles. I just had a talk with Mr. Grant from the club. The representatives of the record companies have been there. They say you need some work. Also, the people I have talked to are not impressed with the tape that Jonathan made. They do not think it truly represents the band. Maybe if we had something better on tape by a professional like Pat Johnson, we could convince them. These people need to hear singles that could play on the radio. Live shows are just not enough. Our tapes, up to this point, have been pretty poor. Pat said the same thing. He's thinking of finding us a single, maybe one written by Rod Stewart, Elton John, Cat Stevens, or someone else."

"What do those assholes in the record companies know anyway? They wouldn't know talent if they heard it." Bill's disgust was apparent.

"Well, if all the labels have passed, what is the point? Why don't we just give it up?" Gloria questioned with frustration.

"I know I've had about enough of this," Jeff said.

They all nodded in agreement. They were all feeling dejected and disconsolate with long faces to match their mood.

"I just don't wanna sign this contract. I want a real contract with a real label. But I don't wanna break up!" Jason exclaimed.

"Ah, come on guys, I guess we gotta give up something to get something," Frank conceded.

"Without a label and little interest I might have to consider moving on," Jeff said. "I believe in this band, but how much time must I spend? I can get another gig. Bill and I can do studio work, you know."

"It's pretty fuckin' frustrating playing these silly Top 40 gigs." even Bill agreed.

"Pat also says he could place songs with other recording artists if we have any we think would be good for someone else. Part of the deal includes publishing."

"I don't wanna give up any of our songs at the moment, but I do have some that don't suit us. Perhaps we could see what he could do with 'em." Jason thought out loud.

"He says he has good connections and is good at placing songs. Let's give him some of the stuff we don't use. He can give it to other artists, and we can make some money as songwriters. Ya know what I mean?"

"That works for me." Mike's ears perked up.

"Look, let's give this a shot. He has the connections. He'll make us a professional tape. What do we have to lose?" Frank sounded desperate. "Look, we all know this band is great. It'll just take some time for someone else to appreciate it. Let's go for it, and not forget what our dream is. Besides, I can't believe you're all quitters after a few disappointments. You're really ready to call it quits? Just go to the party and think about it. I don't think anyone wants to disband. We've worked too hard to get this far. We're closer than ever. Just let's keep on truckin'. We will conquer. Just wait and see."

They decided to wait for the party to make their decision. No one really wanted to break up.

The band left for the party in their van as it was the only vehicle large enough for everyone to fit. Frank and Eric went by themselves and would meet them there. They were in the hills of West Hollywood overlooking the Sunset Strip. The lights of the whole city were laid out below them. It wasn't far from the band house but a world away. It was a steep winding road up in the hills that they sometimes wondered if the van would even make it. They never realized that these roads went so far up into the hills behind Hollywood. Finally, they saw the house in the distance—all lit up. In front of the house there was a row of cars—Rolls Royces, Ferraris, Mercedes and the like—lined up as boys in red vests hired as valets searched for places to park the cars on any available place on these small winding streets.

"I can't believe they have valet parking," Jason said excitedly from the back of the van while peering over the shoulder of Gloria in the front seat with Mike driving.

"You guys are sure late," the valet said. "Help is to report to the back door. Are you guys with the caterers? Serving?"

"We *are* invited guests." Jason said in his most arrogant and bitchy tone, showing his invitation and practically throwing it in the valet's face.

"Oh, excuse me sir," the valet apologized and opened the door.

They had all exited and were ready to enter when they heard a voice from a car calling their names. It was Frank driving a shiny new black Porsche Targa with Eric sitting next to him in the passenger seat. "How do'ya like the new wheels?"

"Bitchin' wheels,'" said Jeff

"Boy, drug business must be doing well," Mike announced as Frank and Eric exited the car.

"Can't complain, can't complain." Frank laughed. He threw the keys to the valet and started in.

They looked up the stairs to see two large doors. They stopped. It looked more like a castle than a house. The band looked like Dorothy and her entourage approaching the door to the wizard's castle in the <u>Wizard of Oz</u>. When they reached the door, Frank knocked. The doors opened.

"Invitation please." A man in a tuxedo with white gloves and outstretched hand asked before opening the door completely. They could hear the loud sounds of a party in full swing coming from inside. "Thank You."

The doors swung wide open revealing a large room filled with people. On the opposite side of the room the lights of the city sparkled behind two stories of glass which showed off the magnificent view of the city from downtown to Santa Monica. Below, the pool was all lit up. There was a fireplace in one corner. Two story beamed ceilings allowed large modern works of art dramatic resting places on the soaring walls.

"Check out the Jasper Johns," Bill commented pointing to one of the largest works of art that hung over the leather sofa. "I love his use of color. That must have cost him a fortune."

The group looked at each other, puzzled. "How does he know that?" Jason whispered.

"Maybe from his days in New York with Andy Warhol and the artist community. Who knows?" Mike answered. The rest of the group giggled, shrugged their shoulders, and continued on.

It was like some Hollywood glamour movie of the 1940s. All they needed was Fred Astaire and Ginger Rogers to come dancing in. The five stood there rather stunned, gaping at this palace. A waitress dressed in a black and white French maid's outfit walked past with a tray of champagne. She offered them a glass bringing them back to reality. Each grabbed a glass just as a waiter in a tuxedo and wearing white gloves walked past with a tray of hors d'oeuvres. He held out the tray offering them crackers with cheeses or caviar.

Pat Johnson almost ran into them as he was crossing the room in his usual hurried manner. He first sighted Gloria. "Welcome, I'm so glad you could make it. Please make yourself at home. Food is downstairs. There is also a full bar downstairs in case you prefer something other than wine or champagne. Please feel free to mingle." He gave Gloria a big hug, kissed each cheek, and pulled away. He clapped his hands three times to get everyone's attention. "Your attention everyone!" still clapping his hands in a rather flamboyant fashion. "This is my new find. They call themselves 'Hollywood'. Isn't that so apropos? Please welcome them."

"I think he's gay," whispered Gloria to Jason. "These are the kinds of men you ought to be picking up."

Jason laughed. "I'd certainly at least like to hang out in his circles."

The bands eyes were directed to the crowd in the center of the room. "There are all kinds of stars here." Jason whispered to Mike. He looked at the others in the band to confirm that he wasn't the only one feeling rather embarrassed by the introduction in the presence of some of his rock idols and people whom he had only seen on album covers or in concert with his binoculars.

Frank was the first to begin his exploration of the house. He vanished into the crowd. The rest of the band gradually made their way around the house, first to the downstairs for a drink which they all needed. The bar area was more crowded and louder than upstairs. The talk all seemed to be music related. They overheard people discussing their next album, managers discussing tour plans, industry people discussing albums, tours or other music related information, and record company executives discussing new bands and new record deals. Against one wall there was a full spread of food: hot dishes, full deli platters with meats, cheeses, and the like.

Just then Frank whizzed by. "The coke is in the bedroom sitting on a mirror if you want any. Isn't this awesome?" He vanished again into the crowd.

The band finally made it to the bedroom. Sitting on the dresser was a large pile of cocaine—large enough to have filled a coffee can. More than they had ever seen before. They were still unaware of the extent of Frank's dealing—to them he was still a small time dealer. On the mirror were rolled up hundred dollar bills to snort the coke. People were helping themselves, then leaving. Each of the band members did a line and left. The family room, if you could call it that, had a full ongoing disco with music and lights. There was more activity here and the band felt a little more comfortable. They began to indulge in drink and drugs.

Jason and Gloria went outside by the pool. Jason looked up. "There sure are a lot of stars out tonight." Gloria looked at him and giggled. Jason, realizing his pun, began to laugh, and then became serious.

"You know, we have to sign this contract," Gloria started.

"Yeah, I know. If we don't, there will be no band. Everyone's tired and ready to quit unless something happens," Jason conceded. "I just hate to sign the wrong contract."

"Frank read it, and so have all of us. We're not stupid. It seems all right to me. Doesn't it to you?"

"Yeah, it seems all right. We really have no choice." Jason felt trapped.

"But look at all this. This isn't such a bad start. We could be a real part of all this. I mean, how can we pass it up?" Gloria said.

"Um, yeah, I guess I'm just a little skeptical. I'm not so sure about this contract. But, this is what we gotta do," Jason agreed. "But for now, let's party."

They noticed Bill standing in the corner by the pool smoking a joint. "Having a good time?" Jason inquired.

"Yeah, OK. Good drugs. Just can't relate much to these people. But it's OK, and the caviar is good and so is the champagne."

Jason looked at Gloria. "The caviar is good? How the fuck does he know good caviar and champagne from bad?" They laughed, shrugged their shoulders, and walked away.

As they entered the disco room, they noticed Jeff with a woman on each arm obviously having a good time. Then they saw Mike in the corner sipping a drink and not looking too happy.

"What's wrong?" Gloria asked.

"Oh, this seems so phony to me. All this kissing, and let's do lunch shit. Nobody really listens to each other. They only listen to themselves, and how important they are. It reminds me of those assholes that I knew when I was growing up—arrogant, uncaring, egotistical, and self-important."

"Ah, cheer up. It's only a party. Relax a little. Don't take things so seriously. I'm gonna grab a drink. Gloria, stay and talk to Mike." Jason vanished into the crowd.

It was late in the evening. Gloria and Mike were both having a wonderful time. They were both very high and generally intoxicated from the booze and drugs. They decided to round up the crowd to leave.

They discovered Jeff as he was leaving a bathroom with a tall blond woman who could easily have been a model. He was zipping up his pants, smiling like the cat that had just swallowed the canary. Gloria knew what he was up to. Bill was snorting coke in the bedroom, but they couldn't find Jason.

They went into the backyard. On the grass by the pool they noticed a figure dancing and singing to himself as if he were Gene Kelly. As they got closer they noticed it was Jason. He was singing chorus after chorus of "If they could see me now" from Sweet Charity, belching every other world, obviously extremely intoxicated.

He noticed the band. He ran over to them, gave each a kiss, and then started ranting and raving about how fabulous the evening was. Mike and Jeff tried to grab him to help him out, but they were also so drunk they could barely stand either. The three stumbled towards the side exit so as not to make a scene when they left, falling and laughing the whole time. Gloria went to get the van, but Jason had just had too much. When he saw the trash cans he decided that this would be the best place to relieve himself. He unzipped his pants and started to pee on the trashcan. Just then all the booze caught up with him. He just couldn't control himself and started throwing up in the trash can. For ten minutes he just stood there puking. Finally, he stopped. He stood up, zipped up his pants, but immediately stumbled. Mike and Jeff caught him. They grabbed him under the arms and carried him the rest of the way to the van.

As he passed the parking attendant he looked over. "Well, you sure are cute," he said in a drunken, slurred speech. "I'm gonna be a big star you know. Why don't you come with us? I'll give you the thrill of your life." Jeff and Mike quickly threw him into the van. Then they sped off home.

Monday the band met Pat Johnson in his office. He had the contract that his attorney had drafted. They immediately all signed it. It was the motivation that the band needed.

38

"WAR, WHAT IS IT GOOD FOR"

Edwin Starr

"It's been months, and we've got nothing but a lousy tape of two songs that we recorded in two days. Not really the professional tape you promised." Frank was pounding on Pat Johnson's desk with his fist while Eric sat silently listening. "All we keep doing is playing that dive once a month while still doing our fucking Top 40 shit." The office staff, hearing his loud voice and noticing his anger, approached to restrain him. "And I've had just about enough of this. It's time you got us a record deal, like you're supposed to—like you promised." Frank noticed the approaching staff.

"All right. All right." Pat motioned that he was in control.

"But I want some action—and fast. We're not waiting any longer. I have my ways."

"Don't come threatening me with your bullshit. You know as well as I do that every label in town has been approached, and no one is interested. So stop playing Mr. Tough Manager. Grow up and try to become professional and get your act together. It's time you got a dose of reality. You are still a bunch of kids pretending to be rock stars. You haven't improved in months. This is a business you know, and you need to sell your product to the labels just like you sell anything. Just like toilet paper, or soap, or cereal. Not only do you need good contents, but you also need good packaging—the whole look and attitude. You need an image. You need musical direction and a lot of other work. Most importantly you still need a single. You should try to get your act together before you come getting in my face. Let me do my job. You need to do yours and the band needs to do theirs. Besides, I've placed a few of their songs with other artists which are on albums or are being recorded now."

"What the fuck are you talking about? We *are* ready. You just can't land us a deal because you're not as big as you think you are. We want more than our songs being played by Rod Stewart and shit. We want our own recording contract. You'll see. We'll get you. We're gonna make it—with you or without you."

"You forget. However you make it, I still have a contract. You're stuck with me, like it or not." Pat walked quickly to the door to escort him out. "I have no more to say. You need to leave now."

"You son-of-a-bitch!" Frank stormed out of the office.

He and Eric rushed downstairs to the car. "That asshole! He's just giving me a hard time."

"He ain't doing shit. He's just along for the ride. He knows the band has potential, but he's got us signed to his production company, and there ain't nothin' we can do."

"Well, we're late for Mr. Grant. You'd better cool out. You've been doing a lot of coke lately. You've been getting a little strung out. I think you should watch it."

"I can handle it. Don't worry." They sped off in silence to the club.

Eric and Frank entered the club and went straight to Mr. Grant's office.

"Where's my shipment? And why the increase?" Mr. Grant spoke first.

"Look, the price is going up. There's nothing I can do," Frank spoke convincingly to Mr. Grant. "My suppliers are asking for more money. What can I do?"

"I think you're taking a little too much off the top for your cut. I suggest you talk to your sources and ask them to reconsider. We have ways of eliminating the middle man."

"You trying to threaten me? Just who the fuck do you think you are, you son-of-a-bitch?" Frank jumped up with his fist clenched.

Mr. Grant's thugs approached, only to be motioned off by Mr. Grant. "You small time pushers are all the same. A little power and it goes to your head. I need that shipment by tomorrow. Now get out."

"Wait. What about your promise to help my band? You never made good on that one. Did you?"

"What the fuck do you mean? They've been here. They've seen your band. If you weren't so busy trying to be big shot drug dealer you'd know who some of these record company people were. Do your homework and tell your band to get its act together, then maybe they will get signed. You know for every band out there that makes it there must be hundreds that don't. They're all after that big pie. What makes your band so special—so different? They're just like all the rest—nothing new, nothing different—but just arrogant enough to think they are. Now get out, or I will cancel your dates *and* my orders, and put you and your band out in the cold." Mr. Grant motioned his thugs to escort him out. With one on each side they grabbed his arms lifting him up so that his toes barely touched the ground and carried him out the door.

"This just doesn't seem to be your day," Eric said as they left the office.

"Yeah, let's do it. I need that shipment by tomorrow. Call your contacts, same place, tonight."

"They can't do that. We need to arrange this. I can't just call 'em up and tell 'em where to be and with what."

"Then I will. Let's go."

"This is Frank. Yeah, you know, Eric's partner." Frank was in the band house now with a phone in his ear." Don't give me that cloak and dagger shit. I need my shipment and I need it tonight! Same place, in the desert. Midnight. We arrive by plane as usual." There was a pause as the person on the other end of the line spoke. "What d'ya mean you can't make it? Look, I need this shipment. Be there or I'll go public. I'm sure the world would love to know that the FBI and DEA are both dealing drugs……. You're damn right that is a threat! I could blow this whole operation sky high! See you at midnight!" Frank slammed down the phone.

"I need a hit." he took a sniff of cocaine from his vile with his spoon.

"What's shakin'?" Mike asked as he entered the room with Bill during a break from rehearsal.

"Same old bullshit. How're rehearsals going?" Frank inquired.

"We're working on a new tune. I think it's gonna be great, but what's happening with Pat Johnson?"

"Uh, let's go to the garage with the rest of the band. We'll have a meeting. I only want to repeat this once." He stormed out of the room.

"I hear you've got a new tune you're working on. Well, I just came from Pat Johnson's office. It wasn't too pleasant. He ain't doing shit. It's time we got it together and did it ourselves."

"What's going on? I don't get it." Jason questioned.

"Um…Well, basically he said no one has been interested. Says that we need to work on our sound, our image, and a single. I must agree, but we'll show 'em. I want an advertising campaign. I wanna show Hollywood that they're wrong. The band that bears their name is gonna make it. The town will not get the best of us. I want you to think of your look."

"Not the flower shirt shit again," Gloria said in disgust.

"No! More outrageous. Go for it! Gloria, you're sexy; show it off, show some anger. Maybe a black leather outfit or something. Jason, be flamboyant, be a star, be fabulous. You are all stars, now just look like it. None of the t-shirt and jeans crap. You saw how those rock stars looked. They look like stars, and it's time you looked like stars as well. Ya know what I'm sayin'?"

"That just seems so phony," said Mike

"Yeah, but I do think we could dress a bit better," commented Jason.

"But we are just musicians," said Bill.

"Well, do you just wanna be musicians or do you wanna be rock stars," barked Frank.

"Come on guys. Let's dress up a little better."

"Yeah, I guess we can do that."

"Now that's the spirit. I also want a complete campaign for advertising. We can make up fliers and plaster the city every time we play—you know telephone poles, sides of building. We can make a party of it after those late night gigs. We need to be putting up signs. I want crowds. I want a buzz in this town the likes of which it has never seen. I'll be putting some ads in the local trades and music magazines. Although our crowds have been adequate and building, I wanna see mania. I want it so that they can't ignore us anymore. Next, I wanna get rid of P.J. Productions. They're nothing but low life. We need an attorney. Does anyone have any ideas or connections?"

"I know one," Bill piped up timidly. Everyone looked at him in amazement. "An old friend of the family. I ran into him recently at a gig. Just so happens that he says he does entertainment law."

"Great, let's set up a meeting and see what we can do. Now, I gotta split. Big deal. Remember what I said. We have a gig starting Monday. Come on Eric, we have an appointment to make." Eric and Frank rushed out to make their big deal.

The lights of Hollywood and the rest of the sprawling metropolis of Los Angeles seemed to stretch out to infinity as Frank and Eric winged their way to their desert rendezvous in Eric's Cessna airplane. It was 11 P.M. They had one hour to make their rendezvous at midnight.

"Look at that city. You know I'm gonna crack it." Frank looked out the window of the small plane. "This city will be mine. But sometimes when I'm feeling like I'm on top of the world, it all seems to come crashing in on me. Ya know what I mean?"

"Yeah, it's been rough," agreed Eric.

"And then, I begin to doubt myself—and this band. I mean I can make it doing drugs and be quite comfortable, but I want more. I want a legitimate business, and I aim to prove I can do it. I'll show those bastards. I'll show 'em I can pick talent also. I think these guys are great. Don't you?"

"Yeah, I think they could make it, but you've already got it made. Why the nonsense with the band? You could do it without 'em," Eric said.

"You know, because I know they need me." Frank turned toward Eric. "And I kinda like being needed. They feel like home, like family. I'm sort of their Ward Cleaver, their Father Knows Best, and they're my kids. It's kinda fun being dad once in a while. I guess musicians are really just big kids at heart. They never learned to grow up. But that's what keeps them creative. Sort of like Peter Pan. Because once you have to grow up; all that creativity leaves you; and you begin to worry about life, responsibilities, and all that. That's why I try to protect them and shield them from the world. You know the harsh reality of everyday living. All they see and hear is their world of music. It's kind of a wonderful ignorance and innocence. I wish I could be like that. They'll never have to know the hardships we endured; the horror of war that we had to deal with. You know, all that we went through in Viet Nam. Jeff is the only one who understands that, but he was never captured. He was never a prisoner or anything."

"Yeah, boy, do I remember those days." The hum of the plane engine now reminded Eric of the sound of planes in Nam. He was reminiscent and strangely talkative for a change, unlike his normally quiet demeanor. "Um, I thought we'd never get out alive." Visions of the Viet Nam War played in his mind like a newsreel or some harsh war movie showing the horrors of combat. "I remember going out for missions. Dropping bombs on villages. I never even knew if they were friends or enemies. We would do a fly-by and watch the whole jungle or village blow up, leaving destruction behind us, then on to our next target. The night missions where especially wild. I could see the whole landscape light up from the bombs. We did that so many times it was like we were invincible, like it just did not matter. I guess you have to become pretty insensitive. And then I was hit. It was daytime. My plane went down in the jungle and crashed through the trees. I thought I was gonna die. The plane was torn up by the vegetation. Then it stopped. Somehow I survived. I couldn't believe I was alive; pretty badly mangled, but alive. Next thing I knew I was surrounded by the Viet

Cong. Guns drawn. Two guys picked me up by the arms and dragged me to their base where they put me in the jail. I became a prisoner of war. Never thought I'd get out of that alive. I was only there a couple of days when they brought you in and threw you in the prison cell with me. What were the odds?"

"Yeah, I'll never forget the day I was captured." Frank was reliving that time so long ago. "We had been on so many missions and seen so much combat. That hot steamy jungle with the air so thick I almost couldn't breathe. We had no idea who was our enemy or who was our ally. I can't believe that we just shot and killed them all. I still have visions of those women and children pleading for their lives. Villages going up in flames. We thought we were invincible. Then that awful day. I was walking down that path to the village and then boom, the battle was on—guns and explosions everywhere. It was chaos. They seemed to come out of nowhere. We were certainly taken by surprise. We were scrambling for our lives." Frank paused almost in fear as he relived his biggest nightmare. "On that day the Viet Cong appeared. It seemed like hundreds of 'em."

"War is hell, they say."

"Six soldiers surrounded me. They motioned me up and led me to their base. I was captured and thrown into that awful place with you. At least you were a familiar face."

"I think the only reason that they let us live was to see if we knew anything—they wanted information," Eric continued. They had never discussed this part of their life before, and it was now just pouring out. Something they both needed to get off their chests.

They had left the lights of the city behind and the darkness of the desert stretched out before them, enveloping them in a sea of black with only a few stars visible.

"We were both interrogated pretty intensively." Frank's voice got quieter.

"Yes, and extensively. Tortured within an inch of my life. I was stripped and beaten—whipped until I passed out from the pain. I remember coming to in the cell all bruised, cut, and hurt. And you tried to ease the pain, as I did for you. We were stripped naked of our clothes, our dignity, and our humanity. I really didn't think we would make it, but I never let 'em know anything."

"Me neither." Frank turned and stared out the window into the darkness. "I remember us sitting in that hut, fearing for the worst, dreading that they'd return and take me or you for more interrogation. Almost wishing they would just kill me and get it over with. Sweating like whores in a church. No food, little water—just each other."

"Uh, I didn't think I was gonna make it either." Eric stared straight ahead. "I still have nightmares. I can see that small cell they had us in: no windows, just blocks of concrete, a dirt floor, and a steel door. I remember the darkness. The only light was the sunlight that came in from the cracks in the concrete and that small slit in the top. The sweltering heat was oppressive. I can almost feel the heat as the sun heated up the cell during the day. I can still feel the sweat pouring off me, like being in an oven. Of course there was no bathroom, just a bucket. Certainly took away any dignity or shame or inhibitions. That little bit of water and sometimes a plate of rice was all we survived on. The sound of bombs and guns off in the distance. I sometimes still wake up in a sweat, fearful that I'm back there again. Even to this day I still jump when I hear a loud noise.

"It was pretty horrible." Frank turned to face Eric. "We were there quite a while. I scratched the wall when I could see it change from daylight to night just to keep track of the days."

"I remember being rescued. Can't believe how happy I was to see the American troops."

"Yeah, I never thought we'd get outta there alive," he repeated himself as he relived those horrible moments.

"Me neither. But you know, it somehow made us stronger."

"We had to endure. We had no other choice." There was a silent pause for a few moments.

"But you were there for me." Eric turned to Frank. "You, uh, made me strong. You helped me to endure. I probably wouldn't have made it without you. You were an inspiration. I guess I never did thank you. If it weren't for you I probably would've died. You made me hang on. You were always positive, never complaining. How could you be that way?"

"Well, you just make the best of a bad situation. You know, when someone gives you a lemon, you make lemonade. We had to make it Eric. We had to survive. I can tell you now I was scared shitless as well. I just did not show it. You know, you can't always be brave. I needed the support as much as you did."

Eric was silent. He looked straight out the window again. Then he continued. "They certainly did break us down—humiliated us. I think it was all part of their plan to deprive us of our humanity. We were stripped bare emotionally and physically. I think, it's difficult enough to admit to your own weaknesses, but when others see them it leaves you vulnerable. We saw each other at our worst, but instead of breaking us down, it made us stronger. Those were desperate times, and all we had was each other. Ya know, for the longest time I was ashamed and embarrassed by what happened to us there. It was a camaraderie born out of fear, uncertainty, vulnerability, circumstances, dependence, and need. During that time, at least for myself and I think for the both of us, we did need each other, even if for no other reason than for moral support and survival. I never brought it up before because I *was* always embarrassed. We were like two scared school girls, clinging onto each other for dear life. Two scared army soldiers thrown into the worst of situations. I thank God it was you there."

"You were there for me too, ya know." Frank was showing signs of true emotion for the first time. "I too tried to forget what had happened. Ashamed of how we had behaved before we were caught by the enemy. I never thought I could do those things. You know, actually killing the women and children. It seemed right at the time. Then, spending all that time in the prison camp with you, thinking about what I had done and what I had become. I grew to dislike myself. It was a difficult time in my life. I may have appeared strong, but underneath it all I was scared. I too felt weak and vulnerable. We had to rely on each other. I hate to say it, but when we were rescued I was relieved when they split us up. For then I wouldn't have to face you and the reminder of what had happened. I knew that I'd never forget you, but I felt as if you had seen too much of myself: my vulnerabilities and frailties. And I too was embarrassed and ashamed. All I wanted was out. I'm glad you are around now, and that we can talk about it. In a way I miss those times, for they truly touched something deep in me."

There was a moment of silence as they both reflected on their past.

"Enough of this shit. We have business to take care of and some material to get—and there's our drop. Let's land, but let's never speak of this again and especially not tell anyone else."

"Agreed."

Eric knew when they were getting close to their destination. The plane dropped in altitude. They could see the headlights of the cars lighting the make shift runway in the middle of the desert. Eric made his approach and landed the plane. It rolled along the runway gradually slowing. As soon as the plane came to a complete stop, two cars approached. Eric and Frank got out of the plane. Two feds were standing next to the cars with guns drawn.

"It's only us, Eric and Frank," Eric shouted out in the darkness.

"OK, come forward," a voice said, but they could not see who it was. "Look, no more of this going public shit. There's more at stake here than you think. We get what we can get, and that's that. I let you know in advance. I have no control over when the bust will take place, and you don't either. We give you first crack at it, but we can only take it from the big busts. We never know how much we can take off the top. You don't like the arrangement then you can do your shopping somewhere else."

"Look, you're in the vulnerable position, so you better start listening."

"You don't like it, you can go elsewhere." The fed in the black suit who seemed to be the spokesman stepped forward.

"This guy's getting a bit big for his britches. Maybe we should put him in his place," a voice from the shadows was heard, obviously the brains of the operation.

"Or out of commission," came another voice from the shadows.

"We can't afford exposure," another voice from the shadows whispered.

"I heard that! Are you threatening me? Don't even try buster! I have a few tricks up my sleeve also! Now hand over the stuff!"

"Don't even try!" barked the two men with guns pointed at Frank and Eric.

"Sorry. Perhaps we got off on the wrong foot. I'm just looking to sell some good material. You guys are making a fortune by getting me this stuff that you confiscated. I serve as a way to get rid of it at a healthy profit. I think an arrangement that works for all."

The man from the shadows stepped out in the light of the cars headlights. He put his hand up ordering the men to lower their weapons. It was Russ. "Yes, I think this arrangement works for everyone concerned. Eric, have you forgotten who you are dealing with? We've been doing business together way too long—all the way back to our Viet Nam days when we were running drugs. Frank, you ought to know how serious I can be since you were on my base. So don't pull this shit on me. We're business partners. Now let's take care of business and get outta here."

"Sorry," said Frank.

"Ok, bring him the stuff. You got the money?"

Frank handed him a suitcase filled with cash. He checked it out and closed the case.

"It had better all be here," said the fed.

"Don't worry, it is," said Frank. Frank and Eric took the large plastic bags of drugs from the other feds who were unloading it from the cars.

And with that the transaction was made.

"It's pretty good stuff. You'll see the bust on the news tomorrow. It was a big enough bust that it should make national news. They're reporting a huge bust, but we got more than half of it. We got there early and took the best pickings."

"This'll do."

"Until we meet again." Eric and Frank jumped into the plane and took off into the night. Frank was pleased that he could return to Mr. Grant the next morning with his shipment.

"WHAT'S GOIN' ON"

Marvin Gaye

It was only a few days later when a large black limousine pulled up in front of Frank's beach house. Three men in black suits got out and went to the door. It looked like some sort of gangster movie. They knocked. Frank answered the door with Eric sitting behind him on the sofa. They immediately recognized Frank.

"We need to talk," said the tall thin man in the suit standing in front.

"What d'ya guys want?" Eric questioned as he approached the door to see what was happening.

"We have some business to discuss with Frank—privately." the man in the suit said He strong-armed Frank down the stairs and toward the limo.

"OK, I'll see you later Frank." Eric stood there stunned.

"Get in!" he said. They put Frank in the back seat and drove off.

Eric, knowing that this could mean trouble, immediately ran downstairs, got into his car, and followed them.

They drove for about twenty minutes toward Long Beach and the Los Angeles harbor. Eric followed not far behind keeping enough distance so that they wouldn't know that they were being followed. Long Beach was about 35 miles south of Los Angeles not far from the South Bay section of the city where Frank and Eric lived. Only The Palos Verdes Peninsula separated South Bay from the Long Beach area.

He continued to follow the black car as it drove nearer to the harbor. Eric could see huge ships and container vessels docked and ready to unload their cargo from faraway places. Huge cranes and stevedores stood ready to unload all the foreign goods that were being imported from around the world but mostly from Asia. As he got closer, he felt like he was like driving through a dockyard movie like <u>On the Waterfront</u>. The docks themselves and the surrounding storage areas were loaded with whatever America wanted: container boxes filled with all kinds of foreign goods, acres of automobiles, or whatever. In the distance the war ships of the Long Beach Naval base shipyard stood ready to leave for ports unknown, ready to spread the word of democracy throughout the world. They drove by massive oil refineries that looked like something out of a science fiction movie with its maze of metal, pipes, tubes, and storage tanks. The flames of exhaust gasses burning off excess could be seen for miles. These were huge industrial factories located near the ship yards where oil tankards brought crude from around the world that would be processed and refined to satisfy America's thirst for gasoline. This was certainly a working part of Los Angeles.

To the west, the hills of Palos Verdes rose where neighborhoods and houses got nicer the farther up the hill you climbed.

They arrived at an industrial section in San Pedro. The streets were lined with warehouses with a few manufacturing plants and other small factories. The limo stopped in front of an old run-down metal building. The old faded sign above it read 'Barcelona Automotive.' Eric stopped about a block away to keep a safe distance.

Eric saw the guys take Frank out of the car. With guns drawn, they walked Frank towards the run-down auto shop. Eric kept his distance. This was beginning to feel like a really bad gangster movie. All it needed was James Cagney and a couple of tommy guns.

They took Frank inside the building. It was a dark, grimy building. It looked like at one time it had been an auto repair shop, and it had all the grease and grime to prove it. Now it looked more like some sort of warehouse. It was mostly empty inside now except for a stack of boxes which was stored in the corner. There were no windows and only a dim light lit the inside of the room. There were a few tools left from when it had been an auto repair shop, but that seemed like a long time ago as evidenced by the dust and cobwebs. They took Frank inside and threw him on the greasy, dirty ground. Frank stayed there on his knees, looking up at the four men.

The obvious leader of the group slowly walked up from behind. Frank heard every click that his shoes made on the concrete floor. He motioned to the other two to back off as he approached. His name was Carmine. He stood over Frank with his arms crossed. "It's time to pay up."

"Uh, what d'ya mean? I, uh, told Vinnie that I'd get his money later. What's the fuckin' rush? There is no problem here. Uh, you know I'm good for it."

"Vinnie is tired of waiting. He did your old man a favor by getting you in the business, but he doesn't like a double crosser." The man was pacing the floor while the other three stood at attention, eyes focused on Frank.

Frank could see the guns under their suits. He knew they meant business. Finally, they drew their guns and started waving them in Frank's face. "Vinnie gave you the drugs in good faith. Now it's time to pay the piper. We've already given you a thousand tabs of acid, ten pounds of cocaine, and 50 pounds of pot. Time to pay up."

"You know I don't have the money. It takes time to sell those kinds of quantities. I'll, uh, have some of it next week. Tell Vinnie he just needs to be patient."

"Not good enough. We've been promised this way too long. We have our orders. Let's teach this guy a lesson." The two other thugs proceeded to beat him with their fists and their guns while the leader looked on with arms folded.

Just then Eric stormed in. Frank was on the floor while the three thugs were beating him.

"What's going on here?" Eric questioned.

Carmine turned. "Your buddy here owes us some money. This is between us and him. I suggest you butt out." Carmine had just been standing there watching; supervising the beating. "Let him go guys, I think he gets the message. We'll catch up with him later. Watch your step, or Vinnie will be talking to your Pop. We will get our money some way."

Carmine turned and started to walk out with the two guys following. They left, got into the large black limo, and sped away.

Frank sat on the floor; bruised, bloody, and dirty.

"What the fuck was that all about?" Eric asked.

"It was the mob, you know the Mafia. They've been my other main suppliers up to now. I've kept them from you because they don't like outsiders. I didn't want to get you involved. I owe 'em some money. I got in a bit over my head. I've been using their money to pay the feds since they require payment upon delivery. Also, I've been using the money to support myself and the band. This band goes through a lot of drugs and money. Just thought I could keep owing 'em; paying them only a bit at a time. I didn't realize I was so in debt. I guess it just caught up with me."

"Shit, man, you shouldn't be fuckin' with 'em. And who is this Vinnie?"

"Vinnie is the south coast godfather—a real tough customer."

"What was that shit about your dad?"

"Oh, he and Dad have been in business for years."

"I thought your dad ran an automotive garage."

"Yeah, you're looking at it. It's just a front for the Mafia. It's mostly used as a warehouse now. They run a lot of drugs and contraband through it. The business is actually a front for money laundering and shit. I don't think there's been a car in here for years."

"Let's get the fuck outta this dump," Eric said.

"I need to talk to my dad. Can you just drive me there? He lives not far from here."

"Sure," said Eric.

They got into Eric's car and left. Frank was trying to clean himself up as Eric drove up the hill. The higher they drove the nicer the area became until what had been an industrial area became a very wealthy neighborhood with large homes and tree lined streets. They were driving into the rich section of Palos Verdes. It was a large peninsula that rose like Mount Olympus in the south part of Los Angeles between Long Beach and South Bay. It had expansive views on all sides that overlooked the city on one side, the harbor on one side and the ocean on the far side. The views could be magnificent. It was where the wealthy lived—somehow above the workers and low class people, who they looked down upon. It was as if they were somehow above the people down below.

They arrived at a large iron gate which gave the only view of the house due to the huge wall that lined the street on both sides of it. Beyond the gates was a huge green lawn with a large circular driveway that led up to an enormous house that stood in the center up on a hill. It was a mini mansion with three columns along the front.

"Wow, I see what you mean," Eric said in disbelief. "I guess he sure didn't get all this by fixing cars."

"Yeah, he has a lot of real estate holdings. But mostly the whole thing is to hide the money and goods for the mob. They're more powerful than you think. I just went into the family business, but mostly I deal with the drug side."

Frank pushed the button to the intercom to gain entry.

A woman's voice answered. "Who is it?"

"It's Frank, Mom. Open the gate."

The gate swung open. They drove up the driveway to the huge house which was more impressive as they got closer. It was like driving up to "Tara", the mansion in <u>Gone with the Wind</u>. They stopped the car, got out, and started up the stairs just as someone opened the door. It was a striking woman. She was fully dressed even at this hour of the day. Her hair was done up in a huge beehive hairdo. Eric couldn't help but notice all the jewelry that she was wearing that early in the morning while just sitting around the house.

She immediately noticed Frank's injuries.

"What happened?" She said with a true voice of concern. She showed Frank into the house.

"I need to talk with Dad immediately." Frank stormed into the room.

"But you're hurt. Let me at least tend to those wounds," She said. She ran into the bathroom and returned with a wash cloth, bandages, and first aid cream.

"Luigi, it's your son, Frank," she hollered.

A very large man entered the room. He was dark, obviously of Italian decent, with black hair and black eyes. He was wearing a suit and tie.

"So, what gives? And who is this?" he asked.

"Oh, this is my friend Eric. We're doing some business together. You know the band I told you about, as well as the family business."

They all exchanged salutations. The conversation continued while Frank's mom tended to his wounds.

"I need to talk with Dad." Frank got up leaving his mom standing there. He walked down the hall to enter his Dad's office followed by his dad and Eric.

"Vinnie and his goons gave me a bit of a roughing up. You need to talk with him and get him to lay off."

"What is their problem?" Luigi took out a large cigar. He offered one to Frank and Eric who both declined. He lit it, went behind his desk, and sat down in a big overstuffed desk chair. He leaned back and stared at Frank, waiting to hear what was going on.

"I did some business with 'em, and they want their money. You know I'm good for it. Just get them to knock it off. I just need some more time."

"They roughed you up pretty good, must be some pretty big quantities. Sounds like you are into 'em for a lot of money. I'll have a talk with 'em. But you know son, don't fuck with them! There is only so much I can do. They mean business. You had better pay up. I know family is important—but business is business."

"I just need a little more time."

"I'll see what I can do." He got up, slapped Frank on the back, and put his arm around his shoulders as he led him out of the room. "But you had better get your shit together."

"Thanks Dad. Let's go Eric."

Frank and Eric got up to leave. They said goodbye to Frank's parents, went outside, got into the car, and drove off.

"I can't wait till the band makes it big, so I don't have to deal with all this drug shit."

"LONG TIME GONE"

Crosby Stills and Nash

Monday morning came too quickly. Frank and Eric had dressed for the meeting Bill had set up with his attorney friend. His name was Steve Gold. He was a junior partner in a large law firm. They arrived at the office building on Wilshire in Beverly Hills. A long list of names filled up the door to the office suite. They stood to make sure they were in the correct place. They opened the door and entered the reception room. It was cold and business like with large overstuffed leather sofas for people to sit in while they waited. A few gold records lined the walls. The coffee table had the latest entertainment trade magazines like Billboard and Variety. Behind the receptionist were dark wooden double doors leading to the inner sanctum of the law offices.

"Frank Barcelona and Eric Watson to see Steve Gold. We have an appointment."

"Thank you," the receptionist replied. Frank noticed her beauty and professionalism. "I'll see if he's ready. Go ahead and take a seat. I'll announce your arrival." She picked up the phone to make the announcement.

A few minutes later a handsome well dressed and well groomed man probably in his late twenties or early thirties entered through the doors. His obviously expensive suit looked like it was tailor-made with the finest fabrics. A white shirt and tie completed the ensemble. His brown hair was combed and styled with the latest hip but still business-like manner.

"I'm Steve Gold. You must be Frank." He held out his hand. "And you must be Eric." They shook hands. "Bill has told me a lot about you. He came by last week. We had lunch and were able to catch up. It was great seeing him again."

"Yes. Did you receive the package?"

"You mean a copy of the contract? Yes, I have. Let's go to my office. Do you want something to drink?"

"No Thanks. Let's just get to business." Frank and Eric followed as Steve led the way to his office. His office was large with floor to ceiling windows and a view of the city. He took his seat behind a glass topped desk. Gold records lined the walls.

"After reviewing your contract with P.J. and doing some checking on my own, here is how we stand. The contract is pretty iron clad. He has you tied up for years to come. All he must do is approach one record label a year. This year he has done more than that. He has done his work. It seems that most of the record companies are aware of the band, at least the ones I've contacted which is quite a few. They're all well aware of your band. They've heard your tape and have seen the band perform, some many times. Basically, all he has to do is sit there and wait till the band is ready and good enough to get signed. Then make his move. The contract is very one sided. For instance, he gets all the publishing. He gets 25% of everything including the gross points or percentages and advances on the album, live shows, and any other income the band can generate. Everything is at his option. Basically, the band has no say. We can blow some smoke his way, maybe settle by giving him the publishing but releasing the album options which would leave you free. I'm not sure what we can get, but it's worth a try. Chances are he won't want to fight since the band has had no industry interest at all so far. He has also placed some of the bands songs with other artists. That is one thing he's good at and known for. So I think that you should at least stay with him to do your publishing. At least they could be getting songwriter's royalties even though he is keeping the publishing, but in a way he does earn it. As a publisher, he's quite good and has some good connections. We're not getting the publishing back, so I say let him have it. We can all make some money." Steve leaned back in his chair.

"I hate giving him anything." Frank got up and started pacing. "I just wanna nail the bastard! He won't lift a finger for us anymore." He stopped, looked out the window, and then turned. "But I guess you're right. Let's get rid of him as much as possible. Let him keep the publishing if that's what it takes. After all, the band members who have written songs have been making a little bit of money from the songs he sold to other artists under this publishing deal. I wouldn't want to deprive them of that."

"In the meantime, what is happening with the band?"

"Not much, I must admit. Apparently, as you've confirmed, no one is interested. Do you have any suggestions?"

"Well, I do have a few friends, but if I can be so blunt and candid."

"Uh, please do."

"The tape that I heard does not do the band justice. And live, although exciting, the band lacks image and stage presence. You know—showmanship. You are a good bar and party band, but not really an album band. You need more of a show when you perform live. But most importantly, you need a single or some other hit material. I haven't heard anything that would go on the radio, and radio play sells albums."

"Everyone has their criticism," Frank said in disgust. "I have tried to get them to at least dress a bit, but they think it just looks phony. They look better than they used to, but I agree, they could look better."

"Well, take it or leave it. But I've seen these bands come and go. I get to the clubs to see what's going on, and you know the record companies are there also. What they want is something special, something great, some hit singles, something that they can sell—like a commodity. I think your band can be that with some work, some new songs, or maybe some revamped songs. You need at least one hit single and a dynamite show. I mean really something different. Sell yourselves. It's not just music you're selling here, it's the whole package. This is rock and roll, not the philharmonic. What sells is songs, sex, and image. Look at the stars and tell me I'm wrong."

"I guess you're right."

"I do know of a producer. He's just arrived here from England looking for work. He's looking for a band to start from scratch. Produce a demo. Really do something with. I can introduce you and see how it goes. He has a lot of great ideas. It might help to make that difference musically. He has extensive studio background with some of the majors. He worked at EMI studio in London with The Beatles, The Stones, Pink Floyd, and all the biggies. He's just starting to break into producing from engineering. His named is Derek Elliott. I'll have him get in touch if he's interested and not too busy."

"Can't hurt. Have you had lunch yet?"

"No."

"Care to join us? We can talk more."

"Sure, I can spare time for lunch." He got up from behind his desk and made his move toward the door. "There is a restaurant close by. I hope it's suitable."

They were seated in the restaurant. Steve continued the conversation. "The band seems to be doing well in the Hollywood club scene. You have developed a good following and seem to be doing fairly good box office. The industry is aware of that. That's a good sign. You ought to keep the momentum going. You seem to be playing the Hollywood clubs only about once a month which is good to keep the interest level up without becoming overexposed. I would, however, recommend that at least for now you keep a low profile with the record companies and other industry people. Many of them have seen you or heard you already between Jonathan Cooper, P.J. Productions, and just playing in town. Most have passed, are not interested, or don't think the band is ready for a record deal. It'll take something new to get their attention again. What you do have going for you now is the crowds and the audiences. The industry people will hear about it from club owners, from the street, and from their representatives who are constantly in the audience checking out new acts. Trust me. Believe it or not they're out there a lot. Let them hear the street buzz. Have that work for you. Just as a suggestion, work on new songs, a new tape, and a new show. Then really hit the industry once you're ready. Don't wait too long because you don't want to lose the momentum. You need to come back with something new and exciting. Something that'll make the fans and especially the industry people take notice. Give them something to talk about. Work on new material or revamp some of the other stuff and work on a new show. Perhaps work with Derek, or whomever. Once you get your new or revamped material and a new show together—then give them a blast. Do a new and improved showcase. Make it a real scene and a real event. Cause a buzz, but make sure you're ready. You only have a few chances in this town. I can offer my help wherever possible, but before I stick my neck out, I wanna make sure it's right. Remember, in this town your reputation and your ear is only as good as your last success or failure, and all the A & R guys are in fear of their jobs. It's easier for them not to sign an act that might fail than to miss a good act. They must be very careful."

"A & R?" Eric asked unaware of the term.

"Artist and repertoire, they're the guys in charge of signing new acts and overseeing the albums of their artists. Basically, they're the liaison between the artist and the rest of the record company departments. You know, they become in charge of certain acts which they sign and coordinate with all other departments—art department, publicity, promotion, distribution, advertising, etcetera, etcetera. I can see you're fairly new at this." Frank nodded in agreement. "Well, being a friend of Bill's, I'm willing to help as much as I can, but only when I feel the band is ready."

"Thanks. We can use all the help we can get." With the mention of Bill, Frank's interest was piqued. "But how do you know Bill? He has never spoken of you until recently. None of us know much about him. He pretty much keeps to himself and is pretty quiet. Sort of a mystery to us all, but we respect his privacy."

"Bill and I go back a long way." He paused, eyeing Frank and Eric with suspicion. "Not sure how much I should tell you, but you are his manager. Bill and I grew up together outside of Boston. We were sort of school buddies."

"But you certainly seem from a different world than Bill. And you became an attorney. It seems hard to imagine that you both came from the same background. It must've been difficult working your way through law school."

"Oh, I didn't have to work. My parents sent me to Harvard. Uh, my parents are not poor, quite the contrary, they're quite wealthy, as are Bill's parents."

"Bill comes from a wealthy family?" Frank and Eric looked at each other stunned.

"Sure, you didn't know?"

"As I said, Bill keeps pretty much to himself." Frank responded waiting for Steve to continue.

"Bill's full name is William Franklin III of the Boston Franklins, a very prominent and very wealthy family in Boston. We were both old money, Boston aristocracy. It was sort of like those movies of wealthy privileged people. You know, the other America. Huge mansions, children in uniforms going to private schools, summers in the Bahamas or in Europe, yachts, the best colleges, fancy parties, cotillions—all very rich and proper. It was a different world. We really had everything. It was the life of The Great Gatsby. Our families hung out with people like the Kennedys, the Rockefellers, and the Vanderbilts. A life of privilege, money, power, and prestige."

"It all sounds wonderful," Frank said as visions of one of the movies of the rich and famous passed before his eyes. "But what happened?"

"Well, it's not as easy as it looks with all the high expectations that are placed on you."

"Well, you've certainly done well for yourself. What the fuck happened to Bill? He lives like a pauper." Eric asked.

"Bill basically wants nothing to do with his family and that life. I shouldn't be telling you this, but he gave it all up, disowned his parents, and has nothing to do with them and that life that he left."

"When did that happen?" Frank asked.

"He left home during his first year in college. Gave it all up and went to New York City."

"Yeah I know about his drug problem."

"Well, the drugs basically burnt him out, but it started even before that. This isn't the same Bill I knew and grew up with. The Bill I knew was bright, personable, highly intelligent, and well-mannered, although it took some time to get to know him. Bill was kind of a regular guy, but he was brought up to be aristocracy, something he really did not like. There are still some remnants of the old Bill in there, but only I can detect it and only occasionally, knowing what exactly what to look for and also having the history to bring them out in him. He never did quite fit in though. His family was very strict. They had very high expectations for him—expectations so high that no one could ever have lived up to them. His dad, especially, was pretty hard on him. I really felt sorry for Bill. It was pretty rough for him growing up, never being able to please his dad no matter how hard he tried. I think it just got to him. He became somewhat rebellious even as a teenager. I think it was because of that that he never really fit in. He just felt alienated. He became reclusive, kept to himself a lot. We were still friends, but he really distanced himself from the rest of the rich kids. He started getting into drugs when he was in high school. After all, he could easily afford them with his allowance. There was a lot of pressure on him to be successful. I think that pressure was just too much for him. After his bust, his parents hired an attorney in New York. You met Brent when he dealt with the band bust."

"Uh, oh yeah. He's the attorney that Bill knew. He went to court for us when the band got busted," Frank admitted.

"Yeah, that's Brent Richmond. He told me all about it."

"I just thought he knew him from his drug bust in New York. I didn't know that they were friends."

"He was a friend of mine and Bill's as well. Bill thought and still thinks that Brent was doing him a favor since we were all friends growing up. We actually knew each other way before the New York drug bust. Brent did get him off in New York, but that was before he moved here.

Brent was able to get him off easy on the drug charge in New York, of course with a little help from daddy's money and influence. Basically, Bill's drug charge was bought off—but he doesn't know that, and he never should. He would be furious if he found out that they interfered and angry at us for letting his parents know and allowing them to get involved. So please, keep this to yourself."

"Our lips are sealed, but we are flabbergasted. It does somehow make sense though. We always wondered how Bill knew these attorneys and other things. So you three grew up together."

"Yeah, the three of us grew up together and hung out together. When we got into high school we all got into music. We thought we were gonna be rock stars. Bill got his guitar, I got a bass, and Brent played the drums. Music was our common thread. It was kinda fun. We thought we were Cream. I think the first song we played was 'Sunshine of Your Love.' Some great memories. We were just a bunch of kids jamming and playing in the basement like we were rock stars. But at least for Brent and me, we gave it up. It was more of a hobby for me, but I liked music which is why I got into law and was really excited about getting into entertainment law. As time went on, we had less and less time to play. Then we all went to Harvard."

"Bill went to Harvard?"

"Yes, but Bill only went for one year. We needed to study. Brent and I did become attorneys—eventually graduating from Harvard Law School. Brent went into criminal law and I went into contract law. Brent and I are still good friends. We even have some mutual clients. We both made the move from New York around the same time."

"What happened to Bill? Why didn't he finish school?"

"Bill was just different. He never made it past the first year—home problems, personal problems. He just had a different calling."

"But what made him quit school, go to New York City, and give up all that in the first place? Sounds like he had it made with Dad and the family money."

"Not always as easy as it seems. He had a falling out with his family."

"Can you tell me what happened? Bill is very secretive about his past. It would certainly help me to understand him better."

"I guess I can tell you, but keep this to yourself. If Bill found out he'd kill me. When he was in college he met a girl, nice girl, her name was….Debra I think, or something like that. She worked as a waitress near campus. They met and fell in love. But she was from a different class. She was not a debutante or blueblood. Bill was brought up to take over his father's empire. This also meant being around the right people, and goin' to the right parties—you know, the country clubs, the cotillions, and all that social stuff. I think he liked it for a while, but it got old. He grew to resent it. And again, Dad was pushing him all the way. He had some big shoes to fill. Dad wanted him to become an accountant and get his MBA so that he could run the businesses. Dad had his whole life planed out for him. Then he met Debra, and he was quite happy for the first time in his life. Debbie represented a different lifestyle, one that Bill envied and wanted—a simpler life, free from all the pressures. To him, she was freedom: freedom from the expectations, freedom from the pressures, and freedom from all that Bill had grown to hate. Bill wasn't doing that well in college either. He spent more time getting high and seeing Debbie. Needless to say Dad and Mom didn't approve. They blamed her for leading their son astray which is entirely not true. I think his parents drove him away with their demands, but they'll never admit to it. Anyway, they didn't like her. She was a rather poor, common sort of girl. Her father was a factory worker, struggling to make ends meet. They lived in the poor part of town. Not the sort of girl that their son, a Franklin, should be involved with. Bill had decided to run away with the girl, leave his family, give up the money and privilege for the woman he loved. In a way he was very noble. Sort of like <u>Wuthering Heights</u> in reverse. She represented a different life style, and one that Bill longed for. He also got more into drugs at the time. He became very anti-establishment and anti the whole rich scene. Personally, I think it was mostly the pressure that drove him away. He just couldn't handle it anymore, and this was his way out.

There were problems, but things were going OK. Everything was fine until Daddy stepped in. They felt they had to intervene. Dad was very controlling. It was all about power, and Dad was losing control. Dad knew that with money there is power, for you see, when you talk big dollars everyone has a price. Anyway, Daddy got to Debbie's family first, before Bill and Debbie left. He offered the father a better job somewhere out of town in one of his factories or something, along with a lot of money and a house. The only stipulation was that they leave immediately, and his daughter would never see Bill again. Being poor, as they were, they accepted the offer. One day, Bill arrived at her house only to find it empty with only a note saying they had to leave for financial reasons, but that she would always love him. Bill was furious. He went home very suspicious. I think he confronted his dad. Somehow, he discovered what his father had done. After having it out with his parents, he left home with his guitar and a back pack on his back.

They, and even we, lost touch with him for a long time. I guess he went to New York and really got into the drug scene there. Then one day, he contacted Brent and me in New York. He told us that he had gotten busted for drugs and needed our help. Brent and I were both practicing law in New York by that time, but I dealt with contract law, so I couldn't handle the case. Brent dealt with criminal law, so he was able to work some deals. Bill thought Brent had taken care of everything, but actually his parents were very instrumental in helping to get him a reduced sentence. Even bought off the judge with some of the friends they knew in high places. I always kept in touch with Bill after that. He moved out here about the same time I did. I left a law firm in New York when I was offered a job to work in entertainment law here in L.A. I got in touch with Bill, and we've been in contact ever since. After all, we are old school chums. I've seen the band a few times. I still hear from Bill's parents from time to time. They're still interested in what he's doing. I'm their only contact with Bill. If it weren't for me, they'd have no idea at all what was happening with him. I, however, keep in contact because he's an old friend and our families are all friends. Please don't think me a spy for I'm not. His parents are sorry for their mistakes. He knows my parents talk to his parents. But he never asks, and I never volunteer. He basically has disowned them."

"Gee, all this time we thought he was some poor waif with no family."

"Please don't tell him I told you. It could jeopardize our relationship. I only told you because I thought you should know as managers of the band."

"I appreciate your honesty. Now, I must let you get back to your office."

Frank arrived back at rehearsals to find them just coming to an end. As he walked in, the band was packing up the gear. "Finished already?"

"Yeah, for today." Bill looked up from putting away his guitar. "I'm gonna do some writing. How'd it go with the attorney?"

"He thinks he can get us off the production deal by giving him the publishing. He also knows a producer friend he wants us to meet. Says he can help our sound and maybe make a good demo."

"Is all this getting us anywhere?" Jason asked disgustedly.

"Just look how far we've come, and we're real close. But here is what I want to do—not play the Star for about three months. That'll give us some time to get our show together, and I really want a show this time—a whole new act. It'll also give us some time to work with the producer, get some new material, and get some advertising. Then do a real industry showcase. Make it a real buzz. I want this to be special, a real event, and a whole new band. Think about it. But for now, I think we all could use some time off, just a couple of weeks. Our next engagement is a Top 40 gig and that's not for two weeks. So let's take a break. No writing songs. No fixing guitars. Nothing. Just your own time away from music. You guys have been doing nothing but music for a long time now. You all need a break. I, for one, plan to party and get laid. Jeff, you up for it?"

"Sure, I could use a good buzz and some good pussy. Mike, what about you?"

"No thanks. Ya know. I've been thinking about my mom a lot lately. Wondering what she's up to. I think it's time for me to go and see her. Time for me to go home. She probably thinks I'm dead by now. So I think I'll go and pay her a visit."

"Gloria, how about drinks at Studio 69. We haven't seen Chuck or Greg for a long time. You know, I bet they're still together after all this time. I think I'd like to go back for a visit. After all they were close friends at one time. I've just lost touch. They helped me through some pretty rough times, but with all the rehearsing and gigging."

"You mean that gay bar we used to play at? Sure, maybe I can find some little queer boy to fulfill my fantasy." Gloria laughed. "Just don't leave me there alone with no way home."

"HOMEWARD BOUND"

Simon & Garfunkle

Mike arrived at the diner. He could see his mother inside the window. She was still working at the same place even after all these years. It was dark outside. He knew it was near closing time. He stood and stared for a while watching her work as she wiped down tables and counters, put things away, and replenished other things. She was an older woman than he had remembered, but it had been quite a few years. Her long black hair had almost completely turned gray. Mike had remembered what a beautiful woman she had been, but she now looked older and tired. Her thin model's figure was now overweight and dumpy. He was very nervous as he approached the door. So much time had passed since he last saw her, but he knew that it was time to reconnect with her. He had to see her again. He opened the door and stood there. His mother's back was to him.

"Sorry, we're closed," she shouted, not even looking back.

"Um…Even for your own son?"

"Michael!" she turned "Is that you?" the tears were welling up in her eyes as she ran to Mike. She put her arms around him. For a long time they both just stood there embracing each other in silence. Finally, she spoke again. "Is that really you?"

"It's really me, Ma."

"Oh, I've been so worried." The tears were now streaming down her cheeks. "I'm glad you are all right. It's been too long. But what happened to you?"

"I'll tell you about it at home. Get closed up, and let's split. It's time I came home."

They arrived back at the house Mike so well remembered as a child. It somehow seemed smaller than he remembered and not so full of life. Mostly the same furniture he had grown up with was still there, but it was now old, worn, and tawdry. He walked through. His room was the way he had left it so many years ago. Perhaps in anticipation of his return.

"Just the way you left it," she said.

"Looks great, mom." They sat down on the sofa.

"So what happened? Why did you leave? Where did you go?"

Mike began. "Well, what happened was I got this girl from school pregnant. You might remember her. Judy was her name. But I just wasn't good enough for her. She wanted me to pay for the abortion, but I had no money. I knew she'd come to you, and you couldn't afford it. So I figured the best way was to split. I didn't want to be a burden to you anymore. I had burdened you enough in your life. I know I stood in your way of making it big in movies. This was just the last straw."

"Michael, I love you. Nothing you could do would ever change that. I never had any regrets having you. You were the best thing that ever did happen to me. I just couldn't understand why you would leave. I never want you to feel that you can't come home again. This is your home too. Never let those people scare you again."

"Thanks Mom. I guess I just didn't want to disappoint you."

"You would never disappoint me. Judy did come to me. She made her threats. I told her there was no way she could prove you were the father, betting you weren't the only one. Eventually, I did get her to admit that she wasn't sure who the father was. She wanted someone to foot the bill for the abortion, and you were the likeliest candidate.

She ended up marrying some other guy, football player I think. She probably nabbed him the same way. I guess we'll never know who the true father is."

"Yeah, I guess we won't. He's probably raising my kid. At least he's able to take care of it. Something I couldn't do. I didn't have the money that they did. She wouldn't marry me because I wasn't good enough. Since then, I've been running for all this time, waiting to come home when I had made it. I wanted to prove myself to those people. Let them know I was just as good as they were even though we didn't have the money. I think it was all high school pride and nonsense. I've just grown up a little bit. I'm not out to prove anything anymore, because I am OK just the way I am. However, I am sorry I've put you through all this. I now realize that I always did have a home to come to, and that I should never be ashamed of it. I'll never let other people ruin my life again."

"I guess we all must grow up sometime."

Just then a knock came to the door. Mike's mother answered it. In walked an older man, about his mother's age. He was well dressed and distinguished looking with a hint of gray hair. The man noticed Mike sitting there.

"Oh, I didn't know you had company, I'll leave." The man began to exit.

"No, come in, Jack. This is my son Michael."

"Don't do this Margaret," the man said nervously. Mike reached out his hand to shake.

"Michael, this is Jack, Jack Carver—your father."

Jack lowered his head. "You shouldn't have. You promised." Jack whispered.

Mike stood there speechless for a moment. "What d'ya mean? My father's dead!"

"See what's gonna happen," he remarked sadly.

"The boy deserves to know the truth. He has lived without a father for years. I think it's time I was honest with him. After all, what can it hurt now? It's all over. The truth is out. Your wife passed away. You have provided for us generously for many years. You even paid for all this. I think he deserves to know. You see Mike, Jack and I met when I first came to Hollywood. I was struggling to become an actress, as you know, but it's difficult getting work in Hollywood. I tried but didn't really get very far. He was a movie producer at the time, still is, one of the biggest. He's the studio head actually now, but back then he was just a producer. When I met him he was married to the studio owner's daughter. We fell in love and had a long time affair."

Mike envisioned some Hollywood movie with a big producer having an affair with the pretty actress.

"Unfortunately, I became pregnant. He couldn't leave his wife because it would ruin his career. So he agreed to take care of me and my son. I couldn't have afforded this house and everything on my salary at the diner. It was just a job to keep me busy and for extra money. Jack has been very generous. Over the years, we were always in constant contact. The affair continued year after year. After his wife died, we were able to start seeing each other again, but this time not in hiding."

"But what about the airline pilot?" Mike asked.

"All made up. Some guy I used to know and date. It was done to protect you."

"I can't believe this. My father is a movie producer. This is too much." Mike was in shock. After all these years he had a father, a real father—a little too late, but nonetheless a real live father.

"You never knew it, but I did watch you grow up. I just had to observe from afar. I couldn't take the chance of ruining my career. I used to see you at school every once in a while. Sometimes I went to your concerts when you performed in the band. I even read some of your papers Margaret sent me. Sometimes I'd even watch you as you walked home from school. I loved your mother very much. I love you very much. I know I haven't been much of a father, but I hope you'll forgive me. I hope in the future I can be more of one. I came here tonight to ask your mother to marry me. I think it's time. Of course, I'd like to include you. A bit late to adopt you as my son, but we could be a family. That is, if you'll have me after all this time." Jack reached out his arms and the three embraced for the first time as a family.

"Oh my god," said Gloria as she sat in her apartment one evening. "I can't believe it. I'll get there as soon as possible." She hung up the phone in tears and quickly called Frank. "I may need some time off. What's our upcoming schedule?"

"Why, what's wrong?" Frank asked.

"It's my dad. He's in the hospital. He had a major heart attack. I need to fly to Texas to see him."

"Well, we're pretty booked after next week, but lemme see. I'll check the schedule."

"Thanks."

"We have two more nights to finish out the week here. Our next gig is in Pasadena in two weeks but nothing until then. We were just gonna rehearse. That gives you some time to go see him. I hope that'll be enough. You just need to be back for the gig in two weeks."

"Works for me, thanks," said Gloria.

It seemed like the longest couple of days in her life. They finished on Sunday. She flew to Dallas on Monday morning. She let her mom know when she'd be arriving.

Mom met her at the airport. Gloria saw her standing there. She ran up and gave her a big hug. Both burst into tears. They embraced for a long time as other passengers passed by on their way in and out of the airport.

"It's lovely to see you dear. It has been so long. Thank you for coming. You look wonderful."

"How is he?"

"Doctors say he had a major heart attack, but he will be OK."

They went to the parking lot and proceeded directly to the hospital.

"I haven't told your father yet that you were coming. I thought it would be a good surprise. They say he's gonna be all right, but it was a pretty major heart attack."

They arrived at the hospital. It was a white sterile building which looked like most hospitals. Mom took her immediately to the Cardiac Care Unit. Gloria peeked in. She could see her dad in the hospital bed. He was in a hospital gown lying down with all kinds of tubes and wires connected to him. Monitors and other hospital equipment surrounded him. He looked so helpless and pitiful, not the man she remembered.

She took a deep breath, got up her courage, and entered the room.

"Uh…Hi Dad," was all she could say.

"Is that you Gloria?"

"Yes, Dad, it's me."

"I can't believe it. How'd you know I was here?"

"Mom told me." The reunion was awkward with neither of them quite knowing what to say.

"I didn't even know you and your Mother spoke."

"Only occasionally, but she always knew how to reach me."

"It has been a long time."

"Uh, Yes, I know Dad. Sorry to hear about your heart attack."

"Doctors say I was lucky, got it in time. It'll affect me, but at least I'm alive."

"I'm glad to hear that," said Gloria trying to hold back the tears.

"I have missed you so," her father said.

"Uh, me too Dad."

"Guess I wasn't always the best of fathers, but I tried my best. You were my little angel."

"Thanks Dad." Gloria went over to give him a hug that lasted for a long time. Tears were now streaming down both of their cheeks.

Finally, Dad spoke again "I think we were too much alike," he said trying to make his amends. "You were as strong willed as I was. I never planned on that."

"You raised me to be independent, and I guess I was a bit rebellious."

"You were a firecracker. At least you stood up for what you believed in."

"Yeah, you're right."

"I don't think we'll ever agree on politics or many other issues, but I guess I need to at least respect your opinion. This has made me realize what is really important in life. You are my daughter, and I will always love you." Gloria could see that her dad was really reaching out to her.

"Um….and I you Dad." They both hugged again, tears still streaming down their faces.

"So what're you doing?"

"I'm in a band in L.A. I'm a singer. We play all the time all over the city, mostly at night clubs. We're trying to get a record deal. I wish you could come out and see us some time."

"My daughter, a singer in a band—probably one of those loud, noisy rock bands."

"Yeah, Dad, it sure is."

"Well, I still don't understand that music, but I guess that's for the younger generation. We had our music. I guess you have yours as well. But a singer. I'm very proud of you."

Gloria could not believe what she was hearing. She had returned home to her family.

Gloria was able to spend a couple of days there getting reacquainted with her mom and dad. It was truly a heartfelt reunion. She returned home to L.A. happy that she had been reacquainted with her parents after all these years.

42

"THIS IS YOUR SONG"

Elton John

"This is Derek, everyone, Derek Elliot, the producer I told you about." Frank said. He entered the rehearsal studio followed by a tall thin man in his early thirties with a short beard and light shoulder length brown hair. His sport coat and freshly laundered and pressed dress shirt contrasted with his tennis shoes and slightly faded although obviously expensive designer jeans which had also been pressed.

"He's a producer from England. Bill's attorney friend, Steve, invited him along. He has worked with some of the best in England as an engineer—the Rolling Stones, Rod Stewart, The Beatles, Elton John to name a few. Most of the albums he has produced never did that well over here, but I've heard 'em, and they sound pretty impressive. You can all listen to 'em later."

"Ullo," Derek said in his English accent while making the rounds, shaking hands as each of the band members introduced themselves. "Heard your tape. I think there could be some potential there. I'd like to hear more if possible. Perhaps you could play a set of your own material."

"Sure. We have a lot of cover material as well. Some of which, I think, are good enough and different enough to be on our own album.

But for now, we'll just play the original songs," Mike stated as he plugged in his bass.

Frank got out two chairs and placed them in front of the band. Due to the limited space, they were practically in the middle of the set up. The band returned to their places. Derek placed the clipboard he had brought on his lap, took out a pen, and prepared to write. The band began their set while Derek sat with arms folded and a blank expression on his face, only occasionally writing down things on paper. He remained silent for the entire set.

"Well, that's basically our set." Frank stood up to get some kind of reaction from Derek who remained lost in thought.

"Well, I can see some potential. That tape I heard certainly does not represent the band. It does not do you justice. I think we could work together. I'd like to give it a try. Is the band open to suggestions?" The question was an open one for anyone to answer.

The entire band agreed with a shrug of their shoulders and nod of the head.

"If you have a tape of all your material that I can listen to, that would be a great help. Even a rehearsal tape is adequate. I just want to hear the songs."

"I can get you that on our way out." Frank edged toward the door.

"We rehearse most weekdays from noon to six. We gig at night—mostly Top 40 stuff. Then about once a month we do the Hollywood clubs like the Star. We've been developing quite a following."

"I would like to see an originals gig. Let me know the next time you play. I'll see you all lata'. I must be going for now. Ta. Frank, can I see you for a moment?"

The two walked outside, leaving the band to themselves.

"I don't know if Steve discussed with you my normal production deal." Frank nodded that he hadn't. "It's probably premature, but I like to get these things out in the open from the start so there are no problems later. Once the group is signed to the record company, I get three points on the album, appropriate points on the singles, $20,000 advance on my points recoupable from the sales, and full producer credit. Of course, all of this is moot until you get a record deal. But when that time comes, it is something to take into consideration. Steve can work all that out. But, I think I can whip them into shape. I'd like to do a demo tape. I assume you can arrange that. I don't think the tape I heard properly represents the band. I think something fresh could make the difference. From what Steve has said everyone's already heard and passed on the old tape anyway. You need something new."

"That can be arranged. Also, we're playing the Star this Monday. I think it would be to your advantage if you could see the group perform live. It's quite a good show."

"Sounds great. I'll be there. Perhaps we can meet again with the band next week once I've had a chance to see them live and listen to the tape, and you've had a chance to discuss my terms. I can make it back on Thursday of next week to work with the band prior to going into the studio."

"Sounds like a plan. I'm sure we can arrange everything to your satisfaction." Frank shook his hand, turned, and marched back to the rehearsal studio.

"Who the fuck was that?" Jeff was the first to ask.

"Like I told you, he's an up-and-coming record producer. He's quite good, and Steve highly recommends him. I've already met him for lunch and we seemed to get along."

"Yeah, well, first off, I don't want some person to come in here and change my music—turn us into elevator music or something," Jason replied.

"Yeah, and what does this guy get out of it?" Gloria said defending her pocketbook again.

"He's asking for points on the album which he will produce. Ya know, a percentage of the sales. Just like you get. It's a pretty standard deal."

"But haven't we already given away a lot of points to P.J.? What's going on with that?" Mike asked.

"Steve is working on that now. He thinks we can get out of it, but it'll take some doing. I spoke with him today."

"You know, we can't just keep giving away points, first to P.J. and now to this Derek fellow. Then you, as a manager, get a percentage.

That doesn't leave us with much. From what Steve says, an average deal is only about 10 points, a great one is 12 or 13, but that is usually only for bands with some clout or who have been around for awhile." Bill spoke up with assurance having obviously spoken with Steve recently.

"Let's at least give this guy a chance," said Frank. "If it doesn't work out, it doesn't work out, and we just walk away. I'll talk to Steve and see if we can at least delay the process to see if Derek is on the same wave length as we are. Now for some good news. Attendance at the Star and the other Hollywood clubs has been up. We're more and more in demand. Those fliers, ads, and everything else are starting to pay off, but we need to continue. Steve has recommended that we continue to develop our audience but lay low with the record companies until we have a chance to revamp our show. They are aware of us, have seen and heard us, and have passed. We need something new to regain their interest. In the meantime, we need to keep building our audience and the momentum. My hope is that we get a large enough following that the record companies can't help but take notice. With a large following, they'll have to know that this band is popular, and something people will want to see and buy. When they see how popular we are locally; hopefully, they'll see how this could be translated on a nationwide basis."

"It's pretty tough rehearsing all day, playing some casual at night, then on the way home tacking up posters of our next gig," Jason added hoping someone would alleviate that task. "I mean, we are musicians."

"It'll all pay off eventually. Eric, Mark, Pete, and Alex have been doing a lot of that as well. In fact, we need to think about paying them something pretty soon. They could also use some help. They've been making pretty good money dealing and helping me with the drug business, but I know they'd like to stop doing that at some point and just do music stuff full time. Eric has virtually worked with me as the manager on everything: going to meetings and helping me out. I know Eric doesn't necessarily need the money that bad since we do OK with the drug money, but I think we should at least offer him something. Mark, Pete, and Alex have turned out to be excellent roadies. They're learning a lot. They know the set as well as you guys and consequently make the sound and lights and effects an integral part of the show. I mean they're always running errands, fixing cords, setting up, and tearing down, or fixing stuff. That's a lot of work. I know they love it because they love the band and they believe in the band. But it's time we paid them a bit more. Keeping them with drugs and having them doing so much dealing and shit is not enough."

"Yeah, they've all been great, a great help," Gloria agreed. "As soon as we can make some money, we'd be glad to pay them more. We're still struggling as well, without much extra money. But, we'll keep it in mind."

The next meeting was arranged with Derek once he had seen the live show. He walked in. He could sense the tension.

"I want you all to rest assured that all I'm interested in doing is to make this band sound better. I have no intention of changing the band. I hope to bring out the best in this band and allow you to fully reach your potential. It sometimes takes a third ear to hear it. Musicians are so often caught up in it so much so that you are unable to hear the flaws. Perhaps just a simple change of arrangement or something minor can make all the difference. After hearing your tape and seeing your set both live and here in the studio, I think I have an idea of what you are trying to do. I think the biggest problem is that everyone is trying to play like a soloist. You must remember that this is a band, not a collection of soloists. You must think of the sound of the song and what makes it work. Not just showing off to that drummer or guitar player in the audience. I think that you can all have your solos and a chance to show off at some point, but only at the appropriate time. Make the songs stand by themselves. It's a problem I face with a lot of bands. As musicians, they don't know when to stop playing and therefore play too much. Economy of notes, play only those which are necessary. Sometimes less is more. The song is the most important thing especially in getting a record deal, air play, and being accessible to the public. I hope you all agree. Any questions?"

The band looked at each other and nodded in agreement. No one had really talked to them this way, but it somehow made sense.

"Now then, if we're all in agreement, I guess we can get started. I do, however, have one last rule. I take this very seriously, and hopefully you do as well. I'd prefer that there be no drugs or alcohol during rehearsals and especially in the studio if we get that far. Personally, I'm not into drugs, but I know how most bands operate and how the rock and roll business is. I'm not naïve. I just don't wanna waste anyone's time. I know that you, like most bands, do your share of drugs. But for me, this is serious work. In fact, I've walked out of quite a few recording sessions with some pretty big acts, who will remain nameless, because there was just too much drug use going on. Either it was a big party, or they thought they sounded great but in fact the opposite was true. Nothing was getting done. So my policy is no drugs. Do them on your own time. Any problems with that?"

"None at all. We do our share of drugs, but not when we're working. We've been that route and are happy to hear you say that actually. So, I think we're on the same wave length." Mike spoke as the rest of the band shook their heads in agreement.

After a few minutes of idle talk while the band got plugged in and tuned up, they were ready to start. They had played about five songs when Derek stopped them.

"That's enough for now. I hope you don't mind if I make some comments. We'll start working on individual songs. There is some really good material here, but it's getting lost. I'd like to woodshed each song individually. Really work it out."

Everyone agreed that any help would be appreciated.

"The third song in the set, I didn't get its name. Can we start with that one?"

It was played.

"Now just play the chorus. It's a great line, but it's getting lost in the clutter. Remember the concept of less is more. We need to break it down, maybe even do it with a half time feel to give it some variety and somewhere to go. The most important thing is the melody in the vocal line. I'd like to hear some vocal harmonies; you'll need to work on those. Now, try it with the keyboard playing the chords for pitch, but instead of playing chords, try interval runs like arpeggios. Bass should be playing less, a sort of half time feel against the vocals. Now drums, be sure your kick is exactly on with the bass, not a counter figure which you are currently playing. The drums and bass should always make for a strong bottom and play together. Guitar, I want you just to follow the lead line. Try something strong and ballsy, but make it simple, like a simple riff."

"Wait, this is gonna change the whole feel of the song. This is too much. You're changing our music. We want it our way," Jason objected, defending his own song.

"Bloody 'ell. Please just gimme a chance. If you don't like it, we can work out something else or take some ideas and not take others. Just hear me out."

"Yeah, let's at least give the guy a chance," Mike spoke up. "We all know how you feel about your tunes Jason, but let's at least listen to what this guy has to say." The band agreed as Jason conceded.

"Now for the intro. Let's try just starting with the keyboard only, kind of a classical type introduction. Just do two turn arounds of the theme before the vocals come in. Then try the first verse with piano only."

This certainly made Jason feel much better for it gave him a chance to show off his playing.

"On the second verse add the bass and drums, but you need to make a strong entrance. I need a strong power chord from the guitar. Then fade. The only other thing this song needs is a hook. Jason perhaps you can come up with something. Ya know, something really catchy that you go away singing. I'd also like to hear a bridge added. Some sort of a transitional part of the song that is different from the verse and chorus. Then a short turn around between the verse and chorus. Maybe something like a half step progression which will lead to the chorus and make the song build. Let's try a standard type arrangement for now: intro, two verses, chorus, bridge, verse, chorus, intro, chorus, and out." The band worked for an hour on this one song trying to make it better. The interaction between the musicians and producer became stronger and stronger and the song began to sound better and better. In fact, the difference was amazing. They played it over and over as he made suggestions. Once finished, the song sounded better. It still kept its integrity but made much more sense arrangement-wise, musically, and sonically. It sounded like a real song.

"You know, I hate to admit it, but the song does sound a hell of a lot better," Jason admitted.

"Next, the song has some strong emotional content. It tells a wonderful story. But the way you play it, I just don't believe it. Don't get me wrong, you all play the notes right, but it just has no feel. You need to tell the story. Make me believe it. This is mostly the singer, but applies to the whole band. It's not just about getting the right notes; it's about making it believable. Now try it like you mean it. Take the emotion and the story in the song and tell it through the music. It's not just the song but the delivery as well. You need to take me or the audience there, on a journey, convince me that what you are singing and playing about is true and real—that you are not just playing a bunch of notes. Now try it again."

"But I thought we *were* doin' that," Mike protested.

"Needs more."

The band played the song like they never had before, not just with technical ability, but with feeling.

"Now you are getting there. Now, exaggerate it. The audience is dumb; you have to bombard them with the feeling. I still don't believe it's enough. And when you do get there, you have to do that every time you play the song."

"Uh, yeah, I see your point now," agreed Jason.

"Now, for the next song, try the first one on the tape."

The band played the first song

"Yeah, that's it. Now let's try something different again. First off, that's a great opening guitar line—a very cool riff. Feature it. Make it louder and more defined. Establish it as a theme. After you've established the guitar line, bring it down under the vocals. It can still sound strong and powerful, but it needs to be in the background. Maybe something crunchy and rhythmic to keep the song moving and to keep the groove—but something that won't detract from the vocals. Might even be only a few notes or part of the chord, but even if it's the whole chord, make it staccato—you know, short, so that the song still thumps. Heavy, but in a different way. We can return to the really loud guitar part later in the song, but really build back up to it. Then let it rip again. That'll give it some direction and dynamics. In fact, the whole band needs to come down during the verse so that we can hear the vocals. The trick is to not lose the intensity, but to make the verse and the vocals sit right on top of everyone's playing. This you should do with every song. It was something I noticed on everything you played. But not to worry; it's a very common mistake that a lot of bands make. Bring it up again at the chorus and whenever that guitar line comes in by itself. Then really crank it up. The time for the band and the music to get really loud and really lay into it is when there are no vocals. Use some dynamics, but don't lose the intensity."

Derek continued. "Cool, now for the ballad. Try starting with an acoustic guitar just playing individual notes of the chord like a melodic arpeggio: no strumming, just finger picking. After that's established maybe a simple flute line Jason. No drums or bass yet. Add some tinkling cymbals during the first verse when the vocals come in, but nothing else: no bass, no flute, no keys. When it goes to the chorus, I want a big power chord from the guitar. Just hit it then let it fade. Also, that's where you add the drums and bass. Also, the keys can enter here, but play some sort of string line, something that sounds like violins, perhaps on the mellotron. After the second chorus when you go to the center lead section I want you to break it down. Start out quiet with a flute solo that builds to a guitar solo. Really make it soar. Then back down to the acoustic guitar line but played on the electric. Then on to the next verse but with the whole band. At the end, have it return to the acoustic guitar thing to come full circle. That'll give it some dynamics and the song will go somewhere. Make it a journey. Remember keep it simple. Also, I think it really needs some vocal harmonies during the chorus."

They worked on this song for another hour. It too sounded better.

"Next, the second song—that rockin' song. This is Bill's chance to shine. Try having the guitar coming in at the beginning very strong, really establish that line. Really rip into it."

This made Bill quite happy. Seldom had he been told to play louder.

"Then, at the verse, drop out to let the bass and drums take over. They can keep the rhythm and keep the groove. The guitar should enter later, half way through the verse. Start with some lead lines or screaming notes but only around the vocals. Play off the vocals, but keep it to a minimum with just a few chords or notes, then fade away. By not playing or playing less it will even feature the guitar more as it will become more noticeable. In the other verses still keep it sparse. Then really kick it at the chorus, but as always keep it under the vocals. Then really rip into your guitar lead. That is your moment."

"That'll work." Bill was happy.

"I want you to try this with all your material, so next time we can continue working."

"We have a gig tonight. Are you interested in coming?" Eric asked.

"Sure, I'll be there. Have a good gig tonight. Ta."

Jason went to Derek after the rehearsal. "I really dig working with ya. I must admit I had my doubts, but I think this is gonna work out great. I can't believe we've been playing and rehearsing those songs for all these years, but we did more to improve them in that time than we did in all that time before. It's truly incredible. Thanks for your input. I'm truly looking forward to working with you. When will we see you next to work on the songs?"

"A couple of days. You know what to do now. I'll give you some time to work on these things yourself. Then I'll come in to make changes. Once we've reworked all the material, we can decide which songs to take into the studio and produce a new tape."

"Sounds like a plan," Gloria agreed.

"Thanks," said Jeff.

Derek made his exit.

Moments later Frank walked in.

"You should hear what this guy has done!" Jason shouted.

"That bad, huh?"

"Fuck no! The stuff sounds fucking incredible. Check it out. You just won't believe the difference."

The band played the songs with the changes.

"Sounds fuckin' fantastic!" Frank offered. They were all abuzz talking about how much better the songs were. Frank continued. "He really has made a difference. I guess this means that you have no problem with his terms."

"Hell no. He's gonna make this band sound fuckin' awesome," said Jason.

All chimed in with enthusiastic agreement.

"I saw him on my way out. He wants me to pay for some studio time in about a month. He said he'd set it up. I guess you guys will owe me some more. I hope this ends soon. I can't keep supporting this band. You know it costs money. Besides, did you know that you guys are up to a pound of pot a week? That's getting a bit expensive."

"Sorry," they all apologized.

"Anyway, we'll talk about it later. I've got some problems of my own. Do ya know where Eric is? He was supposed to meet me here."

"Haven't seen him," said Jeff

"Tell him I'll be home and to call me immediately."

"Sure enough boss. Will we see you tonight? You know we're planning a big party afterward. We need it after working so hard."

"Probably not. Eric and I have other business to take care of. Besides, it's just another Top 40 gig. You can handle it with Mark, Pete, and Alex in case you have any problems." Frank turned and left rather preoccupied.

"LISTEN TO THE MUSIC"

The Doobie Brothers

It was almost a month to the day when they finally entered the studio. They had to work it around their bookings. This was one of those weeks that they would be playing in Hollywood for one night only which prevented them from booking a whole week at other Top 40 clubs. Derek had booked two weeks in the studio planning to only get four tracks done. Derek warned them that they would be working for at least twelve hours a day just to get everything completed. The first week would be for laying down the tracks with the second week reserved for mixing and picking up problems which did not require the whole band to be there the entire time. They had worked on all the songs in the set but had decided on the four that they felt best represented the band and were the best and the most commercial.

They found the address, entered the studio, and began to set up. It was a very nondescript building that could have been any sort of a warehouse, factory, or any other industrial type business with no windows and a plain front. They entered the first room which was the reception room and lobby with a couple of sofas and chairs and a coffee table. The walls were covered with gold records. Behind a glass window was an office where a young woman worked answering phones and doing paperwork. She was a young and beautiful woman who looked more like she should be at a nightclub than a place of business. She told them to load in through the back. So Mark, Pete, and Alex took the truck to the back of the building where a large load-in door was located. The band just entered into the studio. They first went into the control room where they found Derek getting ready. It was a smallish room filled with recording equipment. A huge sound board dominated the room. Tape machines and other devices lined the back wall. In front of the board were two panes of glass that looked into a huge room with walls covered with carpet. That was the actual recording studio where they would be playing. Mic stands and equipment lay around waiting to be set up for the sessions.

The road crew began unloading the truck.

"Wait! Drums and bass only first. No amps—just instruments." Derek stopped them from unloading all the equipment. "We can lay some scratch piano and guitar, but they'll only be for reference. I'm gonna have you play in the sound booth, not the studio. You can plug directly into the board. Right now, I'm only interested in getting a good drum track. We might possibly get a good bass track, but that is secondary. One thing at a time. I don't want any interference."

The band looked puzzled.

"Everyone will get their turn, one instrument at a time. So we'll lay final tracks for everyone else later. I mean we will lay the tracks so the drummer has something to go by, but we'll probably not use them. We'll record them for good later."

"Uh, you mean we won't really be playing together?" questioned Jeff.

The band was still wondering about his methods.

"No. We'll concentrate on one instrument at a time. Try to get the best performance for each track. It is a bit tedious, but in the end it'll make it sound better. It makes for better separation. It allows me better control when I do the final mixes. First drums, then bass, then guitar, then piano, then anything else. Vocals will be last. Don't worry; you'll all have your chance. Everyone will play along once but only for scratch tracks, ones that we won't keep. They'll do their tracks that we keep some other time. Saves time in the long run. Once we get a good drum sound we record all the songs. One of the biggest challenges is trying to get a good sound for each instrument: bass sound, or guitar sound, or whatever. That's just how I work, and we only have a limited time. Trust me."

"I guess we'll give it a try. Uh, works for us," Bill stated relying on his expertise.

"Yes, you are the studio master," Gloria agreed a bit confused.

Once the microphones were finally set up all around the drums, they began to get the drums and bass sound. The bass and guitar were being sent directly to the mixing console without the use of an amplifier. After many hours, it was time for a take. It took many hours before one was kept. Derek proved to be a real perfectionist, not allowing any error or even hesitation on tape. The time had to be perfect as did every note and every emphasis. The bass and drum had to be exactly together—as if one instrument. Sometimes they were able to play together for a final take, but other times they decided they would have to go back and redo the bass track since their main goal was only to get a good drum track. Derek even resorted to the use of a metronome to assure perfect time for the basic tracks. It took a long time, but finally they had completed the basic drums and bass for one song.

"Man, this guy is a tyrant," Jeff stated as he came into the control room wiping the sweat from his shirtless body. The band took a break after a long session, while Derek made phone calls. He's really making me work. Either I play too hard, or too soft, or not in time, or he changes the eighth notes to triplets, or something. Besides, I'm used to playing as a group, not all by myself, on my own with just the reference track. It's hard to get the same feel without everyone playing and getting into the groove. Also, only hearing the other instruments in those headphones and not live is real strange. But I guess he knows what he's doing. It sure is different from playing live—a whole different animal."

"Yeah, but you ought to hear how it sounds. It's fucking incredible!" Jason could not contain his enthusiasm. "Your drums never sounded better—like musical thunder. Strong but not just pounding noise."

"Yeah, he even made me tune my drums. I can't remember when the last time that I did that was. It just doesn't seem like rock. It's too exacting. It's hard for me to get into a groove and get the intensity and energy. There should be more feel. I prefer to just beat the fuck outta the drums."

"I think that is the challenge—getting the feel when playing under these circumstances. But you are getting that feel, believe me. You'll see. It's gonna sound fine." Mike patted Jeff on the back to signal a job well done. "I think for the first time, we're really sounding like an album. You know. Those tapes we did for Jonathan and P.J. sounded like shit compared to this. But what do you expect when you go in and record the way we did—real half-assed. This is gonna sound like an album—and a fucking good one. Besides, you're gonna have to learn to get that same feel and energy without the interaction. I guess that's what being a professional is all about."

"I guess you're right. It's just so different from playing live. Just wait until you're in there recording. You feel like such an idiot, like a little kid who can't do anything right. Everyone staring at you and listening to every note and every error. It's really intimidating. Like playing in a fish bowl."

"Coming from you," Gloria said, "it must be heavy. I mean, you can fuck in front of an audience, but you can't play the drums in front of us."

"You know what I mean? You can hear every mistake. It's so grueling. He wants things exact, precise, and perfect without loosing the energy. He's always telling me there's not enough feel, or too much feel, or time was off, or whatever. At least he's nice about it, but it sure is hard work. But in the long run, I think it will pay off."

"I think it's good. This is probably the first time we've really listened to each other's playing this intently. Really hearing the different parts that each of us are playing and how they go together." Bill was showing true signs of excitement, unusual for someone who rarely shows any emotion.

For the remainder of the week, they put down the tracks for all the songs, one instrument at a time. They started with drums, then bass, then guitar, then keyboards, then other instruments, like woodwinds, tambourines, or whatever. Lastly, were the vocals: first leads and then the harmonies. The band, being used to playing live and as a group, felt that it was a strange way to record, but it seemed to work, and it did save time instead of trying to set up each time for a new song.

During the next week everyone had their turn in front of the master, trying to do their best to perform—but no one could even come close to getting it in one take. In addition to mistakes, or tuning issues, or problems; many times parts were changed as the tracks progressed. New and different parts were added or changed once the basics were completed. Bill was the most relaxed of all, just playing along and doing what was required. His true talent and professionalism came shining through. Jason, on the other hand, just tried too hard. Many times it was his song at stake. He had to play it perfectly. However, his own expectations and inability to live up to them created a lot of frustration. Many times his nerves got the best of him. At one point he even ran out of the studio in tears, unable to continue. But after some kind words from his cohorts and the understanding coaxing of the producer, Jason felt better and was able to continue. Finally, they were ready for the vocals. After a few tries Derek decided to have Gloria do them alone in the studio without the rest of the band watching, so he sent them all away. The wall of eyes only made her more self-conscious of every note. It made her voice falter. It was like playing under a microscope. Eventually, all band members had their turn to play.

After each session, they had returned home more excited than before. They would pick up their usual dinner of a pizza. Then spend hours rehashing what had gone on that day. The spark was in the air. There was real excitement again in the band. They spoke for hours about the material. Now, they knew how to make the songs sound better which would make the band sound better overall. This renewed their enthusiasm, and the fact that someday they would make it together—a pact they had always kept. The inspiration had returned. It was this band against the world, and they were going to come out on top. They would return the next day ready to work.

"I know I've heard things I never did before, and I think it's the same for everyone. This is a valuable learning experience. I think we should make it a practice to woodshed all these tunes. Once we've finished in the studio, we need to go back and work on all of our material just like we've done here. I know we've done this a lot already, but now I think we really know what we have to do!" Mike exclaimed enthusiastically.

All agreed; it was time to really take a critical look at their material, rework it, and make it better.

At the end of the week they had each had their turn in the studio. They were finally called into the main control room to listen to a play back.

"I start on mixing the songs tomorrow. I do this alone. You can give me all your input beforehand, but only me and the engineer will be in the studio for the mix. No one else."

"But! what about…" Mike started to say.

"Sorry, that is just how I work," Derek explained, while rewinding the tape. "I think all the tracking is done. I'll make rough copies so you can listen to them at home tonight. You can make any final comments or suggestions before I start to mix. Keep in mind that this is not the final mix. I'll mix the tracks later, but you can at least get a rough idea of what it'll sound like when put together," Derek explained. He hit the play button.

They couldn't believe their ears. It sounded better than any of them expected. It was like it was ready for an album.

"The tracks sound fucking incredible!" Jason was the first to speak up.

They all agreed. The whole room was buzzing about the sound of the songs. This brought them to a whole new level.

Derek worked that recording console just like a musician. In a way, he was as important as any of the musicians. He translated that music to tape, and in doing so, his artistry fully showed through. It was truly magic what he did with the songs.

For all, it was an exhausting and taxing experience. But the end result was a professional sounding tape of four songs of which they could all be proud. Derek had done his job.

Once completed, a band meeting was called in the studio to listen to the final mixes and discuss their next step. They sat in silence, listening to each track as it played. Excitement was bubbling underneath like a volcano about to blow. Once finished there was at first complete silence. They were stunned, and for the first time speechless. They looked at each other in amazement.

Finally, Frank broke the silence. "Sounds fucking incredible!" he remarked. He got up to shake Derek's hand. He wanted to be the first to compliment him on a job well done.

Then the volcano blew in an explosion of excitement. They all agreed it was amazing. The room broke out in a cacophony of enthusiasm on how good it and they sounded.

"I'm truly excited. I don't see how we can miss now with a tape that's this good. They've got to sign us. We've got it made now, thanks to Derek," said Mike.

Everyone applauded and offered him their compliments. They all expressed their excitement about the finished product.

Frank began. "I've brought all of you here for a couple of reasons. First, to listen to the tape; but more importantly, to help us in our planning. As you may have noticed, I've also brought Steve, the attorney who introduced us to Derek. He's here to listen and to give us some news. But first, I wanna congratulate Derek and the band on a job well done."

"Thanks," said Derek.

Steve took the floor. "Derek, you've done it again—incredible job. First to business. I've been talking with the P.J. Productions' attorneys about the contract. They're playing real hard ball. They refuse to give up any publishing but have agreed to take only one point on the album if we get a record deal or three points if they sell it to the label. That isn't so bad. They are a good publishing company as you've found out from them placing some of your songs. That's one thing they do very well. Therefore, I recommend you stay with them for publishing. However, the good news is that they have agreed to let the band sign directly with the label therefore bypassing the production company and releasing you from that part of the original contract. You see, that contract signed you to P.J. and P.J. would then sign to the label. All royalties were to go to them first. Then they could recoup their advances and take their percentages and finally pay the band. However, under this new agreement, the record company must be instructed to pay them their percentage first and directly which should be no problem. They would get no other monies from the band, just the publishing and a point or one percent of record sales after recouping costs. You see what P.J. does is take all these bands, signs 'em, makes tapes, and if they sell they can make some money. This usually happens with publishing. However, they have had some minor success with bands, but that really goes only so far. They just hang on to their percentages. If the band breaks and makes it big, they're in good shape; if not, they've lost very little. Unfortunately, our hands are tied. One bad bit of news. I did find out that they have shopped the band with the old tape, so they've done their job. I don't know if Frank has told you, but most of the labels have heard the P.J. tape and have passed. I discovered this after doing some checking on my own. So, do ya want me to go ahead and renegotiate with P.J.? I highly recommend it. I think it's a pretty good deal considering the circumstances. You will have to give up all the publishing, but there is no production deal. You know you have to give up something to get something."

"Yeah, sure. Sounds OK to me," Frank assured everyone. "Who needs P.J. anyway? That asshole."

"Well, I guess so. I don't think we have any other options." Mike agreed. The entire band concurred.

"Next, I've spoken with Derek, and he and I are in agreement on this," Steve continued. "We recommend that we shop the tape ourselves. At least we can save a couple of points. From what Derek has told me, he wouldn't be against playing it for some of his people, and I can certainly show it around. I don't wanna leave Frank and Eric out of the picture, but Derek and I do have more connections in the business. I think the companies will be more receptive to Derek and me since we do business with them all the time. Frank and Eric will be more involved in corresponding with the band, sort of the liaison, and they can take over once the band is signed."

"Good—then we're ready to send out the tape!" Mike exclaimed.

"Yes, but I want it to coincide with a showcase date at the Star or one of the other clubs. One month before the date we'll send out the tapes along with a complete press kit showing all the print ads, interviews, and reviews to every record company imaginable."

The band could not imagine the record companies not jumping on this immediately and signing them to a record contract.

"I don't know about the rest of you, but I'm ready to get back to gigging," Jeff commented. I miss playing, and I miss the after gig parties. I'm sure glad we're playing this weekend, and I think we ought to have a big party to celebrate."

All agreed. The band had their own listening party at the Hollywood band house later that week with friends, drugs, and lots of sex.

"ALL RIGHT NOW"

Free

They were surprised when they received the first couple of rejection letters—form letters no less with the usual: "Thank you for submitting, but this does not suit our current direction in music." But they hoped that this would change with the upcoming gig.

The band worked feverishly on all their original material for the next month; changing, revamping, and using the information that Derek had given them to make each song better. Their studio time had been an eye-opening experience for them all. They wanted to make sure every song sounded as polished as the couple they had recorded. They reworked every song in their repertoire to make it better, and the improvement showed.

They did the gig at the Star. There were some record company people there to see what the band was up to. They were hopeful that something would now happen.

"Bloody 'ell. That was fucking incredible." Derek was truly excited as he entered the dressing rooms after the gig. "That was a great set. I like the new songs. And I like the improvements you made on the old ones. Sounds like you've really been working. I'd like to do some more recording. Best start working on 'em right away. All the work you've been doing on the songs is really paying off. They're sounding better and better. You are starting to get it.

On another note I do have some good news. I spoke with some of my contacts at Empire America, part of The Empire Records Group. There is some interest. They wanna see a showcase. Rob Allan, the west coast A & R guy, is a good friend of mine and someone I've worked with. He's very interested. He has discussed it with the head office in New York. The president is flying in from New York tomorrow and wants to see the band while he's out here. Since you don't have any upcoming Hollywood showcase gigs, I thought it best that we book a rehearsal room where you can do a private showcase. I know a good one. It has a large enough stage area. A lot of bands rehearse there before they go out on the road so that they can work out their show. This could be your chance to get signed."

Everyone's ears perked up at the sound of some real interest from a label.

"At last," was all Jason could say feeling again a little more positive. "What have been the other reactions so far?"

"Well, from my end," Steve spoke up, "the reaction has been mixed but encouraging. They are watching with some interest, but no one is biting. They're still not sure they can hear a single. Let's just concentrate on the showcase for now."

The large rehearsal studio which Derek had booked was like a small club. It was a large room with a large stage area but almost no seating. It felt like a real stage. The band was excited for their chance at the big time. They would've preferred a real gig, but this was the best they could arrange. Derek entered with a few people and introduced them to the band. He was followed shortly thereafter by Steve who also made the proper introductions to his friends.

Sunlight was streaming in from the outside. All of a sudden, the silhouette of a large figure filled the doorway blocking out most of the light. He was tall and quite a bit overweight. He entered with a look of power and authority. His long curly hair was a little unkempt while his clothes indicated a person of some financial substance at the same time being casual—expensive, but not stuffy. He was followed by a thin man wearing a dress shirt, sport coat, and designer jeans. The large man stopped, put his hands on his hips, and waited while the thin one continued into the room immediately going to the people he seemed to know. He made the introductions to the large man. They made idle talk about the business and new bands.

Finally, Derek broke up the talking. "This is Rob from Empire west coast A & R."

The thin man nodded his head in acknowledgement.

"This is Mr. Greenwood from New York," Rob spoke while the large man nodded and reached out his hand as everyone introduced themselves.

"We're running late for appointments. Can we begin?" Rob asked.

Derek showed them to their seats. The band took the stage and the crew took their places to operate lights and sound which were fairly minimal. Once every one was ready the set began. They did the show without gimmicks, just performing the songs.

Mr. Greenwood sat motionless with arms crossed for the duration of the set. Rob, the local representative, only moved to whisper during a couple of the songs, and then returned to his static position. The rest of the audience sat motionless so that everyone could watch the band perform. Derek and Steve had their eyes glued to Mr. Greenwood for any hint of reaction. The band played their best for a cold and unemotional audience. It was like standing naked in front a school class while everyone looked at your flaws. They felt as if they were under a microscope again being analyzed, scrutinized, and otherwise critiqued. For the band, they had never felt so nervous in all their life. This was not a friendly audience. But this was a chance to make it big or at least get signed, and they felt inadequate and awkward. Without their audience and the interaction and reaction from the crowd, the live show became a bunch of songs. It was difficult to keep up the energy without the feedback, but they did the best they could. The set ended. Mr. Greenwood and Rob got up, thanked everyone, and left without giving any kind or reaction.

One of Steve's guests followed him outside for a few moments. They could hear some conversation but couldn't make out what was being said. Then he quickly returned just as the band was leaving the stage and putting away their instruments. Steve went over to him, followed closely by Derek. They conferred for a moment, and then approached the band with the other friends they had brought.

"This," Derek began, "by the way, is Rick Martin, of Rick Martin's Headline Management." All eyes were on him now. "I know you must've heard of him, or at least of some of his acts."

They all nodded in agreement. Headline had some of the biggest acts in the music business.

"I invited him here for two reasons: one to get an honest outside opinion of the band, but also to see if he'd be interested in working with the band. In addition to today's showcase, he and some of his people were at the last gig per my recommendation. I thought it would be good for you to hear what he has to say. Get a real unbiased opinion. What do you guys think?"

The band was in consensus. "That'd be great," they all said almost in harmony.

And with that he turned the floor over to Rick.

"Derek and Steve have told me a lot about this band. They convinced me that it would be worth my while to get involved. To be honest, I do see some potential, but I'm also somewhat skeptical. I'd like to give you my honest opinion if that's OK with everyone.

"Yeah, sure." They all were waiting with bated breath.

"By the way, I talked briefly with Mr. Greenwood on his way out to see what he thought. I'm sure you are all waiting anxiously to hear what he had to say. So let's get that over with quickly, and for the most part, I agree."

The band sat motionless, hanging on every work.

"He basically said the band had potential, but you weren't ready to be signed for the big time yet. He thought you were a good party club band but not really ready to make an album. Most importantly, he didn't hear any singles. He wants to see what happens with some work. He did say that he might be more interested if I were to become involved. He thought it would be a good team with Derek and Steve. He said with that kind of team it could be more interesting. He'd be counting on me, Rob his west coast A & R person, and our contacts to make this band ready. Singles sell albums, and they want singles. I must agree, but Derek has assured me that they're there. It's just a matter of time and work."

The band was a bit crestfallen—disappointed that they were not ready to jump at signing the band.

"As for me, "he continued. "I know that you have a manager, and I don't want to step on any toes or cause any problems, but I'm just gonna cut to the chase and lay everything out on the table. I'm willing to give it a chance. But, let me tell you the way I work, and what I see for this band. I was asked for my opinion, so whether or not I end up working with you, I thought I could at least be honest. Here are my suggestions and recommendations, and what I see that the band needs to progress and to get that record deal. That's if you'd care to hear my opinion?"

"Of course we would," they all agreed. All eyes and attention were still glued to every word he said.

"First off, very few in town gigs for three months, or until ready. Just enough to keep your name and audience out there and interested, but nothing for the industry. We can keep them pretty quiet. The band is already overexposed. All the industry people have seen it too many times. When I feel it's ready, we start playing in town again, but these are gonna be events, every six weeks at most. I want people to only be aware of one gig at a time, so that every time they all show up they'll be thinking it may be the last. Also, I prefer that you do not do the Top 40 gigs."

"But that's how the band makes most of its money and supports itself. Plus, we also have a good following at those clubs." Frank stated.

"I understand. That is up to you. Just keep them out of town like you have been doing.

Second, I want Derek to work with you on some new songs to record. I think you have some better ones.

Thirdly, I'll be working with you on getting the act together. We need to work on image, your look, and the show. The whole thing is part of the act, not just the music. All the changes will only make the band better. I want more attitude, more conviction, but most of all it must be authentic. The trick is to make it look natural and unscripted, even if it is. You guys are almost there; it'll just take a bit of work."

"Sounds like you want to change us?" Jason questioned.

"My only goal is to make this band the best that it can be, not something it is not. You must believe it, you must believe in yourselves, and you must believe in the image you are trying to portray. Most of all—keep it real.

I brought some people here today to see the band and to get their feedback. These are people I trust. They see the potential. They'd be willing to work with you if I am involved. Basically, they're doing me a favor. There are some others I'd like to call in as well. I could pull a few strings and pull some favors. However, before we start, I need my contract."

"But what about Frank?" Jason interjected.

"I take it you still wanna keep him involved?" Rick asked.

"Yes, he has been with us all along He's supported us. He's part of the family."

"Well, this is business guys, and there is only room for one manager. However, I only deal with certain aspects of your career. I usually only deal with the big problems—record deals, contracts, tours, merchandizing, and stuff like that. The day to day stuff is not part of my concern. In fact, I'd prefer having someone like him to deal with as a liaison between management and the band. He can continue to keep the band organized. Something he seems to be doing a good job at. Perhaps you'd consider making him the tour manager or some capacity like that. He can continue to help finance the band. Also, I, or my team, do not deal with the Top 40 nightclub scene which I understand is a big part of what you do now. Frank can work on those. I'm sure you can find a place for him. Who knows, in the future he may even work out so well that I can use him for other bands I manage. But for now, he'd be your responsibility. So there are plenty of jobs for him to do. You guys discuss it and get back to me. I think you have a lot to discuss, so I'll leave you now. Let Steve or Derek or even Frank or Eric know your answer. Any one of them can contact me if you decide to go forward." He shook hands with everyone then vanished into the doorway.

Frank turned to Eric. "That guy is trying to steal my band away."

It was the next day when they all decided to meet to discuss what they should do next. "Well gang, we've gone this far. What d'ya all say?" Jason asked.

"I ain't gonna quit now," Jeff was the first to respond without hesitation. "Shit, I'll go naked on stage if that's what it takes. Let's get out there and do it."

Bill and Gloria agreed.

"But what about Frank?" Mike asked, expressing his concern. "I feel real bad about leaving him out."

"Yeah, he has been a good friend and has really helped this band. I hate to fuck over a good friend—someone who has done so much for us—someone who is like family. Where are our loyalties?" Jason added compassionately.

"I agree, but this is for the good of the band. We have to at least check it out." Jeff said.

"Let's be honest and talk to him, but I think we should talk to Steve first." Bill added. "I'm sure there'll be a place in this for him. We'll figure out something."

The first meeting was with Steve in his office to discuss their prospects. The whole band was there, but for this meeting Frank and Eric were not.

Steve started. "The first thing that you should know is that Rick takes 20% as manager, *and* he requires a contract before he even starts. But I think you'll all be happy when you see the results."

"20% of what?" Mike asked. "We don't have much of anything."

"Managers get 20% of everything—live performances, recording contracts, album sales, and merchandising. But he pays all his own expenses, and he does spend his own money."

"But what about all the other people? When do we get paid? What about Frank and Eric and the roadies?" Jason was very concerned. The whole group nodded in agreement.

"I recommend that you keep them for now, that's if you want to. They've stuck with you this long. Frank can be your personal manager taking care of the day to day business, Sort of a buffer from the business side of everything so that you can just concentrate on the music and the show. That's if he's still interested. It takes a lot to make a band into a star. Also, Rick has no interest and won't deal with the Top 40 nightclubs either. That'll be left up to Frank until you've made it big. Roadies should just remain in that same position. I don't think you should really change the organization at all. I'll just be handling the business part with the record companies. You all have worked so hard, no need to give it up at this point."

"What about everyone else?" Jeff asked.

"Everyone gets paid and here is how it's gonna work. Derek the record producer gets only album sales percentages off the top. P.J. gets publishing and therefore you and your manager will get none of that. They also will get one point from the album. Remember there is still songwriting money which the songwriters will get through the publishing company, album sales, and live performances. The manager will get his percentage of album advances and sales, and live performances. I've already discussed this with Rick and he's fine with it. The only other piece in the pie will be your agent who will get ten percent of everything he books which will probably only be your live performances, but if he does get you a recording contact he'll get a percentage of that as well."

"So what does that leave us? You know we have to split all this up five ways. Not to mention that we also have to pay Eric and the Roadies."

"Unfortunately, you must give something away to make it. No manager works for nothing, nor does any agent or producer. These are all standard terms, and you're getting some high level talent. If it all works out, you'll all make some money."

"But Frank was only gonna take 10%."

"10% of what? He never really did anything except book you in those dives. He's a great guy and he helped get you to this place, but you never would go anywhere with Frank. You are dealing with professionals now. Well, is it gonna be forward or backward?"

"I think it's either forward or not at all. We have no other choices," Mike replied in disgust. "So it's onward. Unless I hear any objections I think we should have Steve draft up the proposal, and we'll sign it."

"But first we should talk with Frank and Eric and see how they feel about all this," Jason said with a great deal of concern in his voice.

The meeting was called with the band, Frank, Eric, and Steve. Frank and Eric were quiet. They knew something was up.

Steve started. "Frank, the band has an opportunity to sign with Rick Martin's Headline Management. This could be a great opportunity for them. It puts them into the big time. They really want to do this; however, they certainly don't wanna leave you out of the mix. They'd like to keep you on as personal manager or tour manager or something—whatever you want to call it. You would be dealing with the day to day running of the band, the local gigs, and all jobs that the new management won't do. Even Headline likes the idea of a go between to keep the band organized and be the voice of the band to management. You could work closely with 'em, but they'd have the final say. We'd repay you for all you've done or will do and pay you a smaller percentage. This could be a good career move for you as well. They have many other bands that might be able to use your services if it works out."

The band sat quietly with their heads down. They really didn't like being in this position, but they knew it was the best for the band. You could have cut the atmosphere with a knife. They could just feel the grave disappointment Frank must have been feeling after all he had been through.

Frank sat in silence; stunned at what he had just heard; his head bowed trying to hide the tears. This was the first time any of them had seen this side of him which made them feel even worse.

After a long silence Frank began. "Um…Although I am disappointed—I, uh, certainly wouldn't want to stand in the way of this band making it big," Frank stated. "And that means whatever it takes. I would still like to be involved if there is a place for me. Uh, I'm willing to do whatever it takes. Is there something we can work out?"

"Of course," they all said. They stood up and went over to him to give him a big hug. "We would never leave you out in the cold." They stood in an embrace for quite a while.

"Then it's settled." Steve was happy. "We should meet tomorrow so I can go over some terms."

"Sure," Frank agreed.

"Since we want to keep Frank and Eric involved, we can work out their deal at the same time we work out the deal with Headline," Jeff stated.

Steve continued. "I recommend we get all contracts done at the same time, the one with Rick the new manager, Frank's contract, and the one with Derek. He has been asking for one, and I've just been putting him off. As a friend of Bill's and a believer in the band, I'll agree to delay the bill for my services until you get signed and get some money."

The proposals were drafted. The attorneys came to agreement on the terms and they were signed by the band. Now the machine which was being created started to work.

A meeting was set up with Rick to plan their next step. The band, Eric, and Frank entered Rick's 12th floor office in the 9000 building on Sunset. A large picture window offered a view of the city. The walls were lined with gold records of all the acts he managed. His receptionist showed them into a large conference room. Rick was sitting at the head of the table with a few other people sitting around talking amongst themselves, their note pads ready. She announced their arrival and showed them to their seats.

Rick began. "I understand from Steve that you've decided to join our management team. I welcome you to our company. I'll introduce you to the office staff on your way out. I'll be setting you up with some people who'll help you to get your act together. I brought some of them along today. These people are gonna help you with your image and bookings. I'll be setting up meetings with them at a future date, but I at least wanted to introduce them to you. There'll be others, but I wanted to start here. All these people normally work only on large acts, but they've agreed to lend a hand in this situation based solely on my recommendation. Basically, I'm asking them for a favor. They've heard your tape, and they were also at the showcase and your last gig at the Star. They're willing to help since I believe in you so much. With their help we can create the buzz in town." With that he began introductions.

"This is Sue Stone." A blond well dressed woman in a business suit stood up. She was a large woman, not really very attractive but striking in her appearance and demeanor. As he spoke, she went around the room shaking everyone's hand. "She's a publicist or sometimes referred to as a press agent. Stone Public Relations is her company. She works with all the media—written, radio and television—regarding public relations which means she deals mostly with the press. She'll be spreading the word about you and your band. I use her for a lot of our acts. She'll be working with me on getting you some local press; you know concert reviews, and interviews in local music papers, magazines, and radio stations, and such. I think we can get some press and exposure through her. She can really get the buzz happening since she's well connected with all the press people here in town." She nodded her approval then sat down.

"This is Isaac Cohen." A well dressed rather handsome man in designer blue jeans, a dress shirt and sport jacket stood up. He was well groomed from head to toe which helped to accent his striking and handsome features. His jet black hair was slicked back to reveal a very handsome face. He could have appeared in GQ as a model or as the handsome leading man in any Hollywood movie. As Rick continued talking, Isaac also went around the room shaking everyone's hand. "He's an agent with Creative Artists Talent Agency or C-A-T-A for short. He'll be in charge of booking the band on some live gigs. That is if he feels the band is ready. And believe me; he's as tough as I am. His value will mostly come in later after you're signed, but he'll be a good ally and make the band seem much more legitimate to Empire." Isaac nodded then returned to his seat.

"I'll also be in touch with Rick, the A& R guy from Empire. They wanna keep tabs on your progress. I'll warn you now, however. I will not represent inferior product. This band must be perfect and each song great. I want to see a show that's amazing and timed to the last note, the last word, and the last second—with no surprises. You will not perform until I see fit. It's all up to you. But I'll warn you now; you will do it my way. I do want to say, however, that I do think that you have it in you. Otherwise, I would not waste my or any of my colleague's time. This band could be great, and you could all be rock stars. It's all up to you."

They all nodded in agreement, anxious to please their new manager.

"I've arranged for a small party this Saturday, sort of a signing party as a way to introduce you around. I want everyone to meet in a social setting. This'll be my way of announcing your affiliation to the company. My assistant will give you the information."

That night they drove down Sunset to Rick's house in Bel Air just west of Beverly Hills. The house was a few blocks off Sunset, not far up the hill from UCLA where they had played so many gigs. They turned on Bel Air Rd where a huge gate announced that they were truly in Bel Air. They drove up the hill on the winding road mostly seeing only walls and gates with an occasional glimpse of a large mansion with well-manicured lawns and grounds behind or over the walls or through the gates. This was an area reserved for the very wealthy. Many rich entertainment people lived there including quite a few stars. They looked for the numbers trying to find the correct address. When they finally found it, they didn't see the house at first; it was behind a huge wall covered with bushes. They drove in through the gates that normally would have been closed, but were open this evening to accommodate the party guests. They drove up the large circular driveway that took them to the front of the house. There was a huge expanse of lawn with trees and bushes lining the perimeter. They couldn't believe the size of the house. It was a mansion tucked away in the hills. They were met by valets who opened the car doors for them. The band walked toward the house which was all lit up. They arrived ready to meet their new world head on.

They entered the large contemporary house which seemed to go on forever, with rooms in every direction. Two stories of glass offered them a view of the back yard complete with a large swimming pool, tennis court, patio, and large grassy area—all lit up for people to go out and mingle. It seemed more like a resort hotel than a house. Modern art hung on the walls. The caterers in black pants, vests, and bow ties circled with hors d'oeuvres and champagne. It was a truly high end Hollywood party, somewhat serious, but very elegant. The absence of drugs was obvious. A different scene from what they were used to and expected. All of Rick's staff was there; as were Rob, Sue, and Isaac; and some of Rick's clients, mostly rock musicians. It seemed like more of a corporate business party than a wild rock and roll party, a real change from parties of the past. They were introduced to some of the other acts Rick represented who only had good things to say about him. They noticed Derek and Steve. They were glad to see some friendly faces. Eventually, they mingled and talked with many of the people with the band gravitating more to the musicians and Frank and Eric gravitating more toward the business people—each sharing some common interests. It was a fun evening but rather sedate compared to some of their other parties.

The next day at rehearsal Jeff spoke up. "I sure am glad we're playing at Pier 11 next week. We've been working our asses off. And all this business stuff is kind of a drag. Time to have some fun. I miss playing and partying. After all, I am a musician. This stuff has been hard work."

All agreed.

Since they were playing at Pier 11 the next week they decided they needed their own party to celebrate. So after the gig on Friday night a huge party was organized at Frank's. They had one wild party, like the old parties of the past. They were celebrating their good fortune in their own way.

45

"ALL THE YOUNG DUDES"

Mott the Hoople

The first meeting was with Isaac at his office at Creative Artists Talent Agency, a very large agency that handled all aspects of entertainment. They arrived at the large rather ominous office building on Beverly Boulevard just a few blocks from Beverly Hills in West Hollywood, not far from the Sunset Strip. The entire nine story building housed the agents and operations of C-A-T-A. Frank, Eric, and the band entered the main lobby to be greeted by a receptionist and a uniformed guard.

"Your name, please."

"Frank Barcelona and the band Hollywood. We have a meeting with Isaac Cohen." Frank replied.

She checked her list. "Yes, I have you here. Music is on the third floor. Tell the receptionist there. She'll announce you."

They took the elevator to the third floor only to be met with another receptionist. The lobby was filled with rows of gold records and pictures of clients each autographed by the artists.

"Frank Barcelona and the band Hollywood to see Isaac Cohen," Frank told her.

"Yes, he's expecting you. He has reserved the conference room. Follow me. We can tell him you are here on the way."

She walked down the hall followed by Frank, Eric, and the band. It was a long corridor with many doors. As they walked by, they peeked into some of the open doors. These were very small offices, not much larger than a cubicle, and all almost identical. Most had an agent on the phone or going over the stacks of paper work which were piled up everywhere: on their desks, on the file cabinet behind them, or on the floor. The place was abuzz with the sound of their voices. Everyone seemed to be in a hurry especially those that were almost running down the hallways as if there was an emergency.

The receptionist stopped at Isaac's office. She poked her head in. "Your ten o'clock appointment is here. I'll show them into the conference room."

"I'll be right there," he answered with a phone in his ear.

She continued on her way with the band in tow. As they walked by, each one peeked in and waved. It was a small office, a typical closet of an office that one would expect at an insurance company or other big business with only enough room for a desk and a file cabinet, not the large glamorous office that they had expected for a Hollywood agent. They noticed more gold records and pictures of numerous music acts; some bands, and some single artists each with Isaac at the center or shaking their hands. He, like all the others, appeared to be a hard working agent as evidenced by the mounds of paperwork surrounding him. He was wearing a sport coat, tie, and designer jeans. His black slicked back hair made him look more and more like a runway model or a Hollywood leading man. This contrasted greatly with this less than elegant setting.

They entered the typical-looking conference room with large comfortable chairs, a large wood table, and expensive modern art work on the wall. It was definitely a place to show off to clients, to hold meetings, and do business deals—very different from their personal work space. They were all seated as Isaac entered the room in a flurry of energy. He never sat down but preferred to pace the floor clicking his pen as he talked. He was fast talking and seemed very busy. The meeting was very short.

After introductions were made he began. "Rick has told me how much he likes this band, and because of that I've agreed to work with you and him on bookings. I understand you do some Top 40 gigs. I do not book them. Those you will have to book on your own. I will book the legitimate venues like the Roxy and the Whisky. I have heard the tape and have also seen the band, so I think I know what you are all about and where you might fit. I may have an occasional opening slot for a concert. I'll also be working with Rick in getting the labels interested. Normally, that's the job of an agent, and Rick and I work closely together. When the time comes, I'd be happy to help in shopping the band and in negotiations with the record label. That's all in the future however. If there is anything else I can do, don't hesitate to call. I'll be in touch with Rick. Who should I contact if I need to contact the band?"

"That would be me," said Frank. He handed him his card.

He thanked them for their time, got up, passed around his business cards, and left the room to return to work at his office. The band was not quite sure what had happened. No time for discussion, no time for questions. He just spouted off and left. He was already on the phone when the band passed by his office again on their way out. It was like a whirlwind, but the band felt that he knew his stuff and they were excited just to be in one of the big Hollywood agencies.

The next meeting was with Sue. They met in her office in Beverly Hills. The waiting room was lined with pictures of rock stars, movie stars, and television stars. Apparently she did it all. Oddly enough there was also an old picture of her in a police uniform which the band was curious about. She invited them into the large boardroom. Around the table a large group of people were already there with note pads ready to work. They sat on one side of the table leaving the other side open obviously for the band. Sue was at the head of the table standing.

"Everyone, this is Hollywood, our newest client. I'm sure you'll give them your undivided attention. Most of you have seen them perform, and you've heard their tape. So you know what we're in for, and what this band is all about. Is there one spokesman for the band?"

"We brought along Frank and Eric. They've been our business persons up to this point. Although not real band members, they keep us organized so you can run everything through them," said Mike.

"Fine, please make the introductions." Eric introduced the members of the band and the instruments they played.

Sue followed immediately introducing everyone she had brought in to the meeting. "I've called in some friends of mine to help us get our look together. I wanna use 'em as consultants. They've either seen you, heard your tape, or both. I want you to work with them. They know the business and are experts at what they do. This is Helmut, a photographer, and Maggie, a fashion consultant." A man and woman on the other side of the table stood up. The man was all dressed in black: black pants, black shirt, black shoes, a black jacket, and a black beret. This went along with his jet black hair and extremely white pasty complexion almost devoid of any color. He looked very European. Standing next to him was a woman in a long flowing dress. Her hair was pulled back showing off her beautiful face. She was very severe looking, but striking in a way that she could have been a fashion model.

Then, with the introductions made, Frank and the band took their seats.

"First, we need some press pictures. That's Helmut's department. He's an incredible photographer. He'll be taking you into the studio to take some pictures that we can use for the press. We need something interesting and quirky that gets everyone's attention. Something that represents the band and makes you look like rock stars. We'll have him go to a rehearsal to see how you perform on stage and take some stage shots, but mostly we want him to do group shots for the press. Some 8X10 glossies for publicity and stuff. He'll have to get to know you as a band in order to get the right look for the camera. His job is to bring out the personality of the band and each member individually."

They all shook hands with him in a rather business-like fashion.

"But before we even start taking pictures, we need to give you a new hip look. It's all in the packaging you know." She could see the dissatisfaction in their faces. "You may have the best product on the market, but if it's not packaged properly people won't want to buy it. Think of yourselves as a box of cereal, you are the best tasting cereal money can buy, but you are packaged in a plain box—not interesting, so no one buys it. Your look is like the cereal box—your packaging. It needs to look great and get people interested. Grab their attention. Make you look like rock stars. That's where Maggie comes in. She's a fashion expert. She'll help you work on and develop your look: clothes, hair—everything to make you look the part and to make you look better for the stage and for the press shots. She'll take you around to buy some new clothes. I think you'll like her. She's very hip and has a good eye, good fashion sense, and a good sense of what'll work and what won't. You need something appropriate—something that fits you and who you are, while at the same time making you feel comfortable. You'll need casual clothes but, more importantly you will need stage clothes. She doesn't want to change you, just make you look more the part and enhance your personalities."

Sue continued still sensing their reservations. "Don't get me wrong, I don't want to turn the band into anything that you aren't already. I just want to enhance the group—make you bigger than life. You want to be rock stars. Then start looking and acting like rock stars. Image is everything in this business—and we are selling an image. That means not changing anything, just enhancing and exaggerating everything. Some hip clothes will help but only if they fit your personalities. Let's start with a shopping spree. This jeans, t-shirts, and tennis shoes look is just not gonna do. It makes you look like your mom dressed you to go to grammar school. I've also seen you on stage, and while it's a bit better, it's still too plain. Not flashy enough. You need a better look, one that reflects the band as a whole and your own individual personalities. You are a much more sophisticated band than that look—especially with the music that you play. This look is just so common and ordinary. This plain look just doesn't do you justice. Remember, you are on a stage. Look like stars. Your band sounds like rock stars, now it's time that you all looked like rock stars, no matter where you are going. Something hot and sexy I think. Any thoughts on what you want to look like?"

The band just looked at each other dumbfounded.

"Shit. Not the matching flowered shirts thing again I hope," Bill replied dejectedly.

"No, nothing of the kind," Maggie explained.

"I think we look fine on stage," Jeff commented sternly.

"You look OK for a club band, but you need to look like rock stars, like you should be on an album cover." Maggie now took the floor. "You are way too hip, and raunchy, and sexy for that." She turned to Jeff. "I'm thinking of tight leather pants and a skin tight tank top to show off those incredible arms and muscles for you, perhaps in a military fatigue design." Jeff smiled. She obviously knew how to get to Jeff with flattery. "You are all very good looking and sexy in your own way. We need to bring that out. I want to get to know each of you so that whatever we buy will bring out your personality. I don't want you to be phony, just more exaggerated—more flamboyant. Gotta keep it real, but make it bigger than life. Leather is always safe. Each of you should have leather jackets and leather pants. I also want to try some ceremonial clothes or uniforms; you know military or band type with lots of buttons, epaulets, and insignias. Not the whole uniform but just a jacket or shirt or something with some designer jeans. I know a great costume shop that furnishes the studios with their costumes. They always have a lot of stuff on sale. We can also try the tuxedo look, maybe formal tales with a cut away front with blue jeans. That might be an interesting look for Jason and maybe even Bill and Mike, just not all at the same time. Try to keep a unified look but not all wearing the same thing at the same time. Vary the look and coordinate depending on the gig. I want to try a lot of things and see what works for you."

"But we're just bunch of musicians," Bill said.

"Well, you can be just a bunch of musicians playing in clubs, or you can be rock stars. The choice is yours. I, for one, think you are rock stars."

"Let's give her a try. What can it hurt?" Jason said. "I have always said that we should dress up more."

"Uh, sure why not. We've come this far," Mike reluctantly agreed. "So long as what we're wearing is something we feel good about."

"I'm all for adding some fashion to this band," said Gloria. "You guys could look hot."

"Come on, this could be fun," Jason explained. "And we could use some happenin' clothes."

They all agreed.

Sue continued. "The rest of the staff will be working on press releases; mostly local stuff." She made the introductions to the other people in the room.

The next day the band met with Maggie for their whirlwind shopping spree. They met in Sue's office first to get a game plan.

"Jeff, I still see you in muscle clothes, military tank tops, tight pants, perhaps shorts for when you play. You are very physical, so it has to be confortable, but it can also be sexy."

"Works for me."

"Gloria, you need something real sexy, stiletto heals, skin tight pants, and a skin tight top or shirt maybe with a leather jacket to accent. Jason, something flashy yet sophisticated and classy, leather sport coat perhaps, tuxedo cut away tails, uniform, or just some sexy leather pants and a white shirt with diamond studs—simple but flashy. Mike, I see you more as the guy next door look, but not too funky, tight jeans or leather pants and a hip shirt. Bill, with that thin body we can do so much, you just wait. What d'ya all think?"

"Sounds great," they all agreed.

"Then let's get going."

Jason was the most enthusiastic. Everyone could see that he was truly in his element. He had always wanted to dress up more and for the band to be more fashionable, but it had been a losing battle. The band did not want to appear too gay. So they would often simply ignore him or make fun of him. It was easy for Gloria to dress up because she was the front person and a girl. This was what Jason had been wanting, and he was glad that he had some support for his views.

They began at an army navy surplus store to see what they might have. They found some very formal dress military jackets with epaulets and brass buttons that looked great. They liked the Army, Navy, and

Marine dress blues and Maggie said they would go great with jeans. The got some tank tops for Jeff. They all got some military clothes, t-shirts, tank tops, and other things that they thought would be fun.

Their next stop was at the leather shop where they each bought some skin tight leather pants and a jacket. Each jacket was different to show their individual style.

Next it was on to shops with hip and trendy clothes for men and women. They found some sexy tight fitting clothes. Some with sequins, or studs, but nonetheless much flashier than what they were used to wearing. They bought a few things then were off to the next stop.

The Hollywood costume place was next. They thought this could be fun. There was a large room of for sale items that were mostly surplus and overstock items that they wanted to get rid of. They were too old, they had too many, or they just were not needed. All of these clothes once had been rented in one or many movies. There were clothes and costumes of all types, from ordinary street clothes to real costumes that one would only wear in a movie or at Halloween. They had fun trying on different things, from appropriate to absurd to funny. Maggie could use this for ideas to see the personality of each band member.

Jeff was the first to become playful. He came out of the dressing room in a Roman Gladiators outfit complete with breast plate, helmet, shin pads, and sword. "Where are the Barbarians?" He held up his sword and posed like a warrior. They all had good laugh.

Gloria was next. She tried on a frilly antebellum dress right out of <u>Gone with The Wind</u> complete with hoop skirt, parasol, stockings, and wig. She looked like Scarlett O'Hara. "Well, fiddle dee dee. Where is that Rhett Butler?" She said in a southern accent.

Mike put on some science fiction robot outfit with metallic looking square shaped body piece, hat, and leggings." I am from the planet Music," he said in a robotic voice. "I am here to take over your world."

Bill came out dressed like a superhero with tights, cape, mask, and boots all in black and looking a bit like Batman. "Here I am to save the day," he said sounding more like Mighty Mouse than Batman. The tight suit really accented his skinniness.

"You know, I could totally see you in tights." Maggie remarked.

"With these skinny legs and nothing on my crotch except this swim suit like thing?"

"Sure, not exactly that, but something similar."

"But, I would be so embarrassed."

"Embarrased! You would look hot. Many people think that skinny is sexy, and it is very rock and roll. With the right shirt and jacket you would look real hot. Your guitar would hide your crotch anyway, which could look very phallic, so you could wear anything there. Yes—very hot indeed." Maggie thought aloud.

Jason decided to go 17th century with white stockings, knee high knickers, fluffy shirt with Jabot knot and lace cuffs, knee length brocade waistcoat, vest, and even a powdered wig.

"I am ready to perform the Mozart harpsichord piece," he said in a proper English accent. Everyone laughed.

"You know, how about you get that and just wear the jacket with some jeans or leather pants?" Maggie offered. "Kind of a fun look."

Jason thought about it. He thought it could be fun, so he bought it.

"That's what I mean, try something fun and outrageous then mix it with something else."

They all had a good laugh trying on things that they knew were totally ridiculous and inappropriate and some were just plain funny. But some of these outfits gave them ideas for other outfits and clothes. It created a catalyst for experimentation. Perhaps they could possibly mix and match some of these outrageous outfits with other clothes to create a look. They did like the tuxedos especially the tail coats with the cut away in the front and the tails in the back. They also liked the military, ceremonial, and marching band tops and jackets. They all thought they worked for the band. They were classy, flashy, and fun. Each picked out stuff that they felt comfortable wearing. Maggie said they would go great with just jeans and a t-shirt to dress it down. In the end they all had a good laugh. They were able to find some things that would fit their new look, their new image, and their personalities.

Their next stop was a fashionable girl's store. Everyone thought it was for Gloria and her outfits. Gloria did try on a few things. Then Maggie started picking out wild tops and tight pants and scarves. She handed them to the guys and told them to go try them on. They were dumfounded. They started to giggle.

"But these are women's clothes," Jeff protested.

"What the fuck are you doin', turning us into drag queens or something! I don't wanna look all gay or anything, no offense Jason," said Mike.

"None taken," said Jason.

"Oh, get over yourself. You didn't have any trouble trying on those silly outfits at the costume store." Maggie's plan was working. "Think of this as the same thing, just sexier. Now, just try 'em on. I insist. This is what's hip and now. We want those girls to go crazy over you guys. You are all great looking guys. We want the girls to think you are sexy, and you need sexy clothes for that. These clothes will make you look sexy. For the guys, we have to make you look so hot so that every girl will want to go to bed with you, while at the same time every guy will want to look or be like you. For you Gloria, the same holds true in the opposite sense, every man must want you, and every woman must want to look and be like you. It's a fine line, but something that can be accomplished." Her plan had worked. She had gotten them used to trying on silly and funny things. Now they were to try on sexy girl's things. Their guard was down, so they were a bit more receptive.

They were very reluctant at first. The look totally worked for Gloria. But for the guys, wearing woman's clothes was not something they had really planned on. She shoved them off into the dressing rooms amidst their protesting. The guys were at first quite uncomfortable trying on women's clothes.

Jason, Mike, and Jeff shyly peeked their heads out of the dressing rooms. It took some coaxing, but eventually they came out very timidly with all their new clothes on, looking quite embarrassed and laughing at each other

"You guys look hot," Maggie remarked. "Any woman would want to have sex with any of you. Look at yourself in the mirror."

They looked at each other and started to giggle. But when they looked at themselves in the mirror, they were spellbound. The clothes *were* cool. There were tight pants, hot, skimpy glitter tops, and all kinds of tight, sexy outfits.

"You guys do look great—real sexy," said Gloria. "I'd almost fuck you."

"Actually, I do look pretty hot." Jason was the first to admit as he stared at himself in the mirror. Finally, he looked around. "And so do you guys. I might even fuck you." Jason laughed, and the rest joined in.

"Uh, you know, we do look pretty hot," Jeff agreed. "I'd probably even have sex with myself." He laughed.

"You do that already." Gloria laughed.

"Hey," barked Jeff. "Knock it off."

Just then Bill walked out rather shyly. All eyes turned to look at him. He was wearing very tight pants that left nothing to the imagination and a skin tight shirt both of which complimented his skinny body. They all stopped and stared—their eyes transfixed on him.

"Uh…Is it that bad?" he turned to escape back into the dressing room, but Maggie wouldn't allow it. She grabbed him and led him out in front of the others.

"Are you kidding? You look especially fuckin' hot!" Jason exclaimed." I never thought that skinny body of yours would look good in tight clothes, but with those skin tight pants you really look like a rock star; like Mick Jagger, or Steven Tyler or something. I'd pick you up in any bar."

"Yeah man, you look great," Jeff agreed." But, I'm not sure I like that. You're certainly gonna give me some competition with the chicks."

Maggie motioned for Bill to look in the mirror, coaxing him all the way. Bill slowly walked over to the mirror, feeling very embarrassed and self-conscious. He stood there transfixed, staring at himself as if seeing someone for the first time. Everyone else stood around him, watching him. All were in awe of the transformation. They were all giving him compliments. Finally, he started to smile. At first a shy sheepish grin. As the compliments continued the smile got bigger. It seemed that he even stood a little straighter. It seemed to be a confidence builder for him.

"You know, I always thought I was just some skinny kid. I was always self-conscious, so I tried to hide it behind those baggy jeans and t-shirt, but I guess I do look pretty good." Bill stood staring at himself in the mirror for a long time. His whole look and demeanor changed from the shy quiet type to a strong rock and roll type, standing tall and confident for the first time.

They all cheered at seeing the transformation and continued to give him encouragement.

Maggie had been very clever in luring them into trying on the clothes way outside their comfort zone. Now that the initial shock was over, they were really getting into it. She had been constantly talking with them to see just what their personalities were and tried to match up the clothes with the person, always keeping in mind the overall look of the band. She had made it all fun and not threatening. At the end of the day, they all had handfuls of new clothes, a new hip looking wardrobe, and a new look and image. They had thought they had been dressing up for the gigs, but this was way more than any of them had ever imagined.

"Now for some new hair cuts. These long hair hippie cuts are just not working for you guys. It's not the sixties anymore. We're going to one of the most trendy hair stylists in the city. He's very famous. He cuts hair for all the stars. You may have heard of him. His name is Enrique. He can give you all a new look, but I'll warn you now. He considers himself an artist. So keep quiet and let him do his thing." Maggie looked at her watch "We had better get going, our appointments are in an hour, and no one keeps him waiting."

They drove to Beverly Hills and parked on Rodeo Dr. They walked past many beautiful stores with expensive clothes from designers they had only heard about or read about in magazines. They entered the salon as loud rock music blasted. A skinny flamboyant obviously gay man in tight leather pants and t-shirt entered with arms flailing. He went to each of them playing with their hair, pulling it back so that he could see their faces, then moving it around. Finally, he stepped back, took a deep breath, and looked at them all.

"Well, this is gonna be a challenge. What do you think I am? A magician?" he shook his head in disgust with his arrogance showing through. "You guys look like a bunch of hippies from the '60s. Hasn't anyone told you—it's the '70s," he said with a laugh. He looked at the band shaking his head. He began pacing the floor, his arms flailing as he spoke. "Lemme see, something very rock and roll, very hip. At least you all have good faces, good cheek bones. Yes… Yes… I can make you look fabulous. This could be my greatest transformation." He threw his hand in the air in recognition of his great challenge as if he had had an epiphany. He grabbed Jason, placed him in the chair, and started cutting his hair. They all watched patiently. He set forth cutting their hair one by one. He kept the hair long but a more '70s look with more layering. More of a shag type haircut, long with style. One by one he performed his magic—transforming them into rock stars.

When he finished they all looked in the mirror. They were all speechless.

Finally, Maggie started. "You guys look incredible. I hope this silence is one of approval. I hope you all like it."

"We look amazing!" remarked Jason. The room exploded. They were all so excited with their new look. They couldn't even believe they were the same people—how different their appearance had changed. They spent the next few minutes looking at and admiring each other one by one, and then complimenting each other as well as Enrique. They all agreed they did look better.

Finally, Bill spoke. "I never knew we could look so hot. You are a magician."

The new outrageous costumes and hair cuts were designed to enhance their personalities, while making them look like real rock stars. They were individual, but together they added to the whole look, concept, and attitude of the band. It did not feel unreal, phony, or a sellout. When he finally saw them, Rick approved.

The photo session was set up.

They arrived at the photo studio ready for their photos with all their new outfits. It was a large rather empty room with lots of space. Helmut was busy placing lights while his assistants were placing back drops in various places. The band got dressed and entered the studio.

"WOW. I can't believe it. What a transformation. You guys look great. Maggie has certainly done her magic on you. I'm confident that we can have some good shots of you guys. Helmut told the band to go over and stand in place. He turned on rock music to get the band in the mood.

"Now, the trick is to make it look natural. We do that by placing you all certain ways. I wanna see attitude as well. Just listen to my direction. But most of all, think of yourselves as rock stars."

It wasn't long before the band was in place and the camera started clicking. Helmut barked our directions, moods, and attitudes: sometimes happy, sometimes serious. He told them to make love to the camera, to get angry at the camera, to show their playfulness to the camera. Helmut tried placing their heads this way and that way, very exact very meticulous. He had them look in different directions: toward the camera, away from the camera, up, down, all in different directions. He used different lighting and different backdrops. He took group shots, individual shots, some with instruments, some without. They changed costumes, lighting, and everything many times. They took staged shots, casual shots, and sometimes he just had them act naturally, or silly, or whatever as he shot away. Some color, some black and white. It took hours. In the end he took over 1000 photographs.

The next day they went back to the sound stage which they had rented for the day. They were to simulate stage shots. He had them play, he had them pose, and he had them perform. They changed costumes many times. Sometimes he just let them be natural, other times he gave them exact direction. It was another long day of photographs. He took rolls and rolls of film, both color and black and white.

"I think I have what I need. I'll go over the proofs and be ready to present them to you and Rick next week. Thank you for your cooperation. I think we have some great shots." Helmut left.

A meeting was set up a week later to view the photos and pick the ones that best represented the band.

The meeting was in Sue's office. Rick, Helmut, and Maggie were all there. They began viewing the pictures.

"Man, look at us. We look amazing," Mike was the first to comment.

"Yeah, I'd hardly even know that these pictures are of us. You made us look amazing," Gloria agreed.

The band was excited. The pictures really did make them look like a real rock band. Helmut showed them the ones he liked best which he had already had blown up. Next, he showed others that he thought could also be suitable. Sue, Rick, Maggie, and Helmut discussed the photos amongst themselves as if the band wasn't even in the room. It was almost like they were some inanimate object: a piece of art, or that box of cereal. The band remained silent as they looked over the proofs and pictures. They picked out the ones that they thought best then showed them to the band for approval.

As the band was looking over the pictures, Sue left the office for a moment. Eric noticed a picture behind her desk. "What is it with the picture of her in the cop's uniform?"

"Oh, don't you know?" said Rick. "She used to be a cop in Beverly Hills. That's how she got her start. She got to know the stars and people in the business and in the press because she gave them tickets: parking tickets, speeding tickets—whatever. She was the type of cop that was so friendly and outgoing that by the time she gave you the ticket you were saying thank you. She was so well known and well liked that she was encouraged to leave and start her own business as a press agent by some of the people that she had actually given tickets to or had seen in court. She already had a couple of people that were ready to sign with her, so eventually she did start her own business as a press agent. It didn't take her long to get a rather impressive list of clients. She's one tough broad."

"Don't talk about my girlfriend like that, at least when I'm in the room." Maggie piped in as she entered the room.

"Oh, sorry Maggie," said Rick. Maggie exited the room again. "Sue and Maggie have been lovers for years."

Everyone looked at each other and gave a collective "Ahhhh," as they nodded their heads, finally realizing the relationship.

Sue re-entered the room with Maggie and Helmut. "So what d'ya guys think?"

"We think they're great. You did an incredible job Helmut, and especially thanks to Maggie and her fashion sense."

"I agree. So get me fifty of these in an 8X10 glossy." Rick gave one of the choices to Helmut. "And 50 of these as well. These will be our press pics which will show our new look. Good job guys."

Everyone seemed pleased at the outcome.

"The photos are great and I dig the new look. However, let's not overdo it yet. Let's keep some things for our next big showcase for the industry. Wear some of the clothes so that you can get used to them but save something special for the big gigs. I'll let you know when I'm inviting the industry to see the band."

They all agreed. The band felt great from these experiences. It was like they all experienced a transformation from being just a bar band to being rock stars.

46

"I'M JUST A SINGER IN A ROCK AND ROLL BAND"

The Moody Blues

The band was working hard. They had their work cut out for them. All the music was being revamped with the help of Derek, and they even wrote two new songs. They would only be playing occasionally and mostly out of town gigs per the advice of Rick, just enough to keep their name around. They missed playing all the time, but Rick seemed to have a game plan. They also missed the after gig parties every night but were able to have one if the gig was close to home or at the beach. They had a few gigs booked in the future at big showcase clubs, but these were seldom and few and far between. Per the advice of Rick, they were not showcases for the industry, just enough to keep their name known in Hollywood and to try out their new look.

It was a weeks later that Rick set up another meeting with the band.

"You've got a great look now. Next, I've set up a meeting with a few consultants to help us with the live show." Rick began. "You guys are doing a fine job. I just wanna make it even better, so I've invited a stage director to help. Ken has done sound, lights, staging, and all aspects of putting on a show for rock bands, Broadway shows, movies, and television. He'll work with you and your sound and light crew to put together a great technical show."

"Sounds cool. He can meet with Mark, Pete, and Alex. They know our set backwards and forwards, but let us talk to them first. They may feel like you're taking their jobs away."

"No problem. I want him to meet with them and work with them. I only want to make the show better, and with a few small changes I think we can do that. I am also having you meet with a choreographer," said Rick.

"A what!" Bill asked.

"Choreographer, her name is Sally," Rick stated

"We're not doing steps and dancing." Mike protested. "We are a rock band, not some Broadway show, or the Temptations."

"No, of course not. This is all about staging. Every move on stage is called choreography. They'll help show you how to move, what to say, and how to pace your show. Everything you'll need to make the show even better."

Mark, Pete, and Alex entered the band rehearsal that night. It had been a while since they had seen everyone.

"Hey guys," Mike said.

"Wow! We hardly recognized you. You guys look great," Mark commented.

"Listen, we think you guys are doing a great job. We just wanted you to know how we felt and thank you for your efforts. Our new manager has some ideas of his own though. You wouldn't believe what he has us doing. We've gone out shopping for clothes, made pictures, and hired a stage director to help us with the show."

"Check out the photos." Jason handed them copies of some of the photos Helmut had taken.

"Wow, like a whole new band. You really look like rock stars now," Mark said.

"Also, guys, we have an expert sound and lights guy who wants to work with you in making the show better. It won't take away your jobs; he just wants to make the show more consistent every time we do it.

We've already told him what a great job you both are doing, so this'll be an incredible opportunity for both of you to learn more about sound and lights from a professional. He has worked with some of the biggest acts in the music business and has done work on Broadway, movies, and, television. I hope you'll cooperate with him. But also, you guys know what we want, make sure that's clear to him."

"No problem, sounds like a real good opportunity," said Mark.

"Yeah, we can always learn something new. See what he has to say," Pete agreed.

"Works for me," Alex nodded in agreement.

"Good, thanks for being cooperative," said Mike. "I'm sure it'll be worth your while. This could be a real opportunity for you guys. Play your cards right and make a good impression, and this could work to your advantage. He works all the time and a recommendation from him could mean other gigs."

"Thanks for the recommendation. We won't let you down." They all were excited, thinking about the possibilities.

The meeting was set. Rick walked in with two people. The first was a tall thin dark-haired man with glasses, jeans, tennis shoes, a t-shirt from the last Rolling Stones tour, and a sport jacket. Behind him was a very small blonde woman dressed in leotard shorts, and a long sweat shirt covering up most of it.

"This is Ken and Sally. Ken is here to direct your show. Sally will be here to work on stage movements. Ken is here to work on the overall look and to help with the technical aspects of the show. He'll be coordinating sound and lights and some of the staging."

"Let's just get one thing straight. We're not a Broadway show. We are a rock band, and we wanna keep it that way. We don't want it to look phony." Jason's concern was obvious.

"That is the trick," said Ken. "Making it look new every time you do it, but mostly making sure the lights are right for the song. They should create a mood that reflects the songs itself. The sound also needs to be done right. Who does your sound and lights now?"

"Mark, Pete, and Alex, we'll introduce them to you. We've already discussed this with them. They know the set backwards and forwards."

"We'd like to see you perform if possible. When is your next gig?"

"Sure," said Rick. "Our next gig is at the Hollywood Star next week. We'll make sure your names are on the guest list."

Sally and Ken entered the club. Rick took them backstage to meet everyone. Introductions were made with all the band members and the technical crew. Then everyone was asked to leave so that the band could do their set. Sally, Rick, Frank, and Eric took their places in the audience while the band waited backstage for the crew to be in place. The band played their usual set. It sounded very good, and it had a lot of energy.

"Well, I guess we have our work cut out for us," Ken said to Sally at the conclusion of the set.

"Yes. But they are a really good band, and they do have their look and their set together. They just need some polish."

They walked back to the dressing room to approach the band.

"Do you guys have a tape of the set?" Ken asked.

"Sure." They all nodded in agreement. "We'll make sure you get one."

"I think you are all going for a sort of classy but still a rocking out rock band thing. At least that's what I hear, and so far that's what I see. Am I correct?" Ken asked.

"Uh, yeah, sort of like a cross between the Rolling Stones and Jethro Tull. Or something like that."

"Cool, that gives me something to work with. I can see that you've been playing clubs a lot. At least you know how to work the audience and keep the energy level up."

"Thanks. We try." Mike admitted.

"One suggestion. Keep that small club sound on stage. Play at a normal and comfortable level—one that everyone in the band can hear no matter what size venue you are playing,"

"That'll work I guess," Mike replied. "We just always thought we had to play louder to make sure it was loud enough for the room."

"You do have to play to the size of the room, but when the room gets too big, don't try to fill up the room with your stage amps and loud playing. It just becomes noisy. You should always play at pretty much the same level that is comfortable for you on stage. If the room gets too big, let the PA system make you louder. We can always mic the amps or drums or whatever when needed. For the big gigs, I want a microphone on everyone, every amplifier, every drum. We can then control the sound of everything from the board, not just the vocals but a whole mix. It gives us greater control so that the band will sound better and have a better more balanced sound out in front for the audience which is the most important thing. I will work with and train your sound guy to help him."

"Sounds cool," said Jason.

"Don't sacrifice a good sound and a good mix for volume."

"We should also be able to hear better on stage." Gloria added.

"Exactly! You should sound the same on stage no matter what. The size of the gig or the size of the room should not matter. Let the sound system fill up the room if needed. This will give you more control as musicians. It should always sound the same."

"That does sort of make sense. We have just been playing louder to fill up the room, but we sometimes can't even hear each other." Bill commented.

"I'll meet with Sally and discuss the direction. Sally will work with you directly in a couple of days. In the meantime, I'll be meeting with your sound and lights crew."

Ken worked with the crew. He made sure they knew how to mic the amps and drums and showed them how to mix the sound. He had them practice with the band at rehearsals so that the band always sounded great. He helped with sound cues and lighting cues and in general all the technical stuff that was needed. It was a learning experience for all.

It was about a week later when Sally entered the rehearsal sound stage they had booked where they could work things out. The room was big enough, but it was mostly taken up with a short stage meant to be like a real stage for acts to work out their show. There was very little room for an audience. She took a seat and was ready to work. "OK, show me your stuff. I wanna hear the third song of the tape first. I can't remember the name. Play it like you are playing it for an audience even though it's only me and the crew."

They played it then stopped for comments.

"First of all, most of my comments will apply to every song. So keep this in mind as I critique you. Now, it is a great song with a great message, but I just don't believe it," was her first comment. She walked onto the stage where the band was playing as if she were a musician. "You all look like you are trying to be rock stars, not that you actually are rock stars. That song has some great music in it. It tells an interesting story. Now make me and the audience believe it, and believe what you are saying. You need to make it real and authentic."

"It's tough getting the energy when there is no audience," Gloria admitted. "We play off the audience and their energy a lot."

"Yes, I know that it's difficult, but you have to be consistent. You should not rely on the audience for your energy. It should always be there. You may have to rely on each other for the energy at times, at least that can be made consistent. You guys do a pretty good job of this already. You have the energy. It just looks a bit phony at times. It'll just take a bit of work. It needs to go to the next level. It's a combination of energy and realism. The trick is to make it fresh every time you play it. Take me and the audience on that journey with you—not only with the music, but with the way you perform it onstage. You should be able to do that every time you perform it no matter where you are: a different club, different city, different crowd, or on an empty sound stage. It always has to make the audience feel like they're part of your journey, part of your experience—something that you and the audience has shared together. We do this a lot in acting. If you don't believe what you are playing or saying, the audience never will. The moves are OK—some nice standard rock stuff. They just don't seem authentic. Just make it fit the song, like you really mean what you are saying or playing. Now tell me, what is this song about?"

"Well, it's about a guy and a girl who meet and fall in love," said Gloria.

"Great, the song does a great job of saying that, but your moves do not. You need to sell it to the audience. Now try this. First I want to address the lead singer. You have the biggest job of all. It's your job to relate to the audience. Most importantly, as the front person, you are the connection and the liaison between the band and the audience. Make me believe what you are singing—every word. This goes for every song. It's your number. Tell the audience. Make it believable. I really want to feel that the words you are saying mean something. That you are really talking about some love affair you had."

"This reminds me of the time we saw Grateful Dead. They took us on a journey," Bill commented.

"That's good. Exactly what I mean. Here are some tricks. Go to the edge of the stage and belt out this song to the crowd. Get in touch with the raw emotion." She turned to where the audience would have been, walked to the edge of the stage, and showed Gloria how to perform the song. She looked like she was belting out the song herself. "Sing that song to that person out there. Pretend that the person you are singing to *is* in the audience, and that you are really singing that song to him. You may even have to visualize that, especially if there is no one there. Your moves and expressions need to show it all."

Gloria went to the edge and started to belt it out.

"Better. Next, interact with the band. Get sassy. Rock out with Mike or Bill or whomever, especially during the musical times when you are not singing. I'll teach you some things you can do with the microphone, some cool mic techniques that'll be very flashy. Things like throwing the mic out into the audience, or things to do with the mic stand. There are lots of things you can be doing to increase the excitement. When you are done singing it's also your job to direct the attention to the other musicians when it's their turn. If Bill has a lead, walk to him, transfer the attention to him so that he can have his moment. Same goes if it's Jason, or Mike, or Jeff. You job is to direct the audience's attention. Then when they're done, it's back to you again. You need to take that attention back. Take your moment. Force the audience to pay attention to you again and regain the focus. You are the focal point after all. Keep them aware of what they're supposed to pay attention to, whether it be you or someone else on stage.

Now, for the rest of you. When it's your turn to be featured, take your moment. These things need to be worked out so that the audience knows where to look and where their attention should be directed. When it's your solo (she pointed to Bill), the singer walks back to you as if exhausted while the guitar player takes his moment, or she can walk over to the guitar player and get into it with him handing off the attention to him somehow. Bill, you need to walk to the edge of the stage and show me how that song makes you feel in the same way that you show me with the way you play it. Take the spotlight. Play to the audience." She dragged Bill to the edge of the stage and stood next to him pretending to play the guitar. "The rest of the band should be rocking out together upstage, but not upstaging the lead. At other times, you can be surrounding him, urging him on, or rockin' out with him. But this is his moment and do not forget that. Don't take it away from him. When the song starts with bass, Mike it's your turn to take center stage. Then perhaps return to the drummer. Generally, you and the drummer should be working together. Jason, I want a mic at the front of the stage for you when you do your flute or sax stuff. That is if there is time for you to return to your keyboards. Unfortunately, you are a bit restricted being behind the keyboards all the time. But when it's your time to solo, everyone else should be there rocking out with you. Drums and keyboards should be on platforms above everyone else so that they can stand out when it's their turn. The others can move to the front of the stage, but drums and keyboards are stationary. The rest of the band needs to not only allow this but to bring attention to them when it's their turn. It's all about directing attention to what's important. You know, getting the audience to focus on what you want them to. Now try it again and remember to sing it and play it with conviction and attitude. But most of all keep it real. Think about who's the most important person in each part of the song and feature them—feature whatever should be featured."

They did it again, and really put some emotion into it. They took their places at the appropriate times, moving to the front of the stage or the back depending on whose turn it was. A few times they bumped into each other or got their cords tangled up, but they were really starting to interact on stage.

"Now you're talking. I almost believed it. The trick is gonna be to perform that song the same way every time you play it—with the same intensity, same emotion, same delivery. Remember, you must make it look like its natural, not choreographed. I'll work with you on some exact stage moves and getting around on the stage in an organized fashion so that you don't get your cords tangled. That is what we mean by choreography. Each song should be like a small theatrical event in itself. It's all part of the show. Now on to the next song."

"It's just a fun dance number about a guy who wants to meet a girl at a bar," Mike explained.

"Then make me dance. Show me a fun time. Make me want to dance. Also, show me that anxiety you feel in wanting to meet that girl—or your brazenness—or whatever. Just make it real. Not just random energy standard rock thing, but make the song come alive. Tell the story."

"This is gonna take some work. I think we should try some simple acting tricks. We have a few weeks, just trust me."

"Shit, this chick is tough," Jason said as they packed up after rehearsal. "But I think it's gonna make us even better."

They all agreed.

Sally worked hard with the band for the next couple of weeks. Her experience as a dancer and choreographer really helped in coming up with moves and movement. They worked out on sound stages choreographing each move. Each person had their time in the spotlight. They made sure that cables would not cross or interfere with each other. They crossed the stage at the right moments. Gloria spoke the right words at the right times when the band needed to make adjustments, tune, or change instruments. With much practice and hard work, the set was like clockwork. Gloria learned all the standard rock moves and they all learned how to work with the props as she called them: the mic and mic stand, the guitars, even the drum sticks. With rehearsal and hard work the set looked like it was spontaneous energy even though each move, movement, and moment was planned.

Although hesitant at first, the band was excited and pleased with the changes. What they had accomplished was a more concise, accurate, and professional portrayal of the band and its personalities. Each song was designed to take the audience on a journey which they, the band, would be the leader. Even the band had to admit that the songs seemed more real, and they enjoyed playing them more. They were really feeling them, not just playing them. This was from a completely authentic place. They were selling themselves and their songs as a complete package, and having the time of their lives doing it.

It even created a more relaxed and comfortable atmosphere. Sally encouraged each member to have fun and be themselves on that stage. They all knew each other extremely well, now they needed to bring that persona to the stage to show that person to the world. They had to come out of their shells and be the person that they knew they were inside. They had to expose themselves and their personality. Although it was scary at first, it became easier and easier as time went on. Letting the audience really know who they were was always scary, but when they got in touch with their feelings and put them across on stage it was at times magical.

Ken had been working with Mark, Pete, and Alex in private, helping them with sound, lights, and effects cues, suggesting colors, spotlights, and other things to add to the show. He was getting them acquainted with all the technical aspects of the show. Ken had his own vision of what the show should look like. He met with the band and stage crew many times to make sure their vision was unified. With the help of the stage crew who knew the show so well, they were able to accomplish a great deal. He was a great teacher. They all picked up a wealth of information.

Finally, they were ready to start rehearsing again with the sound and lights. With all the new moves they really had to coordinate the new show. Ken was brought in along with the crew. They spent a couple of weeks perfecting the new stage show so that every move, every sound cue, and every special effect was picked up by the tech crew.

All the changes merely reflected the new-found professionalism, while leaving the integrity of the band intact with just some refinement and polish. Rick and his staff had done their job. He wanted to show their character and individual personalities. He wanted them to be just as crazy and eccentric on stage as they were not only off stage, but also in their own subconscious minds. He did not want them to be someone they were not, but be themselves only bigger than life. It was almost like group therapy. Rick really wanted the band to develop personality, both collectively and individually. He saw them not only as musicians, but also as artists with interesting stage personas which, through his persistence and vision, he could transform into a band who could stand up with the rest of the professional album acts.

They had worked hard, and Rick felt that they were ready to start playing for the industry again. So he had Isaac book them in some more high visibility industry showcase clubs. They played the gigs with a new-found enthusiasm and new found commitment. They continued to play the out of town gigs using all they had learned to develop an even better show. Their confidence was high and they really felt that they had learned a lot which really made them a better act.

"I WENT TO A GARDEN PARTY"

Rick Nelson

With all the work they had done they were confident that they couldn't miss. When they started performing again with all the new professionalism in place, they felt that it would be only a matter of time before a record label would pick them up

Rick felt it was time to do a big showcase. They were booked back in the Hollywood Star. Rick and Isaac invited music industry people including record company executives and Sue invited all the press people. Anyone of importance would be there. This was going to be the gig that got them signed.

The show went great and there was a lot of enthusiasm. The band performed excellently and was using all their new tricks and all they had learned. They sounded great, they looked great, and they had the moves. They had become rock stars.

Rick had also planned an after show party at his house. It was to be a huge event with all the music industry people and the press. A truly gala affair.

The band arrived at the party about midnight. Rick quickly grabbed them and started introducing them to the guests. It was a who's who of the music industry and press. The band felt confident that this would be their shot.

It was about two in the morning when four policemen showed up at the front door.

"We got a report of a disturbance." The policeman said. "Just wanna make sure everything is OK.

"No problem," the doorman replied.

"They walked through the house as all the people smiled uncomfortably. When they walked outside everyone rushed to put out the joints and hide their other drugs. They walked through, smiled, and continued on.

"Everything seems to be in order, thanks," The head cop said and they left with a sigh of relief from everyone at the party.

At about four in the morning the party was still going. Some of the industry people had left but there were still some there including press people. But at this hour, for the band, now the party was more about friends and people important to them. The band was a little more off their guard because these were their friends. They could relax a bit more and enjoy themselves.

Being a warm summer night in California, some people started taking off their clothes to go skinny dipping in the Jacuzzi and swimming pool. These were not the industry people but more the bands guests and friends. They had all had enough to drink and it just seemed the right thing to do. Even the band thought it fun since they had had an exhausting night.

It was around 5 A.M. when the sky was starting to get light. Mike wandered outside to get some air. He was standing on the side of the pool. Most of the people who had gone swimming or in the Jacuzzi had now left and there was one person left.

"You must really like that pool," Mike laughed.

"I'm stuck." He said.

"You're what?" Mike responded.

"Stuck, I have been stuck here for hours."

"What do you mean?"

"Well there must be an intake here because when I was just hanging out here, my nuts got sucked into the intake pipe. It really hurts."

Mike started to laugh.

"It is not funny" he started to cry.

"Well, let's get that thing turned off first."

Mike went and got Rick. There were still about 40 guests there including the entire band, some of their friends, a few record people and a few press people. They all followed Rick outside to see what the commotion was. Rick immediately turned off the Jacuzzi jets hoping that this would free him.

"Sorry, they are still stuck. I think they got swollen." There he sat with a crowd of people surrounding him, laughing, pointing, and making fun of him.

"Well, we will just have to call the fire department or something."

They boy was really in tears at this point.

Rick went into the house to call the fire department.

"Who are you with anyway?" asked Jeff.

"No one."

"No one?" repeated Jeff.

"No, I crashed the party. I have been a fan of yours for a long time. I have seen you at many gigs all over the city but especially in Hollywood and starting way back when you played in Venice at the Surfrider. You probably do not remember me, but I had a thing for Gloria. We had an affair when we met in Venice. Then she dumped me. I never really got over it. I have watched the band since then, at first it was because of Gloria but I also thought that the band was great. So I have been following you ever since."

"You're a groupie for Gloria." Mike laughed.

"Yes, "I guess you could say that. Brad is the name." He sobbed.

"Oh, I kind of remember you." Gloria responded. "I thought I told you to get lost. I can't believe that you have been following me all this time. It is kind of sweet but also kind of sick and creepy."

"Yeah, I sort of remember you as well," replied Jason.

"I just think you are great, and if nothing else, at least I can see you and the band perform. I kind of kept a low profile, stayed in the background. I did not want to bother you especially when you were so mean to me. But I have seen you progress for a long time and boy you guys sure got better and better. I always thought that you had talent and would someday be stars. Looks like now you are really on the road. And when you become famous at least I can say that I have had sex with Gloria, one the members of the band Hollywood."

"Well sorry, but you are not the only one she or we have had sex with." Jeff chimed in.

"Yes, I know, but it will always be special to me."

"Man, our first real serious groupie. Unbelievable." Mike was astonished.

"That is a bit sad and pathetic." Jason interjected.

"Yes, I know," Brad was really crying now. "But I have told everyone I knew and talked about the band a lot. I brought a lot of people to the gigs, believe it or not. So I have done some good for you guys."

"Well, perhaps you have, and for that we will always be thankful." Jason replied which brought a small smile to the sobbing boy.

"How did you get here?" Jeff asked.

"I just followed the limos, parked my car on the street, and hoped the fence. It seemed like a good idea at the time."

A few minutes later the sirens could be heard in the distance.

It wasn't long before fire trucks, an ambulance and two police cars pulled up.

They got out and Rick rushed them to the pool where the boy sat crying profusely.

They two police men who had been there earlier were there. "We were about ready to go off duty, when the call came in. We just could not resist. We just had to see what this was all about."

One fireman who seemed to be in charge assessed the situation. He was tall, at least 6 foot 4 with wide shoulders and a big bushy moustache. He was a large husky man but not at all fat, very masculine and burly. He had probably been a linebacker in high school and assuredly still stayed in shape by going to the gym just judging by his arms and body. A real macho man and with his fire gear on he looked even more masculine. He rolled up his sleeve revealing his large muscular arms.

He reluctantly knelt down by the pool edge put his hand under the water and felt around.

"What were you doing there anyway boy, some kind of kinky thing?" The fire man asked.

"No really, I was just talking with people on the ledge when my nuts got sucked in. I thought I could get them out but the suction made them swell up."

"Well. You sure have gotten yourself into a difficult situation. I am not so sure what we can do." He conferred with the police and paramedics.

"We will just have to crack the pool," he concluded rather confidently.

"You will crack his nuts before you crack my pool." Rick retorted.

Jason went over and whispered something to Rick He then disappeared into the house. He returned a few minutes later with a tub of Crisco, and a jar of Vaseline.

"Here try one of these."

All the firemen and policemen looked at each other and backed off.

"You're in charge," one of them said as they all snickered.

Finally the lead fireman grabbed the jug of Vaseline from Jason and handed it to the boy. "Here try this. It won't dilute in water and should lubricate them enough so that you can pull them out."

"I would if I could, but I can't apply this. I am having enough trouble just hanging on to the ledge with my hands. You will have to try to lubricate them and pull them out."

"Shit man, you have got to be kidding."

"Sorry."

With that the fireman, took it back unscrewed the top, put a liberal amount of Vaseline on his hand and put his hand under the water while his buddies snickered in the background trying their best to hold back complete laughter. He messaged and applied Vaseline for a while occasionally taking his hand out to get more of the gel. It took a long time as everyone stood by, horrified, but amused, trying not to giggle because of the poor boys misfortune. The situation, however, was made even more humorous with this large burly fireman messaging the young boy's genitals with a complete look of disdain on his face.

Everyone could see the look of pain on the boy's face as the fireman worked to remedy the situation and this seemed to be the fireman's only consolation. Every once in a while the boy would scream or say, not so rough for which the fireman just responded with. "You were the one who got them stuck; now be a man and deal with it." The men especially were appalled. They each grabbed their own crotch with a look of pain on their face.

Eventually with a lot of work they were able to free them. Everyone cheered. The fireman saved the day and became the hero of the event although it was something he assuredly would rather forget. They all helped him out of the pool and that was when they all noticed. His testicles were the size of grapefruits. They had swollen up so large due to the suction. They all gasped trying again to hold back the laughter. The paramedics put him on a stretcher and rolled him off into the ambulance.

They thanked the fireman and everyone else as they left the scene. For the next hour that was all they could talk about. All were trying to show sympathy without laughing but the humor was just too much for them.

It was quite an end to an eventful evening. It was after well dawn before it was all over. The party had lasted well into the morning hours until everyone was truly exhausted.

The very next day the party was the talk of the town. There were enough press, radio people and local disc jockeys there to observe the event and it hit the airwaves first to be followed with newsprint. News travels fast in this town. For the next month there were articles in a lot of newspapers and magazines. It began in the local music trades but even national and international trade magazine had articles on the story and there were even some in non-trade magazines and newspapers. They got their fifteen minutes of fame. This was not exactly what they had planned on or hoped for as their first real national news article and it certainly was not what they had expected. They received a lot of fame and notoriety all due to someone's misfortune, and his genitals. The headlines read "Fan hospitalized when his appendage gets stuck in Jacuzzi after crashing 'Hollywood' party." Or "Hollywood party interrupted by fans distress." The articles did talk about the band, but the real news story was the poor party crasher and his genitals. All the band could do was laugh it off.

"After all that time of wanting to get some good press, this was what we get." said Sue in her office in the days following the event. "I was trying to get good reviews and a buzz, which in fact we did get, and some industry interest, but what makes front page headlines. Not the band but their party and some party crasher who get his nuts stuck. But hey, let's run with it. Press is press."

The poor boy was released from the hospital a few days later very sore and with bruised and bandaged testicles but with his dignity hurt more than his body.

The band did get their publicity even though it was not what they wanted at least they could have a good laugh at the whole event

"GOOD TIMES, BAD TIMES"

Led Zeppelin

Disappointment was strong when again, they were still not signed—nor were there any offers. They had high hopes with Rick and the new management team saying they were ready—and ready they were. But still nothing was happening. They tried their best not to be discouraged. Rick assured them that all would come in due time. He kept saying that there was some interest, and the labels were looking, but just not ready to offer a deal yet.

Isaac started to book them into some better gigs. They were even playing out of town gigs in San Diego, San Francisco, Fresno, and Phoenix at some of the big clubs and even some small time concerts as an opening act to some major recording artists. After every gig there was a write-up of some sort in the local trade papers thanks to the efforts of Sue and her staff.

Derek took them into the studio again to record some new songs, one of which they could swear would make a hit single. Everyone was excited about the new tracks. Once the tracks were finished Rick called a meeting.

They listened to the new tracks. Everyone agreed that they sounded great.

"I'm truly excited. I don't see how we can miss now with a tape that's this good. They've got to sign us. We've got it made now, thanks to Derek," said Rick.

Everyone applauded and offered him their compliments.

"I've brought all of you here for a reason, first to listen to the tape, but more importantly to help us in our planning. But first, I want to congratulate Derek and the band on a job well done."

"Thanks," said Derek.

"Well, let's try again. They can't ignore us this time." Jason sounded hopeful despite all their rejection.

"Good, then we're ready to send out the new tape!" Mike exclaimed.

"Not so fast. I have a plan," Rick started. "A plan that should take us over the top. Frank and I have been discussing and planning this for a while. Here is the plan. Before I shop this tape I wanna try something different. I want to book a large concert hall about six months away for you to headline. In the meantime, you will play around town everywhere you've already played and advertise your big concert. We'll invite everyone in your fan base, send out fliers, tell everyone at these gigs about the concert, and get a real crowd there. Then six weeks before the gig, no playing. This should generate a huge crowd. It'll also get the crowd ready and responsive. I'll send out the tape about the same time as this concert is happening. Really do a media blitz. Once the record company hears the tape, sees you on a big stage, and sees the huge crowd reaction they won't be able to ignore us anymore.

Here is how it'll work. You'll need to play at your usual places, the beach, Hollywood, the Valley, East LA, Long Beach, the colleges and really spread the word about your first big concert. We can advertise all over the media, pass out fliers, put up fliers and posters all over town, and really promote this concert big time. I want to give out free tickets and free drink vouchers to our biggest fans. Frank has agreed to buy a whole bunch of tickets. Of course we'll give tickets to the record companies, but we wanna pack the house with fans, especially enthusiastic ones. Let's get them a bit drunk and receptive. Every time we do a gig, and see someone who seems really into the band—give 'em a ticket and a drink voucher, or perhaps two. We'll have our own audience. We all will have tickets to get rid of, including the crew. We'll show the record companies how much energy we can generate when we pack the house with our own people. It'll cost some money, but I think it'll be worth it. You guys will have to be perfect. We need to do a great show with great songs and good showmanship. We need to be careful that this does not get out to the record companies about the free tickets, free beer, and stuff. I'll work with Sue so that we can work out a huge advertising campaign to get a lot of press, print ads, articles about the band, and interviews both in print and on the radio. She can get us some good placement with print ads in Billboard, Rolling Stone, the L.A. Times, and some other magazines especially local ones, but mostly the ones that the record execs read. Even the New York execs will be wondering who we are. I also want to put up a billboard on Sunset announcing the show. Make it something that they can't ignore. They'll see it every time they drive down the strip. Isaac has been in touch with the Santa Monica Civic Auditorium. It's a great venue and a big enough hall to put on a great show. It is also a good central place that'll draw in crowds from all over. It is close enough to get the Hollywood crowd, the beach crowd, the valley crowd, and the college crowd especially the ones near the University where you played so often. I then deliver the new tape and invite the record companies to the gig. With all the publicity, the tape in hand, and the invitation to our big gig, they cannot help but take notice. Finally, I will host a big party after the gig. We invite them all. Also, we invite a lot of celebrities. Between my client list, P.J.'s client list, Isaac Cohen's client list, Sue's client list, and all the people we know. This will be the event of the season. Everyone will want to attend the concert and the party. What d'ya all think?"

"Wow, sounds like an incredible idea," said Gloria. They all agreed. "But how do we pay for all of this?"

"Frank has agreed to bankroll it. I dunno where he gets his money, and I'm sure I don't wanna know. But whatever it is, business must be good. He has agreed to finance the whole thing using his own money.

The band will, of course, have to pay him back eventually, but I think it'll be worth it, and he agrees."

The band worked hard for the next three months; playing gigs and promoting their big concert. The following the band had generated had grown tremendously and, thanks to Eric, who had started a mailing list of fans, they were able to notify everyone. Each fan would receive free admission plus free beer. Most people were happy to get free tickets and free drink vouchers to the Santa Monica gig. They were continually playing to sold-out crowds in all the clubs. It was exciting for the band to be generating such a following, and the gigs were actually fun. Tickets were given out to those who showed the most enthusiasm and who had been their biggest fans. They wanted the crowd to be their crowd—a crowd of people who really liked them. Playing in all the old venues gave the band the opportunity to refine their act and get it ready for the big concert. It also gave them a chance to see all their old friends from all the bars, night clubs, and places they had played in the past. In the meantime, they were doing interviews that Sue had set up and getting reviews from the press. The band couldn't imagine the companies not jumping on this immediately and signing them.

Rick mentioned the up-and-coming Santa Monica gig to the record companies to prepare them in advance of the event. The reaction was reluctant but somewhat positive. Most companies said they would send a representative of some sort, and all wanted to see the band live again. He told them he'd send out the tape once the date was a bit closer. He would follow up with a phone call to find out their guest requirements, so he could send them tickets to the show. All the record company people would receive unlimited drink tabs. Rick wanted to be sure everyone would be there. He felt sure their time had come.

Isaac bargained hard with the Santa Monica Civic Auditorium. He worked out a deal for a reduced price ticket and reduced price drink vouchers. The cost was substantial, but it was an investment that he was sure would pay off. Besides, Frank needed to do something with all the drug money anyway.

Even Mr. Grant, despite his hatred for Frank, was enthused when he heard the tape and helped spread the word. Pat Johnson and P.J. Productions were also on board helping spread the word and the enthusiasm for he still had the publishing and a point on the album at stake.

As the day approached, the excitement built. They would purposely be taking off six weeks before the concert to rehearse the show. They would spend the time working with Derek in the studio, with Ken and Sally on the stage show, and with Maggie on fashion. They would also work on some of the tunes, both new and old. But for now, they had to finish up the gigs to promote their big Santa Monica Civic gig.

Their final gig before the Santa Monica Civic show was at the Hollywood Star. Sort of a dress rehearsal before the record companies saw them six weeks later.

They were there to set up and do a sound check when Mr. Grant heard the noise. He walked out followed by his entourage of body guards.

"New tape sounds great!" Mr. Grant seldom was enthused. He was in need of another band to break from his club. It had been some time since he had discovered new talent. "Frank, I need to see you right away."

"Uh, be right there," Frank answered.

"NOW!" Mr. Grant shouted, then walked away.

"Duty calls." Frank followed Mr. Grant backstage. In a few minutes the band could hear voices shouting from Mr. Grant's office.

Frank soon emerged.

"There is someone asking for you," the stage manager said to Frank. "He said to meet you outside. Said it was important."

Frank walked outside to see what was going on. He returned a moment later.

"Eric, I need to see you," Frank said as he grabbed Eric. They walked outside. "I'm in kind of a bind. I need to take care of some business. Can you take care of the band for a few hours? I'll be back for the gig tonight. I'm trusting you to make sure everything goes well. Tell 'em I'll see 'em later." Eric nodded in agreement. Frank left in a hurry, walked across the parking lot, and got into a large black limo. Eric tried to see who was in the limo waiting for him but could see no one. The limo sped off down the street leaving Eric in charge.

As the evening approached the absence of Frank became obvious. The excitement was growing as the band was getting ready in the dressing room. "Where's Frank?" Jeff asked. "I thought he'd be here to wish us good luck or break a leg or something."

"He's probably out hobnobbing, doing his business thing," Eric lied. "He's here. He's just tied up. There sure is a crowd out their tonight, wait till you see. This is gonna be great. Mark and Pete are in place working on sound and light cues. Alex is back-stage ready. I've been instructed to be your tour manager of sorts, keep the band happy and make sure everything goes smoothly, so Frank and Derek can hang out with Rick and talk with the record execs."

"Showtime," the backstage technician announced knocking on the door.

"This is it guys." Eric left with the band to take his place off stage while they waited to make their entrance. Derek went out to the main room.

At the same time in a distant deserted part of Los Angeles on the Angeles Crest Highway in the Angeles Forest, a limo sped down the winding road, finally coming to a stop in a field by the side of the road. In the darkness, three figures led another man to an open field lit only by the stars and the lights of the limo. They surrounded him with their presence and their questions. Voices flared and tempers rose.

In Hollywood, the band approached the dark stage, trying their best not to look at the audience, but feeling the sea of eyes upon them. The adrenalin was pumping. They entered the stage with their instruments, plugged them in, and took their places.

Suddenly, the first chord was hit. It was like a bomb blast. The show had begun.

On that deserted stretch of highway the scene was very different. In the darkened shadows there was a scene of violence.

Two scenarios were being played out at the same time, one on stage and one in a deserted field. Although for both the band and the victim, they were the center of attention, but in very different ways. For both, the issue was one of power, the band taking it, the victim succumbing to it.

The band continued with their set. It was a show full of energy, excitement, and raw power. A set designed to show the full impact of the band, and the sheer power of their performance.

In that darkened field there was a power struggle of a different kind. Talking was over. The man they had brought there was now experiencing the violence of the men from the limo as he was beaten by them in the darkness.

In Hollywood, the band played a high energy set for one hour. They played like they had never played before, as if their lives depended on it—each song, each chord, each vocal line, each solo more powerful than the last. The music built to an incredible crescendo. This was a powerhouse of a band. The band could feel it, and the audience knew it as well.

The scene in the field was having a crescendo of its own, one of violence. With each power chord of the band there was another blow to the man now kneeling on the ground. It was as if in sync with they music of the band. At the same instant, they both reached their climax, the band's one of ecstasy, the victim's one of pain. At almost the same instant as the band hit their last power chord at the end of the set, far away in a lonely field a shot rang out in the night—then there was silence.

As the last note of the last song reverberated in the hall, the crowd went wild. The audience had left their seats and was crowded along the front of the stage screaming and clapping.

Miles away the limo sped off leaving a lifeless body lying on the ground.

The band returned for two encores.

Then, in what seemed like a split second, the show was over. The band members left the stage with a feeling of exhilaration and great satisfaction. They arrived back in their dressing rooms, adrenaline still pumping, and sweat pouring off each of them. Spirits were high as they congratulated each other. They knew this had been a great show. The excitement was in the air as they heard a knock on the dressing room door. It was Derek and Eric.

Eric was the first to speak up. "Great fuckin' show guys."

"Sounded real good," Derek complimented them in his own dry way.

Steve and Rick knocked, opened the door, and entered at the same time.

Steve started. "That was one incredible show. Great job," he said. He was filled with excitement and trying his best to keep out the crowd of fans waiting outside to offer them compliments.

Rick added. "Pacific Records said they want you to do a showcase for the head of A & R, and a few others companies are interested as well. I told 'em to come see us at the Santa Monica Civic, and then we will talk. I know they were impressed. I wasn't planning on any record companies being here, but I guess word got out. I was hoping to wait until Santa Monica, but these people have eyes and ears everywhere. I even saw Pat Johnson, and boy did he look thrilled. He knows he's got somethin' now. Let's just keep our fingers crossed. This could be the one. Overall, the reaction on this one has been positive."

"That's great news. But where's Frank?" Gloria asked.

"Didn't see him, I was with some other people."

"He's probably back at the band house already. I know he was planning a party after the gig. So, let's get our friends and get outta here. You all comin'?"

Steve said. "I'll meet you there."

They entered the house to find the place ready for a party. Frank had made the arrangements. The keg of beer was there, and plenty of drugs were left, but still no Frank.

"I'm getting kinda worried," said Gloria.

"Frank will show up." Jeff tried to convince them. "He's probably dealing, dicking some chick, talking business, or something else. You know Frank."

"I just don't think he would miss this." Gloria seemed concerned.

"He's probably cooked up some big surprise," Jeff added.

"Yeah, I'm sure you're right," Jason agreed.

It was well after two in the morning, and the party was in full swing. Eric, who had been in one of the bedrooms getting high, suddenly ran out. "Hey everybody, be quiet, turn the TV on to channel 3." But it was quicker to do it himself. He ran over and turned on the TV. The room gradually got quiet.

On the television they heard. "Police expect foul play. He was shot six times at point blank range. Authorities speculate it was done by someone he knew based on the evidence from the crime scene which showed no signs of a struggle. The body was found in The Angeles Forest shortly after midnight. Federal agents speculate that this was in fact the murder site. Frank Barcelona had been connected with organized crime and drug dealing. Federal agents feel the killing was drug related, appearing to be more of an execution than a murder."

The band was in shock.

"Oh my god," Gloria sighed while the rest looked on in disbelief.

"Was Frank that into organized crime?" Jason naively asked.

"Sure he was," Eric answered. "He had a lot of enemies and pissed off a lot of people. The feds, the mob, other dealers, even Mr. Grant."

"This is fucked up!" said Mike.

Gloria and Jason did their best to fight back the tears, while Jeff's emotion turned to anger. Bill stared coldly into space, while Mike just sat there in shock.

Then Jeff started consoling the others. Jason and Gloria were now in tears. Mike and Bill were more in shock than anything.

"This one was for Frank." Mike lifted his glass with tears in his eyes. "He was our friend, and we will never forget him."

A night of drinking and drugs followed to try to ease the pain, but the pain would be felt for a long time to come. Others felt anger at the injustice. Their biggest triumph had been interrupted by tragedy.

"THE TRACKS OF MY TEARS"

The Miracles

It was two days later when there was a knock at the door of the beach house. Eric answered it.

Two men stood there. One was a rather overweight, balding, middle-aged man with black horn rimmed glasses. He was wearing a brown rumpled suit, a white shirt that was also wrinkled, and a tie that was too short reaching nowhere near his belt buckle. Behind him stood a younger man with blonde hair and wire rim glasses. He was wearing a newer looking black suit with a white shirt and black tie.

"I'm Detective Morgan, and this is Detective Anderson." The man in the brown suit took out his badge to show them while his partner took out a note pad. "We would like to ask you some questions about Frank Barcelona. We understand that he lived here, and that you had some business dealings with him. We're trying to complete our investigation." He put the badge back in his pocket.

"Sure, uh. Whatever I can do to cooperate," said Eric. "Are there any suspects? We'd, uh, really like to know who did this."

"The police have none," said the detective. "Where were you the night he was killed?"

"Uh, I was at a gig with the band he and I managed together," answered Eric. "We were playing at the Hollywood Star that night. Frank was supposed to be there, but he left during the sound check in the afternoon and never returned. I saw him leave with some people in a large black limo, but I didn't see who they were. Do you have any details about the murder?"

"We're really not at liberty to tell you much about this case as it is an ongoing investigation. But I can tell you this. He was shot in the head six times at point blank range in a field off Angeles Crest Highway. From the looks of it, he must've known his assailants as it appears he was taken there without a struggle. Did he have any enemies?"

"Oh, I'm sure he did, but I couldn't tell you who." Eric lied.

"It looks like he was pretty badly beaten. It appears to be an execution style murder, staged to set an example. There is speculation that drugs were involved. We have reports that he was dealing drugs, so that may have been the motive. Do you know anything about his drug dealings, or any of his connections?"

"Uh… No, not really. We were always a bit suspicious where he got his money. Thought that he may have been dealing, but he kept that from me and the rest of the band," Eric lied again.

"I guess that's just one less drug dealer on the streets. That's about all we know. Did you or any of the band know or have any dealings with the people he was dealing drugs with."

"Uh, no. He was the manager and the money man for the band. We just thought he had a lot of money," said Eric. "We never thought to ask how he got it. We suspected it might have been drug money, or inherited, or whatever, but he certainly kept that separate from us."

"Do you know anyone who would want to kill Frank?"

"Uh, no, not really."

"We would like to talk with the band. Perhaps one of them knows something. How can I get in touch with 'em?"

"I can set up a meeting. They live in Hollywood. Here's the address. Would tomorrow be convenient?"

"That'd be fine. We'll meet you there tomorrow." They turned and left.

Eric immediately picked up the phone to call Alex. He had grown suspicious of this whole murder and investigation.

"Hello Alex, I need you to do me a favor. Find out what you can from Russ. Something sounds fishy to me."

Alex agreed.

He called back the very next day.

"I got a hold of Russ. He claims to know nothing about it, but he's keeping pretty quiet. He claims that the feds are breathing down his neck as well. He said for our own good, as well as his, we shouldn't have any contact with him, at least for the time being until the heat is off. All of his operations are suspended for now because of everything. Also, he's denying any knowledge of Frank or any of us. He strongly suggests that we do the same so that that we keep our stories straight. It's best that we corroborate our information. Sounds like things are pretty heated up on his end as well. If you ask me, he was sounding very suspicious and acting strangely. I think there is more to this than he wants to let us know."

"Thanks," Eric offered confirming some of his suspicions.

The detectives arrived the next day at the band house—same suits, same routine.

"I understand that he was financing the band as the manager."

"Yes, actually we do have another manager. He was our former manager, but he continued to work with us as our tour manager and to help finance us when needed. We've worked with him for a long time. He has always been good to us. We can't believe he's gone."

"Do you have any suspects?" Jeff asked.

"Not at this time."

"Any details?" asked Gloria.

"Only what you've already read in the newspaper."

"Did any of you know about his drug dealings? Look, we're not here to bust anyone for drugs. We're just investigating a homicide."

"Well, Uh. We were pretty sure that he was dealing drugs only because we wondered where he got his money, but we really don't know anything about that," Jeff answered as the rest of the band shook their heads in agreement.

"Do you know any of his contacts? Anyone he was involved with or anyone who may have wanted to kill him?"

"Uh, No," They all answered almost in a chorus, knowing full well that this was a lie.

"Well, he must've done something to anger his drug connections."

"Sorry, we can't be of more help. We really just did not know much about his drug dealings or that side of him and his business. He really kept that all pretty secret, probably to protect us, if it is in fact true. Our dealings with Frank were purely professional as our band manager," Mike answered.

"Well, at this point the feds has taken over the case. They have requested that we back off. They asked us to just get a statement from you since we already had the appointment, but at this point we're off the case. Sort of strange if you ask me, but they take jurisdiction over our department. It seems they have some interest in this. We may be in touch, but like I said, it has been taken over by the feds, so it really is out of our hands. They may contact you for more questioning. We're just following up. Since you have a pretty good alibi, it seems obvious that you were not involved. We'll pass this information on. Thank you for your time." The detectives turned and left.

Eric was the first to start. "This has all the makings of some Hollywood crime movie with mobsters, feds, double crossing, and no one really knowing who the bad guy is. I've also been doing some checking on my own, and no one is saying much. Did ya notice that they didn't wanna say much about the case? And don't you think it odd that the feds took over the investigation? They certainly are keeping this one under wraps." He paused deep in thought.

"I think I saw the people that probably did this. They took him from the club in a big black limo during your sound check. I just couldn't see any faces, but when he got in he greeted 'em as if he knew 'em. The police even agreed that it appears it was someone he knew as there was no sign of a struggle at the murder sight. No one seems to wanna talk much about it though, especially the police. They don't seem to even care. Their opinion seems to be that there is one less low life drug dealer to deal with. I'm not sure that they don't care or have just been told to keep this one quiet. Other people seem reluctant to talk as if something is being hushed up. I just can't seem to find out much of anything."

The group looked stunned as they listened to Eric's story.

"What else do ya know?" asked Jason.

"Well, I know for myself he was playing hard ball with some pretty heavy players. I know he had pissed 'em all off plenty of times. He was dealing with both the Syndicate and the DEA—buying drugs from both. Also, he had some problems with other dealers, buyers, and clients including Mr. Grant."

"We did hear him arguing with Mr. Grant that day," said Jeff.

"There are many possibilities." Eric continued. "Anyone could've fuckin' done it—the FBI, the DEA, the Mafia, Mr. Grant or his people, or anyone. Frank had a lot of enemies, especially in the drug world. It looks very much like a Mafia hit. But then again, this whole thing could have been staged to make it look like an organized crime hit in order to divert attention. Ya know what I'm sayin'? I know that the DEA knew he was also dealing with the Mafia. Of course, the federal agent contacts are denying any knowledge of the events, but it is interesting that they took over the investigation. I really don't wanna contact his connections with the Mafia. That could be even more dangerous, and I do not want to be implicated. I get the impression that they all just want to sweep this one under the rug and forget about it. Even the police seem strangely quiet about this whole thing. That's why I think the feds may be involved. It really is unclear to me if it was a Mafia hit or a fed hit made to look like a Mafia hit. You even heard them say the case has been turned over to them. Besides that, the fact that federal agents found him in the middle of the night in the middle of nowhere makes me very suspicious. How did they know to even look there? Did they do it themselves and try to hide their tracks? Did the mob do it and inform the police? You heard the detectives. Basically, the feds have told the police to back off and not to investigate any further. There are way too many unanswered questions. Something seems very fishy. It's all very hush-hush. It all seems very suspicious to me. In the end, I'm still not sure if it was the mob, or the feds making it look like a mob hit, or some of the other low life he deals with. Either way, these are people that we do not want to get involved with. They have certainly sent a message and made an example of him. We need to stay away. These are obviously some very dangerous people."

"I'm gonna get the bastards!" Jeff exclaimed.

"You'll end up just like Frank. Let the police, the feds, and the authorities do their thing. Let's leave it alone. But you know we all are gonna miss him."

"Yeah you are right," Jeff agreed. "I had better lay real low for a while. I'd hate to fuck this band up. I think Frank already has. We must now be real strong. Remember what he told us. We can make it. Now let's get out there and do what it takes. Make his dream become a reality. Let's do it this time."

Jeff formed the group into a circle. They all gave a large group hug to each other as Frank had taught them to do before a gig. They took one step back, raised their hands much like a football team and clapped them together as a sign of their potential victory. The drive was really on now to prove they could make it—for Frank's sake.

Eric ran out of the room. His struggle to be brave was wearing thin. He didn't want the others to see him upset. The others just stood looking at each other speechless. They each took a seat and put their head in their hands. Some were silent in disbelief while others were crying over the loss. All were shaken at the events that had transpired.

The feds did question them shortly thereafter. They then closed the case due to lack of evidence. Nothing more was heard about the case making the band and especially Eric even more suspicious. They felt as if they were hiding something or sweeping it under the carpet. For them it was just another low life drug dealer off the streets and one less criminal to deal with. The band and Eric had to drop the whole thing in fear of implicating or endangering themselves. They would have to play it pretty clean for a while.

"So, now what? This is really fucked-up." Jason asked leaving the funeral. He was walking arm and arm with Gloria and surrounded by the rest of the band who were all trying to comfort each other. "What the fuck do we do now? I mean Frank's dead." Tears again started streaming down his cheeks; his eyes already red from holding back the tears.

"We'll be alright." Gloria tried to be convincing while holding back her own flood of emotions. "We'll just have to carry on as before."

"Don't you think we've been through enough already?" Mike too was feeling the pain of loss and desperation. "I mean, this is like the last fuckin' straw."

"I can't believe the shit that I'm hearing—and especially from you two, the original band members. After all, this was your dream. A dream that's shared not only by Frank—but by all of us. This should just make us strong." Jeff was trying not to sound cliché, but he was angered by their surrender. "Frank was my friend also, but we must carry on. This time for Frank. He would never forgive us if we gave up now. He would want us to continue. If nothing else, we should all have learned that Frank was not a quitter. He believed in this band the same way we all do. I don't wanna let Frank down. We're better than that. Now is the time to pick ourselves up and continue on. We all knew this wasn't going to be an easy road, so let's just take it and run. Prove Frank was right. Now let's hear it. Are we in, or not." They all raised their hands for a giant slap then fell together for a group hug—their loyalty reaffirmed.

They arrived back at the band house. Jason immediately went to the practice room to his piano and started tinkling on the keys. It was a way of hiding his sorrow. Mike was the first to follow. They began jamming. The music and words just seemed to flow. For an hour they jammed their hearts out, allowing each their own release for the pain they were feeling—raw and emotional. As they worked, the others walked in one by one. It wasn't long before they had written a new song. The creative juices were flowing. Everyone knew that this was going to be special. It was a power ballad, and it seemed in some way to ease their pain. They dedicated it to the memory of Frank. It was the best thing they had written to date because this song was real, and there was a true emotional connection. They were also able to use everything that they had learned in arranging and putting together a song. The song was called "Are you still there?" It reflected the influence that Frank had on the band even though he was no longer present. His influence and his presence would always be felt. Even in his absence he'd always be a part of the band. By the time they were finished, they were emotionally drained and exhausted, but they each felt better for they had channeled their feeling into music.

Just then Rick, Derek, and Steve entered the room.

"Well, I guess the gig is off," said Jeff.

"Not at all, everything has already been paid for. Frank made sure of that." Rick explained

I wonder if that's the reason he was killed." Eric started. "Frank was not too good with money. He owed people all over town. I know he was spending a lot of his money to finance this gig. His priority was the band. He wanted this for you guys. He may have made the ultimate sacrifice for this band."

"Well, we'll have to do this for Frank. It would've been what he wanted. So, let's get out there and make him proud," said Rick.

"I guess that's one consolation. We just wrote another song. Let us know what you think." Jason said.

They played the song.

"That song is incredible! I want it on the tape. Derek, can you get it ready in time?"

"No problem. I agree. This is the best thing you guys have written. Needs some work, but I think this song could be a hit. We can start recording immediately."

Derek worked with the band for a couple of days. Then he took them into the studio to record the new song. In three days the song was finished. It did prove to be the best song they had ever done.

After a few days, they were back on track.

The Santa Monica Civic date was quickly approaching with only one month to go. Rick contacted every record company as well as all his other contacts and invited them to the gig and to the after-party. He asked the record companies to bring all important personnel and to furnish him with a full count of the number of tickets each company needed so that they were sure to bring all the important departments—promotion, marketing, advertising, and press—not just the A & R people and the presidents and officers. He also had Isaac, Sue, Steve, and Derek call their usual contacts to do the same so that everyone would hear about this event from a number of sources. He contacted Pat Johnson and invited him and whatever guests he wanted to invite since some of them were pretty powerful.

Sue in the mean-time continued working on publicity, press, and advertising. She was paying for print ads and radio spots as promised. They did interviews with local newspapers, magazines, and radio stations. They even offered free tickets to radio stations as giveaways. The local rock magazines, newspapers, and college radio, especially those colleges where they had played, seemed to be the most receptive, and Sue knew how to work them. They too were invited to the after party just to sweeten the deal for what could be a difficult audience to impress. The band loved seeing all the press and advertising they were getting. Everything had to be right. But the best of all was the billboard on the Sunset Strip, right across from the 9000 building. No record company could ignore it. It was impossible to miss. Many had offices there, and their windows looked right at it. They stood there one day smiling with satisfaction while looking up at themselves on that huge billboard, their likenesses perched many feet into the sky.

Two weeks before the gig Rick sent out the packets. It included a tape with the new song dedicated to the memory of Frank; photos; a complete press kit showing all the print ads, interviews, reviews; and an invitation to the upcoming show at the Santa Monica Civic complete with tickets, free drink vouchers; and invitations to the after show party. Every record company and industry person imaginable received it. No stone was left unturned. Rick had created a buzz about this band, the likes of which no one had seen in a long time. Everyone wanted to go and be seen at this concert and the party.

The whole machine was working.

50

"YOU CAN'T ALWAYS GET WHAT YOU WANT"

The Rolling Stones

Finally, the day of the show arrived. It was with excitement that they entered the Santa Monica Civic for their sound check. They saw the huge stage ready for their performance. Sitting on one side of the stage where Jason's equipment was set up was a concert grand piano.

"A fuckin' grand piano," was all Jason could say. He rushed over and began to play. Jason was thrilled. It had been rented just for this show. It was a dream come true. In center stage the drum set was up on a riser about 4 feet above the rest of the band. Jason and the rest of his keyboards were on a riser as well, about three feet off the stage floor. This was going to look like a real rock concert. Derek and Ken were there to help make the show a success. All the crew was busy setting up instruments, while the lights and the sound system were being set up. Frank had thought of everything.

A long time had passed since their signing with Rick and his management company and the band had grown restless again as they waited for this gig. It would be the most important one of their career. The record companies, although friendlier, had come and gone.

Many had shown some initial interest, but eventually they had passed. However, that was changing with the new tapes and with the new songs. Many were showing some real interest again. There were even a few small offers, but Rick wanted to hold out. He knew he could get more offers, so he told them all that there would be no negotiations until after the Santa Monica gig. Everything hinged on this show.

They were hoping the large following they had developed would generate a large audience. All those people they had encountered along the way—friends, fans, groupies, sex partners, opportunists, just people who wanted to party with them after the gigs, the hangers on, and even those looking to get something for themselves out of it—all were important. These were the people that had kept the momentum going and the reason they had come this far in the first place. Many were sure that this band was going to be big someday, and they wanted to have discovered them first. They wanted to be part of that in-crowd. These were the people that were spreading the word of the next big band—for they had seen them before they were rock stars. In a way they all wanted a piece of the fame and glory. The "I knew them when" syndrome.

"It's been a long time since we started this band," Mike stated as he entered for the sound check with Jason. They stood there transfixed as they watched the stage being set up. "Remember that acid trip in the woods?"

Jason laughed in agreement. "We sure have come a long way from those days."

"Yeah, look at us now. Whoever would've thought?"

As they were waiting to set up, Mike turned to Jason. "You know my mom and dad will be here tonight. They decided to see just what it is I do. I guess Dad knows some of those record people from his movie stuff. He even said he'd put in a good word for us. You know he heard the tape and was impressed, even though, as he said, it wasn't his kind of music."

"Yeah, my parents are coming out for a visit as well. They wanna see what I'm up to. They decided to take a vacation to come and see me," Jason replied. "Sure has been a lot of people who have crossed our paths." Jason was reminiscent. "You know that Chuck and Greg from

Studio 69 are coming tonight. It seems like so long ago that we played that little gay bar. They're still together after all this time. They sure have been good friends."

Gloria, having overheard what they were saying, walked up behind them. "Yeah, I even told my parents. They're flying in from Dallas just to see me play. I hope to make them proud."

The band walked onstage to find Alex there with Eric.

"Hi guys. How does it look?" Eric asked.

"Fuckin' amazing," Gloria said.

They all chimed in with words of approval. They were all checking out the stage, the equipment, and the empty seats that would soon be full of their audience.

"I can't even believe this shit," said Jason almost in total disbelief.

"This is gonna be fuckin' great," said Alex. "I even have a crowd coming tonight—mostly friends and family. Even they couldn't turn down some free beers." He joked.

They finished their sound check. They were blown away at the way they sounded. The lighting system they had rented especially for the gig added another dimension to the show. They left the stage confident and ready for the show that evening. They returned home to get ready for the gig.

The excitement was high as the band got ready to leave. The limousines arrived ready to pick them up. Frank had thought of everything. They had been ordered to take them to the gig as well as the after party so that all the band had to think about was the gig. It was the first time any of them had even seen the inside of a limousine. As they got in, they really felt like stars.

"Do you believe this?" said Jason.

"Nope, I could really get used to this,' Mike responded.

"Champagne is chilled and ready for you," The limo driver offered.

"No thanks. This evening is too important to start that now. But keep it chilled. We'll want some of that later."

They were driven to the gig in style. They entered the dressing room. Rick and Eric were already there running all over the place making sure everything was ready. Maggie was there to help them with their hair and outfits and putting on the finishing touches to make sure they looked good.

Jason was talking with Chuck and Greg.

A large group of people entered and asked for Bill. "Hey guys, great to see you. Look, everyone, it's the guys from Music World. Thanks for coming. You know everyone here I think."

"Sure do."

A knock came at the door. "I'm looking for Mike." The familiar head of Speed peaked around the door.

Mike jumped up. "Hey, what brings you to L.A.? It's great to see you!" Mike exclaimed with enthusiasm.

"We got your invite. Sunshine wanted to come down to see some friends anyway, so we thought it would be a perfect time."

"Far out! Come on in." Mike seemed truly happy to see his old friends.

Just then Steve and Brent walked in talking with Eric who was showing them the way.

"Steve and Brent, great to see you!" exclaimed Bill. "But I haven't seen the two of you together in a long time."

"Oh ya know, we're still good friends. We talk and still keep in touch. Steve told me you were playing. I just couldn't miss it," said Brent.

Steve stepped up. "Bill, I have a surprise for you. Can I talk with you privately?"

"Sure." He led Bill into the hallway.

"Your parents have flown in. They'd like to see you. They're waiting outside." Steve whispered to Bill.

"What the fuck do you mean my parents are here? How the fuck did they know where to find me?" Bill snapped back in anger.

"You know they are friends of my parents. I still talk to my parents and word gets around. Your parents called me when they got into town. They were here on vacation." He lied. He had arranged this reunion. "They asked about you. Don't you think enough time has passed to forget about all that? It's time you to let bygones be bygones and start

480

acting like a family again. They really want to apologize and make peace."

Steve pleaded. He put his arm around Bill and walked him out the door. His parents were waiting in the hallway. His mother was overdressed, as he had always remembered, with fur, pearls, and hat; and Dad was in his expensive Brooks Brothers suit.

The mother was first to burst into tears as she wrapped her arms around her son. "We've missed you so."

Bill pulled away at first. His father held out his hand for a shake. "It's wonderful to see you, son. We sure are proud of what you've done. We're sorry for anything we may have done in the past."

Steve interrupted, shaking the father's hand in a subtle effort to silence him as if both were keeping a big secret. "We're looking forward to seeing your show, son."

"Thanks Dad," Bill said with forgiveness in his voice. "It actually is nice to see you, both of you. It has been a long time. I guess it's time I moved on." Bill, in a gesture of acceptance, dragged them into the dressing room to meet the rest of the group—a true act of forgiveness. He introduced them around, much to the surprise of everyone else.

Rob brought Mr. Greenwood to say hello to the band. He was followed by Jack and Margaret, Mike's mom.

They all went up to Mr. Greenwood and Rob to give their thanks. As Mr. Greenwood went to Mike he said. "Your dad tells me you're a pretty good kid."

"Thank you Mr. Greenwood. We'll try our best." Mike responded

"I didn't know you knew my Dad?" Mike said.

"Of course. We're old friends. We've worked on quite a few movie soundtracks in the past. I never knew you were his son until recently. Small world isn't it? Well, break a leg guys." Mr. Greenwood left with Jack and Margaret talking all the way out.

Even Jason's parents were there.

Rick came into the dressing rooms. "Sorry everyone, it's almost time for the show to start. Please return to the audience. I need to get this band ready to get on stage. We'll see you after the show." The crowd exited leaving only the band, Mark, Pete, Alex, Eric, Maggie, and, Rick. They all stood in silence at first. Then Rick said. "Give 'em hell!"

"This one is for Frank," said Rick. They all agreed. They had one big group hug that grew to a big cheering rally. With excitement high, they left the dressing room. The crew took their places, Maggie and Rick took their seats in the audience, and the band stood back stage ready to go on.

The best seats had been reserved and were filled with VIPs. These were mostly record company executives and employees, but also, many other music industry types. It was quite a crowd. Pat Johnson was there still seeing dollar signs in his eyes. So was Steve Gold figuring he'd be busy soon negotiating their record deal. Sue was busy hobnobbing with the local press. Of course Isaac, Helmut, and Maggie, and Sally were also there. Derek and Ken had said there hellos and had taken their places with the crew. Present was every record company they had ever approached, most of whom had passed up to this point. They were now eager to take another look at what the band had become. Of course Rob from Empire was there beaming with delight as he stood with Mr. Greenwood. There were also a lot of invited celebrities from the entertainment industry that had been invited by all the people involved. They all sat waiting anxiously for the arrival of the band. Many were talking with others in the business that they knew like old friends at a convention.

A different section had all their close friends: Sunshine and Speed, Chuck and Greg, all their friends from Music World, and other people who had believed in them all along. Even Doug and Brian, the original musicians when the band first started and was called Axis were there. Both were curious to see what they were now up to. It was also filled with family: Jason's parents, Mike's mom and dad, and Bill's parents. It was also filled with all the other business people who had become so much a part of their lives in getting to this point in their career.

Most importantly the arena was filled with their fans, their friends, and all the people who had seen them over the years or who had followed them in their career. They had watched them grow. These were *their* fans and the people who got them to this point. This was their crowd—their audience.

But most importantly they would be playing for Frank. They knew that even the presence of Frank seemed somehow alive that night for his legacy and his dream had lived on.

The scene and the whole mood suddenly changed as they approached the back stage area. The dressing room had been rather quiet, but as they approached the stage area they could hear the faint sounds of the audience chanting, "Hollywood! Hollywood!" The closer they got, the louder the chanting got. They reached the edge of the dark stage ready for their entrance. They just stood there as if time itself stood still.

Show time approached, the lights dimmed, and the audience broke out into a huge cheer. This was their cue. The band took their places on the dark stage. The show was about to begin.

The show started in an explosion of sound, lights, and special effects—lights erupted, flash pots fired, and fog filled the stage. The opening song was chosen for its power and energy. It even surprised those who had seen the band perform many times before. They filled up that room with sound. The crowd roared like nothing they had experienced before. They looked and sounded like rock stars—for tonight they had become rock stars. They knew they were playing for their lives. They moved on stage like professionals, and every light and sound cue was synchronized thanks to Pete and Mark. Every special effects cue was on time thanks to Alex. The vocals came in as the band backed off just slightly, keeping the intensity but allowing the vocals to soar over the music. The chorus crescendoed and the band played it beautifully. The song ended with a power chord that echoed and resonated so strong that it seemed like the whole auditorium was going to collapse around them. The crowd went wild. It was difficult to hear amidst the noise.

Gloria stepped back up to the mike. "HELLO LOS ANGELES, ARE YOU READY TO ROCK?"

The crowd started shouting as the next song began.

It was another rocking song, one from the tape that the record companies had received. It was commercial and radio-ready, but in the live performance they played it with a higher intensity. The audience loved it and cheered in approval.

Then the lights dimmed. Gloria began. "We'd like to dedicate this next song to our former manager Frank, a man without whom we would not be here today, and who has made this all possible."

Jason walked to the grand piano. He tossed his tuxedo tails over the bench and took his place like he was about to play a Beethoven piano concerto at a classical concert. One lone spotlight shone on him as he began the opening piano solo. The stage floor filled with fog, enhancing the mood. Then Gloria took her spotlight for her vocal entrance. Finally, the lights slowly went up in cool colors as each member made their entrance. The song crescendoed to a dramatic climax, ending in a spectacle of sound and lights. It was an emotional tribute for all. The crowd went wild at its conclusion. This was going to be their hit single, and everyone knew it—including the record companies.

The set went on flawlessly. Every song was performed to perfection. It was a spectacular show with choreography, and sound and lights that only enhanced the experience. It was their coming-out party. The set had highs and low, and the new song about Frank was the biggest hit of all. It was their most exciting, professional, and incredible show to date.

The set was crafted to include a mix of their original material—fast songs, rocking dance songs, slow songs, and even two power ballads, the one for Frank and the song Hollywood which was dedicated to Sarah. After each song, the crowd roared for more, and then would get quiet as the next song began. The show was designed to build with each song more intense than the one preceding. This made for a well-paced rock show. Their final song was a frantic climax to an incredible show, ending with a high-energy frenzy in a blaze of glory—flash pots firing.

The band left the stage. The house lights stayed off with only the amp lights lit on stage.

The crowd roared. "More! More!"

The band stood on the side of the stage looking pleased with themselves, their adrenaline pumping. They entered again for the first of what was to become two encores.

When they finally left the stage for the last time they knew that they had done a great job and were proud of their accomplishment. They had entered that stage as another L.A. band and left that stage as rock stars.

Back in the dressing rooms there was silence. They were more stunned than anything as they put their instruments away.

Rick was the first to enter. "That was fuckin' incredible!!!"

With that, the band erupted in a cacophony of expletives. Words could not explain how they felt that night. Everyone was congratulating each other for a job well done.

"I have never felt anything like that before!" Mike exclaimed.

"Me neither!" Gloria exclaimed ecstatically.

Bill agreed as he put away his guitar.

"I think we were incredible!" Jason exclaimed.

They were high on the experience. Higher than any drugs could have taken them.

51

"I JUST WANT TO CELEBRATE"

Rare Earth

They returned to the limos to get ready to leave the gig and go to the party.

"Before we leave," said Jason as he grabbed a bottle of champagne and handed it to the limo driver. "It's time to crack this bottle of champagne."

"Yes sir." The limo driver grabbed the bottle, opened it, poured it into champagne flutes, and passed around the glasses.

They each toasted each other.

Once they had their toast, they got into the limo and sped away.

It was a short drive from Santa Monica to Brentwood. They were so excited. They were all talking at once, pointing out various parts of the show that they had performed particularly well. The limo was a buzz of energy.

This would be the second part of their evening. The party had been planned as part of the whole event. Since the gig itself did not end until 11:00, it was after midnight when the party really started. It too had already been paid for by Frank. Every record company executive and employee, entertainment person, and press person had been given an invitation. Most were anxious to go because this could be the social event of the season, especially now after the show they had just seen. Everyone wanted a chance to meet the band and congratulate them. For some it was also a way of showing their interest. It was the place to be and be seen—and a great way for all of them to network with each other. The bands friends and family were all there as well, each having been given an invitation.

They drove up to Rick's house in Brentwood only to see a line of limos waiting to let out their riders. What seemed like an army of valets were waiting as each car drove up close to the front door so that they could exit the car directly into the house while their cars were being parked. For this event, they had to use every available space including the front lawn and streets to park the cars.

By the time they arrived, the party was in full swing. The band made their entrance. They stood for a moment by the front door in disbelief. Immediately, upon seeing the band, the crowd erupted in applause. The band motioned a thank you and wandered into the crowd. Waiters and servers were circulating with glasses of wine and champagne and hors d'oeuvres. A full bar was set up in the living room. Rick was making the rounds along with all the other members of the team which included Isaac, Steve, and Sue. Rick was the first to spot the band.

"Welcome. You guys were great tonight. Congratulations. Lemme show you around." Rick circulated through the crowd introducing them to everyone—record company executives and heads of departments, press people, agents, promotional people, and even some of the celebrities. This lasted for at least an hour. Everyone, including the record company people, had nothing but praises and compliments to offer the band. Champagne was flowing, and everyone was feeling the energy of the evening. It was a party like no other.

Once Rick had made their introductions he instructed them to mingle.

"OK guys, meet your public. By the way there is some blow in the bedroom, but keep it quiet. It is only for you guys, and me. I am not going to furnish the whole place with drugs. These people can bring their own."

Rick continued to make the rounds, talking with all the record companies. He told them to call him with a real offer so that they could talk some business. He was really working the crowd, something he did very well.

Jason spotted Rob, the local A & R representative from Empire.

"Great show," Rob said as he approached Jason. "Wanna hit?" He asked Jason showing him his vile of cocaine.

"I guess that'd be OK now that the show is over."

"Let's go out to the back yard. That's where most people are getting high."

They walked to the back yard where there were others talking, smoking joints, and passing the little coke spoons around. He even spied Mike and Bill there passing a joint. Rob gave Jason a hit of blow, then took one himself."

"Thanks, I still can't believe all this," said Jason. "Uh, but if you don't mind my asking, do you really think we'll get a record deal? We've been doing this a long time."

"Yes, I think it's only a matter of time now. I've been pushing for you to be signed with our label for a long time. I've already requested that if you do sign with us that I be your A & R representative."

"I'd like that," said Jason. "You've been around a lot and have been very supportive. Besides, you seem like a pretty cool guy."

"Also, I know that we brought a lot of people to see the show, all the execs and department heads. Something is going on."

"Sounds great."

"Also, I know that all the labels were there in force tonight with many of their department heads. And from what I hear, they all want to sign you as well. Do you really think they would show up if they weren't interested?"

"I guess you're right."

"But if you don't mind me asking, what has taken so long? I thought we would've been signed a long time ago. I really thought we were ready and as good as many of the things out there on record."

"I, for one, have been watching this band for a long time, since the days of Frank and Pat Johnson. I always thought the band had some potential. You just weren't ready. The band just needed some work. You gotta remember that our jobs could be at stake. Signing a flop could be the end of our career, so we all tend to be very conservative. I'm glad you guys stuck it out, and I hope to be working with you soon in the future. The band needed the polish and the fine tuning. When I first saw you, you were just a like a garage band or a club band. You needed to get some great songs, some great singles, get your live act together, and be more professional. We also look at improvement, direction, and dedication. Basically, at this point Hollywood has displayed all those qualities. And you *are* ready. You may not think that we, the record company execs and business people, have been there, but we have. You probably didn't even realize it. But I've seen so many gigs, and every time I saw you guys perform I always ran into a bunch of music industry people. We've all had our eyes on you for a long time. Believe it or not, everyone here has seen you at least once and many have seen you many, many times and have heard your tapes. We were always watching to see if you were gonna do it, to be the next big act. It takes a pretty big investment in a band, so any label is reluctant to spend that kind of money before they think it's a sure thing. We were just waiting to see if you would prove yourselves. And you did. At this point you are now ready to take the next step. Now, I've got to mingle and find the rest of my label."

The party continued well into the night with each band member having a chance to talk with many music industry people, record company people, and press people. This party was more like work, having to network with all these people. It was exhausting, but it felt great.

It only took a couple of days before the phone was ringing off the hook at Rick's office. All the labels were interested now. He decided to keep this to himself at first so that the band did not get their hopes up too high. Finally, he had to tell them. The labels wanted to set up appointments with Rick and the band so that they could show off their operation and what they had to offer.

Rick stopped by the band-house during rehearsal about a week later.

"We have a lot of labels interested," said Rick. "Many want to meet with the band. I've set up the first meeting tomorrow morning, so I want you all to dress nice."

"So, who all is interested?" asked Gloria

"You'll see," said Rick.

Rick picked the band up at 10 A.M.

"So why all the secrecy?" asked Jason.

"Just never you mind. You'll see," said Rick.

'They drove to downtown Hollywood and entered a parking lot near the corner of Hollywood and Vine.

"Follow me," said Rick.

As they walked up to the Capitol Records building, the band was filled with excitement. Jason and Mike looked at each other in disbelief.

Rick walked right up to the guard and said. "Rick Martin and the band Hollywood. We have an appointment with A & R."

The guard looked on his sheet.

"Yes, Mr. Martin. They are expecting you. 12th floor," said the guard.

Jason and Mike looked at each other. They started to giggle, remembering the scene a long time ago when they were walking down the boulevard and this was the unapproachable tower that they were to conquer.

"Man, we actually are getting into the tower. It is just like we dreamed," said Mike.

"Just like Frodo," said Jason. "We even wrote a song about it." The two giggled some more while the rest of the band just looked at them puzzled.

In the weeks to come they had many meetings with many labels. Each record company wanted to meet the band and have the band meet them and their staff including the A & R personnel, but also the marketing and promotions departments, and even the president. Each time these people told them what a great a job they could do for the band. The band was getting the hard sell. For a change the labels were buying, and the band felt they had the upper hand.

Multiple offers were coming in to sign the band to a label. After all this time, the band surely had made it. They were sought after. A bidding war ensued among the labels. Rick was playing one offer against the other, trying to get the best deal that he could. He wanted a large advance, a good budget for the album, and the promise of a certain amount of dollars for promotion and advertising, a subsidy for the band to tour, and a good percentage of record sales or points. The record company would, of course, recoup all their expenses before the band got paid their points, but that was all the reason to get as much as possible up front and to go with the right company who had the staff to promote and market the band properly.

Finally, a meeting was called in Rick's office with all the band members as well as Rick, Eric, and Steve Gold.

"Well guys, we have an offer that I'm pretty happy with. Actually, we have had a number of offers. I'll go over them all with you, but I think this one is the best for a number of reasons. It's from our old friends at Empire. As you know, they've been supportive all along the way. Mr. Greenwood has assured me that they want to do everything possible to make this band a success and to make us happy.

Here are the specifics. They're offering a 5 album deal, $400,000 per album with 12% royalties which is the band's percentage of the record sales. This will increase to 14% at gold and 15% at platinum. Of course the $400,000 is an advance on record sales and would have to be recouped before any royalties or other money went out Remember, it would be recouped at your percentage, not gross sales. The breakdown would be $100,000 per record for recording costs, $100,000 tour support, $100,000 for advertising and promotion, and an additional $100,000 signing bonus. Keep in mind that you have a lot of other people to pay percentages to, but in the end it would be worth it. Also, all other percentages are from what you take, my 20% is from what you make from any source, P. J.'s percentages are based on publishing monies plus 1 point or percent on the album. Unfortunately, Frank is out of the picture, but Eric should be compensated as that team, and he'll continue to work in Frank's capacity. The agent will take his percentage out of the gig and tours only off of the top of your receipts, not the record company money since he was not involved in the negotiations. If all of that is satisfactory, Steve can start working on negotiations."

"Sounds great to us," they all chorused in agreement.

"By the way, I didn't know you had connections at Empire." Rick turned to Mike.

"Neither did I. What d'ya mean?" asked Mike.

"Well, it seems your Dad's name was mentioned. Mr. Greenwood knows him from some business dealings. Not sure if it helped, but at least it sure did not hurt to have him on our side."

It was a month later when Rick called a meeting at his office.

They entered to find Rick at his desk.

"I have an announcement to make." Rick silenced the group for their undivided attention. They all took seats around the office. "I am indeed pleased to announce that we've completed preliminary negotiations for a record deal with Empire. We expect to complete negotiations in the next few weeks. All terms have been agreed upon. Now it's up to attorneys to work out the language. Congratulations."

They all cheered.

"Rob will be our A & R person. It was due to his perseverance with Mr. Greenwood that we got signed. Your contact will always be Rob. He'll be coordinating everything with the label. Through him you'll get to know all the departments.

Negotiations lasted for about another month, but eventually, Steve and Rick were able to work out a great deal for the band. Two weeks later, once the contracts had been drafted, a meeting was called at Empire. The band, Rick, Eric, and Steve along with Mr. Greenwood, Rob, the attorney for Empire, Sue and her press people, and the Empire press people were all there with cameras ready. They all shook hands and the band signed their recording contract. They passed the pen around, looking at each other with incredible excitement while cameras flashed.

They were then taken to a large room with lots of people. A large banner across the back wall said "Welcome to The Empire Records Group." They were first re-introduced to the department heads and a lot of the staff.

After introductions were made, a line of people brought in champagne on trays giving everyone a glass. Mr. Greenwood got everyone's attention.

"We would like to give a warm welcome to The Band Hollywood." He raised his hand with the champagne glass to give a toast to the band.

A rousing roar of applause followed.

"Fucking A!" was all they could say. Their excitement was getting the best of them.

Jason saw Rob. He went over to speak to him. "I still can't believe we're finally signed.

I'm glad you signed with us. It'll be a pleasure working with you. Congratulations." He held out his hand to Jason who nodded in agreement.

"I can't believe it, we've fuckin' done it!" Gloria exclaimed with all the band and Rick surrounding her.

"I can't believe that we've finally made it! We finally got a record deal!" Mike exclaimed.

"Yeah, me neither!" Jason exclaimed

"This is the end of our journey," Mike said.

"Yeah, I feel we've reached the end of our odyssey." Gloria was exploding with excitement.

"This is not the end. This is the beginning," said Rick. "This'll be the real start of your career, and the start of a lot of hard work. Don't think it's all over. You have an album to make, a tour to mount, and a lot of press to deal with. What you've been doing so far is child's play. Now the real work begins."

"Yeah, but we have worked so hard. We finally got it. It took more time than we had anticipated, but at last we're on our way." Mike could hardly hold back his joy.

"Yeah, we're looking forward to that gold record to add to my wall," Rick stated matter of factly.

"I dig the sound of that—WHEN we reach gold, ya know," said Jeff.

The band was ecstatic. They all cheered, gave each other hugs, and patted each other on the back. This was going to be the culmination of all their hard work.

Hollywood; The Band was signed.

ROCK ON…..

www.ingramcontent.com/pod-product-compliance
Lightning Source LLC
LaVergne TN
LVHW041737060526
838201LV00046B/835